To Love Jason Thorn

Ella Maise

First published by Ella Maise 2015

This paperback edition published by Simon and Schuster UK Ltd, 2022

Copyright © Ella Maise, 2015

The right of Ella Maise to be identified as author of
this work has been asserted in accordance with the
Copyright, Designs and Patents Act, 1988.

1 3 5 7 9 10 8 6 4 2

Simon & Schuster UK Ltd
1st Floor
222 Gray's Inn Road
London WC1X 8HB

Simon & Schuster Australia, Sydney
Simon & Schuster India, New Delhi

www.simonandschuster.co.uk
www.simonandschuster.com.au
www.simonandschuster.co.in

A CIP catalogue record for this book
is available from the British Library

Paperback ISBN: 978-1-3985-2158-2
eBook ISBN: 978-1-3985-2159-9

This book is a work of fiction.
Names, characters, places and incidents are either a
product of the author's imagination or are used fictitiously.
Any resemblance to actual people living or dead,
events or locales is entirely coincidental.

Printed and bound in Great Britain by
CPI Group (UK) Ltd, Croydon, CR0 4YY

MIX
Paper from
responsible sources
FSC® C171272

*This book is for everyone who once
loved a boy and felt those butterflies
overwhelm them in the best possible way.
And, well, if the boy didn't love
you back, shame on him!
What a jerk.*

CHAPTER ONE

OLIVE

Up to the day I met Jason Thorn, my dreams were made of fluffy white clouds, pretty pink dresses, tasty apple pies, and of course, our neighbor Kara's big brother.

"I don't want to hear another word about this, Jason. You are always welcome to stay here, sweetheart."

I was about to go down to help my mom set the table when their voices carried up to me and I stopped.

"See, I told you it would be okay. Come on, let's go up to my room."

"Hold on, Dylan. Not so fast."

I heard mom's coffee cup softly clink on the kitchen counter a few seconds before I heard her speak again.

"Jason, are you sure you don't want us to call anyone? Maybe they should check on your mom and make sure everything is okay, or we can call your father and let him know that you are spending the night with us. I bet he would be worried if he called your house and couldn't reach either one of you."

My mom was a soft, compassionate woman—soft as in she carried a heart that was purely made of shiny liquid gold. I'd heard my grandpa tell her so countless times for putting up with my father, so as a child I knew it had to be true. There was also a side of her that could be seen as vicious at times, as she was fiercely protective of the ones she counted as her family.

Other than that, she was a sweetheart, as my father liked to call her. She had this secret way of making anyone smile, even when they were sad about something. I knew that because she always made me laugh when we were at the dentist, which was a big scary place for a six-year-old (almost seven!). If she was in the room, chances were she'd have you beaming up at her in no time.

It wasn't just me and my brother; she had the same effect on my friends too. Whenever it was her turn to pick us up from school, they all looked up at her with these big, silly smiles stretched across their faces. Actually, now that I think about it, they reminded me of Buzz, the puppy Kara had gotten a few weeks before. Oh, how much I loved watching Kara's brother Noah play with that puppy; I'd always thought we could rescue a few puppies for ourselves after he asked me to marry him.

Sigh...

Anyway, I hadn't been allowed to have the puppy in the house, and of course I would never ever sneak him in whenever my mom was out—*sshh, don't tell anyone*—but I did see the faces the little guy made when he wanted something from Kara.

All in all, back then, I believed it was tough to be a kid, but having a mom like mine made everything a bit easier. That's why I'd always wanted to be like her. I'd wanted to make people happy, make them forget about their worries for a while, be their sunshine, as she was ours.

There had been only one teeny-tiny issue...the blaring fact that I didn't have a golden heart because I was never good at being peaceful or graceful, where my mom, on the other hand, was the epitome of those traits.

It wasn't my fault though; it was always Dylan who made me

angry. If blame were to be assigned, it would fall squarely on Dylan's shoulders, not mine.

Dylan was my big brother, the one who kept ruining everything for me, probably since the day I was born. Unfortunately, I didn't remember those early years of my existence, but I was pretty sure that he'd been messing with me back then, too. According to my mom and dad, a few days after they brought me home from the hospital, he told them they should take me back to where they'd found me—next to the garbage cans.

Can you believe the audacity? My loving big brother.

It didn't even end with a cleverly veiled threat either. I remembered myself that he would steal my stroller and run around with me in the park. Why, he was probably trying to kill me with sheer excitement!

At an early age, I'd come to the conclusion that I would get to have my own golden heart when Dylan wouldn't be around to throw me off of my game. Whenever he was around, chances were he'd do something and I'd lose my cool, which would lead to us getting into a screaming match.

There was nothing graceful about screaming your little heart out at someone because they wouldn't play My Little Pony with you.

Jason's carefully chosen words brought me back to the present where I was plastered to the wall just to the left of the staircase, listening in on them.

"Thank you, Mrs. Taylor, but I don't think my father cares about where I'm spending the night. And…um…my mom will probably be okay in the morning. I'm sure she just fell asleep. It's my fault really; I should've checked the time and made sure I was home before six."

"We were playing catch on the street, Jason. Like, right in front of your house. I don't think you are the one to blame here.

And who goes to sleep at six, Mom? Even Olive stays up later than that."

"Dylan," my mom said in a low voice before sighing.

I grinned, feeling proud. I could stay up pretty late. Sometimes I could even go until nine.

There was complete silence for a few moments, and then the feet of the chair scraped the floor as someone got up from the table.

"Okay, Jason." I heard mom's strained voice breaking the thick silence. Who was this boy they kept calling Jason? Maybe he was part of the family that had moved in across the street a few houses down a few days ago?

How come Dylan hadn't introduced me to his new friend?

"You are always welcome in this house. I want you to remember that, okay?"

"Thank you Mrs. Taylor. I appreciate it."

"Why don't you go and get cleaned up while I get dinner ready? After dinner we'll call your dad and make sure he knows you are safe."

"That's not really necess—"

"Let's say it's for my own peace of mind."

"Come on, Jason." I heard my brother murmur. "I'll show you the new video game my dad bought me."

Oh, about that…I'd always thought it was quite rude of him to hoard all the toys. He never let me play with him.

I turned on my heels and was about to run back to my room to check out who the new boy was through the small opening of my door when my mom said, "Dylan, can you stay and help me set the table first? Then you can join Jason upstairs until I call you guys down for dinner."

"Sure, Mom," my brother answered readily. "The bathroom is the second door to the left, Jason. My room is next to it. I'll be right up."

"Is there anything I can help with, Mrs. Taylor? I wouldn't mind."

"Oh, you are too sweet, Jason. How about you be our guest for tonight, and any time you come by after today, you'll give me a hand, too, okay? And you call me Emily from now on."

"Okay, Mrs. Tay—umm…Emily. Thank you so much for letting me stay here tonight. I'll be in your room, then, Dylan." His footsteps started up the stairs.

I stood still and patiently waited for the owner of those footsteps to reach me. Since Dylan wasn't with him, I could say hi and welcome him to our neighborhood without getting into trouble.

Argh Dylan… Just because he was four years older didn't make him the boss of me.

Would he be blond? Maybe he would have dark eyes and dark hair and be all dreamy, exactly like Kara's big brother, Noah, who had turned eighteen just a few weeks before. My mom thought he was a little too old for me, but she had also once said a girl should always dream big. While I loved my mom dearly, clearly she wasn't right all the time.

Anyway, since this Jason seemed to be friends with Dylan, I highly doubted he would be something to dream about.

Suddenly my stomach got all fluttery for some reason. I frowned and smoothed down my dress. Dylan's friend or not, he would be a guest in our house and I thought I should be welcoming since he sounded very stressed out about staying with us.

Tommy, one of my best friends from school, believed that we would get married one day, but I'd never said yes to him. I'd never even gotten excited whenever we were on playdates.

First, I saw Jason's sneakers. I still remember: they were white and very clean for a boy his age. I thought maybe he wouldn't be that bad and make fun of me like Dylan's other friends.

Putting on my best smile, I slowly lifted my head up to meet his eyes. His steps faltered when he saw me hiding next to the wall. I got a good look at him and my smile slowly vanished as my mouth dropped open.

Jason? Jason what?

Butterflies? Were those tiny flutters in my stomach butterflies? The ones my mom had told me about? It sure felt like it. Thousands of them. Were these the same butterflies my mom had felt when she'd met my father?

What was his last name?

I wanted—no scratch that, I *needed* his last name to be my last name.

Not the day after, not ten years or twenty years later. I needed it to happen that day—right at that moment to be exact.

He seemed surprised to see me for a second, but recovered faster than I did. He gave me a stupidly cute smile with a dimple showing on his left cheek.

"You have a dimple," I breathed out, totally lost in that tiny little crevice. It was almost magical.

I closed my mouth and felt the heat rise up to my cheeks. I managed to return his smile with a wobbly one.

"Hey, little one. You must be Dylan's little sister. I'm Jason."

"Hi," I greeted sheepishly as I gave him a small wave.

His smile picked up a notch, and I felt my face flush again. Tucking a loose hair behind my ear, I smiled bigger.

Oh, boy.

He was so cute.

I cleared my throat and extended my hand, just like I saw my dad do when he was meeting someone new. "I'm Olive. My friends call me Liv or Oli because they think I have a weird name."

Quirking his brow, he looked at my hand then up to my eyes as he gave it a good shake. "Do they now?" he asked, and I nodded enthusiastically, hiding my hand behind my back again. "I think you have a good name, little Olive. It would be hard for someone to forget a name like Olive. You have very beautiful green eyes; I'd say the name suits you."

Beautiful?

Beautiful?!

I was never going to wash my hand again.

My smile got bigger, and I believe it was the first moment I fell in love with the mysterious boy who had an adorable dimple and was going to spend the night right across from my room.

"Are you our new neighbor?" I asked. He had to be our new neighbor. I had to see him again.

"Yes, we moved in last week."

I nodded. That was good news—more time for us to be together.

"Since you like my name, would you like to marry me?" I asked.

His face turned red and he opened and closed his mouth a few times.

Finally he laughed and said, "What?"

I shrugged. "My dad doesn't want me to get married for at least another thirty years, but I don't think we should wait that long. So, can we get married sooner?"

He scratched his head and even made that look cute. "I think we are too young to get married, little one."

Crushed, I looked down at my feet. "My dad says that, too. I've always thought I would marry Noah, our neighbor, but my dad is pretty set against that. Even my mom thinks he is too old for me. I think I can wait for you to get older, though." I nodded to myself. "Make sure you wait for me too. Okay. I'm gonna go down and help mom with dinner. Dylan always screws it up. You know," I started, clutching my hands behind my back as my eyes fell to his shoes. "I helped her bake the apple pie and the vanilla sauce earlier. I'll make sure you'll get the biggest slice. You'll love it, and I'll give it to you first."

I knew guys cared about food because my dad had always appreciated a good home-cooked meal. My little heart had fallen in love for the first time and I was hoping Jason would fall for me, too, after he tasted the pie.

He chuckled and touched his finger to my chin. Surprised at the contact, my head flew up, my eyes huge. When I saw his smiling face, I had to bite down on my lip so I wouldn't grin like a little girl, which would surely be a dead giveaway that I was in love with him.

"Thank you, little one. I'm sure it's delicious if you had a hand in it. I better let you go then. I'll look forward to seeing you at dinner."

Passing by me, he tugged a piece of my hair, his smile still going strong on his lips as he headed for the bathroom.

I fidgeted with my hands so I wouldn't wave him a goodbye and sigh like my friend Amanda did whenever she saw Dylan.

Inside, I was dancing on the clouds.

He had touched my hair.

He had touched my chin and looked into my eyes.

Jason.

Our one-dimpled new neighbor. Had. Touched. Me.

Ah...

I was pretty sure he'd fallen in love with me, too. I mean why else would he smile, look into my eyes, and touch me, if he hadn't?

Right?

Right?!

CHAPTER TWO

OLIVE

Seven years later...

"Thank you for letting me have your phone, Amanda," I whispered as I was hiding in my closet.

"Why are we whispering?"

"So Dylan and Jason can't hear me."

"Are you sure you want to do this? I mean, come on Olive, what if he realizes it's you texting him?"

"But I do want him to realize it's me." I thought about that for a second, and then changed my mind. "Well, okay, maybe not at first, but eventually."

Amanda sighed on the other end of the line. "I'm not so sure this is a good idea, Liv. What if he tells Dylan?" She gasped. "What if they recognize the number and think it's me?"

"Oh, stop it. How could they possibly recognize your cousin's number? If you don't open your mouth, no one will know. And it's just for tonight. I won't text him again. My parents are gone, he is staying over, it's the perfect timing."

"Olive!" My brother banged on my door. "The pizza is here, come down if you don't want to find an empty box."

"Break the door down, why don't you," I muttered to myself. Opening the door of my little closet, I yelled back, "I'm coming!"

"Okay, I'm heading downstairs. What time is it?" I asked Amanda, getting up from the floor.

"Nine. When will you text him? You have to let me know what he is saying."

"I can't text you while I'm texting him. I'll be too excited. I'll call you tomorrow to let you know how it went."

"Nope, I'm coming for breakfast then, who knows when you'll call me. Plus, I need to get the phone back to my cousin. They are leaving tomorrow afternoon."

"Fine, then I'll see you tomorrow. Wish me luck."

Throwing the phone on my bed, I took a deep breath and looked at myself in the mirror. My strawberry blonde hair was falling down on my shoulders in soft waves, my eyes were sparkling, and my face was flushed with excitement over the possibility of what might happen later that night.

I looked down at my shaky hands and laughed at myself.

All I wanted for that night was to text Jason and talk to him as if I was someone else, like an admirer. You see, I'd had it all planned for days. I was going to text him, of course keeping my identity a secret, preferably when Dylan was not by his side, and then simply talk to him. Maybe I could ask him who he would want his admirer to be... *Wouldn't it be something else if he said me?*

So far the plan was working smoothly. Depending on how the rest of the night went, I would make my move accordingly.

"Olive!" my brother thundered from downstairs.

Closing my eyes, I took a deep refreshing breath, hid the phone under my pillow, and walked out of my room.

"What are you yelling for? I said I was coming," I said when I spotted Dylan sitting alone in front of the TV.

"Pour the drinks and bring out the pizza," he answered, not even looking at me.

"Why can't you get up and do it yourself?" I shot back.

"Just get on with it already. I'm about to start the movie."

I opened my mouth to—

"Hi little Olive," someone whispered right next to my ear, causing me to jump.

"Jason," I whispered back, my hands jumping to my chest to keep my heart in place. "You scared me."

He chuckled, showing me the dimple. "I know."

I laughed back, my eyes shining with love for the boy I'd known for seven years now.

Tugging at a piece of my hair, he winked and walked past me with a cold water bottle in his hand. He pushed over Dylan and sat right next to him.

Eyeing the small seat next to Jason, I asked, "Do you want anything other than water?"

Turning his head, he smiled at me. "Thank you, beautiful. I'm good."

I melted into a small, very happy puddle on my mother's favorite carpet.

"Stop flirting with my sister, you shithead," Dylan muttered, but I was too occupied with my dreams to tell Dylan to shush— not that he would listen to me.

Grabbing Dylan's soda and a few paper plates for the pizza, I went back into the living room.

"Pour your own drink," I said, dropping the bottle a little too harshly on the coffee table in front of him.

"How many slices do you want, Jason?" I asked, kneeling on the floor and not quite meeting his eyes.

Dylan sighed and muttered, "Here we go again."

He didn't like that I always gave the first slice of pizza—or cake, or pie, or any type of food actually—to Jason.

Putting his water bottle down, Jason reached out to help me up. "You are not sitting on the floor." He pulled me up to the couch. "I'll handle the pizza."

Plopping down next to him, I let him divvy up the slices between the three of us.

"Two slices good?" he asked, giving me the first share.

Be still my heart.

"Yes, thank you."

When he leaned back and shot me another quick wink, I forgot all about my pizza and reveled in the fact that I was about to spend two hours sitting right next to Jason watching a movie. It was the perfect night to text him.

"What are we watching?" I asked, taking a small bite from the huge slice.

"Nothing you'll enjoy. We are already spending our Friday night babysitting your ass so you don't have a say in the movie choices."

"Don't be an asshole, Dylan," Jason murmured with his mouth full.

"So you're saying you prefer to stay in tonight instead of going out with the girls?"

As my eyes filled with tears of embarrassment and something else I couldn't name, I put my plate down and attempted to get up, only to be pulled back by Jason.

"Children," he said in a tone similar to my dad's. His warm hand was still closed over my wrist, keeping me seated—or more like paralyzed. "I promised Emily I would babysit both of you just in case you decided today was the day to kill each other. So, cut the crap and start the movie already. The girls aren't going anywhere, Dylan."

Still embarrassed, I cleared my throat to get their attention. "You guys don't have to stay in for me. I'll be okay, Dylan. You know I don't mind staying alone."

Looking at my miserable face, Dylan finally shook his head and reached for his plate. "Nah, it's okay. Jason is right; the girls aren't going anywhere and we've wanted to watch this for weeks, now is as good a time as any."

The movie started and they both settled back as all my excitement for the night slowly trickled out of me.

When Dylan jumped up and said, "I'll get the lights," I was still playing with the paper plate in my lap.

Could he have a girlfriend?

I was sure he didn't have one. Neither did Dylan actually, not since he'd broken up with his on-again, off-again girlfriend Vicky.

"Don't worry, little one, it's not a horror movie or anything. It's action, you'll like it," Jason whispered into my ear before Dylan took his seat again.

Hearing him use the pet name he'd always liked to call me, I managed to put a sincere smile on my face when I looked up at him.

"Thank you. You guys can leave after the movie, you know. I won't tell Mom and Dad when they come back tomorrow."

"Are you kidding? I was looking forward to a quiet night in. Pizza and a movie with a beautiful green-eyed girl by my side?" He gave me a light shove with his shoulder. "Your brother is the stupid one, not me."

Dylan turned off the lights and hopped back onto his seat. Luckily this time I was melting into another puddle on my mother's not-so-favorite couch. I stayed that way until the end of the movie because Jason's shoulder stayed plastered to mine the entire time.

About to die from sensory overload, I still had a stupid smile on my face as I headed to my room for the night.

Let the texting begin…

———

AROUND 1:30 AM, huddled under my covers, I listened to Dylan's bedroom door open and close for the second time. The TV in his bedroom was on, but their voices were low. Either they didn't want to wake me up or they were about to go to sleep, though I highly doubted that was the case.

Reaching for the phone under my pillow, I tried to get a handle on my breathing and erratic heartbeats.

As much as I was dying to text Jason, I was also scared out of my mind.

My fingers as cold as ice, I quickly sent the first text of the night.

Me: Hi Jason.

Original, I know.

I waited to see if I would hear his phone go off, but I couldn't hear anything. My heart in my throat, I sat up in bed and dropped my head back on the headboard. Maybe Amanda was right. Maybe, this wasn't the best idea I'd ever come up with…

Jason: Who is this?

There might have been a squeak that escaped from my mouth when the phone lit up in my hand without a sound. In the darkness of my room, an unexplainable rush going through my body, I started talking to Jason as a stranger.

Me: I don't think you'd know even if I said my name.
Jason: We can't know if you don't try me.
Me: My name is Michelle. We go to the same school.

> *Jason: Hmm... You're right. I don't think I know a*
> *Michelle.*
> *Me: Can't exactly say I'm surprised.*
> *Jason: And why would that be, my new friend Michelle?*

Already lost in a different world, my fingers stopped flying over the buttons when I heard Dylan's door open and close quietly. Not knowing whether it was my brother or Jason, I hid the phone under the covers so the light wouldn't draw attention.

> *Me: There are always so many people around you. Doesn't*
> *give many opportunities for new people to introduce*
> *themselves, I guess. But then again, maybe you already*
> *know me.*
> *Jason: That's interesting. Our friendship is so new,*
> *Michelle who is not really Michelle, and you're already*
> *lying to me?*
> *Me: I wouldn't say it's lying. Let's say I'm one of your*
> *many admirers and a little shy one at that. Just wanted to*
> *talk to you.*
> *Jason: Let's play your game. What would you like to talk*
> *about?*
> *Me: I have no idea. Maybe you can start with where you*
> *are and what you are doing?*
> *Jason: Easy enough. As I'm already sure you are not a*
> *Michelle, you must already know my friend Dylan, I'm*
> *over his place.*
> *Me: I know of him and I know that you are close friends,*
> *that's about it.*
> *Jason: Would you like me to introduce you two? It'll be*
> *like a second introduction for us, too.*
> *Me: Not necessary.*

Jason: As you wish, new shy friend. What else would you
like to talk about?
Me: Do you have any guesses as to who I could be?
Jason: Oh, another game. You sure are full of games
tonight, mystery girl.
Me: It's not exactly a game for me.

Five minutes passed but no texts came in. When it hit the
ten-minute mark, I got anxious, worrying if he already knew
who I was and had put a stop it. Getting up from my bed, I
started pacing my small bedroom. When the space wasn't
enough, I sneaked out of my room and quietly went downstairs
to grab a bottle of water and distract myself with something
else.

Padding into the kitchen in a tank top and pajama bottoms, I
stopped short when I found Jason staring out the small window
over the sink.

"Jason?" I whispered.

Turning to me, he whispered back, "Hey, Olive." His chocolate eyes looked tired for his young age. "What are you doing up
so late?"

Spying his phone on the kitchen counter, I forced my gaze
away. "Bad dream, I guess. Couldn't go back to sleep." Acting
nonchalant, I opened the fridge and took out a bottle of water.
"What were you looking at?"

"Just at my house."

"Your mom okay?"

"I don't know, Olive. I really don't know." Letting out a deep
sigh, he absently reached for his phone and walked over to me.

"You can talk to me if something's on your mind."

He stopped right in front of me, his eyes almost invisible in
the dark.

"I can?"

"Of course. I know you worry about your parents sometimes. I can listen if you need to."

"You're right, little Olive. I do worry about them, but they are the last thing I want to talk about."

"I'm sorry," I mumbled, looking down at the floor.

"No need to be. Come and get us if you need anything, all right? I don't think we'll go to sleep for a few hours yet." A gentle tug at my hair and he was gone.

I waited a few minutes before I padded back upstairs.

Just as I was about to go into my room and run for the phone, Dylan peeked out of his room.

"What are you doing, Olive?"

Damn it! Didn't he have anything else to do other than make my life miserable?

"What are *you* doing?" I asked back, a little peeved and a little nervous.

He cocked his head, his eyebrows knitted.

"Go back to bed, Olive. It's late."

"I was doing exactly that before you stopped me." I lifted the water bottle in my hand so he could see. "I went downstairs to get a drink, Dylan. I wasn't doing anything."

Neither one of us backed up. Just because his friend was staying over, I couldn't leave my room to get a drink?

"Leave her alone, man." I heard Jason's voice coming from behind Dylan.

"Goodnight, Dylan," I said at last, then slipped into my room without waiting for an answer. Who knew what was up his ass…

Jumping into my bed, I searched for the phone under my covers and had a small freak out when I couldn't find it. I relaxed when I realized it was under my pillow.

The silly excitement rushing over me once again, I checked the messages only to find no new text messages from Jason.

Settling down, I told myself that I would only send one other text and then maybe try my luck in the morning before Amanda came to get the phone.

> *Me: What? No guesses? I'm surprised.*
> *Jason: Sorry, I was busy. Which game were we playing*
> *again?*

Seeing my first opening, I couldn't help myself and jumped on it. Would he mention me?

> *Me: Busy? Busy with what? Already found a new friend,*
> *huh? You really are quick.*
> *Jason: You amuse me. I was cornered by Dylan's sister.*
> *Not exactly in the arms of another girl.*

Not knowing my heart was about to get broken for the very first time, I swallowed the pain the word 'cornered' had caused and forced myself to text him back.

> *Me: It's almost 2 AM, and you were with Dylan's sister?*
> *This sounds good. Do tell me more.*
> *Jason: She is just a little kid. A clingy one maybe, since*
> *she always follows me around, but still a kid. She*
> *sometimes forgets that. I'm much more interested in who*
> *you are. I'm ready to play. Are you ready to be discovered*
> *by me?*

I read the text a thousand times, or maybe it was a million. A tear escaped from the corner of my eye, and I drew the covers over myself and lay back.

Gently, I put the phone down and pushed the covers off of my face to stare at my dark ceiling. At some point it buzzed with two new messages, but I ignored them. No, that's not true, I remember reaching for the phone and deleting everything before the unexpected words could hurt me again, but at that point it was all blurry for me. I couldn't read them even if I wanted to torture myself.

Clingy?

Cornered?

My heart broken into pieces, suddenly I couldn't bear to see Jason in the morning. Couldn't bear to sleep in the room across from him again.

Swinging my legs down from the bed, I didn't realize I had kicked my own phone into my closet door.

Seconds later, Dylan burst into my room.

"Did you hea—Olive, what happened?"

Wiping at my tears, I looked up at my brother and more fresh tears slid down my already wet cheeks.

When he sat down on my bed and gently put his hand on my back, I threw my arms around him and hid my face in his neck. His arms came around me.

Warm and safe.

I heard footsteps at my door, but I was too scared to lift my head and come face to face with Jason. I didn't think I would ever be able to look him in the eye again.

My breath hitching against Dylan's neck, I said, "I'm sorry, just a bad dream."

"It's okay, little sis," Dylan said. He hesitated, then added, "I'm sorry, too."

The next few days were pure hell for me, having Jason sleep right across the room from mine, sitting right next to him at the dinner table. The worst was when I looked at him and found him smiling at me but knew it meant nothing at all.

Maybe it never had.

CHAPTER THREE

JASON

The first thing I saw when I opened my eyes was Emily's worried face hovering over me.

"Good morning," I said, yawning through the words. "What time is it? Did we miss breakfast?" Sitting up on the makeshift bed I'd made use of almost every other day for the last seven years, I rubbed my eyes and tried to wake up.

"Jason. Honey." I heard Emily's struggle with those simple words and became alert at once.

Then my gaze fell on Dylan, who was sitting on the edge of his bed, his head in his hands. I looked up and saw his father, Logan Taylor—a fireman, a man I respected more than my old man—standing in the doorway. His eyes were as hard as steel.

"What's going on?" I asked no one in particular as something ugly started to find its way into me.

Emily, the woman I loved quite possibly more than my own mom, sat down next to me and gripped my hand in her small, delicate one. She had burn marks on that arm, almost up to her shoulder, but they never bothered me like they surprisingly bothered a lot of people, young *and* old.

"Jason, I don't know how to say this."

Another burst of silence.

"Can someone please say *something*? Dylan? What's going on, man?" Still no sound. "Okay, you guys are starting to scare me."

"Logan," Emily murmured next to me, her eyes desperately focused on her husband.

Dylan's father shook his head, dropped his arms, and stepped into the room to sit next to Dylan, right across from me.

When my best friend lifted his head, I saw his bloodshot eyes.

My gaze went back to his father's steely ones. They were easier to look at. Anger was always easier to handle than emotion; I had learned that from my own family.

"I'm ready," I said, keeping my eyes on Logan. "Please tell me what's wrong."

I didn't know it, but I was not actually ready for the words he would give me. Nowhere near ready.

"Son," he started, because that's what I was to him. "You can handle this."

It wasn't a question, but I nodded anyway.

"Your mother overdosed on her sleeping pills last night. She is gone."

I blinked, once.

I nodded.

My voice thick and rough, I asked, "Who found her?"

"Apparently your father came back from his trip this morning. He called an ambulance, but Lorelai was already gone."

"I understand. Where is my father?"

"He is at the hospital. I talked to him a few minutes ago."

Helpless, I nodded again. What else could I do? What else was I supposed to do?

"Thank you," I said, giving Emily's hand a quick squeeze. "Thank you for being the ones to tell me."

Every single person in the room I was sitting in had been

more of a family to me than my own could ever be. I appreciated the fact that I could see the concern in their eyes, their concern for me. I never saw anything even close to it in my own mother's eyes. Her alcohol meant more to her than her own son.

I slowly got up. "I should get back…home, I guess."

But I had never had a home, had I? This was a home. The house across the street? Not so much.

Dylan and Logan got up with me, but I looked down at Mrs. Taylor. Her eyes were full of tears. She had the same shade of green eyes as her daughter, just as striking as Olive's. It was soothing to look at.

I leaned down and, surprising myself, brushed a small kiss on her cheek.

"Please don't cry, Emily. It's okay. It'll be okay."

It sounded more like a question to my ears.

She slowly got up and brushed a tear away, my tear. I wasn't even aware that I was crying. Her warm hand cupped my cheek and she stared right into my eyes. "Of course it will be okay, Jason. You have us."

I nodded.

Unexpectedly, I found myself in Dylan's arms next. "I'm so sorry, man," he said, holding on to me. I felt Emily's hand at my back, a soothing caress. Logan was standing next to us, watching over his family.

I was family to them.

I'd earned that place among them.

———

"ARE you sure you don't want to stay here and finish school with Dylan? I can talk to your dad again," offered Logan.

The Taylor family was out on their front lawn. Even little Olive had come out to say goodbye with tear-filled eyes. I smiled at her. I could see sparkles in her eyes, sad sparkles maybe, but sparkles nonetheless. She was so full of life and had the most beautiful, captivating green eyes. So rich and alive. The kind that you looked at and let yourself happily drown in. I knew some idiot was bound to break her heart very soon, but I wouldn't be there to protect her heart right alongside her brother. I wouldn't be with the people I considered my family.

Instead, I would be in Los Angeles living in an unfamiliar house with a stranger I called Dad who I had never had the chance to get to know. For a quick second I wondered if he was blaming himself for her death. He certainly hadn't been there when his presence could've made a difference. Maybe the ending wouldn't have changed, maybe a few years down we would've still ended up in the same situation, but we would never know. It was too late for everything.

As for what I thought…I blamed life, and him. He was the one who'd chosen to leave us behind when he could've been a lawyer in San Francisco just as easily. He was the one who'd chosen to ignore my mother's quickly deteriorating mental health, or depression, whatever you wanted to call it. And then he'd been the one who'd ignored me when I said his wife was becoming an alcoholic.

In the end, the choices they had made were changing my life.

"He isn't changing his mind. Believe me, I tried," I said finally.

I shrugged. Everything had changed except my dad's decision: we were leaving. Or, more accurately, he was *forcing* me to leave everything behind.

Kicking at the grass under my foot, I stopped in front of Emily, the kindest, most caring human being. A mother who could never be truly mine.

"I don't know what to say," I admitted, words burning in my chest as my eyes continued to look down at my sneakers.

"Jason?"

Warm, gentle hands cupped my face and looked into my eyes.

"Do you remember what I said to you the first time we met?" She smiled, her eyes shining just like her daughter's. "You're always welcome here. That will never change. Los Angeles isn't that far away; I'm expecting you to come back whenever you want to or need to. Do you hear what I'm saying?"

"Yes." I nodded. "I don't know how to thank you for everything you've done for me, for everything you've been for me."

"I don't need a thank you, Jason. Just make sure you come back to us." She hesitated, only for half a second, then pulled me down and kissed my cheeks. "Make sure you take care of yourself." One last look in my eyes, and she let me go.

I wished she wouldn't.

"Son," Logan said as he gave me a quick, unexpected hug. "You heard what Emily said, this is your home too. And you always come back to your home. Don't forget that. We will miss you."

It seemed like I wasn't capable of doing anything other than nod that day.

I glanced at Olive and despite my situation, my lips tipped up.

"Cat got your tongue, too, huh?" She just stared at me with those sad, sad eyes. Olive Taylor always had something to say—always. "You've got nothing to say, Olive?" I asked, chuckling, the sound completely wrong and rough.

"I'm really sorry about your mom, but I hope you'll be happy in LA."

The cold tone and what I was seeing in her eyes didn't match, but before I could say anything, Dylan got up from the steps he was sitting on and Olive hugged her dad's waist, shutting me out.

Even so, I reached out and gently touched her soft hair, tugging it gently before letting it go for the last time.

"I hope so too. And thank you, beautiful, I will never forget you."

A tear slid down from her eye, and before I knew what I was doing, I reached out to capture it with my fingertip.

She closed her eyes and hugged her dad tighter when I touched her, but didn't say anything.

I looked at the teardrop that rested on my fingertip for a long time and felt a tug on my heartstrings.

"Man," Dylan said, saving me from my confusing thoughts.

I released a big breath and dropped my finger.

"This sucks," he said.

I chuckled. "You're tellin me."

"I want you to come back the first chance you get, and you are keeping in touch."

I snapped a sharp salute, causing his mouth to twitch.

Hitting my chin with his knuckles, he groaned. "Oh, man. I can't believe I'm gonna miss seeing your shitty face every day."

"Dylan!" Emily admonished.

"Sorry, Mom." Rubbing the back of his neck, Dylan looked at me sheepishly. "We'll talk?"

"We'll talk," I promised.

"Jason," my father called out from the car waiting across the street.

"I better go," I said, taking a few steps back.

Giving Dylan a quick hug and a slap on his back, I said, "Take care of your family, man."

"You make sure you take care of yourself, too."

My chest heavy, I looked at all of them one last time and walked away. I wasn't strong enough to stride away from them without turning back. In the time it took me to cross the street, I looked back three times.

Did it make me a bad person to be happy to see them sad?

Happy because I felt loved? Loved and welcome as I'd never been before?

How they stood together as a family was burned into my mind as a happy memory, and then I got into the car and disappeared from their life.

CHAPTER FOUR

OLIVE

My emotions waging a war inside me, I clung to my dad and watched Jason get into the black Mercedes. The image of him turning to look at us with a dimpled smile before he got into the car would be burned into my mind as a sad memory for years to come.

Then like every other fleeting moment in life, my first love slowly faded into time.

CHAPTER FIVE

JASON

Eight years later...

Pushing the private back door of the nightclub open with my shoulder, I dragged the giggling mess out with me. Since she was busy pawing at me with those claw-like fingers, she tripped over her own feet, righting herself at the last moment, her giggling getting even louder. Gripping her waist to make sure she didn't face plant in those spiky-heeled shoes, I checked the alley to make sure we were alone. As soon as the door closed and the heavy bass of the music drifted away to a buzz, I took Jenna's hand off my dick and slammed her back against the concrete wall, eating up her moan in a hungry kiss.

Wait, is her name Gemma?

"Take me home, Jason," she said, her words slightly slurring. She wasn't drunk—if she were, I wouldn't do this with her—but for some reason she chose to act like she was. I didn't care for her games. "Take me home and I'll show you a few new tricks."

More giggling.

Jamie maybe?

Fuck!

"This is better, babe. Don't you feel the thrill?" I asked in a low voice as my lips ghosted over her skin against her throat. "Anyone can walk out on us. Doesn't that excite you?"

What the hell is her name again? She hadn't had a big role in the movie, but we'd shared the same set for about a month. She twirled and skipped around me whenever she found me alone in a corner, watching the crew work. She whispered dirty, dirty things in my ear—at least dirty for a girl her age—when no one was around. At last, after countless 'fuck me eyes' had been thrown my way at the wrap party that night, little brunette beauty Jessie (*???*) was about to get the fuck of her life against a concrete wall in the back alley of a club. Looking at her flushed skin and already dazed eyes, I could see that it wasn't bothering her in the slightest that she was about to get fucked like a cheap hooker, out in the open.

That was all she would be for me, and most likely for the others that would come after me—producers, agents, etc.

"Aww, you can't wait to slide your dick into my pussy, can you? I can't wait either. I knew you were crazy about me Jason," she whispered into my ear right before she licked it, trying to kill my ear with the stabbing motions of her tongue.

Christ!

I pushed her face away.

Her high-pitched voice buzzed around in my head, making me too aware of the alcohol I had consumed.

Ignoring her words, I lifted Jenna's skintight silver dress up and over her hips, making sure to caress her toned thighs as she moaned against my neck, her heart racing.

She kept mumbling in between sloppy kisses, but I tuned her out and let myself get lost in her body.

At that point, I wasn't feeling much, just some sort of house music pounding in my head making it too hard to think clearly.

My dick was definitely feeling something as it strained against my jeans, dying to get into her tight pussy.

"You knew you were gonna get fucked tonight, didn't you...babe?"

Damn it! I still couldn't remember her name.

"Yes. Yes. I knew you couldn't stay away." She gasped as my fingers found their way to her...butterfly? What the hell? Normally I wouldn't care, but, well, sue me, I was a curious bastard.

I took a step back from her octopus arms and looked down to find a sparkling butterfly holding two flimsy straps around it wings. Her pussy was open for all to see in her crotchless panties —if you could even call them panties, that is.

"Huh," I muttered. "I guess that makes my job easier."

My dick was still roaring to get into action so I shrugged her hands off my shoulders and took out a condom from my back pocket, pulling it on pretty quickly considering my buzzed state.

Lifting her thigh as high as it would wrap around me, I entered her in a quick deep thrust as she gasped in delight.

"Jesus, you filled me," she said in surprise.

"You like that, babe? Is that what you've been after for so long? Getting filled up properly?" Another thrust and her eyes fluttered close.

"Yeah, it's better than what I've heard." Her voice was all dreamy, which made me hesitant to keep fucking her. I didn't do dreamy. A one-time quick fuck that would get us both off was more my kinda thing. Dreamy led to complicated stuff, and even though I liked to believe that as an actor I could sell a good dream, or hell, even *be* a good dream, I wasn't fucked up enough to think that I would find my own happy ending with my career choice. Not everyone would tolerate the lifestyle I led.

Don't get me wrong, I loved my job. It was the only thing that made any sort of sense in my life. However, everything else? The constant isolation forced on you, the paparazzi hounding you, everyone dissecting your every little move... After a while it felt like there was a noose around your throat that was being tightened by everyone in your life.

Yes. That's exactly how I felt.

Indifferent. Tired.

The only time it seemed like I was breathing again was when I was on a movie set, pretending to be someone else.

In a way, my life was a play.

"Oh my god, Jason. Yes. Yes, I knew it would be like this with you." She moaned as her words slurred. I picked up my pace. This was the only time she'd be getting fucked senseless by me; I should've been focused on her.

"Keep it quiet," I hissed in her ear as her cries started to get higher. "You don't want to get caught getting fucked in the street, do you?"

"I do. I do. Yes! Yes!"

I dropped my head to her shoulder and raced for the finish line. The quicker this was over, the quicker I could get back to my house.

Grabbing her ass, I wrapped both of her skinny legs around my waist and kept drilling into her. Her sharp cries echoed in the dark alley, blending with the music that was coming through the walls of the nightclub her back was against.

"Oh, fuck me, Jason," she screeched in my ear.

"That's what I'm trying to do," I said through gritted teeth. With all her shrieking, I was already sobering up.

I closed my eyes and tried to focus on the task at hand. When she suddenly tipped over the edge to fucking dreamland, I swore and came after her as she kept squeezing my dick rhythmically.

Tipping my head back, I felt every muscle in my body relax and experienced the bliss I appreciated so much, even if it was only for a few seconds.

That's exactly when I heard the running footsteps coming from behind us. Looking over my shoulder, I saw the first of many blinding flashlights.

"Fuck," I swore, my hands quickly getting rid of the condom before they could get to us.

Jenna slumped back on the wall and sighed, an even more doped up smile beginning to form on her lips as she started to fix her hair.

Zipping up my fly, I pulled down her skirt for her as she was too busy already beaming up to our intruders over my shoulder.

Shit! They were almost on us. Thankfully, my body was big enough to hide her from their cameras so I doubted they had gotten any shots of what we'd been doing just seconds before. At best, they would think I'd taken her out for a quick make out session.

"Jason! Jason! Is this a new relationship?" the one with the mustache yelled.

Click. Click. Click.

"Did your love start on set? Are the rumors true?"

"When are you goin' public with this?"

Click. Click.

"Did you start a relationship to promote your new movie?"

"Jason! Talk to us man! What were you guys doing back here?"

A few of them snickered.

Click. Click. Click.

What's-her-name threw her arms around my neck and beamed at the cameras. "How did you find us back here? This was supposed to be secret. We were being clever."

My face a mask of calm, I gently shrugged off her arms yet again and opened the private back door to push her back into the club.

Her eyes were as big as saucers and she couldn't do anything but gape at me as I closed the door on her face and turned to face the paps still shouting questions at me. Thankfully, there were only seven or eight of them.

"Jason! There is a clip of you with Zoey where it looks like you are getting busy in your car. Now you are with Jennifer, any comments?"

Ah! So that was her name.

"Have a nice evening, guys," I said in a bored tone, ignoring their questions. I put my hands in my pockets and they parted for me to pass, their voices getting higher and higher in my head. I didn't specifically hear what they were saying, but I knew I would be getting a phone call first thing the next morning from my agent, Tom Symond, who had become a good friend over the years, and of course my publicist, Megan.

A few minutes later, I was in my car racing back to Bel Air, still as edgy and empty as I'd been at the beginning of the night.

CHAPTER SIX

OLIVE

"Can you please remind me why you couldn't come with me again?" I whispered to Lucy on the phone as I pressed my forehead to the wall in the corner of the white waiting room where I sat, waiting to be called in.

"Babe, calm down. If it wasn't the little bitch's class, you know I'd be there holding your hand every step of the way. The woman already has it out for me; I can't give her more ammo. By the time you get home, I'll have the tequila shots ready to celebrate. Focus on that. It'll help."

I closed my eyes. I was seconds away from throwing up. To calm down and focus on something else, I started to pace up and down in my little corner. *Happy thoughts,* I encouraged myself.

Happy, happy thoughts.

There was a blonde girl sitting on the U-shaped white couch. She'd been busy texting away and then taking useless selfies for the last ten minutes. She was all dolled up and had a so very obviously fake tan that was already going splotchy on her. She hadn't let that thing—that phone that had mickey ears on it—down even for a second ever since she'd stepped in through the doors.

I mean, for god's sake, how many freaking pictures can you

take while sitting in the exact same spot, smiling the same fake smile? I'd stopped counting after thirty.

Looking at her making another pouty face as she squeezed her breasts together with her arms, I groaned.

"I think I'm gonna throw up," I whispered into my phone.

"Oh shut up. Pull up your big girl panties and bra and wow them with your pretty little smile."

"Since you are doing such a crappy job with the best friend gig, at least remind me why Char couldn't come with me?"

Lucy let out a long breath. "Charlotte would be trembling right beside you if you took her with you. That's why we didn't tell her where you were going, remember?"

I did. She was right; if Charlotte were there, they would remember us as the shaking duo—not the best first impression you'd want to make with anyone, let alone the studio people who were interested in adapting your book into a fucking movie.

"I hate you."

"I love you too, my anxious babe."

"Lucy," I started again in a miserable tone. "The meeting was at 2:30, it's almost 3. Maybe I should leave? Maybe they made a mistake scheduling this. I mean, who am I kidding, right? Clearly, this isn't happening. I don't want to wait around to see someone jump out and scream, 'Jokes on you, sucka!' I just wanna come home. Can I come home, please?"

"No, you can't come home. I forbid you to come home before you take that meeting and come back with good news and lotsa money. Now, close your eyes."

"Why?"

"Do it, Olive."

"Fine. My eyes are closed shut. You can come and pry them open if you want to win the best friend of the year award."

"I already own the shit out of that award, babe, so that's a useless threat. Are your eyes closed?"

"Yes," I huffed.

"Ok. Now, imagine you are a river."

"Ahhh," I groaned. *Not this crap again.* "What are you doing?"

"Calming you the hell down."

"By telling me I'm a river?"

"Yes. Now, shut up and imagine that you're a river. You are flowing; no one and nothing can stop you. You feel the sunlight on your…whatever and it makes you happy. You are a twinkle of laughter in the air. Then, you turn into a small waterfall, no, you turn into a majestic waterfall and then yo—"

"Ok, ok, Lucy." I cut her short before she could sputter more bullshit. "I'm calm. You calmed me down. I'm a cold river that hears twinkles of laughter in the air and then turns into a majestic waterfall thing."

"Great, good for you. Now, I saw Jameson's hot ass walk by me so I gotta go and take a bite out of that." I tried to cut in, but she shushed me. "Make me proud and I'll meet you at the house. Byeeeeee!"

I opened my mouth, but she had already hung up on me. I lowered my phone and smiled to myself. She hadn't come anywhere near calming me down, but she always had a way of making me smile.

I looked around the black and white office. Everything looked so expensive: the art on the walls, the furniture, the carpet, even the damn windows looked all expensive and shiny. Feeling naked, nervous, scared, excited—did I mention naked?—I took a step forward to go sit down next to the clicker happy chick, but when I saw her take a selfie stick out of her bag, I decided against it.

Pacing it was.

My gaze landed on the women that sat behind the huge, crescent-shaped reception desk. They all looked like models, not secretaries. Not a single hair on their head was out of place while mine was a crazy wavy mess. I glanced down at my clothes… Well, obviously I didn't fit in with their pencil skirt, blouse, and high-heeled office attire, but I looked good. Just a few hours before, Lucy had forced me to wear a black bandeau skirt with a simple white shirt and a thin leather jacket. Of course, she had tried to force me to wear high heels, but I had gotten away with wearing my lucky combat boots. I liked to think I looked chic and relaxed in a fashionable sort of way. However, it wasn't helping me not feel out of place at all.

I focused on the brunette that had told me that I needed to wait a few minutes because the execs were running late. That few minutes had turned into forty minutes exactly one minute ago.

Please, don't judge me. Normally I'm cool with waiting. Hell, any other time, I would've loved to sit down next to the photo chick and take pictures of her taking pictures of herself and have a laugh about it with Lucy and Charlotte when I got back home. But, minutes had a really slow way of moving when you were about to lose your cool and throw up in front of a handful of strangers. I couldn't be held responsible for all the daggers I was throwing at the model-secretaries.

Hell, shame on them. What kind of cruel people were they that they were playing with my emotions like this? As far as I was concerned, they deserved all the imaginary sharp little daggers.

Finally the brunette met my eyes, held her finger to her ear to listen to whoever was talking on the other the end of her bluetooth thingy, then nodded once.

"Miss Taylor," she called to me.

I closed my eyes, took a deep, shaky breath, and walked over to her.

She was already up from her seat and walking toward me. We met in the middle.

"I'm a river. I can flow peacefully," I muttered to myself.

"Excuse me?"

"Oh, nothing. Sorry." I gave her a shaky smile.

"I'll walk you to Mr. Thomas' office. They are ready for you."

"Thank you," I said, trying very, very hard to keep my hands at my sides instead of doing something crazy like slipping my hand into hers to steal some of her cool.

That wouldn't be weird, right?

She gave me a sincere smile, the first one actually, and led the way down the long hallway.

We turned right, passing more expensive paintings, and some movie posters, then we took a left turn, this time passing a whole bunch of small offices. Each time we passed an open door, I was ready to jump out of my skin with nervousness. When we made yet another turn, I was starting to feel like a hamster trying to get to its treat. Then there was only a big door in front of us.

I came to a halt. Was I really doing this? Was this really happening?

Shit!

Who was I kidding, this was going to be a complete disaster!

I was no majestic waterfall. Not even close.

The brunette stood next to the door and her hand paused on the handle before she pulled it open. Clearly, she was waiting for me to come closer, but I was having none of that. I lifted my eyes up to hers.

Fight or flight?

I was seconds away from flight.

Damn it!

How many turns had we made? Could I even find my way out of that labyrinth of hell without her?

I took an involuntary step back to test the waters and the next thing I knew she was standing right next to me, asking if I was okay, her hand surprisingly strong at my back.

I made an awful, awful mewling sound in my throat and then

started coughing. When I was done with all that nonsense, her face had softened up.

"Sorry," I murmured.

"You are nervous about the meeting?"

"It can't be that obvious," I said, trying to chuckle.

"You have nothing to be nervous about. I loved your book," she stated, shocking the hell out of me.

My eyes widened. "What? You did? You read my book? You actually know who I am? Did you say you liked the book?" I asked, holding my breath. Well, she obviously had good taste; it was a damn good book after all.

"Yes, I did, and of course I know who you are. And right after this meeting, if you accept their offer, a lot more people will know about your story. You hit it big."

I didn't want to hit it big or get bigger. I didn't want to get anything. At that moment, all I wanted was to get in my bed and hide under my covers.

"But you have to go in now." I could see she was waiting for me to move already. "Mr. Thomas has a packed schedule and he is already behind." She checked her dainty little watch then looked back at me. "Go on now, there isn't much time until his next appointment."

I wasn't budging.

Before I knew what was happening, she had opened the door and was ushering me inside.

Catching myself before I fell down on my face, I came to a halt and heard the distinct sound of a door closing. I looked over my shoulder.

She was gone.

The traitor!

I turned around and found myself face to face with three suit-wearing men.

For a second I didn't know what to do, but then I mentally

shook myself off and walked toward them.

I was already in for it, might as well look like someone who knew what they were doing.

The bald one—I was assuming he was Bobby Thomas—came forward and met me halfway, quickly offering me his hand.

"Hello, Miss Taylor, I'm Bobby." He greeted me with an easy smile on his face. If his eyes hadn't been fixated on my breasts, I would have said he looked friendly.

Annoyed, I angled my face and caught his attention. "Nice to meet you Mr. Thomas," I said pointedly.

"We'll have none of that. Call me Bobby. By the end of all this we'll get to know each other much better."

I forced a smile on my face and gently pulled my hand out of his grasp.

The other two didn't get up from their seat, but had their eyes on me again, assessing me.

Walking by my side, Bobby led me to the long table in front of the floor to ceiling windows.

Managing to look around, I noticed that we were in some kind of conference room, which did nothing to calm my nerves down. I was beyond out of my depth here.

"Olive, this is—can I call you Olive?"

"Sure," I mumbled, distracted by his hand resting on the small of my back.

"Great. Olive, I'd like to introduce you to the youngest member of our company, Keith Cannon."

With those pale blue eyes and sharp cheekbones, Keith Cannon made a very impressive first impression.

"Nice to meet you Keith. I'm Olive Taylor."

I smiled up at him and shook his warm hand. He had long, strong fingers. His teeth looked a little too white, a little too blinding to be natural, but it was hard to find natural in LA.

Next to him, a shorter, younger guy who was busily typing

away on his laptop got up and briskly shook my hand as Bobby continued with the introductions.

"This is probably very exciting for you, and if we agree on our terms, he will be the screenwriter for the movie. It's important that we reflect everything in your story onto the big screen as well as you managed to do in a few hundred pages so I wanted you to meet Harry Schuman and hear out his ideas. He is actually here for our next meeting, but we're running a little late today, so since he is already here, we wanted him to sit in on this with you."

I nodded and after the pleasantries took my seat across from them.

"We understand that at this time you have no book agent, Olive. Is that right?" Keith asked.

"Yes," I answered. "This wasn't something I was expecting to happen. At all. I'm an indie author, and as you must already know, *Soul Ache* is my first novel, which makes all this even more surreal."

"We understand that it could be a little overwhelming, but you definitely impressed us with your story and we wanted to get your attention before anyone else could steal you."

"Keith is right." Bobby took over again. "We want you to look at this as the first step of our partnership. You don't have to decide on anything today, but you should know that we are extremely eager to take on this project. You should also be aware that—excuse me." He paused when his phone pinged with a new text message. Lifting his eyes, he absently waved his hand in a gesture that said 'keep going'.

"I need to check on something, but please go on without me for a few minutes and I'll be right back. We might even have a surprise for you, Olive. I think you'll like it."

I forced a smile on my lips and then Boobie Bobby was gone.

"Let's get to it, shall we?" Keith asked and got a nod from both Harry and me. "As Bobby just mentioned, we are interested in optioning your book. But—" He lifted his hand as if to stop me from cutting in.

I'm all ears, Keith. No one is stopping you.

"We wanted to set this meeting so we could get to know each other better and see if we can impress you. After today, if you like what you're hearing, I'd be happy to set up a lunch meeting so we can go over the details and present you with an option agreement for the exclusive rights."

"Okay," I nodded, because that made sense, right? He wasn't saying anything scary, not at all.

Keith nodded back at me with a big smile that showcased his blinding pearly whites again and kept going. "So, essentially, Olive, we want to stay true to your story as much as we can. You captured so many hearts from so many different age groups, so we want to keep the heart of your story. The only difference is that we want to elevate it even more. Polish the main characters, maybe do a few small changes here and there, add a few new secondary characters, big names from Hollywood of course. We haven't decided if we want to change the ending yet, but that's just the details I'm sure you're not interested in." Linking his hands together on top of the table, he looked straight at me. "We want the movie to get everyone's attention."

Somewhere in the middle of his explanation of the studio's intentions with my book, had he just said that I wouldn't be interested in the changes? What on earth was he talking about?

"It all sounds great, but maybe we should take a few steps back," I said. "I really feel like I'm out of my depth here. When you say a few small changes...?"

"I've read your book, Miss Taylor, and while everything was great for a book format, for a movie it won't translate the same way. Making changes will be necessary at certain parts," Harry said, speaking for the first time.

"We'll walk you through everything." Keith assured me,

cutting in. "Usually it takes time—around a year or possibly even more than a year—to gather funding for the movie, to find the right director for the story, the right actors, the production company, and many other steps…but we want to use the buzz of your book to our advantage and keep the momentum going. Since you don't have a book agent, I would highly suggest you to find one or have a lawyer go over the contract we'll be presenting you at our next meeting so there won't be any issues in the future."

"Sure, sure. But what about those changes?" I asked, feeling more overwhelmed by the second.

Keith must have seen something on my face because his smile softened.

"I don't think we asked you, would you like to have something to drink? Something to celebrate, maybe?"

"No, I'm good. Thank you."

"Next time then. So do you have any questions for me?"

I glanced at Harry, but he was having none of it.

"I think I do. First of all, it's very exciting to hear that you're interested in my book, but to be honest, the changes you mentioned you want to make are…I don't know how to put it into words actually. The thing is, I've spent years on this novel. While I do want to see my characters come alive on the big screen, I'm not sure if it's worth it to go through this whole thing only for it to end up completely unrecognizable." Every word in that book held a special place in my heart.

"You are not interested in selling the movie rights?"

"I didn't say that. Actually, I did some research and I believe in some cases authors can act as a consultant. Would that be an option for me? Will I have any say in the making of the movie?"

"Olive, trust me, all authors feel the same way as you do at first, but when the project goes forward and the production starts, everything changes. The screenplay isn't written yet, so we can't really comment on any changes, but I'll definitely make sure that you are included in the process."

Thankfully, I was smart enough to know that having a say in the screenplay and being 'included in the process' were nowhere the same thing.

"Let's talk about the casting," he said while I was still trying to decide how to answer.

"Isn't it a little early for that?" I asked, fidgeting in my seat.

"That's one of the first things we focus on because securing the right actor for the role will change everything. We already have a few names we think would be a perfect fit for Isaac and Genevieve." He checked the notes in front of him. "For Isaac, your main character, we have one specific actor we are trying to get in touch with, but for Genevieve we have a pool of names we are going through. Do you have any ideas, maybe suggestions for the casting?"

"Well, when I picture them in my mind, I don't see them as other people."

Lie, Olive. Lie through your teeth.

"I would love to hear the names you're considering though," I added.

Right at the end of my sentence, the door to our left opened and Bobby walked back into the room with another man right beside him. Keith's gaze shifted toward them too, and before I knew what was happening, Jason walked in behind them, playing with the phone in his hand.

As in Jason *fucking* Thorn.

My mouth dropped open.

Shit!

My Jason.

Double, triple shit!

No, not my, *my* Jason.

Shit! Shit! Shit!

In shock and stuck in my seat, my mouth was still hanging wide open when Bobby chuckled, drawing my attention. I'm sure I was a sight to see.

"Olive, I want—" Bobby's mouth was moving, but none of it was getting through to me.

Remember the peaceful waterfall Lucy tried to trick me into believing I was?

It was gone. All dried up. It was a disaster, really.

I was an avalanche—the mother of all avalanches to be precise.

Jumping up from my seat in a rush, I turned my back to them before Jason could notice me. Maybe I was acting crazy, but there weren't that many Olives in the world. What if he remembered me? Remembered my name?

Damn it!

What if he saw my last name on the book cover that was sitting so prettily in the middle of the table?

Searching for a quick exit, I found none. Surely it would hurt a bit too much if I tried to break the window and jump out. Noticing the bar cart next to the window, I shakily made my way toward it.

Damn that Keith guy, why did he keep calling my name?

Reaching for the pitcher of water that had floating lemon and lime slices in it, I grabbed a glass and started pouring. Since my hands were shaking, some of it didn't land in the glass, but who cared. As soon as it was half full, I chugged it down and poured another one.

Alcohol would've worked much better, but water was doing the trick.

Someone touched my arm, and I was ashamed to say I almost lost my grip on the pitcher, making an even bigger fool of myself.

"Olive, are you okay?"

Noticing it was just Keith, I slowly lowered the pitcher down and clung to my glass.

"Ah, sorry. I don't know what came over me." I tried to smile, but to him it probably looked more like a grimace.

Keith chuckled. "It's not every day you see a movie star this close. I understand your excitement."

He understood nothing. Why was he talking about Jason as if he was an animal in a zoo?

"Let's take our seats again so we can introduce you two. You'd like that, wouldn't you?"

Actually I'd hate that, thank you very much.

There went my hopes that maybe Keith would be nice enough to smuggle me out of there.

"Sure," I mumbled, using the glass of water as a shield in front of my face.

When I glanced at the table, I saw that Harry was gone and Bobby had taken his seat. Next to him sat the man who had walked in next to Bobby.

And *then,* there was Jason…

I tried not to look at him at all.

Dear God, please help me breathe.

Still using the glass as my shield as I kept sipping water, I sat down right across from the unknown guy—who had an amused expression on his face—and then I jumped a little and sloshed water on myself when Keith pulled out the chair next to mine and sat down.

Jesus…get a grip, Olive.

I was ready to jump out of my skin and run away to find Lucy so I could kill her. Surely this was all happening because she hadn't come with me.

Keith started the introductions. "This is Jason's agent, Tom Symond, and this is the author I mentioned to you, Tom, Olive T—"

"So very nice to meet you," I said in a louder voice than Keith's, interrupting him before he could say my last name.

Tom Symond chuckled, rose up, and reached for my hand.

Then I had to get up, too. Don't you just hate being civil sometimes? As we were shaking hands, I slipped and glanced at Jason since he was being so quiet. When I noticed he was looking at me with a frown on his face, I quickly looked away, sat down, and reached for my beloved water glass.

"Jason Thorn is who we want for the role of Isaac. We think he'll be perfect," Keith started up again.

Damn, but the guy talked too much.

"We still have a lot of things to talk about, Keith, so let's not get ahead of ourselves," said Tom.

I nodded enthusiastically. What kind of hell was I in that they had brought in the ONE actor that I would be—

"Olive *Taylor?*"

Oh, god...

Death could be so peaceful. My own heaven. Didn't that sound nice? Breathing was so overrated anyway.

"Olive?" Jason asked again in a surprised voice. There was complete silence in the room.

My stomach grumbled.

Anyone up there? Kill me.

Kill me now.

"Nice to meet you...Mr. Jason Thorn," I said miserably when nobody else spoke for several seconds, silently shaving off years of my life.

Of all the things I could've said at that moment, of all the things I could've been doing instead of sitting there shaking like a leaf...

"Olive," he said once he got up from his seat. There was affection in his voice. Definitely surprise, too, but mostly affection.

All the hairs on my body stood up.

Jason was already rounding the table coming toward me. *No escape now.*

Defeated, I let go of my water glass and pushed my chair back to face Jason.

Once he reached me, only two steps separated us. Two short steps after not seeing him for so many years.

"Olive," he said, his lips cracking into a big grin. His eyes took in every inch of my body, causing me to blush.

Then he was in my space, his hands cradling my already flushed face. Involuntarily, I took a step back, my ass almost sitting on the table. He just came with me.

"Look at you." He laughed, triggering a smile on my face. "I can't believe it, Olive. Fuck, look at you," he repeated again.

The dimple? It was still as heartwarming to see as it had been the first day I'd met him.

"Hi," I said, lifting my hand in a little wave.

He threw back his head and laughed.

Wow.

"Mr. Jason Thorn? That's what you say to me?"

"Yeah, sorry about that," I mumbled, my face heating up.

"Jason?" his agent asked from behind. "You know her?"

"Yeah, I know her," Jason answered, his eyes still on me. "I was her favorite person in the whole wide world. She said so herself when she was eight years old." He tilted his head, his eyes narrowing. "Or was it maybe seven?"

"Probably seven," I muttered and closed my eyes. Yup, I had done that, because he had been exactly that for me.

"Oh, this is a nice surprise," Bobby cut into our unexpected reunion. "We didn't know you two knew each other. This will definitely be a plus for the project."

Jason winked at me.

My heart fluttered.

Then his hands finally left my face alone, only to grab my hand and turn back to Tom.

"You can handle this?"

"Of course, but I think you should stay. We'll keep it short," Tom responded.

What?

"You can take care of everything."

"Jason, wait a minute."

Yes, Jason! Wait a minute!

His gaze landed on Bobby. "I'm in. You can go over everything with Tom."

He was in? In what? IN WHAT? Certainly not my book?

"Are you done with your meeting with Olive?" he asked Keith next.

Hello, people! Am I not still standing here?

Keith's gaze found my startled one before he answered Jason's question. "I'll send you the contract and personally call you to schedule a lunch date. We'll go over the optioning agreement with you and make the necessary changes then."

I was starting to feel dizzy. Had I said okay to their proposal already?

Absentmindedly, I nodded.

"Call me when the meeting is done, Tom," Jason said as he pulled me behind him.

"I can't believe this," he muttered as soon as we were out the door and in the maze again.

Other than being shocked into silence, I just hoped he had been in the building enough times to know how to get out of the damn thing.

One hand engulfed in Jason's, the other flailing behind me with my handbag, I tried to keep up with his big strides.

Is this really happening?

Just when I saw the light and thought we were finally out, I was pulled into an empty office and those dark chocolate eyes of his focused completely on me.

"Olive, you are beautiful," he said after we took in each other in the thick silence. "You've grown up so much."

Fuck.

"I did do that. You look very good, Jason. It's nice to see you."

Was that my voice that was trembling? He was still my first crush and my first heartbreak, but he was also Jason Thorn. *The* Jason Thorn who was only twenty-six and had two Oscar nominations under his belt, but I wasn't going to think about what was under his belt because that would be bad. Really bad. He was one of the most versatile leading actor in the industry. Did I mention he was the best? He was more than just an actor. He was a star—a troubled one, I should say, but still a big, shiny star. Any other woman would be jumping on him if they ever found themselves locked in a room with him, which I believed they usually did.

I, however, was slowly stepping back toward freedom.

"That's it? That's all you're gonna say to me?"

The last day I'd smiled up at him, he had managed to stomp on my heart with a simple text message, not even knowing he was stomping on it. The last time he had tugged my hair as a goodbye had been the last time I'd ever heard from him.

Sure, he had texted and called Dylan for the following few weeks, but after that I don't think even Dylan heard from him again. One year later, we had watched his first movie as a family in the same living room where he had spent countless hours with us.

"I'm too shocked, I don't know what to say really," I blurted before I could say something stupid.

"I am too, but, god, look at you." Another slow perusal of my body. "I didn't even recognize you when I first walked into the room. What are the odds?"

"Right?" I chuckled nervously. "What are the damn odds…"

"You have to tell me everything."

"Everything? What do you mean?"

"Dylan? Is he here in LA. too? How about your mom and dad? Is everyone okay?"

"Yes. They are all fine. Mom and Dad still live in San Francisco. Same house, actually. Dylan is in D.C. He is a teacher, and married to the sweetest girl. Can you believe that?"

I kept walking backwards.

Small steps, Olive. You're so close to freedom.

"Actually, I can." His smile got even bigger as he sat on the edge of the office desk. "He wanted to be a teacher ever since middle school or something like that, and family was always important to him. No wonder he couldn't wait to start his own."

Finally reaching the door, I rested my back against it and waited for the perfect moment to escape.

"God, Olive, you can't even imagine how much I missed you guys."

"When you stopped calling, they missed you too."

He arched an eyebrow. "So, you didn't miss me?"

You hurt me, you big, sexy meanie, I wanted to say.

"Um, sure. Of course."

His dimple disappeared and he straightened. When he started walking toward me, I had nowhere to run.

"What's wrong with you, little Olive?" Reaching out, he tugged a strand of my hair, a gesture so old that it tugged at something in my heart. "I'm not your friend any more?"

He had remembered. The hair-tugging thing he had started doing every single time he saw me was like a warm 'hello' from him. I used to love it, thinking he couldn't keep his hands off of me. I had been in love with him. You could call it a crush, but for me, it was pure love. He'd been my one and only wish on every single one of my birthdays.

"I would've thought you'd be happy to see me, too, Olive. If not happy, hell, maybe a little excited. My ego is taking a real beating."

"Sorry," I said, wincing a little. "It's been a…a weird day, to say the least."

"Still not admitting that she missed me," he muttered almost to himself. His eyes seemed to be taking in every inch of my face, yet I chose to focus on a spot over his shoulder. His face wasn't strange to me, as mine was to him. And I remembered that tender look all too well. Hell, it was just one of the things that made me swoon for him.

"You're a writer," he commented, as if the thought had just occurred to him.

"Looks like it."

He hit me with that dimple again. "Tonight I'll be reading your words."

Panicking, I said, "Oh, you really don't have to. It's not even that good. It's my first book and these people are plain crazy." His smile got bigger and bigger. "I might even be getting punked right now. I'm being serious, you wouldn't even like it, Jason. And what kind of a movie star are you that you have enough time to read a book?"

There was sex in that book! Pounding. Fucking. Sucking. Orgasming.

Oh, dear god. There were words like *cock* and *pussy!*

He chuckled. "Now you've intrigued me even more. I'll have to read it as soon as I get home. Plus"—he lifted a finger when I opened my mouth to object again—"I just said I'm in to the studio execs who are interested in turning your book into a feature film. I think I should know what I'm signing up for, don't you think?"

"Why did you even say that if you have no idea what it's about?"

"My agent dragged me here, saying it was a good choice for me. I'm guessing he knows about your book and I trust him."

"Fine. You go do that. I have to go." Taking a step to my right, I opened the door. "It was so good to see you. Goodbye now."

His eyes lit up. "There's the little Olive I know."

Before I could pull my hand away, he grabbed it as if he was getting ready to walk a kid across the road.

Why did my heart flutter so much every time he touched me even though it was obvious that he still saw me as his best friend's little sister, the kiddo?

"What are you doing?" I asked as I was being pulled toward freedom.

"I'll drop you off wherever you want to go."

"You don't even know where I live. What if it's an hour away? I'm seriously starting to doubt your movie star status."

Again, that chuckle. "It'll be fun. I promise to entertain you the entire hour, Olive."

"It's not an hour. Seriously, I can get there in like no time."

"Then you won't suffer too much in my presence."

"Were you always this stubborn when you were little?" I asked, starting to get a little annoyed about being pulled around like a doll.

"Oh, sweetheart," he said softly, looking over his shoulder, the annoying dimple winking at me. "You were always the little one, not me."

CHAPTER SEVEN

JASON

After pushing a reluctant Olive into my car, I rounded it and got in as she was mumbling something about killing someone.

Amused, I asked, "Are we going on a killing spree?"

I still couldn't believe my eyes, that she was actually there.

Frowning, she looked at me, her hand jerkily pulling on the seatbelt. "What?"

"Easy there killer." I smiled and leaned over her to take care of her little dilemma.

My nose was almost touching her cheek. *Mmm.* She smelled like apples, fresh and sweet.

I felt her stiffen.

My little Olive.

Securing her, I leaned back and my eyes zeroed in on her parted lips. "There you go."

"Thank you," she mumbled, looking anywhere but me. I looked away, too.

"So, you were muttering about killing someone?"

"Lucy. My friend."

"What did she do to deserve such a gruesome death?"

Starting the car, I discreetly glanced at her.

The little girl who had always given me the biggest smiles was long gone. While it looked like she hadn't changed at all, I knew everything had changed. It looked like I wasn't the receiver of any smiles any more.

"I can't be that bad of company, can I?" I asked before she could reply about her friend.

She gave me a small smile. Not one of her beautiful ones that used to light up her eyes and flush her cheeks, but still a sincere one nonetheless.

"No, you are not that bad. You can drop me off at USC, I'll find my friends."

"You go there?"

"Yes."

"Come on, Olive. Don't be like that. Tell me more about what you've been up to. I still can't believe we found each other here out of all the other places in LA."

"A coffee shop or something like that would've been more like it, wouldn't it?"

"Exactly. A studio exec's office? No way in hell."

She chuckled. "It is a little weird, isn't it?"

"Weird? I don't know, probably. You never were an ordinary girl, though."

Stopping at the red light, I faced her. She was looking out the window, her hands resting on her lap in tight little fists. I tugged at a strand of her strawberry blonde hair—which looked much lighter than it had years before—and she looked at me. I smiled and said, "Hi."

She bit on her lower lip and smiled back shyly. "Hi back."

"I missed you, Olive. I didn't even know how much until I saw you." Her smile faltered a bit, but she managed to turn it into a lopsided smile, which looked strangely attractive on her.

The light turned green and I had to give my attention to the road, special cargo and all that. Several minutes passed by with neither one of us saying anything, then we both spoke at the same time.

"Did you—"

"Can I—"

I chuckled. "You go first."

"I just wanted to ask why you stopped calling Dylan. For a while there, he used to get touchy if someone mentioned you. I think he didn't want to show how upset he was. I know it's none of my business and you certainly don't have to answer if you don't want to, but I've always wondered."

When the car in front of me stopped due to traffic, I changed lanes and slowed down. Rubbing the back of my neck, I let out a deep breath.

"You don't have to answer," she repeated before I could form an answer in my mind. I didn't have a good enough reason to give to her.

"No, it's okay, Olive. I know it was a shitty thing to do after everything your family had done for me. To be honest, the first few weeks were really hard. Maybe you remember," I said, glancing at her. "My father and I were never close, and my mother's death didn't change anything on that front. The day I left you guys, he didn't even speak one word to me the entire ride here. When we finally made it, he showed me to an empty room in a big house and went back to his clients. Just like that. I barely saw him, and he certainly didn't care what I was doing. Unfortunately, it only got worse after that. I didn't want to be that kid who only called to complain. And, don't tell your mom, but I think if I had talked to Emily about how I was doing, I would've broken down and cried like a baby when I heard her call me sweetheart in that tone of hers. Lying to Dylan was surprisingly easier." When she didn't say anything, I continued. "And in time, with school and then the movie stuff…"

It sounded lame even to my own ears.

"I'm sorry you had a rough time when you first got here, but you must be so happy now. I'm glad things turned out for the better. When we watched your first movie, I think I saw Mom wipe away tears more than a few times."

"She cried for an action movie?"

"You were shot, and well, I think she cried because she was proud of you."

An arrow straight to my chest. When my mother had passed out from her daily drinking, consequently locking me out for the night, Emily had taken me in. After that night, I'd stayed at their house more than I had at my own. She'd been a better mom to me than my own could ever be. Dylan was my brother and Olive... well, Olive had been my friend, too. They were the only family I'd known. It was as simple as that.

"You really didn't miss me?" I asked, trying to diffuse the heavy quiet in the car. "Didn't wait by the phone for my call? Come on, don't be shy. You can tell me." I watched her out of the corner of my eye.

She laughed. It was beautiful to watch.

"I definitely didn't wait by the phone."

"But you admit to missing me, don't you?"

"Maybe," she said so quietly that I wasn't even sure if I'd heard her right.

When her phone rang, she gave me an apologetic look and answered it.

"Where are *you?* No. Okay. Yes, the meeting is over, I'm on my way back. Ok, I'll be home soon. No! No, wait inside. Lucy, I swear to god, if I find you outside—Hello? Lucy? Damn you!"

"Something wrong?" I asked, amused.

"No, it's okay. Well, good news for you, you don't have to drive me all the way to USC. We're closer to the house."

"Lucy is your roommate?"

"One of them."

"How many roommates do you have?"

"With Lucy, three."

"Is it hard?"

"Not really. I mean, we're all friends, so I guess it's easier than it would be if they were complete strangers."

After she gave me the address, we were quiet for the rest of the ride. Fuck, but I couldn't stop glancing at her. She had the same little nose, that same spark in her eyes, yet she was so different than when I had last seen her. The worst part? She had boobs—boobs big enough that they'd cushioned my arm when I had accidentally encountered them as I secured her in.

Fuck me, but my little Olive—the same little girl I had protected from shitty bullies—was not so little any more.

"Is this the right street?" I asked when I took a right turn.

"Yes. You can stop here. I took enough of your time already."

"Don't be like that. Tell me which building it is."

"Maybe I don't want you to know where I live."

I gave her an exasperated look, and she gave me an annoyed one, which only made me laugh.

She huffed and pointed to an old building. "Do you see those three people waiting there?"

"That old building?"

"Yeah that one."

Coming to a stop in front of the building she had pointed out, I turned off the engine.

"Is this place safe?" I asked, leaning toward her to glance at the building through her window.

"Safe enough." With a quickness I wasn't expecting, she opened the door and got out. Leaning down to look at me through the open door, she said, "Thank you for dropping me off, Jason. It was really nice to see you again. I'm glad we did this. Don't read the book because it kinda sucks if you ask me. Have a nice life. Bye."

She shut the door on my smiling face. *Ah.* She was acting as if she could get away that easily now that I'd found her.

Chuckling to myself, I reached for my Ray-Bans and stepped out of the car. Following her, I watched a girl separate from the other two and run straight into Olive's arms, all screaming and jumping.

The other girl had an equally big smile on her face when she finally reached the jumping duo. The guy? He didn't look that happy at all.

"Start from the beginning, you have to tell us everything. Do they want the movie rights? Did you say yes? How much did they offer? Who will play Isaac?" I heard her friend ask rapidly. I couldn't hear Olive's answers, but I was aware that she was trying to herd them back toward the building.

And she hadn't noticed me—yet.

"Olive," I said next to her ear when her friend focused on the other two and was looking over her shoulder.

"Jesus!" she screamed turning around.

CHAPTER EIGHT

OLIVE

My heart beating in my throat, I turned around to find Jason smiling at me.

"Not so fast, Olive," he said.

Grabbing his arm, I managed to pull him a few steps away. "What are you doing? They will recognize you!"

I chanced a look behind me. From what I could see of the three open mouths, it was already too late.

"So what? I want to meet your friends."

"Jason. Are you sure you are okay? Shouldn't you be…I don't know, a little more concerned about being in public?"

"No one is around. It's okay, Olive. Relax, I won't embarrass you. I promise," he said in a different tone.

My heart clenched. "It wasn't that. I'm sorry. Let's introduce you then."

Lucy was the first one to close her mouth and grin like a cat that was about to bathe in the cream.

"You must be Lucy, the one who is facing a bloody death," Jason said, giving her a sincere smile.

"Yep, that's probably me." Lucy had that starry look in her eyes when she finally shook Jason's hand.

"This is Charlotte, and Marcus." I took over when Lucy finally let go of his hand.

"Nice to meet you guys," Jason said.

When Lucy glanced at me questioningly, I sighed, "Jason had a meeting after mine, and they were running late, and then he was in my meeting so he recognized me and offered to drop me off."

That short but to the point explanation would only hold her off until we got into our apartment.

"You two know each other?" Marcus asked with a confused frown on his face.

Marcus was a completely different matter. He was my roommate *and* my ex, and the more my book took off, the more annoyed he got.

I felt Jason's hand on the small of my back. It was a light touch, but it was enough to make my entire body buzz with excitement.

Stupid, traitorous body.

"Jason was my brother's best friend. He used to practically live with us," I said to Marcus.

"You never mentioned that."

"I'm sorry? I didn't think you would be interested in knowing that."

Lucy cut in. "Oh, shut up, Marcus. I knew, and frankly, that's enough. Would you like to come up?" she asked Jason, softening her tone.

"I would love to, but I'm afraid it will have to wait until next time." Turning to me, he said, "Can I see your phone?"

"Why?" I asked suspiciously.

"I want to get Dylan's number."

Ah, right. It wasn't like he would want mine. Nodding, I took it out of my bag and handed it over.

"Olive." Getting my attention, Char touched my arm. "I'm dying to hear what happened at the meeting and if you said yes, but I have to meet with my study group…" She glanced down at her watch. "In half an hour. I'll catch up with you when I get back, ok?"

"Sure, we'll talk when you get back."

Blowing us a quick kiss, she slipped away.

Before I could ask Jason why it was taking so long to get Dylan's number, Marcus caught my eyes, shook his head, turned around, and left.

"What's wrong with him?" I asked Lucy, making sure Jason couldn't hear.

"Who knows? He is in one of his moods, I guess. Don't worry about him."

Jason handed my phone back, our fingers touching for a quick second.

Those old, childish butterflies I'd thought were long gone? They all came back with a vengeance, which scared me more than anything that had happened that day.

"I put my own number in there and I want you to call me whenever you need anything, ok?"

As if I would ever repeat that mistake again.

"Since I have a feeling you won't do that, I'll make sure to text you as soon as I start reading the book. I'll let you know what I think."

"You're not going to let it go, are you?"

His grin grew bigger. "Not a chance in hell, Olive."

After he said goodbye to Lucy, he looked at me one more time. Then, cupping my face yet again, he pressed an unexpected kiss on my forehead, rendering me completely speechless.

"I'll see you soon," he said, and then he was gone.

"Now," Lucy started as she hooked her arm in mine and started dragging me toward our building. "I'm gonna hold my tongue until we take those stairs up, get in your room, close your door, and lay next to each other on that bed. That should give both of us enough time to take in what just happened. However, when our hearts finally stop going haywire over that fine piece of ass, you'll answer every single question I ask. Is that understood? Nod if it is."

I nodded.

"WAIT A MINUTE. He pulled you out of the meeting? But did you say yes before he dragged you out? Is this awesome movie happening or not?"

I was just as baffled as she was. "It looks like it is."

We were sitting next to each other on my bed, facing the window that looked out to an already darkening sky. My room was only big enough to fit a queen bed and a small closet/dresser, but since my bed was slightly bigger than her full one, it was our regular meeting spot for late night talks and snacks.

"And why are we not more excited about this huge, huge life-changing thing? You're kinda making it sound like it's nothing."

"Seeing Jason eclipsed that little nugget. Oh, Lucy." Closing my eyes, I sighed and fell back onto my pillows. "I acted like a total idiot. I was mortified when I saw him walk in that door, but then why did I feel that rush when he grabbed me by my hand, or when he looked at me as if he was really seeing me? Why did…" I struggled to find the right words. "Why did my heart feel like it was burning?" I threw my arm over my eyes and released a sigh. "But then I remembered how much it hurt to read what he thought of me that night, and I couldn't look him in the eyes. I called him *Mr. Jason Thorn* for crying out loud! I made a complete fool of myself in front of everyone."

Lucy gently lay down next to me and I opened my eyes to look into her stormy gray ones.

"But the waterfall trick worked, didn't it? You were all calm and collected until Hotness Overload walked in and your ovaries exploded along with your heart."

I smiled. "That's one way to put it, I guess."

"Do you still love him?" she asked after a long beat of silence.

I chuckled. "Along with millions of other women. Who doesn't love Jason Thorn?" Lucy ignored my answer and pointedly kept looking at me until I gave up. "He is not the same kid who slept right across from my room, Lucy. I'm not in love with him like that any more."

"I don't believe you, my green Olive." She bopped my nose with her fingertip.

"It doesn't matter whether you do or not. I doubt I'll see him again any time soon." I patted her arm. "Don't worry though, I'll take you to see his next movie. You can still salivate while you are watching his abs. Isn't that coming out like next month?"

After seeing and talking to him again after so many years, wouldn't it be a solid kick in my stomach when I saw him kiss his costar? And right when I was starting to get used to seeing him in a lip lock.

She sighed. "No, still two months away. And anyway, it's not the same as seeing him face to face. Do you think he would've taken his shirt off if you'd asked nicely? I'm forever ruined after seeing him show that dimple to you and then kiss your freaking forehead. If I didn't know you still loved him—"

"I don't love him."

"I would've jumped on him and quite possibly licked that dimple while my hands accidentally wandered to places every girl would give their firstborn to get a peek at." She did a whole body shudder.

"Ahh, don't be disgusting." I made a funny face at her. "And don't do that to *any* guy when I'm around, please."

"Why? Licking is a natural urge. When you think of it, you actually start to learn how to lick properly when you are just kid.

All those lollies and ice creams you licked to death? That was just training. Do you think he wouldn't love it if you licked his dimple and let your hands roam around for bit?"

"He sees me as his sister, Lucy. Of course he wouldn't like having my tongue anywhere near his face, or my hand for that matter."

"Says who?"

"Says every guy who's had a best friend's little sister fall in love with him. When you think about it, it actually does sound a little annoying. There he is trying to have a family moment, which he didn't get at his own home, and there I am popping up wherever he goes, sticking to him like a glue. He was just nice enough not to say anything to my face."

Lucy turned fully toward me, her eyes sparkling with mischief. "Maybe he'll fall in love with you this time around. Then I could see his abs any time I wanted. Damn, I could quite possibly get away with copping a feel."

"I'd say don't hold your breath. I gave up on that dream exactly seven years…four months, and some days ago. Not that I'm counting or anything."

Lucy snorted. "Of course not."

My phone pinged with a new text message and before I could even lift my head off the pillows, Lucy was off the bed and digging into my handbag.

"Who is it?" I asked. "Is it Char? Can you text her back and remind her to buy toilet paper on her way back? There was no way I was going to ask *the* Jason Thorn to stop at the grocery store to buy some toilet paper. Why are you smirking, Lucy? What did she say?"

"Oh, I have a feeling I'm going to love this," she replied with an evil grin on her face as she typed away an answer.

"What are you talking about?"

She threw the phone at me, almost breaking my chin in the process, and ran out of my room straight to her own.

Perplexed, I looked down at the text message I had gotten… and evidently answered.

> *Jason: The Marcus guy, your boyfriend?*
> *Me: No, just the ex. I'm one hundred percent single.*

"I hate you so much!" I yelled as I heard the answering cackle coming from her room. The phone pinged with a new one again.

> *Jason: Good. I don't like him.*

Quickly, I typed back.

> *Me: Why on earth?*
> *Jason: I didn't like the way he treated you.*
> *Me: You only saw him for a few seconds, how would you know how he treats me?*
> *Jason: I have eyes.*
> *Me: How surprising. I hadn't noticed.*
> *Jason: Just got off the phone with your brother after talking to your parents. All is good. He says hi. After dinner, I'm going to download your book and start getting ready for my upcoming role.*
> *Me: Glad you were able to patch things up. Talk to you in a few years.*

"Olive?" I heard Lucy yell from the safety of her own room. "The suspense is killing me!"

"I still hate you," I yelled back.

"Oh, I love you too, but, I meant what is he texting?"

"You'll never know."

She came out of her room and gave me the most innocent look with those pouty red lips and innocent eyes.

Just when she was about to sit down next to me, Marcus appeared at my door.

"Olive, can we talk for a second?"

I straightened up and invited him in.

Lucy eyed Marcus for a few seconds before she looked at me and said, "I'm going to hop in the shower before I go to bed, I have an early class in the morning. Before I sleep, I'm gonna stalk your Amazon ranking for a while. Talk to you later my green Olive."

They threw each other hostile glances as Marcus entered my room and Lucy got out. It wasn't that Lucy hated Marcus as a person—they'd actually been friends with each other longer than they had been with me—she just hated the fact that Marcus had dumped me because he thought I was spending too much time with the fictional characters I'd created in my mind. He never thought I would actually publish, let alone be successful on my first try as a writer. Honestly, neither had I, but that wasn't the point.

Closing the door, he crossed his arms across his chest and leaned back on the wall, watching me with silent eyes. When he didn't like something, he always did that. Always stared you down until you squirmed in your seat before he actually opened his mouth to let you know what was wrong.

"Is this what you want to do with your future, Liv?"

Oh and also, he never ever called me by my full name. He found it ridiculous.

"What do you mean?"

"Char said you skipped a class today."

"Yes," I said slowly, wondering where he was going with that. "I had a meeting."

"Is that what's important to you now? Hanging around movie stars and squealing with Lucy?"

"I know one movie star, Marcus, only one, and Jason insisting on giving me a ride home isn't exactly hanging around a bunch of movie stars. Like I said downstairs, I was seven years old when we met him, as a family, not just me. He was barely eleven twelve himself. He was like a second brother to me."

I wondered how many times I would have to lie with a straight face before the day would end. But it wasn't exactly a lie, was it? He did see me as his sister. It was me and my heart who had muddled the waters in my own head, and all of that aside, I still cared what Marcus thought of me.

Despite what Lucy and Char thought, for the short year we were together, I'd been all in with Marcus. He was intelligent, interested in me, confident in himself, and had a vision for his future—one I wanted to be part of. Having a relationship with someone I already shared a house with had been oddly exciting. And the sex? That was good too, especially when we were sneaking around Char and Lucy.

It had felt like we were right for each other until he decided to slowly tear me down and mold me into something I wasn't ever going to be.

He quirked his brow. "Are you sure? You didn't look like someone who had seen her long lost brother to me down there."

"Why do you do this to me?" I asked, genuinely curious.

He tilted his head. "What do you mean?"

"Question my every move. Undermine my decisions. Make me feel like I couldn't possibly do anything right in your eyes. I published a book, Marcus. People are actually reading it. A *lot* of people are reading it. A fucking movie studio wants to option my book. Why can't you be happy with me? For me? Why are you bringing me down like this?"

"That's not what I'm doing, Liv," he said, coming to sit down next to me. He lifted his hand as if he was about to grip my thigh, but then let it rest on the bed, next to my knee. "You lost so much weight while you were trying to write this book. Hell, sometimes you didn't even have time to shower before your classes, let alone hang out with me. Our relationship ended *because* of this book, because you were more in love with your fictional characters than you were with me. Even when you are not writing, you are lost in your dreams."

"That's not why it ended, Marcus. I'd been writing this book for years, long before you, but you already knew that. When we started something, you *knew* how much it meant to me, finishing this book."

"Maybe that's what you want to believe, but it's not what happened, Liv. I thought once you published, you would take things easier, patch things up between us, but now I can see that it's changing you for the worse."

Shocked, I responded, "I've skipped one single class. How could it possibly have changed me, Marcus? And even if I *was* skipping classes left and right, you also know that I'm enough on top of my classes that I'm graduating early." Neither one of us said anything for a short time. Then I softened my voice and tried again. "Did I unknowingly do something that would make you think like this? If that's the case, if I did something or said something that hurt you, I'm sorry. No matter what happened between us, you know I care about you."

"I cared about you too, Livy."

Past tense.

He rose from his seat and stopped by the door. "When you decide to come back to reality, I really hope it won't be already too late."

"I'm sorry to hear you think like this, Marcus. Truly, I am."

When I didn't say what he was obviously expecting me to say, he nodded curtly and left me alone in my room.

Feeling slightly angry at him for somehow managing to pull me down when I had every right to feel excited about my accomplishment, I jumped out of my bed, pulled the drapes shut, and turned off the lights.

When I was comfortably snuggled under my covers, I closed my eyes and tried to ignore the fact that Marcus still had enough power over me to get under my skin.

Soon enough, I fell into a fitful sleep where I was still a little girl who dreamed and wished for things she could never reach.

————

WHEN A DOOR SLAMMED SHUT with enough force to wake the dead, I startled awake with a gasp. Catching my breath, I had to blink a few times to get my bearings and realize that I was in Los Angeles and not in my childhood home. Patting the bed in search of my phone, I gave up when I couldn't find it and instead got up to check on Lucy.

"Lucy," I whispered and knocked on her door quietly. When there was no answer, I opened it and saw she was already deep in sleep. Closing her door, I padded down to the kitchen to grab a water bottle and get back to my room before I came face to face with Marcus, just in case he was the one who had slammed his door.

When I was safely back in my room, I turned on the lights and finally found my lost phone down on the floor by the bed.

Seeing the two notifications for new text messages from Jason, my heart decided it was time to have a heart attack. I hugged the phone to my chest, took a deep breath, and exhaled. Wanting to be alone in the dark, I turned off the lights again and got back in bed. My phone was still tightly clasped in my hands.

Just like it was years and years ago, I thought.

Now that there was nobody around and I was all alone with

my thoughts, everything that had happened that day seemed like a dream. Seeing Jason's name light up my screen was doing inexpressible things to my heart.

Before I could work myself into hyperventilation, I opened his texts.

Jason: I can see why you didn't want me to read this.

Oh shit!

Jason: Are you awake?

My heart stuttered to an almost stop.
Does he hate it?
He hates it.
The last text had been sent fifteen minutes ago.

I contemplated saying, *Yes, I'm awake*, but decided against it. We had seen each other, talked to each other enough for a day. I didn't want him to see me as the old Olive who trailed after him to get his attention.

If he wanted to say how much he hated my book, tomorrow was just as good as any day.

CHAPTER NINE

OLIVE

Someone poked my cheek. "Wakey wakey, sleepyhead. It's time to get up."

"Go away," I murmured, digging my head deeper into my pillow.

"It's almost nine o'clock," whined Lucy above me. "You have to get up."

I opened my eyes and saw Lucy's upturned face looming over me with an overly bright smile. Quickly, I closed my eyes shut.

"You're like those annoying house cats we always watch on Facebook," I mumbled. "Why do I have to get up? I don't have a class today."

"Because we need to get out and celebrate yesterday's meeting. And I'm not a cat—I'm offended, woman. I'm a cute puppy everyone wants to take home."

Unable to stop myself, I yawned again and reluctantly opened my eyes. Thankfully, she was no longer inches away from my face.

"What time is it?"

"Nine."

"We're celebrating at nine in the morning? Whose brilliant

idea was that? I'm gonna say no. Come back at a reasonable hour."

"Come on, Olive." She pulled at my covers. "You don't have a class, but I do. So get up, get up, get up."

"Jesus, you are like a five-year-old."

"If you don't want me to dump a bucket of cold water on you, you'll get up, get yourself together, and be by the door in less than half an hour."

"Fine," I snapped as I swung my legs down and pushed at her shoulder. "Get out of my way."

She clapped her hands. "That's the spirit I was looking for!"

In twenty minutes, *I* was all ready to go out, but neither Lucy nor Char were ready.

"I'm about to go out and celebrate on my own," I yelled, standing by the front door.

"I'm coming!" Lucy yelled at the same moment Char opened her door and slipped out of her room.

"You have a class, too, Char?" I asked, noticing the big bundle of books she was carrying.

"Unfortunately, yes. Then I have another study session with the girls."

"You sure are working hard lately. Is there anything I can help with?" Char was a shy and sweet blonde who was an English major like me, but unlike me, she had no interest in creative writing.

"That's nice of you to ask with everything you've got going on. I might take you up on that offer when finals are getting closer."

"Of course. Actually, it would help me a lot, too." As much as I hated giving in to Marcus' words, I didn't want him to be right about what he said, especially when I was so close to graduating early.

"Your book is still doing amazing on the rankings!" A jumping and screaming Lucy came barreling toward me.

"Here we go again," Char muttered with a smile in her voice as I braced myself for impact.

Two seconds later, Lucy's arms were around my neck and we were jumping up and down, celebrating her excitement over my book for the…thousandth time? If it wasn't already the thousandth, we were surely getting pretty close.

The truth was I was staying away from checking reviews and rankings and all that stuff because I was scared shitless that all of it would tumble down on me at any moment. Lucy was like a bloodhound anyway; she had refreshed those pages almost every hour, on the hour ever since the book had gone up on Amazon two months before. My fear was also the reason I was trying to lock down my excitement about the possibility of seeing Isaac and Evie on the big screen. Once Dream Catch Studios provided me with the contract—if they were serious about it—and I signed it…then I would either sit down and cry for a few days—happy tears, of course—or I would pull a Lucy and go crazy all over the town—naturally, with her by my side.

"Still in the top hundred?" I asked, the slight tinge of hope in my voice more than clear.

She flicked her hair over her shoulder. "Try top five, woman. You're still killing it."

I'd stayed as the number one bestselling book on more than a few platforms for almost six weeks, and I was still in the top five after two months? I gave in to the urge and completed another jumping session with Lucy, not noticing Marcus leaning against the doorframe and watching us.

Then we were out of there to celebrate with lattes and croissants.

It was well worth every damn calorie that went straight to our hips.

———

IT WAS ALMOST four o'clock when Jason's name flashed on the screen of my phone. I was alone, sitting in our living room, staring blankly at an empty word document, trying to figure out which direction my mind and heart wanted to lead me this time around. Needless to say, neither of them was speaking to me at that moment.

Urging my heart to stop fluttering around like a wild bird in my chest, I took a deep breath and answered the call—at the same time wondering if it was weird of me to get so worked up over a simple phone call.

"Hi."

"Hey, Olive. I'm not interrupting anything, am I?"

"Nope. How can I help you?" I asked before tipping my water bottle against my lips to wet my suddenly parched throat.

"So formal." He clucked, and I could almost see him shaking his head as a small smile stretched across his face. "Soon enough, I'll win you over. You already loved me once; I'll make it happen again."

Sputtering water all over the cheap Ikea coffee table that was stationed in front of the couch, I coughed until I could speak without gulping breaths.

"What?" I wheezed out when what I wanted to say was, *Oh, Jason, I'm still head over heels for you, maybe even more so*.

"What's going on, Olive? Are you okay?"

"Yeah. Yeah," I replied in a rough whisper. "Just water down the wrong pipe. I'm fine."

"Well, okay. You scared me; I thought someone was strangling you."

"Yeah, nothing that exciting."

"Being strangled is exciting to you?"

"Not for me, but definitely for some people. Don't knock it 'til you try it and all that."

He seemed to think about it for a second, then cleared his throat before speaking again. "Ok, we are not going anywhere near that. You shouldn't even know about stuff like that." I did a ladylike snort but he ignored me. "You never answered my texts last night."

"Yeah, I didn't want to bother you." I got up and went to stand next to the window, counting the cars that passed on our street.

"I was the one who texted you; why would I be bothered when you actually went ahead and answered them?"

"It was late. I just thought you would be occupied, or out. Why did you say you were calling again?"

"You're terrible at trying to change the subject smoothly, Olive. From now on, you can answer my texts whenever. I forgot to tell you yesterday, but please make sure no one else gets my number from your phone, all right? It's pure hell when somebody gets a hold of it."

"If you are worried about my friends, don't be. Lucy is the only one who knows my password and she would never do anything like that. She might've looked a little crazy with all the jumping and screaming yesterday, but she isn't someone who would steal your number and then bother you." I paused and thought about it for a second. "However, she might grope you if she ever sees you again so you can worry about that if you want to, but that's as far as she would go. Still, if you are regretting giving me your number, I can delete it right now."

"This trying to get rid of me thing is a huge blow to my ego, Olive. I hope you'll stop before you do some permanent damage."

"I didn't mean to sound…well, mean, I just don't want you to worry about it."

Feeling too wired to just stand in one place, I started pacing the living room from wall to wall. Why wasn't he just telling me what he thought of the book? Even if he'd read a few pages, surely he would have an opinion on it.

"I'm not worrying, and the reason I'm calling right now is because I wanted to let you know that I talked to Keith, the guy from the movie studio, and they will send the optioning agreement to my agent instead of directly to you."

I stopped my pacing. "What? Why would they do that?"

"Because I don't want them to take advantage of you. Tom will go over the contract for us then we'll meet at my house so you can sign it if you are happy with everything they are offering. Just let me know when you'll be free and I'll arrange it. It needs to be in the next few days because I have to leave for Canada on Friday. I'll be out of town for a few months."

"Oh," I mumbled, mostly to myself. That little piece of news settled down in the pit of my stomach, so I bit down on my thumb and tried to come up with the right thing to say. "This is too much, Jason. Despite what I said yesterday, I'm sure you don't have this kind of time on your hands to babysit your old best friend's little sister."

He coughed and roughly cursed on the other end of the line.

"You okay?" I asked.

"Yeah. Sorry. Look, this isn't about Dylan. This is about you. Wouldn't you let Dylan help you if he was in my place? At the very least, you can see me as a stand-in for your brother. I won't let anyone take advantage of your work, Olive. You'll get what you deserve and nothing less."

What he'd just said hurled me back to my heartbroken fourteen-year-old self again. It looked like no matter how much I grew up, he would never see me as anything but a sister.

I dumbly nodded and realized he couldn't see me through the phone so I forced my mouth to open and give him the words.

"Thank you, Jason. I appreciate it," I said, in a dull tone. "Uh, I have to go right now. My friends are waiting for me, but I'll text you to let you know which days I'll be free. You can arrange the time according to your schedule. I don't want to be a bigger burden then I already am."

"Olive," he said, softening his tone. "You couldn't be a burden to me even if you tried."

"Thank you. Goodbye Jason."

Before he could say anything else, I ended the call then powered off my phone completely.

It was a childish and stupid move, but I didn't want to risk hearing his voice again on the off chance he decided to call me back while I was busy feeling sorry for myself.

Later that night, after I had a long talk with my mom, I learned that she had asked Jason to look after me. Since he was being cast as Isaac, she had thought we would be working together. I had to explain to her that I wouldn't be involved in the filming process.

After doing some research on the subject, I'd already learned that no director wanted the author to get in the way of how he wanted to shape the movie. He was the big dog and it would mean nothing to him whether the author was happy with the process or not.

Details of the movie aside, I wasn't sure how I should feel about Jason helping me out as a favor to my family.

I spent some time thinking about what I should do…okay, maybe not a lot of time. After all, who in their right mind would pass up the chance of spending more time with Jason Thorn in his own house? I mean…come on. Even though I wasn't as brave as Lucy and wouldn't grope him at first contact, there would be no stopping me from ogling his body and that damn dimple of his.

I was done feeling sorry for myself.

"Bring it on, Jason Thorn," I muttered with a renewed confidence in myself. After all those years, I'd become the master of loving him from far away. It would be stupid of me not to take advantage of our situation.

Reaching for my phone, I sent him a quick text letting him know that I had no classes on Thursday.

After I went through my nightly routine and returned to my room, his answering text was sitting pretty in my inbox.

> *Jason: I'll pick you up at 6 PM and we'll wait for Tom at my house. Until he can join us, please try not to bruise my ego more than you already have, Olive.*

I fell asleep with the biggest grin on my face.

CHAPTER TEN

OLIVE

Thursday morning, I slowly woke up from my dreamless sleep and became aware of a heavy arm lying across my stomach.

"What the hell?" I said groggily as I forced my eyes open and found Lucy sprawled all over me.

At the sound of my voice, she snuggled closer and threw one of her legs over mine.

"Lucy," I groaned, trying unsuccessfully to push her away. "Go back to your own bed, dammit. For once let me sleep in peace."

"I can't," she muttered, not even bothering to open her eyes. "Jameson fell asleep after our sexathon. I might have accidentally fried his brain. No matter what I do he won't budge." Her face snuggled closer to my breasts. "Mmmm. How do you make your boobs feel so soft yet so firm? I love sleeping on them. Best. Damn. Pillows. Ever."

"I'm thinking I should sleep with my door locked from now on."

"I can pick locks, remember?"

"Right. Well, I can't go back to sleep with you pawing all over me so go back to your own damn bed."

"I can't sleep in the same bed with him." Blindly, she patted my face. "This is comfy. You go back to sleep too, you are breathing too much."

"Sorry to inconvenience you, you crazy octopus. Why the hell can't you sleep in the same bed with him?"

"Because." She stretched out the word as if she was talking to a child. "It was a one-night stand and he is breaking the rules. If I fall asleep when he is in the same bed with me, it will turn into a relationship."

"And what is wrong with that again? You salivate every time you see the guy, not to mention this is probably the 20th time you've had a *one*-night stand with him, which isn't the way one-night stands work at all. Have a relationship with the guy for god's sake and save us all the trouble, please."

"Aurmm yu sleepmy," she mumbled, already falling asleep on me.

"Lucy!" I yelled, loud enough to wake her up.

She jolted awake, her sleepy eyes meeting mine. "What? Where are we going? Who's dead?"

"You are about to be if you don't get off me."

"Tonight, you need to fuck Jason Thorn's brains out or we're gonna have to find someone to get you laid. Like pronto." Huffing, she turned her back to me and comfortably settled down, hogging my pillows and muttering, "Always so selfish about her boobs."

"I'm starting to feel sorry for Jameson."

"Don't. Unlike you, he got it good and hard last night."

"Please stop talking. I don't need the details."

"Not giving away any details, you prude. Just saying, it was pretty satisfying, and you could use some of that satisfaction, too. I'm still sore in all the right places."

"Got it. Thanks. Now, go back to sleep. I'm begging you."

When there was no answer from her—which was a big surprise—I closed my eyes and hoped I would get a few more hours of sleep.

A few minutes later, Lucy spoke up. Again.

"Olive? Are you awake?"

"No," I groaned.

"Good. Are you going to fuck Jason Thorn's brains out tonight? Because I do want details of that. Like every little dirty detail. Is he fat and curvy? Short and fat? Veiny? Thick and long? Can you imagine how lucky you'd be if that was the case. Be honest, you never sneaked into the bathroom when he was taking a shower? I bet even at eighteen his junk was impressive."

"Are you done? What time is it anyway?" I mumbled.

"6 AM."

"I'm going to kill you."

"Sure you will. And no, I'm not done. I want more details. I *need* more details. Like how does he kiss? Does he kiss the way he kissed in *Fast Money* or does he kiss the way he kissed in *What's Left of Me?*" I could feel her turning in bed to face me, getting more into it. "I mean it's important to know these details, you know? What's the reality? Will he gently cup your face when he kisses you? Or will he thread his fingers through your hair and roughly hold you against his body?

"You've spent a lot of time thinking about this, haven't you?" I asked finally.

"Who the hell doesn't?"

"If I ever find out any of it, I'll make sure to let you know so you can die in peace. Can we please go to sleep now?"

"Can I spoon you?"

"Will it get you to sleep faster?"

"Promise."

"Just the arm."

"Just the arm," she repeated.

She snuggled closer and slowly put her arm around my waist. "Thank you."

Trying to be as gentle as possible with my words, I said, "I think Jameson is a keeper, Lucy." Under the tough exterior she showed to the world was the sweetest and most romantic girl I'd ever known. She was even mushier than I was, and that was saying something. The only problem was that she never trusted a man enough to show her weaknesses. Despite that, the guy sleeping in the room right next to us was proving to be a stubborn one. I always liked a guy who knew what he wanted and wasn't afraid to tough it out until he got it. In this case, my money was on Jameson.

"And *I* think we need to come up with a plan on what you should do with Jason Thorn." I started to protest, but she talked over me. "No, hear me out. You are a knockout who has brains, and you already have a connection there."

"Can we talk about this some other time?"

"Before you leave for your date tonight?"

"It's not a date, we're just going over my contract with his agent. It's a…work thing."

"You say tomato, I say tomato."

"God, you talk too much in the mornings."

After that I completely tuned her out and finally, after several minutes of trying to engage me in a conversation about Jason, she gave up and let us get some sleep in peace.

———

"I THINK I'm a little in love with your car," I said a few minutes after I got in Jason's car that night.

"Yeah?" he asked, smirking.

"Yeah. I love the midnight black, and the red leather accents.

Oh, and his eyes are so cute when you look at him from the front."

"Him? My Spyder isn't a he, woman, and nothing about her is cute. Sexy? That's a hell yes. Cute eyes? No."

I shrugged.

I'd had Char distract Lucy for me as I escaped from the house before she could corner me and discuss her newly made plans. She'd even made a list with the title *How to Get Jason to Fall Crazy in Love with Green Olive*. Her reasoning behind the importance of the list? She needed him to fuck my brains out. In her pretty little mind she thought I was her best bet for getting some answers to her questions. All in all, having effectively escaped that line of thinking, I felt pretty good about the evening. There was nothing worse than having Lucy making you her pet project. I was already struggling with being near Jason as it was; I didn't need to think about how certain parts of him looked when he was naked.

His home was on a hillside overlooking a breathless view of Beverly Hills. Strangely, up until I saw the beautiful, ornate steel gates, I hadn't felt out of place with him. After he did something on his phone I couldn't quite see, the gates opened and he drove up the driveway, stopping the engine when we reached the enormous white doors of his home—or small mansion was more like it.

"Wow." I breathed out as I stepped out of the car. "This is amazing, Jason." Looking around in awe at the well-kept garden that surrounded the place, I had the sudden urge to take off my shoes and simply walk around on the grass.

"You like it?" he asked with an odd, innocent smile on his handsome face. "You don't think it's over the top?"

"You're a full-blown Hollywood star, Jason," I said, unable to take my eyes off of every little detail around the house. "It would be disappointing if you had a run-down house. Your girlfriends must go even more crazy over you after seeing this place." As if a sincere smile from him wasn't enough to make you hand over your soul to the devil.

"You're the first girl I've brought here."

I glanced around one last time and walked to his side. "What do you mean?"

He scratched the back of his head then gestured for me to follow him to the front door.

"I guess you could say I'm a little weird about that. This is my home, my escape from a demanding industry, in a way. I'm constantly surrounded by thousands of people when I'm off somewhere filming. Forget about filming, everyone knows every detail of my life whether I want them to or not. When I come home, I want this place to be untainted by all that. I don't even have a staff that's around 24/7. I like my privacy a little too much," he said as he opened the door and invited me in.

A little too excited about seeing his home for the first time, I stepped inside. "So…you're saying there are no outrageous Hollywood parties in my future? Damn, I was hoping to snag an invite."

He laughed. The throaty sound was entrancing.

As we walked through a narrow hallway, our arms almost touching, I couldn't take my eyes off of him and his smiling eyes.

"How about I'll promise to take you with me if I'm ever invited to an outrageous Hollywood party?"

"Yes please."

When the hallway came to an end and I saw the open plan of the living room and the kitchen, I gasped and walked ahead of him straight to the floor-to-ceiling glass walls that revealed not only a killer view, but an expansive backyard with an infinity pool and a hot tub.

My face an inch away from the glass window, I felt Jason come up behind me. "Can they bury me here? Will you let them?

Please? I just want my ghost to sit over there and look down at the city, and maybe walk around the grass every now and then. I won't bother to haunt you at all."

He chuckled again. "I didn't think you'd enjoy it this much."

"Are you kidding me? I would give pretty much anything to come to this place at the end of every day." Giving the pool a longing look, I faced Jason.

"Seriously, this is amazing, what you've accomplished, what you've built for yourself. It will probably mean nothing to you, but I'm proud of you. So proud to have known you when you weren't such a hotshot." Giving him a small smile, I shrugged. "I'm also glad that you lived with us for as long as you did back then. Otherwise I wouldn't have gotten the opportunity to annoy you as much as I probably did when I was a kid."

I felt a familiar tug on my hair as he hooked his arm around my neck and drew me to his side. I let my shaky hand rest on his chest, near his heart. When his lips touched my forehead and he didn't loosen his hold on me, I closed my eyes and let my heart enjoy the peace.

When he drew back, my heart was going a mile a minute. Looking into my eyes, he smiled. "You have never in your life annoyed me, Olive. If I didn't have you looking after me, who would've always given me the first and biggest slices of those pies you made with your mom?"

I chuckled. "Do you remember the first time you came to our house? I promised you the biggest slice of the apple pie and ended up giving you half of the damn thing. I can still see the shock on your face when I brought it over."

His eyes twinkled with laughter. "How could I forget? You looked so pleased with yourself, just waiting in front of me to hear what I thought of your baking skills."

"Yeah, well, I wasn't so happy when my mom swooped in and took the thing right out of my hands before I could give it to you."

"You brought me five slices worth of pie. After your mom's dinner, I barely had enough room to eat one piece." His voice had gone quiet when his eyes met mine.

"Well, I was heartbroken," I said, equally softly.

His dimple beckoning me to take a very, very small taste, Jason's eyes looked down at me with such a warmness to them that I didn't know what to do or what to say for several seconds.

Could I handle being his friend?

Could I ignore my heart begging and screaming against my chest?

Did he even want to be my friend, or was this just a one-time-only favor kinda thing?

The loud ringtone of his phone burst our little bubble, and he took his arms away from me to answer the call.

"Tom? Yes. Take your time, we'll be okay. Fine, call her and come up with a new strategy then." Ending his call, he turned to me. "He'll be here in an hour or so. I had Alvin bring in Chinese takeout, you hungry?"

"Alvin?"

"My assistant. You'll meet him soon enough." As he padded toward his beautiful kitchen, I followed a few steps behind him, admiring the way his shoulders moved with every relaxed step.

Don't look at his ass, Olive. Just don't.

Outside the glass walls, the sky was slowly darkening, and suddenly the entire back patio lit up with dim lights, making the entire place look…magical.

"Olive?" Jason called my name in an amused tone when he spotted me straying toward the glass panels to take a closer look.

With a sigh, I made it back to the long kitchen bar as Jason took out more than a few takeout bags from one of the cupboards.

"What's for dinner?" I asked hopping onto one of the bar stools and almost sliding right off of it.

Jesus, why in the hell would they make the seat so small?

Trying to be all covert about it, I pushed myself up on the foot rest again and tried to sit on it sideways so it would look like I was actually sitting comfortably on the stupid thing.

As my arms started to burn from trying to balance myself, I gave up and jumped down before I fell off again.

After taking off my leather jacket, I rounded the huge island and came to stand next to Jason.

Peering into one of the boxes, I asked, "Oh, chicken chow mein, do we have beef, too?"

"Thankfully, we have two beef chow mein and two chicken chow mein, and all this extra stuff."

"Great. Can I help with anything?"

"I'm trying to find the chopsticks," he muttered as he emptied all the bags on the counter. "Can you check the drawers to your left? I should have some extra ones somewhere in there."

"Sure." Picking up all the empty paper bags and setting them aside, I leaned down and tried to figure out how to open his drawers. Since there were no handles, I lightly pushed at the first one, and it opened automatically.

I rolled my eyes.

Rich people.

It was full of knives, impressively organized by size, but no chopsticks, so I pushed it back.

When I lightly touched the second drawer, suddenly the third one snapped open, hitting me just below the knee. I gasped in pain and had to take a step back with the unexpected force of it.

The only problem was, instead of finding my balance like the graceful human being I was supposed to be, the back of my thighs hit another drawer Jason had opened behind me, and I lost my balance. In that split second, I accepted the fact that I was about to fall right on my ass; I just wished it didn't have to happen right in front of Jason fucking Thorn.

However, instead of feeling my ass hit the floor, I felt one hand firmly close around my left boob as an arm hugged me right under my breasts. For a moment—for a *looong* moment—both of us stood still, my bottom parallel to the floor. Jason's hand flexed on my breast as if he was checking the size of it, and the other dropped lower toward my stomach.

"Fuck," he cursed in a raspy voice right next to my ear, and the word sent shivers down my spine.

Please, how could I have not closed my eyes to live that shiver to the fullest? And so what if I did arch into his touch just a little bit? Maybe barely held back a moan? Who could blame me? I was just a human, after all.

When he suddenly pulled away his right hand from my stomach as if touching me had burned his skin off, my legs shook and I reached for the first thing I could grab on to.

His hand.

The one that was still covering my boob.

And fine, if you really need me to admit it, at some point I might have kind of squeezed his hand and that might have inadvertently forced him to squeeze my boob. Or maybe I had groped myself with his hand? Who the hell knows, and more importantly, who the hell cares? Hands touch boobs all the time, all over the world. I bet, at that exact moment, a lot of boobs were being touched.

"Olive." He growled and his chest—*oh, dear god, his chest*—hit my back, holding me firmer against him.

One deep breath.

Two deep breaths.

His hand was still on my boob, and my hand was—not so surprisingly—still over his when I said, "I'm so sorry. Just…just give me a second to get my balance back."

His arm wrapped around my middle again and he hoisted me up.

When I was no longer parallel to the beautiful hardwood floor and felt like I could master standing straight all by myself again, I reluctantly let go of his hand, which was resting comfortably on my breast.

As soon as he made sure I was okay, he lifted both his hands off me and slowly took a few steps back.

Not knowing what to say, I looked down and saw the damn chopsticks sitting in the open third drawer.

I cleared my throat, a few times actually. "I found them."

"Great," he said a few seconds later, his voice all rumbly.

Jesus! Talk about dreams coming true.

Not having the courage to look at him, I snatched up two sets of chopsticks, pushed the freaking drawer closed, and walked back to the glass panels.

Even though my face was probably as red as a frigging tomato, I was grinning like crazy. When I noticed there was no way I could figure out how to open the panels, I decided it would be wiser to wait for Jason before I brought the house down on us.

Two takeout boxes in his hand, he came to stand beside me with a small remote control.

When all the glass panels surrounding the living room and the kitchen area opened up, I took my first step out to heaven and took a deep breath of the crisp air.

"It smells amazing," I said in a low voice, not quite having the courage to look at his face yet.

"It smells…like grass," he said.

"I know. I love it." I took a few more steps. "Can we sit by the pool?"

"We have a table." He pointed toward a big table on the patio.

"I saw that, but I want to dip my toes in."

His hand touched my back and he guided me toward the pool.

Pushing the chopsticks into my pocket, I took off my shoes, bent down, and rolled up my jeans. When I was happy with the length, I straightened up and stood at the very edge of the pool.

"It's amazing up here, Jason." When he didn't answer, I glanced back and saw him taking off his shoes and socks. I bit down on my bottom lip to keep myself from smiling and turned back to face the amazing view.

Taking the chopsticks out of my pocket so they wouldn't break when I sat down, I lowered myself to the ground and dipped my legs into the pool.

I closed my eyes and turned my face up toward the sky with a small smile on my face. There was a quiet splash of water, and I knew Jason was sitting down too.

"Thank you for inviting me up here," I said finally, opening my eyes to glance at him.

His eyes were already on me. Smiling back, he shook his head and handed me my dinner, grabbing his chopsticks before I could hand them to him myself.

"You are different from what I'm used to. Different from the little kid I remember," he said as we started eating our dinner in a comfortable silence.

"Different how?"

"I don't know yet."

I thought about it for a minute, then in a conversational tone said, "Maybe it's the boobs?"

Choking on his food, he coughed for a good minute while I sat there serenely, looking straight ahead.

At last, in a strangled voice, he said, "Yeah. It might be the boobs."

Yup, he had noticed my boobs.

Score one for my boobs!

————

WHEN TOM FINALLY CAME AROUND, it was almost nine o'clock.

"I'm sorry I've kept you guys waiting for so long. I was with another client."

"Please, I should be the one thanking you for sparing time for me in your hectic schedule, and I have no idea what percentage you take for these kinds of things, but please let me know so I can—"

"That's been taken care of, you don't have to worry about it," Jason cut in.

"But—"

"It's okay Miss Taylor—"

"Please call me Olive," I interjected as I reached out for the papers he had pushed in front of me.

Smiling, he continued. "Olive, it's a pretty standard contract, but we'll still go over it so you can decide if there is a clause you aren't feeling comfortable with."

I nodded. I knew nothing, nothing at all about this stuff.

"The first good news is," Tom started as Jason got up from his seat next to me to get Tom a drink. "This project is never hitting the 'development limbo'." When I stared at him blankly, he explained in a bit more detail.

"After a producer or a studio options the movie rights to a book, the timeline is usually around twelve to eighteen months or sometimes even longer to get the production started, and even after that, there is no guarantee that it will ever happen. In your case, they want to capitalize on the buzz that's been going around your book, meaning since they've already secured a big name like Jason, the rest of it will come through quickly."

Reaching up, he accepted the whiskey—or maybe bourbon, either way they both tasted terrible—from Jason and kept going.

"Jason will be in Canada for a while for another shooting, then he has press junkets with the other cast members of *The Witness*. Because of that, they are aiming to start filming when Jason is back in the city. So, Olive, if you sign the contract, this is definitely happening. The casting for the smaller characters will get done while Jason is in Canada, but they will hold off on choosing the right person for Evie until Jason can spare a few days and come back to LA." He turned to look at Jason. "We need to arrange your schedule accordingly. They want you to sit in on the auditions for Evie and do a screen test with the remaining few. You can come back on your day off from the filming."

"Screen test?" I asked, looking between Jason and Tom. When I said I knew nothing, I meant it.

"A screen test is a method they use to determine the suitability of an actor or actress for the role. Since the book is centered on Jason and Evie's relationship, they have to have a strong on-screen chemistry. It doesn't matter if someone aces the audition. They need to see how she works with Jason, so he'll have to come here for those last steps of the audition process."

"They don't want me to audition at all?" Jason asked, frowning at Tom. "I can do a reading from Olive's book instead of waiting for the screenplay to be done."

Tom took a sip of his drink and shook his head. "Since they know you are interested, they want you in it, and you've already established yourself as a strong actor. They don't need you to audition. But the other stuff…" Tom glanced at me before hardening his gaze on Jason again. "The other stuff we need to talk about. Otherwise, everything you've worked on will go up in flames. You haven't seen your contract yet; the studio has some restrictions over your personal life."

"Fine. I get it," Jason snapped at him. "Leave my shit out of this. You'll get your say tomorrow at our meeting. Just go through Olive's contract tonight." Jason's harsh voice made me turn to look at him. Without saying another word, he got up and disappeared from our sight.

A little confused, I had to force myself to focus on Tom when he started talking to me again.

According to my contract, I wouldn't have any say on the final script. If they ended up changing the end—like they had hinted—I didn't have the right to throw a fit over it. Since I was a new author and not yet established, Tom didn't see a way where he could get them to modify that specific clause. The option fee was a flat fee, but the initial 'purchase price' for the movie rights would be three percent of the initial funding—with a cap of course. That was something Tom had already negotiated for, and I would be getting paid when production started.

In the end, we decided that there were only a few points worth negotiating before signing it, and apparently, the most important one was where and how they would be using the author's credit—meaning, my name and the book's title.

When we were finally done with everything, Tom left, and I found myself alone with Jason again.

"They actually want my book, Jason," I said, hugging my knees as I sat on the fancy couch.

"They had you in their offices, Olive," he reminded me as he came to sit next to me. "Of course they want your book. Did you have any doubt?"

"Yeah. I think up until this moment, I didn't take them seriously."

"And now? How do you feel?"

Resting my temple on my knees, I looked at him through blurry eyes. I was having trouble containing my smile. "You're probably going to freak out, but I might start crying at any moment now."

I could already feel my nose tingling.

He stood up and offered me his hand. "Come on, I'll give you a big hug. If you are going to cry, well, you deserve to have a hug while you cry."

Can I swoon? And maybe take him down with me so we could do some naughty things?

Smiling through my tears, I took his hand. As soon as I was on my feet, I threw my arms around his neck and hugged him. My toes were barely touching the floor.

I had worked so hard and for so long on that book. My heart was in every page of it. My secrets, my dreams, my tears. It had taken a lot of time for me to be happy with every single sentence that I'd written.

And now that same book had brought me to Jason's arms.

Swallowing, I leaned back and looked straight into those warm brown eyes. The same eyes I'd stolen glances at across the dinner table when I was old enough to know I was irrevocably in love with my brother's friend. Those same eyes I'd shyly met when he was only a kid. Those eyes I'd watched on the big screen for years, longing after something I'd never had, missing something only he could make me feel.

Feeling happier than I'd ever felt in my life, I smiled. "My story will be on the big screen."

"It will." He smiled back, his dark brown eyes holding my gaze. The day after, I would obsess about how long he had looked into my eyes, but at that moment...I chose not to question every unexpected little glance, every extra second of eye contact.

"Thank you so much, Jason. For everything, thank you so much."

"I didn't do anything, sweetheart. This is all you."

"The book, yes, but this." I gestured to the copy of the contract I would be signing if the studio accepted the changes we wanted. "This I would've screwed up if I had to do it all by myself."

"We both know that you'd have been perfectly fine, Olive."

There was a slight hesitation on his part, but when he pressed another precious kiss on my forehead, I closed my eyes and held on to him tighter, certain I would have trouble letting him go this time around.

CHAPTER ELEVEN

JASON

"Okay guys, we need to make this quick. I'm going straight to the airport after this is done," I said as soon as I entered my publicist's office. Alvin was right behind me, typing away at his phone at an inhuman pace. I assumed he was making sure everything was ready for our arrival in Canada.

"Alvin," Megan said as she got up from her seat across from Tom. "You are waiting outside. Close the door behind you."

After getting a quick confirmation from me, he was out of the room.

"Okay. Lay it on me. What's the damage?" I took my seat in the middle of the leather couch, draped my arms over the back, and forced my body to relax. This part of my job, talking about my image, my fuck-ups…this was the part I hated deep in my bones.

Megan gathered some papers from her desk drawer then took her seat again. They both had equally grim faces.

"What?" I asked when they glanced at each other, obviously trying to decide who should go first.

A few seconds passed and Tom sighed; any man would wilt under Megan McDowell's hard stare. She was the best publicist out there, the toughest of them all, but that didn't change the fact that she was the only woman Tom had a soft spot for.

"Megan got an email this morning and it changes everything."

"Explain."

"Last week, did you have sex with Jennifer Widner...in that alley, before the paps swarmed you?"

There was no use denying it. If I did, they couldn't do the job I paid them to do. So, I didn't. "Yes. They couldn't have gotten any shots though. It was a close call, I'll give you that." I checked my watch. "Anyway, you both saw the pictures from that night. It was implied that we were having sex, but they didn't get the shots. You already gave me a lecture on it, Megan." I stood up. "If this was just to remind me to behave in Canada, there's no need."

"Sit down, Jason," Megan ordered in a curt tone.

Tom was rubbing his forehead; something serious must have happened for him to show his discomfort so openly. Not much stressed him any more after working for me from the very start of my career.

"What's going on here?"

She handed me a piece of paper. It was a copy of a single email sent to Megan's email account.

I read the contents of it. Then I read it again.

"Is this a joke?" I asked, raising my eyebrows.

"Unfortunately, it isn't," Megan replied. "You're being blackmailed."

I looked down at the paper in my hands again. "For two million dollars?" I balled up the paper and tossed it away. Leaning forward, I looked straight into Tom's eyes. "If you're playing me, if this is something you two concocted together so I'll get scared and clean up my act, you tell me right now, Tom. If I find out later, you won't be happy. Neither one of you will."

Tom's jaw hardened and I saw his hands form into tight fists.

"You think I would do this to you? On top of everything else, are you out of your mind too?"

"I'm not stupid, Tom. That alley was empty. If someone was filming me having sex with Gemma, or whatever the hell her name is—"

"You don't even remember her fucking name?"

"I would've seen it," I continued over his rising tone. "Those paps came out of fucking nowhere *after* we were done. By the time they got to us, it only looked like we were making out or something."

"Obviously someone was there, Jason," Megan countered and drew my attention from Tom's angry face. "What good would it do us to make it look like someone is blackmailing you? Stop acting like you know nothing about this industry. Whether it was a pap or some stranger just walking by, they have you on tape."

"I'm not paying anyone anything," I spit out. "We don't even know if they have what they say they have."

"I replied to his email, asking for proof," Megan countered. "I'm hoping we'll hear back today. As you've already read yourself, if you decide not to pay, he'll sell it to whoever pays the big bucks. I'm sure they'll be more than happy to take it off his hands. We will send cease and desist letters, but once it's online, you know that whatever you do it will always be out there, and that will screw your career in a matter of seconds. At this point, we're beyond damage control."

"Is this a new kink?" Tom piped up. "You have to fuck them out in the open, where anyone can get a free show?"

"Watch it," I warned him wearily, all the fight seeping out of me.

Clearly not done with me, he got up from his seat and started to pace in the expansive room.

"This is the fifth incident this year," he said, rubbing the bridge of his nose. "Only this year, Jason. The first few, we managed to squash, but if there is a video and you refuse to buy it before it goes to a tabloid or a news outlet, there is nothing, *absolutely nothing* we can do to sweep it under the rug this time. Do you understand what I'm telling you?"

Stopping next to me, he continued on his tirade. "Do you even grasp the fact that you've lost two projects? Two very important projects with some big names, and you lost them because of the constant negativity in the press. They aren't talking about the movies you're making. And now this? You're not a useless reality star, Jason. Stop acting like it. If you were forty, I'd say you were going through a midlife crisis, but you have no excuse for your recent behavior. None." He waited for an answer, but I wasn't giving one. "What do you think will happen? None of the studio executives are happy with you. The press junkets you were supposed to do? The whole European tour for *The Witness*? You are kicked out. They don't want you to be the center of attention when you are supposed to be there to promote their fucking movie. You'll only go to the opening in London. You're fucking up your entire career."

I said nothing. Up to a point, he was right. Of course I knew that. I was literally fucking my career away for nothing and I had no compelling explanation. I wasn't damaged because my mom had committed suicide, or because my dad had died from a heart attack while he was in bed with a highly priced call girl. They didn't have that kind of a hold on me. They had been my biological parents and that was the end of it.

"I get it, and you are right, which is why I gave you my word that I would cool it down."

"Cool it down?" He laughed. "You're not getting it, my friend. Your little Olive's movie? The one you are surprisingly excited to be a part of? Forget about it. The second the public sees this video, the studio will cut you out. I told you they had restrictions. They don't even want you to have a relationship while you're filming and promoting their movie. Do you think they'll be okay with having your video out there while they are getting ready to announce your involvement with the adaptation?"

I sat up straighter. "You told me yourself they don't want anyone else. They want me to play Isaac."

"Yes, Jason." He nodded and let out a sarcastic laugh. "That's exactly what I told you. I'm surprised you were actually listening to me."

He lost his smile and gave me a hard look, waiting for something.

The meaning of what he was trying to tell me finally sinking in, I sprung up. "She signed the contract, damn it! They can't give up on it just because I screwed up. This has nothing to do with Olive's book."

"You're right, it doesn't. But what do they care? Olive signing the contract means nothing at this point. It is just an option. You know how these things work; let enough time pass and the rights will revert to her."

From the corner of my eye, I saw Megan rise up and get on her computer.

"They only reached out to Olive Taylor because I told them that I would get you on board. You've read the book. I know you've read the book. Think about it for a second. It's almost as if it was written for you. Why would they want someone else when you are the perfect fit?"

Turning around, I faced him again. "What the hell are you talking about?"

"Sometimes you can be so stupid," he said, groaning. He approached me as if he was nearing a dangerous animal. "You said you were childhood friends with Olive, right?"

I nodded curtly. "I practically grew up in the same house with her. Her brother was my best friend."

"Yeah, well, I believe her inspiration for Isaac was you."

"No."

"Why the hell not?"

"I don't do drugs, I never did. You know this. And Genevieve is Isaac's friend. They never live in the same house. Olive was…" Even though she had been my friend, I couldn't quite say it. "Olive was my friend's sister. It's different."

He rolled his eyes. "So what? She is a writer. She uses her imagination. That version of you does drugs. This version of you fucks everything that moves. In public. That version of you is her friend. This version of you was her brother's friend. It's the same fucking thing! The movie isn't about drugs. It's about Isaac and Genevieve. Maybe she wanted to write a happy ending for the boy she was in love with when she was a kid. What the hell do I know?" Taking a breath, he lowered his voice. "All I'm saying is, the execs wanted you because you were perfect for the role: Hollywood's troubled boy finally falling in love on the screen. Isaac is a strong character; he would've changed things around for you. Opened up new venues. I wanted you in this project because it was going to help your image in the public's eye if it was done right. You might see it as just another movie, but the viewers would've seen more than that. In the end, they would've left the theater thinking about all the heartache you'd gone through. Finally, they would've seen a different side of you, someone who is capable of love."

"Now you're just trying to piss me off."

"You think so? Show me one stable relationship you've had in the last few years."

I ran my hand through my hair and picked up the pacing where Tom had left off.

"It doesn't mean I'm not capable of love, Tom. For Christ's sake, why are we even talking about this? I'm just not looking for anything serious, especially not with someone who is in this industry. And don't talk to me as if you don't know my schedule.

I don't have time for a serious relationship. It isn't as if I never had any love interests in the movies I've been in."

"Don't give me that. You've never been in a relationship with this intensity—on screen. Sleeping with your costar while you are running away from bullets and bombs doesn't count."

Megan waved her hand at us and her voice stopped whatever Tom was about spew. "I think you guys need to see this."

I reached her side right after Tom did. There was a video on the screen. She clicked play.

We were all silent as we watched the forty-second video.

"That's it?" I asked once it stopped before either of them could start up again.

Megan spun in her chair to face me. The fire in her eyes was visible from that close. "That's it? That's what you have to say?"

"It's a fucking forty-second video some creep took with his phone's camera. What do you want me to say?"

"So," she started, linking her hands in her lap. "What you're saying is, no one will understand that this is you"—she glanced back at the screen—"clearly fucking Jennifer Widner's brains out? Because my eyes are working perfectly fine, Jason, and I can see your hips pumping into her while her dress is scrunched up around her waist. I can almost make out your dick going into her." I winced—not exactly what you want to hear coming out of your publicist's mouth. "Or are you telling me you were just dry humping her out in the alley? Because if you are about to suggest we tell the media that, I'll have to inform you that it won't work because we can clearly see the condom you are throwing away when you realize there are paps around. Which is exactly when our little camera man zooms in on your face and then the fucking CONDOM you *filled*."

I flinched and got back to my seat without making any further comment.

"Do we know if there is more to the video than that?" I heard Tom ask Megan.

"It doesn't say. Thankfully, there is no sound."

"I'm not paying him," I said from where I was sitting, interrupting them. I looked away from their blank stares. "I'm sorry. I won't do it. He can sell it to whoever he wants. I won't make him rich. For all I know, he will just forward it to everyone after he gets his money."

Tom walked toward me and sat down. "Look, Jason. This isn't a joke. This will ruin you. If this had been the only thing, you would've been fine. Hell, we would be laughing about it. But the pictures with Zoey in your car and everything else before that... They won't let this one go that easily, not when they have proof like that."

Leaning back, I looked at Megan. "You have the best team in Hollywood. Do something. Hell, find me a good girl to date, someone to go grocery shopping with at Whole Foods hand in hand every now and then. Divert their attention from this. Jason Thorn dating someone would be more of a shocking story than a blurry sex tape," I added with disgust.

"Do you think everyone is stupid and won't see through the publicity stunt?" Tom asked, getting all worked up again. "Every idiot is getting into a fake relationship these days. No one will buy it with you." His eyes flicked toward Megan, who was staring at me silently. "Aren't you going to say something?"

She shrugged. "He's right; dating someone won't help you deal with all this crap. With the timing of this, they'll see right through it. However, if we find someone—"

A knock on the door interrupted her sentence, and a second later Alvin's head popped in. "We're going to miss our flight, boss. We need to leave right now."

I waved my hand. "I'll be out in five minutes."

When he closed the door, I gave all my attention back to Megan. "You were saying?"

"You're not going to like it."

"So far you haven't said anything I liked, why change it now?"

"If we're going to lie about a relationship, we have to go bigger than that. You have to do something that will pretty much swallow this whole thing up along with your previous transgressions."

"Out with it," I said impatiently.

Tapping her long fingernails on her desk, she let out a long breath. "We'll have to find you someone to marry."

I stared at her blankly. Then, looking at Tom's interested gaze, I laughed. "I think you've both lost it. I'm not paying you to come up with a stupid solution like that. They won't believe that I went ahead and got myself a girlfriend, but they'll believe that I married someone for love? Do you even hear yourself?"

"You're not paying the guy off." She shrugged. "So I'm telling you that having your pictures taken with a fake girlfriend won't make all this go away. You have to do something big and stop all of this at once. And what does it matter to you? I'm not telling you to fall in love with her. A fake girlfriend, a fake wife— it'll practically be the same thing for you. The only difference is you'll have to live in the same house for a few years."

"Live in the same house? A few years?" I laughed harder. "You're crazy. Tom, you can't possibly agree with her."

"Do you have a better idea?" he shot back. "The public's perception of you has to change; if this is the way to do that…"

Glaring at them both, I got up from my seat and walked to the door. I was tempted to fire them both on the spot, but they were the best, and apparently I wasn't in a place where I could do whatever the hell I wanted any more.

I stopped by the door. "I'm not paying anyone. Let him

release it to whoever he wants." Opening the door, I saw an impatient Alvin lifting his brows and tapping at his watch.

"Jason." Tom's resigned voice stopped me from moving farther.

"If this…*after* this gets out, you'll still get offers, but trust me they won't be the same offers you're getting right now. You've been playing with fire, and frankly, you're about to go up in flames."

My grip on the door tightening, I turned to face the duo. Over the past few years, we had built a good relationship among us. They knew who I was and where I wanted to go in this industry, and I always appreciated their guidance. They had never cornered me like this. They always offered me options.

"I want Olive's movie," I said to Tom. "Do whatever you have to do to tie me to it. Leak the news today before this goes out if you have to. I don't care what you do, just do something so they can't back away."

It was reluctant, but he nodded. "I'll do my best."

To Megan, I said, "I don't like your solution, Megan. I get where you're coming from, but…anyway, it doesn't matter. I have to think about it. I assume you don't have any blushing brides ready for me to choose from?"

Calmly, she shrugged. "I might have a few names."

"Of course you do," I muttered. Ignoring her, I continued. "When I get back from Canada, you can show me your list and I'll think about it more. That's about all I can do right now."

I turned around to leave.

"Jason, in Canada you have to—"

"Don't worry, Tom," I interrupted him. "I'm not planning on letting anyone come near my dick. Not any time soon anyway."

CHAPTER TWELVE

OLIVE

"What are you doing in there, Olive?" Char asked.

I drew my head out of the freezer and looked at her over my shoulder. "Have you seen my ice cream? I hid it behind the peas, but it's not there."

She laughed. "I'm afraid you're too late, I saw Lucy inhale that last night."

"Damn you, Lucy," I muttered, giving up on my search.

"Are you nervous?"

"Nervous? Who, me? About what?"

Tilting her head, she waited expectantly.

Rolling my eyes, I mumbled, "He hasn't been gone that long, just a few months, and he texted me every now and then, but yeah, I'm excited to see him again." Even though I knew I shouldn't have been, I was. "And as if that's not enough excitement for my fragile heart, I'm gonna meet the casting director and actually be there when they pick who'll play Evie. I'm definitely freaking ecstatic about that."

"You're so lucky. I wonder who'll come in to audition for her. If Keira Knightley is there, you have to take pictures. A ton of them. From every single angle."

"Ah, Char," I said as I hopped up on the counter empty-handed. I wanted to eat ice cream to calm down my nerves. "Talking about Keira Knightley isn't helping at all. If I see Keira Knightley, I'm going to embarrass myself even more than I did the last time they saw me, and I don't want to think about that."

Walking around me, she opened the refrigerator and took out two small boxes of apple juice—taking advantage of a sale, we had bought them the day before. Handing one of them over, she jumped on the counter right across from me.

I sighed. "My savior."

"I would offer alcohol to take the edge off, but I'm thinking that wouldn't be very helpful in your state."

"No, it wouldn't," I said, with a wince. "I'll drink to my heart's content when we go out tonight. Still coming, right? Don't bail on us like you did last time. It's karaoke night."

"No bailing necessary. I wouldn't miss karaoke night. So, how does it feel to be an early graduate? What are your plans now?"

"I haven't decided how I feel about it yet. I'm happy, of course, but a little sad, too, I think. I paid off all my student loans with the money I made from the book, so that's something. I feel as light as a feather. Don't have a lot of money left in the bank, but at least I won't have to worry about loans."

She shook her juice box before jabbing the straw into it. "Yeah, I'm not looking forward to paying student loans every month. I wish I had the time to write a book, too."

It wasn't anything I hadn't heard the past few months. I'd quickly learned that when you write a book, and surprise, surprise, you're making money off of it—even if it's only fifty bucks a month—suddenly everyone around you turns into a writer. Of course, they're a much better writer than you, only they don't have the time to sit down and go into la-la land because they are so very busy with real life already.

"Oh, you're thinking of writing a book?" I asked mildly as I inspected the juice box in my hand.

"Well, I'm English lit, too, so yeah, I've thought about it. I mean, even you wrote one," she chuckled nervously.

Raising my eyebrows, I looked at her. "Even *I* wrote one?"

"Oh." She went poker-faced. "That didn't sound right. I just meant, you never mentioned that you were writing a book and then *bam*, you published it on your own. It was just surprising."

Lucy had been my beta reader since the day she'd stolen my laptop to see what I was always working on, but I hadn't had the courage to share my words with anyone else. It wasn't because I didn't like Charlotte, it was just because I was too nervous about the whole thing.

In the silence that followed her words, she took few long sips from her apple juice before putting it down on the counter. "Anyway, the reason I asked about your plans…I was wondering if you were thinking about moving out?"

"Moving out? Of here?"

"Yeah. I mean we have one more semester, but since you're gonna have money coming in from the movie, too…" She shrugged. "I just thought maybe you'd get your own place."

"You trying to get rid of me, Char?" I asked, slightly amused, slightly wary.

"Of course not." She jumped down and tossed the box into the garbage can; she hadn't even finished it. "You know Lily, right?" I nodded. "Well, her boyfriend tossed her out so she is looking for a place to stay for the rest of the semester. I said maybe your room would be vacant if you decided to move out."

"Sorry to hear that about Lily, but I'm not considering leaving. I like living with you guys."

"Oh." She looked genuinely confused. "The way you've been acting around Marcus lately, I thought you were uncomfortable here."

"Marcus was my friend for a year before we started our relationship; we've been living together for almost three years now. I'm not uncomfortable around him, Char, we just don't hang out together as much as we used to. Other than that, I have no problems with him. He is the one acting weird after this book deal happened."

"I understand." She avoided my eyes.

"Well," I started, edging off the counter to get down. "I'm glad we did this."

"Are you angry at me?"

"No. Is there a reason I should be?"

"No. Then can I ask you something else?"

I settled back again. "Sure. About?"

I pulled the short straw into my mouth and sighed a happy sigh when the cold apple juice hit my tongue.

"Jason Thorn."

Intrigued, I gestured for her to go ahead. Charlotte didn't ask many questions. She watched. She listened. She was shy to the point that it was painful to watch sometimes.

"When you saw that video of Jason in that alley…"

My face fell. Why was she even asking me about that?

"Were you upset?"

Do birds shit?

What the hell?

Letting go of the straw, I raised an eyebrow. "Where are you going with this, Char?"

"Nowhere." Avoiding my eyes, she played with the coffee machine I had bought with Lucy the day I got my first payment from Amazon. "I just don't want to see you get hurt. He is a movie star, Liv. I saw you two together that day—when he was dropping you off—"

"You left as soon as you met him Char."

"I know. I know. But I see how excited you get every time you're talking about him."

"So?"

"Marcus thinks you're—"

"I don't care what Marcus thinks, Char. And to answer your initial question, yes, I was upset to see it, but not because I was jealous or anything like that. I don't have a say in his life. Hell, I'm nothing more than a friend or an old friend's sister to him right now." I shrugged. "I'm not stupid enough to think otherwise. So what if I enjoy hanging out with him, wouldn't you? It's not news that he, um, enjoys having sex, for lack of a better word. Did all those people who bashed him on TV and online think that he was a virgin or something?"

She nodded thoughtfully. "I heard that after the video was released, he was booted out from a few movie projects, and there were rumors that he was actually losing his role in your movie, too."

"Obviously, he didn't." I hopped down from the counter and tossed the now empty juice box into the garbage can.

"Well, still. It seems like he is a ticking bomb. I just hope that he won't ruin your movie, too."

The apartment door opened, and Marcus and Lucy walked in.

I focused on Char. "He is a damn good actor, Char. He can have any role he wants. They'll forget about the video in a few weeks when some other celebrity cheats on his wife with the nanny, then everyone will focus on them instead. What's gotten into you today?" I asked, frowning at her.

"What do you mean?" she mumbled, not looking at me.

"Hi, Liv," Marcus greeted me on his way to the fridge and oh-so-casually brushed a kiss on my hair.

Startled, I turned to him as he took a water bottle from the fridge and walked right out. "What was that?" I asked to his back, pulling myself together.

He glanced back over his shoulder. "I said hi. Or is that banned, too?"

Lucy bugged her eyes at me from the doorway.

"Something is wrong in this apartment today," I announced.

My phone pinged.

Thank god!

"My Uber is here. I'm leaving."

"But I just got here!" Lucy whined. "You didn't even hear what Jameson did to me today." She widened her eyes at me. "In an empty classroom!"

"He rocked your world?" I asked, raising an eyebrow.

She gave me a wolfish grin. "That he did."

"See, I'm all caught up now. Text me when we're leaving for karaoke night, and I'll get back here to get ready."

I grabbed my purse and walked out the door, not meeting Marcus' eyes.

———

FINALLY REACHING the building where the auditions were being held, I got out of my Uber and stood there to stare at the building for a moment. Was I excited because I was about to see my characters come to life? Or was I excited because I'd get to spend some time with Jason again?

"Olive!"

I turned around to see Jason getting out of his car. The way he stepped out and closed the door of that ridiculously sexy car of his...then, as if in slow motion, put his Ray-Bans on...

Damn...

Mini orgasm attack.

Then he got closer and closer, and I got an even better look at my dimple—mine, because I was staking my claim on that damn thing. After all, I'd seen it before all of his loving fans. First come, first served, right?

"Hi," I managed to sputter when he reached me.

"Hi to you too."

We just stood there and stared at each other for a moment, his smile getting goofier.

Should I hug him? *Could* I hug him? Was that even allowed? Why was I so weird?

Finally, he laughed and said, "Come here." He gave me a sideways hug and looked down at me. "I might have missed you a bit more than you missed me, Olive. It's good to see you."

Not the best thing he could've said, but then again I'd take anything that came out of his mouth when he was hugging me.

With my head tilted back, I looked up at him. Reaching up, I lifted his sunglasses and finally looked into his eyes.

"Nice to see you, too, Mr. Jason Thorn."

Laughing, he kissed my temple. Had his lips lingered for more than two seconds, or was it just me? Did those two extra seconds mean something? Why go for the forehead and not the cheek? Did it have a different meaning?

Different meaning or not, my heart gave a happy sigh and the butterflies pretty much fainted from all the excitement Jason was giving them. I closed my eyes and savored the moment.

After we reached the floor where the casting crew was situated, he took his time to introduce me to everyone. The whole setup had a relaxed vibe, nothing scary at all. The casting director, Bryan, his assistant, and a cameraman to tape the auditions were the only ones left behind, and Jason seemed to know them all.

"I'm not late, am I?" Jason asked after shaking hands with everyone.

His eyes on the papers in front of him, the casting director waved his hand over his head. "Just on time, as always. Have you looked through the script we have ready?"

The script is ready?!

Jason nodded at Bryan and took the papers the assistant handed him. "I got them this morning." After turning a few pages, he asked, "Which scene do you want to go over for this?"

"We'll try the first time he finds his way back to Genevieve."

"Ok. Great." Glancing at the corner where I was sitting, Jason looked at me and winked.

I gave him a lame thumbs up and smiled.

Clearly amused, he shook his head and turned back to the director.

"Who's coming in for Evie?" he asked no one in particular.

"We're down to three names. We'll see how you do on camera and then go from there."

When I saw the first actress, Claudia Colbert, walk in, I was very proud of myself for not losing my cool. Even though nobody was paying attention to me, I still thought I deserved a pat on the back.

She was wearing a simple white tee with black jeans and Toms. Her hair was in a ponytail that was effortless in a way I could never achieve, and from what I could see, she had no makeup on. While us mortals had to have at least some concealer on, of course she'd been blessed with great skin on top of everything else.

She shook hands with Jason, talked with the director for a few seconds, then took her place in front of the camera with her script in her hand and waited for Jason to take his place.

"You guys ready?" Bryan asked, giving them all his attention as he got up and sat down next to the cameraman.

Both Jason and Claudia nodded.

"Let's start reading from the top. I want to record the ending from two different angles so we'll stop and take the last part again." When they started reading their lines, Bryan was watching them through the little screen that was on the table. I tried to lean to my left to take a peek, but they were in my way, so I settled back and focused on hearing Isaac and Evie for the first time.

"How could you leave me, Evie?" Jason asked, already sounding like a different person—tired, broken, hopeless. He was becoming Isaac right in front of my eyes.

Claudia took a step toward him and tilted her head to the side. "I've never left you, Isaac. I tried, but I can't leave you. But I won't come after you either; I won't force this on you."

Jason's voice turned harsh as he laughed. "Force this on me? What is this, Evie? Is there even anything left of us in you?"

She took another step toward him and lifted her hand, but then dropped it as both of her hands formed fists.

"Do I disgust you now? Is that why you can't touch me?" Jason all but spit the words at her as his eyes took in her movements.

Claudia flinched and shook her head, her voice beaten and small. "I don't want to hurt you any more."

Jason dropped the papers and clasped Claudia's wrists, lifting them up and pulling her against his chest in one quick move I wasn't expecting. "You think your touch can hurt me? You killed me the moment you let me go in your heart, Evie."

"Isaac," Claudia murmured, and when she looked up at Jason, there were tears swimming in her eyes.

Holy cow! If only I had some popcorn and tissues.

"You were the one who left me," she continued. "You broke my heart into so many pieces that I never fully recovered, Isaac. But none of it matters, does it? You aren't here to stay. You will never stay."

Whooaaa there!

That was most definitely not my dialogue. They had turned a perfectly romantic scene into a cheesy one.

She looked heartbroken.

I saw a teardrop fall from her eyes and Jason let go of her wrists as if they had burned him.

"I came back. I came crawling back to you," Jason choked out. Leaning down, he cupped her cheeks in his hands, forcing her to look at him. "Evie. You're my only one."

They both closed their eyes and rested their foreheads against each other's.

"Take me with you," she whispered into the silence. "Don't leave me bleeding again. Don't let them take you away from me."

Jason kissed her nose, her eyes, and then drew back a few inches, his hands still holding her face. "Say you still love me, Evie. Give me the words."

She stood up on her tiptoes and whispered her love for him against his lips. Then they were going at each other as if the world was ending.

Well, mine kinda ended anyway. I was supposed to watch this take place in front of my eyes two more times with two different actresses? What in the world had I been thinking when I'd told Jason I would love to come along?

Someone say cut, goddamn it!

Then it was over and they parted. Bryan thanked them and asked for another take from a different angle. I refused to watch it for the second time. Seeing the same scene in a movie set would be a different story, but in here, with only a few people around…it looked intimate, real. Each and every one of us was an outsider, intruding upon their moment.

Finally, Bryan was happy with what he got, and after thanking Claudia, they sent her away.

I watched the same thing happen with two other beautiful, very well known, very talented actresses. The third one, Lindsay Dunlop, pretty much blew it out of the park. Bryan asked her to do three different scenes with Jason. At the end of it all, they had their Evie, and Lindsay was smiling just as big as Jason.

Even though I wasn't being specifically ignored or anything, I was still sticking out like a sore thumb sitting in the corner like that. I had a feeling I was just there because Jason Thorn had brought me in. They didn't care that I was the author at all.

Feeling overwhelmed with the kisses, the acting, the words…I sneaked out of the room—not that I needed to sneak out. No one gave a damn about what I was doing.

I was digging into my bag looking for my phone when someone came around the corner and collided with me. I stumbled back.

A second of shock, then I yelped in pain.

I glanced down at my front and saw that my entire shirt was soaked with some kind of green liquid. It smelled like coffee, but it was green.

Scalding green liquid.

"Jesus! Are you okay?" someone asked.

"Oh, shit! Shit! Shit!" My eyes burning with tears, I dropped my bag onto the carpeted floor. Peeling the shirt away, I started to blow on my skin to find some relief.

Some girl came running to the guy's side.

"Sir, is everyth—"

"Go get me something to clean her up with," the guy snapped at the girl.

"Olive Taylor?" He softened his voice for me.

Hearing my name, I looked up and saw Keith, the exec with the bleached teeth, hovering over me.

"Oh. Hello," I said, my lower lip slightly trembling. I peeked into my shirt and realized my chest was already red.

Wonderful.

The girl reappeared next to us and handed Keith a wet towel.

"Let me," Keith murmured, taking a step toward me.

I was in too much pain to decline his help, so I pushed my

hair out of the way and let him gently press the cold towel onto my skin.

"Thank you," I murmured. "That feels great."

He met my eyes and gave me an apologetic smile. He was probably in his mid thirties, but for his age, he looked good—minus the teeth situation. When he slowly reached the swell of my breasts, I swallowed and looked away.

Maybe a wet towel wasn't the best solution, but it was working. For now. I still had to lose the shirt somehow. It was completely soaked through and right then competing in a wet t-shirt contest was not on my to-do list.

Just as he opened his mouth to say something, someone grabbed my wrist and I was wrenched away from Keith. My head jerked up and I saw Jason pushing me behind his back, glaring daggers at Keith.

"What the hell do you think you're doing touching her?"

"Jason!" I gasped, a little belatedly. His hand was still around my wrist, but his touch was gentle.

Keith appeared calm, but upon hearing Jason's tone, he raised his brows.

"Jason," I said, tugging at his arm, trying to get his attention. "There is coffee all over me, he was trying to help."

"It is smoothie, Olive," Keith said looking at me with a small smile.

Hot smoothie?!

Seriously?

"By groping your breasts?" Jason growled. He looked down at me with his flushed face and I frowned up at him.

"Jesus," he exclaimed when he finally dropped his eyes enough to get a look at me. "Jesus!" he repeated. Looking into my eyes, he asked, "Are you okay, Olive?"

"I'll be fine." I looked at Keith over his shoulder and decided an apology was in order.

"I'm so sorry. I wasn't looking where I was going. Thank you for your help." I looked at Jason, lifted my arm, and eyed my wrist that was still in his grasp. "If you can let me go, I'll just leave."

He didn't let me go, but at least his face wasn't flushed with anger any more.

Glancing at Keith, he said, "Sorry, man. When I saw you two…I assumed wrong."

"Understandable. She is your friend."

Jason's mouth tightened.

What in the world is going on?

"I hope we'll see each other soon, Miss Taylor," Keith said to me and walked away from us.

Jason dropped my wrist and gently brushed the hair that had fallen over my shoulders away from my chest.

"We're going to the emergency room."

"No, we're not. What's wrong with you?" I asked, genuinely curious. "He was helping me. What did you think he could be doing out in the open like this?"

He had the decency to look away.

"How can I help?" he asked instead.

I sighed. "You should go back in there, Jason. I was leaving anyway." Again, I peeled the shirt away from my skin. If another Uber was close by, maybe I could make it back to the apartment without being seen by too many people.

"We're done with the reading." He put his hand on my back and urged me forward. "Let's go. I should have an extra shirt in my car. We'll look at the damage as you change and then decide if we're going to the emergency room or not."

"Fine, Mom," I mumbled, and he gave me a dark look.

"Your car really looks adorable from the front," I said, once we reached the parking lot.

"It's a Venom GT Spyder, Olive. It's *not* an adorable car."

I shrugged behind his back. To me, the eyes and the small mouth looked adorable.

Unlocking the doors, he leaned in and reached for something behind his seat.

A gray t-shirt.

"Take off your shirt," he said, straightening up and turning to me.

"What?" I gaped at him.

His fingers reached out to lift the hem of my shirt, but I slapped his hand away.

"What are you doing?" I hissed quietly as two girls hurried passed his car, their phones glued to their ears.

"Olive," he started. "I need to see how bad it is. Take it off."

His hands came at me again. I slapped his hand harder.

"You want me to take off my shirt out in the open?"

He met my eyes. "We're in the parking lot. No one who isn't supposed to be in here is allowed to be in here. No one will see you between the SUV and my car. Go on."

He reached at me again.

So, naturally, glaring at him, I slapped his hand even harder.

This time he laughed.

"Don't make me take it off for you, Olive. I don't want to hurt you."

"Your car doesn't even reach your chest, Jason. I doubt it will do much to hide me from sight."

"Face the SUV. I'll turn around and cover your back. Or we can go straight to the ER. Your choice."

"No," I snapped.

"Then do as I say."

I narrowed my eyes at him. "You're annoying." After a short staring contest that only ended up making me hot, I was the first one to turn away.

Grumbling under my breath, I gingerly lifted my shirt off of my stomach and took it off. It wasn't hurting as much as it had a few minutes before, but I wouldn't say no to rubbing some ice cubes on my chest either. Dropping the shirt to the ground, I…

Shit! The extra shirt was still in his hands.

"Hand me the damn shirt," I whispered, looking to my left to see if anybody was walking around.

"Why are you whispering?" he asked right over my shoulder, his hot breath tickling my neck.

The annoying-hot-jerk chuckled when I squealed and jumped around.

"You were supposed to turn around," I accused him hotly.

His eyes dropped to my chest. His jaw hardening, he quickly looked up and away.

"What is *that?*" he gritted through his teeth.

Covering my breasts with my forearm, I snapped, "They're breasts. What does it look like?"

Did he think they were too big? He probably did. I definitely didn't have those small elegant breasts where you could go to bed without wearing a bra.

"Why aren't you wearing something white and simple?"

Despite the stupid situation, I looked down at my chest and laughed. "Why do you care what I wear? And what is wrong with this one?"

He looked up at the sky. "It's…it doesn't…do anything. You can see through it."

"So?" I asked.

"You aren't supposed to wear stuff like that."

"Says who? I'm sure you must've seen much better stuff than this." I took a deep breath and let it out. "Just give me the damn shirt, Jason," I said impatiently. "It wasn't my intention to disgust you or embarrass you or whatever it is happening right now."

"Disgust me?" His eyes shot back to my eyes. "Olive," he said, taking a step toward me.

I cut him off before he could tell me something brotherly and piss me off, or—even worse—break my heart even more.

"Jason, there are people around. Please give me the shirt so I can cover myself."

His jaw ticked, but he handed me his shirt, and I quickly pulled it over my head.

"Thank you."

He took yet another step and I plastered my back against the SUV behind me. He lifted the shirt up, just a little. This time I didn't slap his hand away. He'd already seen more of me than I'd been ready to show him.

He gently touched my stomach, then started running the back of his knuckles over my slightly irritated skin.

That thing that resides in your chest? Took wings and flew away.

The other thing that was in my skull? Turned to complete mush.

I sucked in a breath, my heartbeat suddenly slowing down to the point where I wasn't sure if I was still alive or had stepped into heaven. When I lifted my head up, he was staring down at me —*right* into my eyes.

By then I was the perfect example of one of those 'My body is ready' gifs.

"It doesn't look as bad as your...chest area," he said, softly dropping the shirt over his hand.

He didn't back away.

I didn't look away.

His hand was still in there.

On my stomach.

Under my shirt.

Then he sighed and pulled it away. Suddenly I could breathe again.

Instead of begging him to take me right against the car like I desperately wanted to, I said, "I'll be okay. I'll put something on when I get home. It's not as bad as it looks."

He wasn't happy, but he opened his car door and helped me get in.

Jason Thorn, my childhood crush and now movie star, had touched my stomach, gently, and I wasn't hyperventilating.

Huh...

Maybe I was getting the hang of this obsession/love thing.

CHAPTER THIRTEEN

JASON

I t had been one hour since I'd dropped Olive off and I was once again sitting in Megan's office, working on damage control. So far, I'd looked through twelve headshots, recognizing some of the girls while having no idea who the others were. The one thing I knew for certain: I didn't want any of them.

"I'm starting to doubt your PR skills, Megan," I said after dropping the photographs back on her desk.

She stared at me blankly as she took a sip of her green tea and slowly put it down on her desk.

"It's been what? A month? Two months? You still haven't decided on a girl, Jason. I'm not asking you to make a lifelong commitment here. Pick one so we can draw up a contract and move on from this."

"I'm not marrying some bloodthirsty new actress who will be in this just to get more exposure. I'm not signing on to carting her around to events and all this publicity crap. Marrying her will be enough torture on its own."

She tilted her head. "Why exactly do you think we're doing this, Jason? It will be a win-win for both sides. Why else would they marry you?"

Ouch.

"In your case, you need the positive exposure. You need to remind the public and frankly everyone in the movie industry that you're not just some exhibitionist and in fact a damn good actor. In her case, whomever you decide to marry, she'll use you for her own gain, whatever that is. That's how the game is played."

I rubbed my forehead and leaned back in my seat. "I don't like this, Megan. I don't like it at all."

"Look, Jason," she started, leaning over her desk. "You're an amazing actor. You have the potential to become one of the bests in this industry, but that's not what the media is circulating any more. Have you read the tabloids lately?"

"You know I don't touch those."

"Yeah, *you* don't, but people do. They love the gossip, they love to learn the dirty secrets of celebrities, and they definitely love to tear them apart at their first mistake, and every time after that. Those facts will never change. Whether you like it or not doesn't matter. You've been in this game long enough to know the rules." She stopped and took another sip of her tea. I wanted to take that damn cup and throw it against the wall. "Do you know what they'll read tomorrow?"

"What?" I snarled.

"A special interview with a college girl from Canada. Apparently, you two fucked all over the place in Toronto, and she is giving the inside scoop on your relationship." She raised an eyebrow, waiting for my answer.

Dumbfounded, I shook my head. "What college girl? What the hell are you talking about? I haven't touched anyone since the alley incident."

"That's not what she is saying."

"And now you're going to believe the tabloids over me?"

"It doesn't matter what I believe. *I* know you didn't touch anyone because I've been in contact with Alvin." My eyes narrowed and she shrugged. "In order to protect you, I need to know what's happening in your life before others can learn about it. So, yeah, of course I'm keeping tabs on you. The point is, tomorrow everyone will eat up the story. It doesn't even matter whether it's true or not, or that there are no exclusive pictures attached to the interview this time around. Everyone will believe it simply because, well, it's what you do." Another shrug. "It's the first thing that pops into their minds when they hear the name Jason Thorn."

"There are no exclusive pictures, blurry or not, because nothing happened in Toronto." I sighed. No matter what I said, I knew I couldn't win. "You're giving me a damn headache, Megan."

"I wish a headache was your only concern. Any publicity isn't good publicity in your case, Jason. Denial can only work up to a certain point and they are not having what we're serving them anymore. You want to be known for your work, not your personal life. That's what you told me when you hired me, and you were right, because that's the only way you'll keep getting the big roles. Otherwise you'll just get lost in this circus because no one will be interested in having you on their team."

"And marrying some girl will solve all of my problems." I gave her a bitter laugh and rose from my seat. The sky was tinged with pink and soft orange hues while in there, in that office, my own world was filling with dark clouds.

"I didn't say it will solve all your problems at once. It all depends on how you act *after* you're married. You're gonna have to play the good husband role for quite some time. No stepping out on your wife either. I don't care if you add a clause into the contract, agreeing to have sex just with each other, but you're not going out there to take out your dick and keep doing what you've been doing."

"I'm not having sex with anyone," I growled.

She waved her hand, dismissing me. "Of course, before all that happens we'll have to make it look like you've been dating for a month or two before you get married. Leak some cozy photos of you two together. Then we'll come up with a good story and you'll elope or something."

"A good story," I repeated, running my hand down my face. "My entire fucking life is turning into a horror story."

"Well, next time you'll remember to keep it in your pants and we won't be in this situation again."

"Thanks for the advice," I mocked.

"Go home, Jason," she said wearily. "I have to make a few phone calls and see who else I can add to your 'future wife' pile."

"Great," I muttered, heading toward the door.

"I'll be waiting for you at 4 o'clock, tomorrow. Don't make me chase you. You have to choose someone so we can start shaping the story. This isn't something that can happen overnight."

I headed out without saying another word.

————

Me: What are you up to?
Olive: I'm about to scream for Mercy for the second time tonight.
Me: What?!
Olive: LOL! Not that kind of screaming. Unfortunately, it's only karaoke night and Lucy wants me to celebrate the movie deal by singing my heart out. We're doing Charlie Puth's 'Marvin Gaye' in ten minutes, for the second time... I believe it'll happen a few more times before the night ends.

I WAS BACK AT HOME, but the longer I tried to relax and read the mostly complete script Bryan had given me, the more I was starting to feel like a trapped animal in my own damn home—which soon enough wouldn't even be my own home. I would be sharing it with an unknown roommate.

Trying to forget about my own life, I'd decided to text Olive to see if she was free to talk about the script. After all, nobody knew Isaac better than her, and even though I'd read the book thoroughly, twice, it would help if I could get deeper into Isaac's head. Maybe ask what she was thinking when she was writing from his point of view. She could give me details about his past, things that only she could know.

As for Isaac's unfiltered sex scenes in the book…I didn't think I was ready to go there with Olive. After reading the book, I understood why Olive didn't want Dylan or her dad to read it. Both of them would either have a heart attack, or simply have trouble looking into her eyes again, which would be a great tragedy. Her eyes…they were one of a kind, alluring and intriguing in a way that made you want to get closer to her just so you could study and memorize the depth of the colors, find those hazel specks hiding in the bright green and watch how they sparkled when she smiled at you.

The night she came to my house to meet with Tom, I found out that I had no trouble at all looking at any part of her body, including her eyes, which probably made me a complete bastard.

Reading her last text again, I realized what I was feeling was disappointment. I'd been eager to talk to her, to pick her brain, to see her again. Wasn't that why I had invited her to sit in on the screen testing? Hadn't I felt happy when I'd seen her standing in front of the building, smiling at me as I jogged to her side? And in that brief moment, hadn't I completely forgotten about Dylan being my friend, and Olive being his little sister?

Not liking where my thoughts were heading, I tossed the

script aside and shook my head. Maybe not having sex was getting to me. My phone pinged with a new text from Olive.

Olive: What are you up to?

I smiled and walked outside as I texted her back.

Me: Enjoying my freedom while I can.
Olive: What does that mean?
Me: Nothing important. I have part of the script so I was actually thinking of calling you to see if you were free to discuss Isaac. Pick your brain a little.
Olive: I've been with Isaac for almost three years. He's been my day and night. He is so broken, but still perfect just the way he is. Let's talk about him. Let's talk about him for hours.
Me: Are we still talking about the same Isaac?
Olive: There can only be one Isaac in my heart. Though he gave his heart to Evie, he'll forever be in mine.
Me: I'm thinking you're a little on the drunk side, little Olive.
Olive: It's Long Island Iced Tea night!!! And I don't want to be the little one any more, Jason :(I want to be big Olive. I've grown up, I'm not clingy or sticky anymore.

Not having a clue what she was talking about, I hesitated for a short moment before calling Alvin.

"Hi Alvin."

"Hey, boss. What's up?" There was a rustling sound in the background.

"Sorry man. Bad timing?"

"It's fine. Did you need something?"

"Yeah. I need you to find me a...a college bar, probably. They are having a karaoke night."

I could hear his laptop come to life. "O-kay. Is there any way we can narrow that down? Otherwise the list will be longer than you'd want."

"It should be somewhere near USC. I'll text you her address so you can check the bars around the apartment, too."

"And this 'her' we're talking about is Olive Taylor?"

"Yes," I replied distractedly as I walked back into the house. If I was going out, I would need to change.

"You're not considering going out to find her in a bar, are you?"

"And if I am?"

"I'd say you must not have enough of Megan chewing your ass and you're jonesing for more."

I laughed. "Don't worry, she won't hear about this." I stopped next to my bed. "And if you don't want to get fired, you're not reporting that to her either. Get back to me as soon as you can. I'm texting you her address."

Ending the call, I texted him the address of her apartment and went to my closet to change into something more college-y to blend in with the rest of the frat boys.

Fifteen minutes later, I was on my way to attempt to find Olive in one of the five bars Alvin had texted.

———

IT WAS at the fourth bar that I finally found...something. And by something, I mean Olive and the friend she had introduced me to that day—Lucy? Charlotte?—up on the small makeshift stage just about to start a song.

She looked...damn it but she looked good. Her hair had clearly been haphazardly put into a messy bun, but there were still a few locks that had escaped and were resting over her shoulders, framing and drawing attention to her beautiful smiling face. She was wearing a short dress, which seemed to sit a little tight on her breasts.

Why the hell am I looking at her breasts, again?

Shit!

When the music blasted, they started swaying to the beat. Then reaching up, she let her hair loose, shook her head, and looked at her friend with a big smile on her face as she mouthed something I couldn't understand. Just as she had said on the phone, they started to sing 'Let's Marvin Gaye' from the top. Then started the slow hip and shoulder movements. The saps who were lined up in front of the stage ate it all up, catcalling and whistling.

Looking down at the floor, I pulled down my baseball hat, trying not to draw attention to myself. I walked in farther and found a dark corner close to the stage. I wanted to grab a beer from the bar, but it wasn't worth getting recognized for. As soon as I knew Olive was safe with her friends, I would leave. My hands in my pockets, I leaned back against the wood wall and watched the whole thing with bewilderment, amusement, and fascination.

When Olive smiled and bit her bottom lip as her friend took over the song, I was completely mesmerized by her.

Sucker punched.

Then the chorus came and they were singing together again. At one point, Olive gave her back to her friend, glanced over her shoulder, and with a playful look on her face, winked at her. I would have bet millions of my dollars that every hot-blooded male's attention was on her, not her friend, but it didn't even look like Olive cared for any of the attention she was getting. Even though her friend was a fiery brunette, she couldn't hold a candle to Olive's beauty. If they had the chance, more than half of those idiots would go after her without a second thought.

Without even realizing what I was doing, I walked closer to the stage. Blending in had been easier than I'd thought it would be, so I didn't see a problem with being more in the open.

A college bar wasn't exactly the place people would expect me to hang around, after all. Even if a few of them thought I looked like someone they knew, with the amount of alcohol in their system they wouldn't remember a thing by the morning, and if someone started to take pictures, I would just head out.

My eyes glued to the stage, specifically on Olive, I didn't see the guy next to me and took an elbow in my side. Grunting in pain, I lowered my baseball cap just to make sure no one could see my entire face. I couldn't stay there the entire night, but I knew I wasn't going anywhere until I talked to Olive and made sure she wasn't pawed by any drunken idiots.

I didn't trust any of those bastards not to pull anything on her as soon as she was off the stage.

As much as the crowd was getting heated, Olive and her friend seemed to enjoy singing to each other, laughing and smiling the entire time. When they were at the opposite ends of the stage, Olive crooked her finger at her friend and I found myself a few steps closer to the stage.

Damn it, Jason!

When she screamed for mercy, I was right there with her. My phone started buzzing in my pocket. Seeing Megan's name on the screen, I ignored her call. Suddenly, flustered and angry for some reason, I was about to turn around and leave when I heard someone yell, 'I'll give you all the healing you need, all damn night babe!'

Stupid shitfaced bastards.

So, I stayed.

I would drop her home myself. That way I would feel better, knowing she was safe.

When they were finally done with the song, I was more than ready to deck a few guys I had set my eyes on. Dylan would want me to, wouldn't he?

As soon as Olive got down from the stage, the guy I'd seen when I'd dropped her off at her apartment took her hand and led both the girls to the end of the bar where a few more of their friends were sitting. Heading toward them, I noticed Olive pulling her hand out of his and linking her arm with her friend's again.

When I was almost by their side, my eyes met with her friend's—the one she had been on the stage with—and she recognized me at once. Had someone else also recognized me? Taken pictures? Was that why Megan was calling?

When I was standing right behind Olive, her friend's grin had become too big for her small face.

That one was trouble.

I cleared my throat, but Olive didn't hear me, not with the stupid blasting music—none of them did. I glanced at her friend, but she was looking anywhere but me.

Sighing, I put my hand on Olive's waist.

The touch felt familiar—maybe a little too much.

She whirled around, her hair smacking me in the face; it smelled like fruit. Edible.

Fuck me.

Not edible.

Not my little Olive.

When I was safe from the hair attack, she was staring at me with a frown on her face, then she slightly lifted my baseball cap and recognized me at once. Her expression turned from cute fury to a fucking beautiful smile.

It was good to know she knew how to handle strangers touching her: hit them in the face with the hair whip and then frown up at them until they slithered away. My only hope was that they wouldn't carry her away along with them.

"Jason!" She beamed up at me and threw herself in my arms, trusting me to catch her.

Grunting at the unexpected weight, I had to take a step back to steady us. Laughing, I nudged her chin up from where it was buried in my chest.

"You smell soooo good," she slurred slightly. "Did you come to see big Olive? I'm not so little any more, am I, Jason? You saw that, right?"

She looked so vulnerable and hopeful that I had a hard time finding the right words to speak.

My hand acting on its own, I cradled her face and watched her close her eyes for two seconds then softly open them up to gaze right back into mine.

"No. I guess you're not that little any more, my little Olive."

She scrunched up her nose. "You're still calling me little." Shaking her head, she said, "You need sooo much help with finding the right nicknames. You always did."

Laughing, I leaned down to her ear and asked, "Do I, now? Would you like to volunteer to help me on that front?"

She nodded eagerly, her smile blooming again.

It was damn impossible not to smile down at her.

For a moment, we stood there glancing at each other and my smile slowly melted away.

I was doing something wrong.

I was *feeling* something wrong.

Then thankfully, her friend was there, clearing her throat as she put a hand on Olive's back.

"Lucy," Olive yelled over the music excitedly as she steadied herself against my chest and saw her friend.

She was definitely a little drunk.

I wanted to tug her closer.

Lucy smiled at her. "Maybe you should let Jason take you home before somebody recognizes him here. People seems to be looking your way," she added, looking at me apologetically.

I glanced around and sure enough, there were a few people close by, whispering as they kept their eyes on us.

"I should?" Olive asked.

"You definitely should," Lucy repeated, patting her arm.

"Okay," agreed Olive and turned to face me. "You should take you home before somebody recognizes me, Jason."

I smiled. "Okay, let's get you home then, you little drunk." My eyes fixed on her lips, I reached up and wiped the moisture away, dragging her mouth open slightly.

She bit down on her lip where I had just touched her.

Holding back a groan, I looked at her friend. "Thank you, Lucy. I'm sorry if I intruded upon your night. I was just worried about her."

"It's okay. We can do this any time, and she's already on her way over to a major hangover, better we cut her off now. She is a lightweight."

I could see that, and for some reason, I preferred a lightweight Olive to a heavy drinker. Nodding, I gripped Olive's hand to steer her away from her friends, but her other friend, Charlotte stopped us.

"Here," she said, handing me a key over Lucy's shoulder. "Olive doesn't have one on her."

"Char, I love you," Olive exclaimed, and pushing Lucy out of the way, gave her friend a big hug.

"Hey," Lucy yelled.

"I love you, too, Olive." Charlotte laughed a little stiffly. "I'll see you back at the house."

She nodded and came back to my side, holding her hand out just like she had done when she was only ten years old.

The memory hit me in the back of the head out of nowhere.

When Dylan and I had found her sitting on the school steps, she was silently crying because some kid had made fun of the burn scars on her mom's arms. While Dylan had flown up the steps to find the little shit who had upset his sister, Olive had simply held out her hand, silently asking me to stay with her.

My eyes on her upturned hand, my mind stuck in a memory I hadn't even been aware I remembered, I reached for it, just like I'd done years before, and held on tight.

I felt more eyes on me, so I looked to Lucy's left and saw the guy, Marcus, sizing me up with a not-so-happy look on his face.

Ignoring him and saying goodbye to her friends again, I pulled Olive out of the bar and onto the street.

Clean air.

When we reached the black SUV, Olive suddenly stopped. I looked back at her.

"What's wrong? Are you feeling sick?"

"No." She squinted her eyes. "I don't think so. Where is your car?" She looked to her right and left, trying to spot my Spyder.

"I didn't take the Spyder out tonight, that would be too telling. Come on, this is mine, too."

"Oh, man," she groaned, her face crestfallen as she started petting the car. "This monster is yours, too? How many cars do you have?"

"Five," I answered, amused at her tone.

She groaned louder and her shoulders slumped, but she didn't object when I unlocked the door and helped her in.

"You're getting farther and farther away from me, Jason Thorn," she mumbled as I was trying to buckle her in.

Misunderstanding her meaning, I laughed and said, "That's because you are drunk. I'm right here. Let's get you to your bed so you can sleep it off."

"Let's," she murmured, right before I gently closed the door.

———

Our drive to her apartment was quiet as she dozed off in the passenger seat. I parked the car in front of the building and jumped out to help her down before she fell on her face. When I slowly opened the passenger side door, she was still sleeping. I was considering whether I should carry her upstairs or if that would be pushing it when some jackass drove by us and someone leaned out the window and shouted something at us.

Fucking idiot.

Olive's eyes opened with a small frown.

"Jason?" she asked, her voice all drowsy and sexy.

Shit!

"Yeah, it's me, sweetheart. Can you walk if I help you?"

Her face still confused, she almost toppled down the seat when she tried to take a step out into thin air.

"Whoa, easy there," I said, gripping her waist. Her dress had ridden up and it seemed insistent on flashing me her white lacy underwear. "O-kay. I think it's way past your bed time, Olive. How about you give me a little help so I can get you up while you are still intact."

"What are you doing here?" she asked, her eyes half closed.

I locked the car, sneaked my arm around her waist, and half carried her up to their apartment as she hung on to me.

When we were finally inside, I had trouble locating the light switch and eventually gave up on it altogether. Fuck eyesight, especially when my friend's sister was almost half-naked in my arms.

"Olive? Are you awake enough to tell me which room is yours?"

"Huh?"

"Sweetheart," I mumbled, taking her weight as she rested her head against my chest. I gripped her chin and tilted her head up. Her eyes opened.

"Jason." She looked at me as if she was seeing me for the first time. There was that smile again.

"Hi there," I said, brushing away her bangs from her face.

She put both of her hands on my chest and hiccupped. "Hi."

I chuckled and held her up as her knees buckled. Regaining her balance, she looked around for a moment then turned her huge eyes at me. "What are you doing in here?"

"Came to drop you off. Can you show me your room?"

She lifted her hand and pointed to her left.

"Where are Lucy and Charlotte?"

"They're still back at the bar, remember? People were starting to notice me so I had to leave with you. I'm sure they'll be here soon enough."

She half shrugged and yawned through the motion.

We entered her room and I stopped short. This was her room? Just a bed against the wall? Not that she had any space for anything else, but still. Glancing to my right, I saw a small dresser in the corner, but that sad piece of furniture didn't even count.

"Sorry," she said in a small voice. I had no idea how she'd guessed where my thoughts were, but she hit it right on the nose. "Considering where you live, this apartment"—she gestured to her room with her hand—"this room must look very small to you."

"Come on," I said, ignoring her words. As soon as I lowered her on the bed, she grunted and fell to her side.

"Can you put my legs on the bed? Please? I don't think I have it in me to lift my arms and get undressed."

"Believe me, that's good news for me," I muttered quietly and kneeled next to her bed. I didn't think it would be wise of me to deal with a half-naked Olive. Pulling the high heels off of her feet, I gently gripped her ankles and lifted them up.

Either way, she didn't need to get undressed; her legs were right there for all to see. As if that wasn't enough torture, she stretched her arms, groaned, and started to turn her hips this way and that way, causing her dress to shimmy up. Leaning over her, I pulled the edge of her dress down a little and my knuckles caressed the soft skin of her thighs.

A soft moan escaped her lips and I froze. I was fascinated by the goose bumps that had appeared on her legs after the small contact. While I was distracted by that soft moan and her legs, she chose exactly that moment to flip onto her stomach and hug her pillow.

"Goddamn it!" I cursed as I tried to pull out my hand from underneath her. When I finally managed to do so after palming places I shouldn't even get close to, I let out a long breath and straightened up.

Then I saw her round ass. "Oh, for god's sake…"

"Jason," she mumbled when I was still staring at her sleeping form.

A small, helpless growl escaped from my lips. "Yes?"

She smiled, but her eyes were still closed when she asked, "Will you stay in Dylan's room again? I know you were his friend and not mine, but I used to get so excited when you stayed over. Even after you broke my heart, I couldn't hate you. Not really."

Thinking she was talking about me leaving after my mother's suicide, I sat down on the bed and brushed away the few pieces of hair that were covering her face.

Looking around the room, I saw a neatly folded blue throw on the edge of her bed. Since I knew it would be damn near impossible to lift her from the bed and get her under the covers, I opted to use the throw to at least cover her legs.

Instead of leaving like I should've done, I took a minute to watch over her. Then I leaned down and brushed a small kiss on her temple. "I'm sorry for breaking your heart, sweetheart. I never meant to hurt any of you."

Trying to be quiet so I wouldn't wake her up, I hesitated to leave once I was at the door. Her breathing had deepened and she looked like *my* Olive.

Not *mine* mine…but still…maybe… Oh, I was *fucked*…

I wasn't ready to admit it aloud, but I might have liked touching her bare skin a lot more than I should have, both at the parking lot and just then.

Either way, I wasn't in trouble. I shouldn't be.

At least not yet.

Hollywood heartthrob Jason Thorn spotted getting cozy with a mystery beauty

Just weeks ago, the movie star shocked everyone when the back-alley footage of him and Jennifer Widner, 25, having a quickie was revealed all over the media outlets. While it was taken down rather quickly, it's not something we'll forget any time soon.

However, in these photos, Jason Thorn, 26, seems to have forgotten all about his costar Jennifer, and his alleged Canada quickie, who was all over the tabloids just last week. While we have yet to identify the young woman in these intimate pictures, Jason seems completely enraptured with her.

An eyewitness claimed: 'Her shirt looked completely ruined and Jason was helping her out of it in the parking lot. We thought they were about to get busy right there in the open—the heat between them was that palpable. While she looked a little flustered, they couldn't take their eyes off of each other. After she had the shirt on, Jason caressed her stomach. We were shocked when Jason Thorn just backed off after the short but intimate touch. They looked completely in love with each other.'

After seeing these snaps of the pair, our team agrees, especially the one where Jason is greeting the mystery woman with a kiss on her temple. Anyone else swooning?

The rumors are still circulating that Jason has lost two major roles because of his sexcapades making the rounds. However, he doesn't seem too worried about it. Wouldn't you agree?

The pair was photographed leaving together, but our sources say they didn't head to Jason Thorn's pad in Bel Air.

So far we haven't heard anything back from Jason's reps. Do you think this is just another fling where the mystery woman will end up in another alley with Jason Thorn? Or does it look like the movie star is changing his ways for the lady in question? It would definitely be a first, don't you think? Either way, we'll keep you in the loop.

CHAPTER FOURTEEN

JASON

"What are you doing here at eight in the morning, Megan?" I half-growled as she entered my house. "I thought our meeting was at twelve o'clock." Rubbing my eyes, I tried to focus on her as her heels snapped with efficiency down the hallway and into the living area. She looked way too ready to start her day, where I was still hoping to get rid of her quickly so I could get back to bed.

"You haven't been online," she guessed correctly and dropped her purse on the ottoman.

"I was sleeping, Megan. In fact, I'm still sleeping. Can't this wait until our meeting?"

"I'm afraid not." Bending, she fished her phone out of her bag. "You might want to put something on. Not all of us want to see you half-naked in the early morning." She waved her hand at my body dismissively.

I yawned and looked down at my naked chest.

"What is this about? I'm still keeping it in my pants if that's what you came here to check."

She texted someone on her phone, put it down, and picked up another one of her phones. It was too early to handle her.

"Tom will be here in a few minutes," she said, not looking up from her phone.

"Great," I yawned again. "Just what I needed at this hour, both of your faces up in my—"

"Stop whining and go change while I make a call. I'll let Tom in."

"The bastard already has his own security code; he can let himself in. He better be bringing me some coffee and breakfast."

"Tom said he'd call Alvin over, he'll bring whatever it is that you like to have."

"Now you are handling my own assistant, too, Megan? You don't have enough people around you to control?"

She gave me a hard look, dismissing me without another word.

"Just great," I muttered under my breath as I left her to do whatever the hell she was there to do.

When I emerged out of my room, freshly showered and properly clothed as per Megan's wishes, Tom and Alvin had joined Megan in the living room and were having a quiet conversation.

"What is this emergency that couldn't wait a few more hours?" I asked no one in particular as I sat down right across from them.

"We have to make a statement," Megan started as she crumbled a muffin and took a small bite. Alvin handed everyone their coffee. After thanking him and picking up my own blueberry muffin, I tried to give all my focus to Megan. "I didn't want to say anything without talking to you first."

"Then why are Tom and Alvin here? And a statement about what?"

"I thought Tom would want to be in on this convo." She gave a small shrug, keeping her eyes away from Tom. "And you trust his opinions."

"You haven't been online yet?" Alvin asked, hiding a smirk behind his coffee cup.

I raised an eyebrow.

"And I was the one who called Alvin since if you give the go ahead, he'll be one of the few people who is in on this," Tom said as he gave Alvin a hard stare.

I glanced back at Alvin, but he gave me a shrug that clearly said, 'I have no idea what's going on either.'

"Are you about to tell me I'm going to die or something?"

Megan and Tom shared a look I couldn't even begin to decipher. Taking a sip of my black coffee, I waited for them to spill whatever it was they couldn't wait to tell me.

"I think we found your girl," Megan finally announced. Tom was still avoiding my eyes.

"This is about that?" I scratched my stubble and leaned back in my seat. "I thought someone else had come out claiming I had sex with them in the elevator or something like that. What's online then?" I asked, relaxing into my seat even more.

Megan tilted her head as Tom sighed. "Is there another girl about to come out and claim that, Jason?"

I gave her a grin. "I don't think so."

She raised an eyebrow and waited for something that wasn't coming.

Tom broke our eye contact by repeating her earlier words.

"She is right, Jason. I think we found the right girl for you. This is the perfect opportunity for us to use. We can't miss this."

"I believe that's something I'll decide, not you, and certainly not Megan. And what opportunity are you talking about?"

Megan powered on her tablet and looked me square in the eye. "You need to think about this before you make a decision. We couldn't have spun a better story than this and we didn't even do anything. This is pure, organic PR. If you think about it, you'll see that yourself. This is the perfect solution, Jason. All I'm asking is for you to think about this. Do you understand me?"

I looked at her unblinkingly and said, "I can see that whoever this girl is, the idea of her being my doting wife is exciting you for some reason, but I told you before, Megan, I won't marry some girl and haul her around to events to get her noticed. If I'm about to share a house with her, I should at least get along with her as a person."

Tom smiled. "I don't think that will be an issue with this girl."

After rubbing my temple, I sighed and extended my hand to Megan. I had dug my own grave, and now it was time to lie in it. "All right, give it to me."

Wisely, she handed me the tablet without saying another word.

When I saw the first photo of me kissing Olive's temple, I looked up with a frown on my face.

"What is this? Someone took Olive's picture yesterday?"

"Keep scrolling down," Megan said.

I scrolled down as she'd instructed, and all I could see were pictures of Olive and me from the day before. Before we headed into the building as I was jogging to her side, me kissing her temple, a zoomed in photo of her closed eyes—in a damn red circle—as I was kissing her temple. It didn't end there. There were the pictures of her after she had changed into my shirt. As my anger started to rise, I was thankful that they hadn't managed to get any shots of her while she was half-naked in her bra, but they did have shots of me caressing her stomach as we clearly stood a little too close to each other. I hadn't noticed that I was standing inches away from her lips.

They weren't the best quality, some were even blurry, but every shot looked intimate.

And blurry or not, we were beaming at each other.

"What the hell is this? Who took these?" I asked, only then noticing that Alvin was looking at the photos over my shoulder.

"They were either taken by someone who works in the building or just someone who was visiting. No one knew you were going to be there, and the shots are not high enough quality to be from a pap," said Megan. "There is an article attached to it. Read it."

Agreeing with her assessment about the images having been captured a bystander, I scrolled farther down and got to the article.

My anger reached a whole other level. I rose up from my seat and tossed the tablet on the couch between Tom and Megan.

Everyone was silent.

"I have to call Dylan and their parents. If someone tells them about this, they'll misunderstand."

"Dylan?" Alvin asked from where he stood, his arms crossed against his chest.

"Olive's brother. My *friend*," I clarified, glancing at Tom. That bastard knew I was friends with Olive's brother.

"We can use her," Megan interrupted before I could even think of where I'd left my phone the night before.

"What did you just say?" I asked softly. Surely I hadn't heard her right.

Tom silenced Megan with a sharp look. "Come on, let's just sit down for a minute, Jason. Like you said, it's pretty early. I'm sure neither her nor her family has seen anything yet. You'll call them as soon as we are gone."

Even though I didn't want to admit it, he was right. I wouldn't want to alarm Olive's mom and dad by calling at an ungodly hour, especially when there was a definite chance that they knew nothing about the photos.

I sat my ass back down and reached for my coffee. After I

swallowed almost all of it down, I got up and tossed the cup into the garbage can in the kitchen.

"Ok, who has this?" I asked when I was back and my temper was slightly more under control.

"It dropped online after midnight. I tried calling you, but you weren't answering, which is why I thought I should come here in the morning instead of waiting for our meeting. We need to get ahead of this and make a decision."

"You were right, thank you for not waiting until our meeting. I don't want them to learn about it from someone else. I doubt Olive has seen it either. At least not yet, not after her night out."

Alvin coughed behind me and walked toward the kitchen. "Since you are having this meeting early, I'll go and rearrange your schedule."

"What night?" Megan asked, looking at Alvin's retreating back.

I waved my hand. "Just in case I missed someone taking pictures of me, I was in a college bar with Olive. She was celebrating her movie deal with her friends and I was in and out of there with her in ten minutes tops. Other than her friends, nobody recognized me, so there is nothing to worry about."

"Jason, was that a smart thing to do?" Tom asked. "Especially when you are trying to lay low? They could've written you up with a college girl if they had gotten a whiff of your scent in there."

"If they had pictures, trust me, they would've released them with the rest of this. I was okay."

Megan's sharp eyes were still on me. "So, what is your decision?"

"Decision? About what?"

"We have an opportunity here, Jason. It's up to you if we use it or not, at this point. If you accept, all I'm going to do is release who she is to the media and give a short back story of how she is your childhood friend—"

"She is my childhood friend's *sister*," I growled.

Megan just kept going. "And how she is the author of the adaptation... Well, everything will fall into place even easier than we expected. No one will assume your marriage is fake. All they'll see is two friends falling in love after seeing each other again after so many years. The public will love the story. It's the perfect cover, Jason, and you know it."

"No, Megan. No matter how perfect this all sounds to you, I won't use Olive. No."

"Who said you'll be using her? Your PR team will be using your story. Not you. She is your friend isn't she? Wouldn't she want to help you? You're already friends, so what if you live in the same house for a few years?"

"She is right, Jason," Tom jumped in. "I don't think Olive would mind helping you, and I'm sure you remember what I told you about the book... I think she might be more than okay with this."

I dropped my head into my hands. Olive, my wife? Dylan would skin me alive. Him aside, I didn't even want to think of what her parents would think of me.

"Here." Tom handed me the tablet again. "Look at these photos and tell me I'm not right."

"The chemistry between you two speaks for itself, Jason. You already look half in love with her in these. It wouldn't take much to make people believe that you married for the right reasons," said Megan.

I grabbed the tablet from Tom—maybe a little too forcefully —and glanced at the website where our photos were plastered.

Funnily enough, we did look in love.

Yeah, I was definitely in trouble.

CHAPTER FIFTEEN

OLIVE

"**W**ake up! Wake up! Wake up! Wake up!"

"Go away," I groaned, tossing a pillow over to where the sound was coming from.

"You have to get up, Olive. You're all over the internet."

Of course it would be Lucy trying to wake me up. It was never the sweet Char. Why, you ask? Because Char wasn't a cruel person. Not like Lucy. Lucy had a real problem with people sleeping peacefully. *She* was a problem all on her own.

"Awesome. Goodnight," I mumbled. I turned my back to her voice.

The bed sank with her weight when she sat next to my hip.

"I don't think you're getting it, Olive." Her hand gripped my shoulder and she forcefully turned me on my back. She also had the power of a she-hulk even though she was only five foot three.

"I don't want to get it. My head hurts, Lucy," I pleaded, narrowing my eyes at her as I slowly pulled the covers over my face. "Come back in a few hours and I'll listen to whatever you want. I'll even nod."

"Fine. I guess you don't care that your cozy pictures...with Jason Thorn...are plastered all over the internet."

"What?" I shouted as I sat up a little too fast for my poor brain. "Ow, ow, ow."

"Here." She placed her laptop on my lap and waited for me to take a look with an annoyingly awake and excited face.

As I scrolled down, with each picture I saw, my eyes got bigger and bigger.

"Holy shit," I mumbled when I started to read the article.

"I know, right? You're gonna have Jason Thorn's dimpled babies. I'm gonna be the cool aunt. I'll babysit. I'll come and watch your half-naked husband while I'm babysitting."

I laughed; granted, it was a little forced, but it still counted as a laugh. "Are you on something?" I scrolled through the pictures again. I couldn't stop looking. "What are you talking about?"

She looked at me as if I was stupid, then sighed and made herself comfortable in my bed—*again*—by lying down beside me.

"You have to stop getting in bed with me," I mumbled, trying to push her off the bed.

"He is in love with you, you are in love with him. This is happening." She brushed her palms together. "My dreams are coming true!"

"*Your* dreams? Please, tell me what you're on so I can make it my life mission to join you in la-la land one day."

"Oh, shut up." A sneaky maneuver and she was right under the covers with me, stealing my pillow. I pushed at her legs and got down from the bed.

"What am I gonna do?"

"What do you mean?"

"It's not Jason who looks in love in these photos, Lucy, it's me! Can't you see that?"

"And...?"

"And he'll never talk to me again. Dylan will lose his head when he sees these."

"Clearly you've gone blind from typing away at all hours on

your laptop." She rolled her eyes and made herself even more comfortable on my bed. "You both look smitten with each other."

"Babe?" I heard a voice right outside my door. I made my eyes go as big as they could.

"Jameson? Again?" I mouthed to Lucy.

Then Jameson's head peaked in.

"Oh, here you are." He didn't even knock! "I thought I heard your voice." He opened the door wider, and I got a good look at his naked chest, and then lower…

"Oh god! Jameson, your penis!" I screamed, my eyes hurting. "Put some clothes on for fuck's sake!" I groaned as I covered my eyes with my hand.

"Oh, hi, Olive. I didn't see you behind the door." He laughed. "I thought Lucy had sneaked into your room to get some sleep."

I peeked through my fingers. Lucy was just lounging in the bed, enjoying the view with a satisfied smirk on her face. Then I glanced at Jameson; I tried not to look down, but well, isn't it always impossible to do that? Well at least he was covering his man parts with his hand, not that he was doing a good job of it.

I groaned louder.

"Babe, I have an early class. If you're good, I'm leaving."

She shrugged and Jameson winked at her.

"Congrats on the book, Olive. Can't wait to see the movie."

"Thanks," I muttered, looking over his shoulder instead of in his eyes. When Jameson finally left and I heard Lucy's door open and close, I turned back to look at Lucy. Her hair was all mussed up and she had a mischievous grin on her face.

She wiggled her eyebrows. "He has a good size on him, doesn't he? Which is why we don't call it a 'penis' like you just did. That's almost like an insult."

I shook my head. She was impossible…but, yeah, he did have a good size on him. *Good for her.* "Is that why you made him your boy toy?"

"And you wouldn't? Didn't you see the size of his monster just a minute ago? And those tattoos? Damn…even thinking about it is ma—"

"If you finish that sentence, I'm going to deck you, Lucy."

She laughed and opened her arms. "Do your best, mystery beauty."

I groaned and leaned my back against the door, just in case. I didn't want to have a second look at Jameson's man parts.

"What am I gonna do?"

"Nothing."

"What do you mean nothing?"

She shrugged and patted the bed. I walked over and sat down, trying not to fidget any more than I already was.

"You, my lovely friend, are going to wait until Jason calls you," she said.

"What makes you think he'll call?"

"His people must've seen this already. Trust me, he'll call you when he sees it."

————

IT WAS three hours later and I was lounging on the couch with my laptop glued to my fingers.

Someone unlocked the door and my head flew up. Seeing that it was just Char, I greeted her.

"Hey. You're home early."

"Yeah, Professor Kindley had an emergency and ended class early." Tossing her handbag and her notebooks into her room, she came to sit next to me. "What are you doing?"

"Blankly staring at the screen."

"Nothing new, huh?"

"Nope. I start writing a few pages, but then I go back and delete everything I wrote. I think I might be a one-hit wonder.

It's like all my creative juices just dried up. Or maybe I was never creative in the first place, and the one I wrote was just a fluke."

"I'm pretty sure it doesn't work that way, Olive," Char said as she started massaging her temples.

"Headache?"

"Yeah. I haven't been feeling well ever since I opened my eyes."

"You want me to cook some chicken soup for you?"

"Nah, I'm good. Thanks though. Do you have any idea of what you want to write, or you just can't find the first words?"

"Oh, I'm finding the first words, alright, but I can't get into the story and end up just tossing the whole thing."

She looked at me with her bright blue eyes. "Then it isn't the right story for you to write. You'll know when it's the right one."

"I'm not so sure about that. My fingers are itching to write, but I have absolutely nothing. Nada."

"Let me know if I can help you with anything. Plotting or otherwise."

I put my laptop down on the floor and got up. "I'm going to make you tea." I said over my shoulder. "Your voice is starting to crack."

She groaned and reached for my laptop.

"Did Jason call about the photos yet?"

"Nope." I filled the kettle with water and while waiting for it to boil, I opened the cupboard to choose from the teas we had. "Do you want herbal tea or just regular black tea?"

"I'll have herbal tea, please." She whistled softly. "You should see the comments on these photos."

I looked up to see Char scrolling through the photos again. Taking down two mugs, I put the tea bags in them. "They're talking shit?"

"No," she replied, looking over her shoulder. "Actually they think you guys look adorable together. More than a few say you are his new girlfriend, a new actress or something."

I snorted. "I'm adding honey to your tea and I don't want to hear any complaints about it." Char hated honey with a passion; whenever she got sick we had to practically force it down her throat. I reached for the boiling water and poured it in our mugs.

"Thanks, mother Olive."

"You're welcome, beautiful child of mine." Grabbing the mugs, I walked back to the couch and handed her the herbal tea.

The laptop still on her lap, she extended her neck and sniffed at my tea. "What are you having? It smells better than mine."

"Just black tea, Earl Grey." Sitting next to her, I glanced at the screen.

"This one is my favorite," said Char, scrolling down to another picture, the one where Jason's hand was out of sight and under my shirt. "You both look lost in each other."

"Well, we weren't lost anywhere, I had weird hot smoothie spilled all over me and he was just making sure I was okay. I don't know what kind of a creep took our photos, but they somehow managed to capture something that wasn't even there. They are a good stalker, I'll give them that."

"I think I'm with Lucy on this one," she admitted, and I sharply turned to look at her, almost spilling hot tea all over myself, again. "Ok, don't kill me yet," she said, lifting her hands as if to ward me off. "I just don't think you could capture something like this if there was absolutely *nothing* there. I mean, it's not like you are still in love with Marcus, right?"

"Of course not. And well, we already know that I'm still in love with Jason so both Lucy and you are seeing that."

"Olive." She closed the laptop and placed it next to her. "You probably don't want to give yourself false hope, but…"

"But…? But, what?"

"Jason isn't really looking at you as if you are just his best friend's little sister. At least not in these photos." She gestured toward the laptop. "Of course I have no idea how he is treating you when you guys are together."

I waved her off and took a sip of my tea. "He is just—"

My phone starting ringing and Char lifted an eyebrow as I looked at her in panic.

"Where is your phone?" she asked.

"I don't know, in my room?"

The phone kept ringing.

She tilted her head. "Well, aren't you gonna get it?"

I shook my head vehemently. "I'm scared."

"Of what?"

The damn phone stopped ringing and started back up again.

"It could be Dylan. I can't deal with him right now. God knows what he'll say. When we were kids, he didn't like me running around Jason that much so he sure as hell won't be happy about those photos if he sees them."

"What if it's Jason?" she asked.

That was even worse. "Well, if it's him, what if he's angry?"

"At you?" She frowned.

"Doesn't matter at who."

Thrusting her mug at me, she rose up. "You're being ridiculous."

Both mugs in my hand, I yelled after her. "Char, don't look! I don't want to know. Please."

"Too late," she said. Keeping her eyes on me, she leaned against the door frame and answered my phone.

"Hi, Jason. No, I'm Olive's friend, Charlotte."

Making a sad face at her, I shook my head and whispered, "I'm not here. Out! Out! I'm gone. Say I vanished."

Charlotte rolled her eyes. "Uh huh. Yes, she is right here. Of course. Take care of yourself."

I groaned loudly.

She dropped the phone next to me and grabbed her mug from my hand.

"I'm gonna go and try to sleep this headache off. Thanks for the tea. Talk to you later."

"Traitor," I announced. "The minute you trust someone, they turn into a traitor. All of you people are traitors!"

She closed her door without a second glance.

Sighing, I steeled myself and reached for my phone.

"Hello?"

"Who is the traitor?" Jason asked in an amused tone.

"All my friends," I replied tiredly. I closed my eyes, letting my heart do its own thing and flutter at the sound of his soft yet still rumbly voice.

He chuckled. "How are you doing, Olive?"

"Still breathing, so that's something."

"You weren't *that* drunk yesterday. Still got a hangover?"

"No, no, I'm fine. It's nothing, really. I'm just having trouble writing."

"Hmmm. Did you see the photos? Is that why you can't write?"

I thought about pretending I had no idea what he was talking about, but in the end, I didn't think I could wing it.

"Yeah, Lucy showed them to me this morning," I admitted.

"Are you angry at me?"

I frowned and took a sip of my tea. "Why would I be angry at you?"

"For the things they wrote in the article, and well, getting photographed with me. It's become a part of my life so I'm used to not having any privacy, but you didn't ask to be plastered all over the internet. Did you talk to your parents? Did they see them?"

"Yeah, no. I'm hoping they won't come across them. And if they do...well, it was nothing after all, right? I'm sure they already know that. It's not like we are having a secret relationship like they are saying."

"Right."

Drawing my legs up, I rested the mug on my knee. "And, hey, at least they said I was beautiful in the article. That has to be good for my ego, right?" I laughed awkwardly. After all, it had felt good to be called beautiful, especially when standing next to Jason.

"Of course you are beautiful, Olive. You don't need to hear it from the tabloids to believe that."

I pretty much melted and became one with the couch.

"Thank you," I mumbled when I could form words. "Are *you* angry at me?" I asked when there was a gap of silence.

"Angry at you? Why the hell would I be angry at you?"

"I don't know." I leaned forward and put the mug on the small coffee table. "After all that other...stuff that came out, maybe you didn't want to be seen with...hell, I don't know." Silently, I hit my forehead with the palm of my hand...and then hit it again.

"No, sweetheart, I'm not angry at you."

Sweetheart?

Melted for the second time.

"Now that we've established that neither one of us is angry with the other, I wanted to ask you out to dinner," he said.

"Dinner? Me? Like *out,* out?"

"Yes. I have something I want to talk to you about and thought maybe we could go out and have a nice dinner together. Better than being cooped up in my house."

"I don't think you can ever feel cooped up in your house, Jason. If you do, there is something very wrong with you." His house was pretty much heaven on this earth, at least for me— especially when he was in it, too.

He was smiling; I could hear it in his words when he spoke.

"I'm glad you like my house, Olive. Even though I agree with you, I think for this, I would like to take you out."

"Should I be scared? Are you going to give me bad news about the movie or something? Because it pretty much sounds like that, and I'm not a big fan of bad surprises."

"Everything is going great with the movie. The filming starts in a few weeks. You'll be at the set with me so you can see it for yourself."

At that, I sat up straighter. "I am? I'll be on set with you?"

"I thought you'd want to see; was I wrong?"

"No. No. I would love nothing more than to be there. If you can take me with you, I promise I won't even bother you. Even once would be amazing."

"We'll talk about it more tonight at dinner, okay? You're free?"

"Yes. Yes. Dinner. Tonight?" My schedule was wide open for him. In any case, the only date I had was with my laptop. "Where should I come?"

"I'll be there around seven o'clock. You think you can be ready?"

I lowered the phone and checked the time. It was almost five o'clock.

"Of course."

"Great. I'll see you later, sweetheart."

Sweetheart…

Gah… He was *my* sweetheart.

"Yeah. See you later."

Hanging up, I ran to Char's room.

"He's going to take me to the set!" I announced as soon as I threw open the door. She was on her phone, texting. "Oh, sorry. You busy?"

"No. No. Come in." She waved me in and pushed the phone under her pillow. "So you're going to the set. When?"

I walked in and sat at the edge of her bed. "He said the filming would start in a few weeks. God, it all feels so surreal, Char. I think I'm starting to freak out on the inside. It's actually real and it's actually happening." I was already bouncing on the bed.

She smiled. "It definitely is real."

"He said he wanted to talk to me about something so he's taking me to dinner tonight. I should get ready. I have to hop in the shower first." I rose up, but didn't move. I wanted to ask for her help, but she'd been acting weird lately. One day cold, one day hot... I didn't know what to make of it, but thought it was the pressure of the last semester.

"When I get out can you help me pick something to wear? I've been staring at my laptop the entire day, I feel like a mess."

"Of course. You go ahead and get into the shower. I'll be in your room when you get out."

"Thank you, Char," I said and kissed her on the cheek.

She smiled. "You don't have time to get mushy. Go ahead."

I skipped all the way to my room.

———

THAT NIGHT when Jason picked me up, I was a big ball of energy. I could've used a pep talk from Lucy, but she was studying with other girls from her class, and Char was...well other than being sick, she wasn't the best person to go to when you needed a pep talk.

When Jason called me to let me know he was just a few minutes away from the apartment, I chose to wait for him outside to avoid Marcus' intense glares.

His Spyder pulled in, and I practically ran to the passenger side before he could get out.

"Why are you waiting outside? What's wrong?" he asked as soon as I was inside.

I took a deep breath and his scent hit me. My eyes rolled into the back of my head.

"Huh?" I asked distractedly. "Yeah. Nothing. I didn't want to make you wait."

"You look beautiful, Olive," he said, his eyes moving over me slowly.

Since I had no idea where he was taking me, Char had thought it would be the safest bet to keep it simple with a black dress. I ran my hands over my thighs, smoothing and pulling the dress down a little in the process, which wasn't all that helpful, so I linked my hands in my lap and let it go. While it felt like it was too short at that moment, I knew it looked good on me when I was standing. I especially liked how it looked from the side; the dress curved around my ass perfectly.

"Where are we going?" I asked after I was buckled in and he pulled away from the curb.

"I thought Soho House would be best for privacy. At least we won't get photographed."

"Oh, the private club thingy? You have a membership?"

"Yeah. I'm not a huge fan; I prefer the privacy of my own home, but sometimes I have to meet industry people there for lunch or other business meetings."

"I understand." Did that mean we were about to have a business meeting?

The rest of the ride was awkwardly quiet. Apparently neither one of us had anything more to say, which I didn't think boded well for me.

After he pulled into the garage and completed the check-in, he casually put his hand just above my bum—practically jump-starting my heart—and guided me to the elevators.

When the silence became too much, I asked, "Is everything

all right?" I didn't mind comfortable silences, but I had a feeling that something else was going on with him. He looked distracted.

He was frowning when he looked down at me. "Yeah. Why?"

I gave him a sad smile. "I don't know. You aren't talking. You seem tense and not so happy to be here."

His eyes softened and he gently tugged at my hair. "It's not you, Olive. Just had a stressful day."

Nodding, I swallowed and looked away from his warm eyes.

Exiting the elevator at the top floor, we walked up the stairs and through the somewhat crowded bar, and then into the coolest dining area I'd ever seen in my life.

The entire rooftop was filled with lush olive trees and other plants. The lanterns and twinkle lights hanging through the branches lit up the whole space and created the perfect setup for a romantic evening. But, from the look on Jason's face, I could see that this was far from a romantic evening for him. Trying to ignore the beautiful view of LA, we followed the front desk girl to a table that was mostly out of the sight of the other patrons.

"Jason!" some guy yelled just as we were about to sit down. I couldn't see the owner of the voice, but Jason waved at someone and sat down across from me.

"One of the producers of my last movie," he explained with a smile on his face. I smiled back at him.

Without any further conversation, we ordered our drinks and food, and then I simply waited for Jason to spill the beans.

"I thought you would enjoy the atmosphere here," he said right as a waiter brought our drinks. Jason had downed his whiskey before the poor guy could even place my Lemon Drop in front of me. He ordered a new one for himself and suddenly pushed back his seat and rose up.

"I need to say hi to a few people, I'll be right back," he said and walked away from me.

Staring at his back in shock, I reached for my cocktail, took a sip, and then another big one.

The waiter came back with Jason's second drink, but Jason hadn't returned yet. I had to force myself to smile when he gave me a snobbish look.

"Awesome," I muttered, taking out my phone to text Lucy.

> *Me: I'm sitting on a beautiful rooftop, surrounded by olive trees and twinkle lights—alone.*
> *Lucy: What do you mean alone?*
> *Me: I don't know what exactly, but something is wrong with Jason. We just sat down, ordered our food and drinks, and he jumped up and left to say hi to a few people.*
> *Lucy: That doesn't sound too ominous. I'm sure he'll be back.*
> *Me: Well, it is. He's been acting weird from the moment I got into his car. No eye contact, no nothing.*

I leaned forward a little to see if I could spot him. Sure enough, he was standing next to a group of ten or twelve people who were having dinner. A beautiful blonde woman joined the group and instead of sitting down, she came to stand next to Jason when she saw him. She touched his arm, leaned in to whisper something into his ear, and said something funny enough to make Jason throw back his head and laugh. Then his hand sneaked around her waist…and I sat my ass back down.

Perfect.

Remembering I wasn't out with Jason but with *Jason Thorn* didn't ease my worries. I'd take the other guy any day.

> *Me: I don't think I'm feeling well. I want to come home, Lucy.*
> *Lucy: Hey, it'll be okay. You are a cat. A purring, content*

one. I'm sure he wanted to talk to you about the movie.
Didn't you say so yourself? If he upsets you, I'll kick his
ass, don't worry.

There was no way that cat crap would work this time.

Before I could text back, Jason returned to the table, muttered an apology, gave me a strange look, and reached for his drink again.

Feeling deflated, I played with the edge of the table and kept sipping my drink as I tried to focus on the beautiful view.

At some point, he asked a few questions about how my new novel was coming along, and I answered all of his questions with unnecessarily long answers. Eventually though, I gave up trying to engage him in conversation when he started texting with his agent.

Our food came—we had both ordered salmon—and—surprise, surprise—we ate in silence.

If picking at the poor fish counted as eating, that is.

My phone vibrated twice, but I didn't check to see who it was. No matter how many times she texted, I was no cat—especially not a purring one. Halfway into our awkward and very disappointing dinner, I gave up on the food too and just leaned back in my seat to gaze at the city skyline. I hated sulking in general, but sitting across from Jason and sulking…well, it was all kinds of wrong. Even so, there was no way I could act like I was having the time of my life at that moment either.

"Olive?"

So lost in my own head, I flinched when I heard Jason's thick voice.

"Yes?"

He tilted his head and furrowed his brows. "Are you okay?"

"I don't know. Are you?" I asked back.

He scratched at his stubble. "What do you mean?"

"You've barely said a word to me ever since we sat down, Jason. Not that you were a chatterbox in the car, but you literally spoke maybe twenty words to me. Since you were the one who invited me out, I have no idea what's happening, but I'm going to wait until you finish your dinner so you can take me home. Better yet, if you can tell someone to call me a cab...do they even do that here? Anyway, if they do, I can get myself home."

A few tables to our left, a group of people roared with laughter, drawing my attention away from Jason. Why couldn't we be laughing with joy like that? Jason was going to take me to a movie set, the movie set that was being set up for the world *I'd* created. I was going to see Isaac's room, touch the bed where he woke Evie up in the middle of the night just because he couldn't wait to kiss her for the first time. I should've been the one laughing my ass off with joy, not sulking in front of a sex god.

He wasn't my sex god, but I was in his vicinity, and God had given me eyes for such occasions after all.

I glanced back at Jason and saw his troubled expression.

"Fuck me," he muttered almost to himself.

I would happily fuck you if that's your problem.

Reaching for his second glass of whiskey, he drank the last bit in one big gulp, pushed his chair back with a loud noise, and came to my side.

I had to crane my neck to look up at him.

He offered me his hand. "Come on. I can't do this here with all these people around. Let's go."

"Go where?" I asked, my eyes suspiciously jumping between his hand and eyes.

Clearly done with waiting for me to decide, he pulled back my chair while I was still sitting in it and took my hand himself.

Grabbing the small clutch I had borrowed from Char, I let him pull me away from our sad table and tried to ignore the warmth that was traveling all over my body from feeling his warm skin on mine again.

Even holding hands with him could count as accomplishing childhood dreams, right? And it had already happened more than once. I should've counted the night as a success. Only I had no idea what was coming next.

Talk about childhood dreams…

CHAPTER SIXTEEN

OLIVE

Instead of driving me home, he drove us back to Bel Air, to the heaven that was his home.

"Do you want something to drink?" he asked as soon as we were inside.

"I'm good. Thank you."

"I'll get something for myself then."

He poured himself...I didn't even care what it was at that point. I just stood in the middle of his living room, hugging myself and generally feeling like crap.

"Maybe you should've dropped me at home, Jason," I said when he kept his back turned to me. "I don't think this night out was a good idea. If this is about you taking me to the set, or, hell, I don't know, to tell me that you think my book is crap...or maybe it's about the photos, that would make more sense, bu—"

"Stop, Olive. Just stop," he interrupted me.

He finally left the bottle of alcohol alone and walked to my side. Cupping my cheeks, he looked into my eyes. "Your book was amazing. You're amazing. Stop thinking badly about yourself. I have to...no, I need to tell you something, or ask you something. Hell..." He let my face go and turned his back to me, again.

"I'm already making a mess of this. I just don't know how to say it…where to start."

"Well." I dropped the clutch onto the comfy looking armchair. "I'm half convinced you're trying to tell me you have to kill me, so it can't be worse than that. Just tell me and get over with it already."

He raked his hand through his already sexily messed up hair and let out a deep breath. "You're right. Okay. You liked sitting outside last time, so let's go out." Grabbing my hand, he walked us outside.

"You have chaise lounges," I said when we stepped outside. There were six of them and they looked gorgeous next to the pool. There were also more than a few giant cushions, the ones that you can curl up and comfortably sleep on. "You didn't have them the last time I was here."

"Yeah, I asked Alvin to find something comfortable to sit on for when I had guests who wanted to sit close to the pool instead of at the table."

He had gotten them because of me?

I was unable to hold back my smile.

We arranged the cushions closer to the pool and sat down facing each other.

"I've danced around it enough, so here we go," he started. I sat up straighter, ready for whatever he was about to throw my way.

"My publicist wants me to get married, Olive."

Wait. *What?* I wasn't ready for *that!*

"Come again?"

"I lost a few jobs after the alley video scandal; apparently they don't think I'm serious enough about my work, and no major studio wants to deal with that. They didn't want the negative press around me to affect their movie, so they ended my contracts. Tom thinks that'll only be the start if things don't change."

Wait. What?

I was barely hearing a word of what he was saying. He was getting married?

Was I cursed? Because there was no way this was fair. I'd long ago given up on my childhood crush, but now after seeing him again, spending time with him again...*now* he was getting married to someone?

"Wait a second." I shook my head. "I don't understand. What does that have to do with you getting married?"

"It's what they do in this industry, Olive. They paint you a life for the public. They shape you into something new, something that fits into their standards. It's all an illusion. Sometimes even in your private life you have to keep acting. You get a new girl-friend; your publicists sit down and draw up a contract. Everything ends up in a contract. Everything is binding. Of course there are real couples, too, but it's tough to find that with someone in this industry."

"So why not get a girlfriend?"

A pretend girlfriend was still bad, but a wife?! I'd read enough romance novels to know that those marriages always had a shot at a real love, and what woman in her right mind wouldn't fall in love with Jason after spending some time with him?

He shook his head. "No. They think the media will see right through that, and if the public and everyone else thinks I'm playing them, it'll only bury my career deeper into the ground. Long story short, Megan thinks that if I get married and act the part for a few years, everyone's opinion about me will change. In the meantime, I'll be able to focus on my work instead of dealing with the ripple effects my actions cause in the media."

My heart sinking further and further, I tried not to show what I was feeling—*pure agony*—on my face.

"Then congratulations are in order, I guess," I said, properly taken back. "Wow. You're getting married. You already announced it?"

He laughed, and it wasn't a happy laugh. Far from it. "Yeah, no."

Not looking at him, I leaned to my left and pushed my hand into the pool water. It was a chilly night, but I was hardly feeling anything.

"My publicist and Tom have been showing me headshots of some new actresses for quite some time now, but I couldn't choose one." He continued to break my heart. "Well, now they chose someone for me."

Headshots? That was freaking hilarious. Choosing a wife by looking at headshots? Obviously, Hollywood wasn't my thing. Where is the love, people?

I forced my lips to tilt up. "Who is the lucky lady?"

Instead of answering me, he said the strangest thing. "Do you remember the first day we met? The first day where I found you hiding next to the wall upstairs?"

My smile turned genuine. "Bits and pieces." False. Of course I remembered that day.

"Then," he said as he shifted in his seat. "Let me answer a question you asked me back then." He paused, then said, "Yes."

I stared at him, clueless. "What?"

Had I asked him if he liked pie or not? I didn't remember asking anything.

"Yes to what?"

"You don't remember," he mumbled as he scrubbed his stubble. Taking a deep breath, he reminded me, "You asked me to marry you…so…would you like to marry me, Olive?"

I laughed. Like a big LOL laugh. Then I saw his face. "What? You're serious?"

A big, giant lump took residence in my throat, almost to the point of suffocating me. Could he hear my heartbeat? See how my hands were starting to shake? "You're not serious, right?" I asked at last, my smile long gone.

He gave me a sarcastic laugh. "Apparently our photos made everyone believe that we were in love with each other, and since we already have a past, Megan thinks the public won't question our marriage. The opposite actually."

"Our marriage?" I managed to choke out. He was actually serious. It was right there in his eyes.

"If you accept that is."

"Wow." I scrambled up to my feet and walked away from him. "Wow."

A part of me was screaming inside me to jump on him, monkey style, and shout 'Yes! Of course, I'll marry you. YES!' until my voice grew hoarse so he would get the point. After all, I'd been wishing for this moment ever since I was eight years old, hadn't I? The other part of me…well, there was no other part of me. Apparently, I was just one giant, mushy, Jason Thorn lover.

I jumped when Jason's hand touched my shoulder and he turned me to face him. I hadn't even heard him get up.

"I'm most likely screwing this up. Let me explain a little more before you answer."

I must have nodded, because he continued.

"If you accept, we'll get married in a week or two."

I gave him a sarcastic laugh. Did he think giving me that information would help? Because it didn't. Not at all.

He kept going. "Of course, you'll live here with me until the divorce."

We weren't even married yet, and he was already planning for a divorce?

"In the contract I've signed with the studio for *Soul Ache*, they added a clause that says I can't be in a relationship while we are filming the movie and through the promotion phase of it. However, since you are the author, us getting married would be a priceless promotion for them." He stopped talking and looked into my eyes. "Megan and Tom think you might have had me in your mind when you wrote your book."

My heart literally stopped beating, longer than it should have. I stood frozen until he spoke again.

"But that can't be true, right?"

"Of course not." I shook my head.

"Right. Well, the public will think like Megan and Tom," he muttered, his eyes still searching mine. "They think the executives will be happy about the news since it will only draw more attention to the movie. When the story gets out that we're together, everyone will talk about how, after so many years, we found each other again, how the movie star fell in love with the author of their own story. In the movie, practically all they'll see is me falling in love with you. The more they talk about us, the more your book and their movie will be mentioned. And, well, you'll be the girl who made me give up my old ways."

I opened my mouth, but he stopped me and took my hands in his.

"Yes, this will help me get everyone off of my back so I can get back to doing what I love doing without all this media crap, but it can also be a good thing for your career, too. Your next book is pretty much guaranteed to be another bestseller before you even finish writing it."

I didn't like hearing that. Not at all. I didn't want people to read my words just because I was married to their favorite movie star. I wanted to make my own path, not walk in Jason's shadow.

"The truth is, Olive, I'd take marrying you over marrying some girl I don't know any day, some girl who is just looking to get a piggyback ride by marrying me."

Lucky, lucky me.

Wasn't that the marriage proposal every girl dreamed they would get from the love of their life?

"We are friends, right?" he asked when I kept silent.

Still shell-shocked, I was trying very hard to keep up with him. I nodded. I guessed we could be called friends. "It might be fun living together again. You'll have your own room right across from mine, just like the old days, except this time there is no Dylan to bother you. I'll mostly be gone, filming." He looked around his heavenly backyard—if that expansive space could even be called a backyard, that is—and gave my hands a squeeze. "You can have this place all to yourself, Olive. It would be easier to write here instead of in a house filled with roommates, right?" His eyes came back to me.

"I'm not even writing," I said stupidly.

"What?"

"I think I'm fresh out of creativity. Nothing new is coming, so that might have been my first and only book."

He tilted his head and showed me his hypnotizing dimple.

"Maybe when you move here I can help with your creativity issues."

My eyes got stuck on his mouth.

What the hell is that supposed to mean?

I forced my eyes away from his lips. I was dreaming of an alternate world where we were kissing. When the love of your life asks you to *freaking* marry him, you laugh with joy, maybe even shed a few happy tears, and eventually kiss, right? But this wasn't my childhood dream coming true, was it? No, this would just be living in the same house with Jason Thorn, acting like we were in love only when were out in public, maybe holding his hand, kissing him on the cheek.

Could my heart survive Jason Thorn?

"So, what do you think?"

"About?"

"Marrying me…"

Did he really not see how I felt about him? Not even a little?

"I'm not sure if I'm capable of thinking right now, Jason," I admitted.

"You'll be saving me, Olive."

But what would happen to me in the process? That was the real question. My heart was willing to go along with what he was proposing; after all, there was no way I could attend his wedding knowing it could've been me up there standing right next to him —even if it was a lie. But my mind wasn't thinking any of that; it was giving out all kinds of warning signs.

"Can I think about it?"

"Of course," he said, letting my hands go.

I was cold. Very cold.

Not knowing what to do with myself, I hugged my elbows and looked down at my feet.

His finger tilted my chin up and he ducked low to capture my eyes, so I gave them to him. He was smiling then, his eyes kind. "It's okay if you don't want to say yes. It's not something I thought I would do this year either."

Was he getting closer to me? Involuntarily—yeah, no, it was very much voluntarily—I took a step forward to close the distance between us. His eyes were my beacon.

What did he see in *my* eyes?

His gaze dropped to my neck. He lifted his hand and his fingertips touched the arch of my neck. I stopped breathing and swallowed. His gaze jumped up to mine as if the motion startled him. Then his fingertips trailed up and around my neck and tangled in my hair, his gentle, unexpected touch causing my body to tremble.

My eyes fell closed and I breathed in his scent.

He was standing so close to me.

To my heart.

His thumb caressed my cheekbones and I tilted my head into his touch.

"Olive," he whispered.

That voice…

I shivered, got wet… My body did all kinds of things that always happen in romance novels.

He was going to freaking kiss me!

If it happens, don't freak out, Olive.

You're a calm waterfall, a purring fucking cat.

At first, he rested his forehead against mine and we just stood like that for a moment, breathing each other in.

Gently. Slowly.

His nose touched mine.

Then, nothing. Absolutely NOTHING! His phone started ringing and his hands stiffened against my suddenly heated skin. For a moment there, it had felt like he was right there with me and there was no one else in the world other than us—but then, nothing.

His damn phone was a cock blocker after all.

His eyes still focused on me, he took a few steps back, answered his phone, and only then broke the eye contact. Had his eyes darkened? Was I starting to see things?

I lifted my fingers to touch my lips. How could I feel like his lips had caressed mine even though he hadn't even touched me?

I walked back inside to where I had left my clutch and picked it up.

When Jason came inside, I was ready to leave before I did something stupid.

I was going crazy.

CHAPTER SEVENTEEN

OLIVE

The moment I was in my apartment, I walked straight into Lucy's room. My hands were already covering my eyes when I said, "For the love of all the cute puppies out in the whole world, if there are any penises dangling, tuck them away."

I heard Lucy's laugh. "I'm alone, you dork."

Dropping my hands down, I closed her door and leaned back against it. Lucy straightened up in her bed and put down her laptop. "What happened? You never answered my texts."

I took a deep breath and then slowly let it go.

"Jason asked me if I would like to marry him."

Lucy stared at me unblinkingly.

Lifting my hand, I looked at it and then up to Lucy again. "My hands are shaking."

"Excuse me?"

"My hands are shaking," I repeated.

"Not that. Could you repeat what you said before that? I don't think I got that."

"He asked me if I would marry him."

"Okay. Am I dreaming or are you really in my room, telling me that Jason Thorn proposed to you?"

I covered my face with my hands and groaned.

"Could you come here for a second?" Lucy asked calmly.

After a few steps, I was sitting right beside her. Reaching out, she pinched my leg.

"I already tried that on my way over. Not a dream."

"Holy shit!" she breathed out, covering her mouth with her hands. "Holy shit, woman! Did you put a spell on him or something? Damn but you're fast."

"Lucy, I need you to listen to me very closely, can you do that for me?"

"Sure, I believe I'm capable of hearing what you are about to say. By the way, I'm very impressed and equally shocked right now, if you couldn't tell."

"Yeah, I don't think you'll be that impressed after you hear the whole story."

Hugging her pillow to her stomach, she motioned for me to go on.

"Apparently the alley—"

"No, wait!" She pressed her finger against my lips and jumped down from her bed. "I'm gonna get the tequila I hid in the kitchen. We need shots to celebrate."

"We are not celebrating anything, Lucy!" I hissed behind her back, but she was already gone.

When she came back she was holding two shot glasses and a half full tequila bottle. She handed me the shot glasses and poured the tequila.

"We're not celebrating," I said again.

"Fine. Bottoms up anyway. I need alcohol in my system to listen to this. Humor me."

We took the shots and she took her seat, the tequila bottle clutched tightly in her hands.

I started again, "Apparently the alley video did more damage than we had thought."

"How come?"

"No questions," I warned.

She opened her mouth, but I closed my hand over it before she could ask anything else. "I need to tell it all at once, okay? I'm having a hard time staying calm right now as it is. I'm letting you go, but no questions."

She nodded, so I pulled my hand back.

"Ok, here goes nothing. Like I said, apparently the video messed things up big time for him. Because of that, his publicist and agent want him to marry someone." Her eyes grew huge, but instead of speaking, she took a mouthful from the bottle, grimacing when it burned down her throat. "You know, become a family man or whatever the hell they are thinking. So they have been showing him headshots. Freaking headshots, can you believe that?"

Keeping silent, she nodded enthusiastically.

"Well, I can't. Anyway. Long story short, he didn't like any of the potential brides they were showing him. Enter me. When our photos went public and everyone seemed to think we were blissfully in love, his publicist suggested that I would be the perfect bride-to-be because of our past together. He said no one would think it was a publicity stunt to clear the negative press around him. He must agree with their brilliant idea because he asked me if I would like to marry him and become his roommate."

"Can I talk now?"

"Yes, please."

"Good. Okay, just a second." She took another swig from the bottle and offered it to me. I took two big sips.

"So, you said yes, right?" she asked as I was wiping my mouth with the back of my hand. "Tell me you didn't say no. Because if you did, I might have to punch you in the eye and I doubt that would look good on the cover of those tabloids."

"I freaked out and left."

"Clearly you've lost your mind."

Pushing me away, she got up from the bed and placed the back of her hand on my forehead.

"You don't seem to have a fever."

I slapped her hand away.

"What am I gonna do, Lucy?"

She leaned down so we were eye to eye and emphatically said, "You're going to marry Jason *freaking* Thorn of course."

I fell back on her bed. "I don't think that's a good idea Luce."

"Why the hell not?"

"It's not going to be a real marriage. What if he br—"

"No." She shoved her finger in my face. "You're not gonna start with all the what if this happens, what if that happens crap."

"Did you hear something?" I asked, rising up from the bed.

Tilting her head, she looked back at her door and listened. "I'm not hearing anything."

"Sounded like someone opened a door. Who's home? I'm not supposed to talk to anyone about this. I got my warning right before he dropped me off."

"Marcus isn't in and Char is not feeling well. Last I checked she was sleeping."

I relaxed. "Still, let's keep it down."

"This fake marriage, this is your opportunity, Olive. This is your chance to make him fall in love with you."

"I'm not sure if we are still talking about the same thing here."

"Look," she started in her, 'I'm a very patient person' tone. "You're still in love with him, aren't you? Always have been, and I believe, always will be. I saw those photos, Olive. He is into you. You can't fake that kind of chemistry. Okay, maybe he is not in love, at least not yet. I'll give you that much. But you have to give yourself a chance. You said you'll be living with him for crying out loud. What more do you want?"

My reluctance already dissolving, I turned my hopeful eyes up to Lucy. "You're right. I know you are right. I want to marry the fuck out of him. But he is also *the* fucking Jason Thorn, Lucy. If he was a normal guy, just working a normal job, I wouldn't even think twice about it. But he is Jason Thorn. I mean, he could do much better than me."

She smiled. "But he chose you, didn't he? And what the hell, let's say it didn't work out. What do you have to lose? Your next ten books are already bestsellers if you marry the guy."

"Why are you the second person to say that to me tonight?" Falling back on her bed, I released a long breath. "I want to marry him so bad, Lucy."

Lucy climbed up and lay down next to me.

"What's holding you back?"

"I think I'm scared. To be that close to him, to fall in deeper. He already broke my heart once when I was just a kid, and he didn't even know he was breaking it. This time around he'll ruin me." I closed my eyes and took a deep breath to clear my mind. "I came this close to jumping on him and holding on for dear life." I lifted my hand and gestured how much with two of my fingers.

Turning on my side, I looked at Lucy. "Did I ever tell you that I asked him to marry me? The first day I saw him at our house? When I was eight years old."

She propped herself up on one elbow and studied my face. "Nope. Tell me now."

I recounted everything I could remember from that day. "Even I had forgotten about that, but apparently he still remembers."

There was a moment of silence.

"I think I'm going to say yes."

"Damn right you are!"

"Should I text him or something?"

She chuckled and whacked a pillow on my face. "No dumbass. Let him think about you until he hears back. You'll tell him tomorrow."

I pushed the pillow away from my face. "So, what am I supposed to do now?"

"Go to sleep?"

"Yeah, I don't think that's happening any time soon."

"Do you want to make a plan?" Her eyes were twinkling with mischief.

"A plan for what?"

"A plan for how to make Jason Thorn fall in love with you."

"I'll pass."

"But it'll be fun!"

"I have no doubt about that, but I already have a plan." Scooting down from the bed, I backed away toward the door. "I'll just love him right to his face."

"That's my girl! Show 'em how it's done."

"If it all blows up in my face, you'll help me pick up the bits and pieces of my heart, right?"

She jumped down from the bed and gave me a big hug.

"Hoes over bros. Always."

"Great to hear. I'll just go and try to calm down in my room."

"I'm still gonna make a list of what you can do to him. Just in case you need it. There is this thing I do to Jameson that makes him extra, extra horn—"

"Okay, love you. Have a great night."

Leaving Lucy's room as quietly as possible, I lay down on my bed and watched the ceiling for hours before I finally fell asleep with a small smile etched on my face.

The mystery beauty is not a mystery anymore!

Ahhh, sorry ladies, looks like our very own sex god Jason Thorn is out of the sex pool for now.

You remember the mystery beauty he was caught with recently? She is not a mystery any more. We've learned that the strawberry blonde is Olive Taylor, a childhood friend of Jason who is also the author of the new New York Times Best Seller that is being adapted for the silver screen. Can you guess who the leading actor is? You guessed right! Jason Thorn will be taking on the role of Isaac, a troubled actor who reconnects with his first and only love who he left behind years before. Do you think Miss Taylor wrote the book to get her old friend's attention? If so, it definitely seems to be working for her. After claiming the number one spot on every bestseller list, is she laying claim to our bad boy, too?

The couple, who have been the talk of the town this last week, were spotted at the exclusive hotspot, Soho House. According to our source, the pair had a lovely dinner together in the main dining area. "They were talking to each other with their eyes, and they were absolutely beaming with happiness. They were definitely on a date," the source adds. "There is no way they are just friends. Their interaction was intense."

The hunky star left Miss Taylor's side only once, and that was to greet a group of business associates who were having dinner just a few tables away from them. The romantic outing ended early when Jason decided he couldn't wait to finish his dinner, grabbed the bestselling author by her hand, and ran for the exit.

"It was the most romantic thing I've ever seen in my life. One minute they were smiling at each other, sipping their cocktails, the next minute they were hand in hand running for the exit," another onlooker said.

You think Jason is in love with his childhood friend? The people who watched their every move on the hot date seem to think so.

Do you think he'll keep her? Will she be the pop to his sexy corn?

CHAPTER EIGHTEEN

JASON

"The damn bastards are quick," I said after reading the article they had on us. I put the tablet on the table, next to my empty lunch plate. "The thing is, I have no idea who these onlookers are who watched yesterday. The way they are describing things…the only true thing on there is that I only left her side once. The rest is complete bullshit. We barely said a word to each other the entire meal." I shook my head and reached for the French fries on Tom's plate.

"The way they are telling the story works for you so I'd say stop complaining."

Licking the salt on my thumb, I kept silent. I had made a fool of myself in front of Olive the night before. I'd thought I would breach the subject while we were having dinner, but for some reason it seemed wrong to ask Olive to marry me as if we were out on a business meeting. In the end I'd still fucked it all up, but at least we'd been alone when it happened. It wasn't like it would have made a difference if I'd gotten down on one knee and asked her to marry me to save my career. There was no good way to ask someone to marry you so they could help you get out of the grave you'd dug yourself into.

Speaking of that, I still hadn't heard back from Olive.

"She hasn't answered yet. Don't get too excited."

"It'll be a huge boost to her writing career. She'd be a fool not to say yes. It'll change her life more than it'll change yours," Tom interjected.

"She is not like all these women you know," I said, gesturing around the café.

"All these women?"

"You know, the women in this industry, or the models you seem to enjoy every now and then."

He raised his eyebrows. "And can I ask what makes her so different?"

I shrugged. "She is Olive. I know her. If she accepts—and that is a big if—it'll most likely be because she wants to help me. I think she is also half in love with my house, so that's definitely a plus on my side."

Tom snickered and shook his head. "You're a blind son of a bitch."

Frowning, I asked, "What the hell is that supposed to mean?"

He sighed and held his hand up. "Nothing. Don't get all worked up on me, but I have to say, you're also a lucky son of a bitch."

"I'll ask again, what do you mean?"

"I *mean* your Olive is not exactly hard on the eyes, is she? Even when you are screwed you luck out."

"Yeah." I cleared my throat. "She is beautiful." And she was all grown up, too, which was a dangerous combination for me.

"So far the only thing Megan has leaked to the media is that you were childhood friends and you're playing in the movie adaptation of her book. Everyone is running with their own version of the story. If Olive says yes, you'll have to be seen together a few more times and start playing the happy couple in front of the cameras. Then we'll leak the news of the marriage after it's all done."

"Are you my publicist or my agent?"

"I seem to be doing everything for your sorry ass these days."

"Yeah, well hopefully they won't be talking about me for much longer. I'm tired of reading my name and seeing my face in the tabloids."

Our waiter came by and picked up our empty plates.

"Is there anything else I can get you?"

"I'm good, thank you." I looked at Tom. "You?"

"I'll have an espresso," Tom said.

"Were you able to get in touch with Jackson Merritt?" I asked when Tom was sipping his espresso.

"You know you lost another contract after the interview with the Canadian girl. Your next year is wide open right now. Maybe we should consider the offers you're currently getting instead of going after the directors and movies you want to be a part of. They are not bad offers."

"Nothing happened with the damn Canadian girl. How many times do I have to repeat myself?" I growled, getting the attention of people close to our table.

"Keep it down."

"I worked hard to get where I am, Tom," I said, lowering my voice. "Just because I messed up in my personal life doesn't mean I'll lay down and let everyone pull me to pieces. I'm damn good at my job. I'm getting married and keeping a low profile, aren't I? If it's not going to help my situation, why am I doing it?" I reclined in my seat and looked right into Tom's eyes. "Since my schedule is open, I want to be in Jackson's movie. Just a few months back, they were after me for the lead role and we had to decline because it was clashing with my schedule. Now it's not. I want that part. Make it happen."

"Easy there," he said, pushing back his espresso as he leaned toward me. "We still have time before we go after it with all we have. Let's just see how everything settles down in a month or two. If they don't come on their own, then we'll go after them. You used to trust me, Jason. That's why we work well together. I won't come to you with a role that won't take you a step ahead of all the others, but you have to let me do my job." His eyes hardened on me. "We can't let others see how all this crap is affecting your career and you. Just keep it in your pants, get Olive to marry you, and we'll get you back on track."

Tired of my own damn life, I rubbed my forehead and decided to listen to Tom.

My eyes fell to my phone when it started vibrating on the table, Olive's name flashing across the screen.

"It's Olive," I muttered to Tom, my eyes briefly meeting his.

"O-kay. Why are you not answering?"

"What?" I looked up at him with a frown on my face.

"The phone. Aren't you gonna answer it?"

"I will," I replied, but made no move to answer it. Instead, I picked up the phone and glanced at Tom again. "What's happening right now?"

He looked just as confused as I felt. "You tell me, buddy."

I thought about it for a second or two, then laughed. "Fuck me, but I think I'm actually afraid to hear her say no. I'm not sure I'll go through with this genius marriage plan of Megan's and yours if Olive isn't in."

The phone stopped vibrating in my hand.

When Tom laughed, it was a big, 'hey people, look at me, I'm having the time of my life' laugh. *The bastard!*

"You like her, don't you? You actually *like*, like her."

He was starting to get on my nerves. "Of course I like her. She's always been important to me."

He lifted both his hands up, his laugh dying down to a chuckle. "I should've known… You didn't even put up a fight when her name came up, not like you did with all those other girls. You son of a bitch. Oh, this is going to be fun to watch."

"Shut up," I snarled at him.

Rising from my seat, I walked away from our table and dialed Olive's number when I was standing in the little garden that served as the café's backyard for smokers.

"Jason!" she answered in a terrified voice.

My entire body locked. "What's wrong?"

"Jason, I…I'm stuck here. There are people outside the café."

"Calm down, Olive. What do you mean there are people outside?"

"I mean there are ten or maybe more people camped right outside of the café. I'm mortified, Jason."

"Okay, sweetheart. Take a deep breath, and start from the beginning."

She did as I said, took a deep breath, and seemed to calm at least a bit. "Okay, sorry. I'm at a café called Dreamers, it's near campus. I was supposed to meet with Lucy and Char for lunch between their classes, so I brought my laptop and came here early, hoping to get in a few words while I was waiting. I'm sorry I'm rambling."

"It's okay. Tell me who is waiting outside."

"Well, Lucy and Char couldn't make it, so I decided to head back home since I couldn't get into my story, but the paparazzi is here, Jason. I didn't even notice them before I walked outside, but one of them yelled my name and started snapping pictures and asking questions. I'm back in the café right now, but they are still out there."

"Fuck," I muttered, turning to head back to the table. "Did you see the news about us?"

"If you mean the stories where they describe what we ate last night, then yes, Lucy shoved them in my face this morning. What does that have to do with this?"

"Give me a second," I said to Olive once I reached Tom. Then I told Tom, "I need to leave. Paps are camped outside the café she is in, and she can't leave."

"Do you need me?" Tom asked, his business face back on.

"No, I'll handle it. I'll call you later, okay?"

"Fine," he nodded. "But don't forget to call Megan after you have your answer from Olive. She has to handle all this and start spinning."

I grunted, grabbed my car key, and left the café as quickly as possible.

"I'm on my way, Olive."

"Thank you. How did they even know I was here?"

"Someone must've recognized you and tipped them off. There is already a hashtag on Twitter going on for us."

"Perfect." She sighed. "I don't have a car, Jason. I walked down here. It's a ten-minute walk, but I can't just walk with them trailing me."

"No. You stay put, I'm coming to get you. I'm sorry Olive, I should've known this would happen. Text me your exact address. Now."

Ending the call, I got into my car and floored it.

———

I ENTERED the café in a big commotion. Olive was wrong. There were at least twenty paps waiting outside and I knew more than anyone how relentless they were. When they saw me coming in for the save, they knew they had struck gold.

Looking around the interior of the café, it only took me a few seconds to spot Olive almost cowering behind her laptop in the corner.

I rushed to her side.

She noticed me and jumped up to her feet, her face as white as a sheet. "Thank you for coming so quick," she said in a low voice, her eyes darting around.

"Are you okay?" My hands acting on their own, I cupped her face and gazed into her dazed eyes.

Her hands landed on top of mine for a brief moment as if she wanted to assure herself that I was there with her. Then just as quickly, she dropped them down. "I'm fine. I just didn't know what to do, what to say to them. They were all yelling at once, and the owner of the café isn't happy about this." She discreetly motioned to her right with her head. "They already asked me to leave once."

My eyes darted around and I saw a stern woman standing behind the counter, staring at us.

I turned back to Olive. "We'll leave in a minute. My car is parked just around the corner."

"Jason, I look like crap." She looked down at herself and touched her hair, which was in a messy bun on top of her head. To me she looked just as beautiful as she had the night before. "I just came here to have lunch with the girls. Call me vain, but I don't want to see myself plastered everywhere like this." She gestured to me, and added, "Especially next to you, not when you look like that."

"Jason Thorn? Are you really Jason Thorn?" someone asked. I turned around to see who was talking to me.

"Oh, you are. You really are. Can I take a selfie with you? I just have to show this to my friends, they will never believe me if I don't have proof."

I forced a smile on my face and nodded. "Of course."

I never turned down a fan who was asking for an autograph or a picture. It wasn't my thing, but at that moment, I wished it was. I took the damn selfie with her face inches away from mine as she hugged me as if we'd known each other not merely for seconds but for months.

As soon as she left, five other people found the courage to approach me and asked for autographs and pictures.

When I turned back, Olive had sat down and was looking down at her closed laptop. I knew we needed to have a quick talk before more people swarmed us. At this rate, we were bound to have trouble leaving the place if everyone started posting that I was here.

I took Olive's hand in mine and pulled her up.

"Where is the bathroom in this place?" I asked as I grabbed her laptop with my free hand.

"There," she pointed to a narrow hallway in the back.

I dragged her behind me and made sure to lock the door to the tiny bathroom once we were inside.

"If we stay longer, more people will hear that I'm here and we'll have a real problem on our hands. We need to leave right now."

She nodded.

"But before we go out there, I have to ask you… I'm sorry, I don't want to pressure you, Olive, but I need to know so I can either—"

"Yes," she interrupted me in a rushed but clear tone. "If you are talking about the…thing you asked yesterday. It's yes."

My heart sighed. Smiling at her, I relaxed. Her hand was still in mine so I squeezed it. "Yes?"

She nibbled on her bottom lip and my attention shifted from her bright eyes to her full pink lips. "Yes," she repeated a little softer.

I cleared my throat and forced my gaze away from the danger that was her inviting lips. "So we are doing this?"

She smiled and nodded. "I think we are."

My eyes still on her, I reached back, unlocked the door, and was about to step out when she pulled me back. "Wait, give me the laptop." I had completely forgotten about it. I handed it over to her and she pushed it into her huge handbag. I went for her hand again, but she drew back.

"Just wait."

We were gonna get stuck in the damn bathroom.

Reaching up, she took a small clip out of her hair and it all came tumbling down around her face. Pushing her fingers through it, she gave it a few good shakes, and then looked up at me with a pretty flush on her face.

I groaned. Damn it, now all I could think was how it would feel to have her vibrant hair wrapped around my hand. Damn it all again—now with her sexy bed hair, she looked like she had just been fucked. By me. Which was the exact conclusion the paparazzi would come to.

"You shouldn't have done that, Olive."

She glanced at the mirror. "Do I look worse? This is all I got. I'm sorry."

"All you got would probably kill me, so I'd say this is more than enough. Come on, we need to leave."

This time she was the one reaching for my hand.

"We are not saying one word. Don't look directly into the cameras, just follow my lead and we'll let my publicist handle the rest."

She nodded and we stepped out of the bathroom. There were a few people waiting for us to get out, but for the first time in my career, I apologized and turned all of them down.

The moment I stepped out of the café with Olive clinging to my hand, the paparazzi were ready for round two. Every single one of them were shouting random questions at us, snapping pictures nonstop.

Olive was looking at the ground and her steps were hurried, but I still had to slow down a little so she could keep up with my long strides. Suddenly she lifted her gaze and our eyes met. We both smiled at each other. Before I could enjoy the moment myself, every pap around us saw the quick exchange between us and went into a frenzy, yelling our names louder.

Even though the paparazzi were in our way, we finally made it to my Spyder in one piece and I opened the passenger side door to help Olive in.

As I finally drove away from the madness, I knew exactly which shot they would use the next day.

CHAPTER NINETEEN

JASON

"That was something," Olive said after a few minutes of silence had passed.

I glanced at her out of the corner of my eye to make sure she was actually okay. "Welcome to my world. You okay?"

She lifted her arms in front of her. "A little bit on the shakier side, but still in one piece. You?"

"They rarely get to me any more. You get used to walking down a street with cameras flashing all around you."

"Comes with the job, I guess."

Unfortunately, it did. Most of the time, I could get away with wearing sunglasses and a baseball hat and simply blend in, but it didn't work every single time. "I think we should head straight to my publicist's office. We need to plan how we're going to handle this."

"Now?"

"Yeah. Running away won't work. We can't be trapped in a café like this a second time. They won't just trail me; they'll focus on you. The more we stay silent, the harder it'll be to shake them off."

"I'm sorry, I should've handled it better," she said in small voice.

Taking a left turn, I kept my eyes on the road but reached out to grasp her hand. I was starting to do that a lot lately.

Holding her hand. Keeping her close. Breathing her in. Touching her. Looking at her ass. And more importantly, fucking *seeing* her.

"If anything like this ever happens again when I'm not around, I want you to call me immediately. If I can't come myself, I'll send someone who can help you. If we're going to do this, I need to know you feel comfortable. I don't want you to be scared to go out because of me."

"It's okay, Jason." She covered my hand with her small one. "If you tell them who I am, or that we're together, I'm sure they'll eventually back off."

I sighed. "I don't think so. That will probably take some time. This is too juicy for them to ignore."

When she pulled her hand away, I had to pull away, too.

I handed her my phone and asked her to dial Alvin's number.

"Is everything okay, boss? Tom just called me and said you might need help."

"It's okay, Alvin. We handled it. Can you find out where Megan is? If she is at the office, I want to go straight to her. Olive is with me, and I think we need to sit down and have a talk."

"Give me a few minutes and I'll get back to you."

When Alvin called back, I was halfway to Megan's office.

"She is not at the office, boss. She is wrapping up a lunch meeting at Chateau Marmont."

"Fine then we're heading there."

"I suggested the same thing, but she said you'd need to have a private conversation. She said to tell you she'll be back at her office in fifteen and to meet her there. Do you want me to get back to her?"

"No it's fine. I'm minutes away, we'll wait for her."

When we made it, her assistant was already waiting for us and led us into Megan's office.

"I know I didn't ask, but I hope you have time for this," I said to Olive once we were alone.

"The meeting? Yes, of course. I know I have to sign things." She gave me a questioning look. "At least, I'm assuming I do."

"You don't have to sign anything you don't want to Olive. I trust you."

We were interrupted when Megan's assistant came back to let us know Megan was a few minutes away and to ask if we wanted anything to drink.

We both declined.

"What is she going to talk to us about?" Olive asked once the assistant left.

"Aren't you going to sit?"

She looked around as if she was only then seeing the big sectional on the far left side of the office and the set of armchairs in front of Megan's desk.

"I'm good," she said after a moment.

I walked up to her and held her by her shoulders. "She won't leak anything we don't want her to leak. For that, she needs to talk to both of us. Basically, we have to come up with a game plan for the marriage thing. That is, if you are absolutely sure, Olive."

Rubbing her palms up and down her thighs, she nodded and looked at me. "I am. Like you said, if nothing else, it'll be fun."

I let my hands wander down from her arms and linked our hands together.

"It'll most definitely be fun," I murmured, her beautiful eyes pulling me in.

"That is exactly how I want people to see you," Megan said as she barged in.

Olive gave a slight jerk. I sighed and looked at the ceiling.

"Hello to you, too, Megan." Dropping one of Olive's hands, I turned us to face my dear publicist. "Olive, this is Megan, a beautiful pain in my ass."

Megan's smile was sort of savage, but she still reached out and patted my cheek. "You would be lost without me."

"If you say so," I muttered and gave Olive's hand a squeeze.

She was already smiling at Megan and I was having a hard time looking away from her lips. She gave my hand a tug, but I didn't see why I should have to let it go so I held on. When she turned those green eyes on me with a small frown, I had to force my hand to let hers go. Immediately, she extended her hand to Megan and they shook hands, exchanging a few pleasantries.

"Okay, let's sit down and have a chat," Megan said as she took her seat behind her desk.

Olive chose to sit on the edge of her seat, her body giving off all kinds of stress signals: jumpy legs, cold hands, lip biting…

Lip biting could be fun, though. I could make lip biting into a fun activity for her.

"I assume you've come to an agreement," Megan interrupted my thoughts—and good thing she did.

"Yes," Olive agreed and turned her eyes on me, waiting for an answer.

I smiled at her and stole a small one right back from her.

"You should save the googly eyes for the press. You don't have to act around me, too."

I could've killed Megan right then. Olive's startled gaze flew away from me, and I could hardly get her to look at me for more than a few seconds for the rest of the meeting, which wasn't anything exciting at all.

"First and foremost we need to apply for a confidential marriage license and get that out of the way. We don't want them to find out about it on their own."

"Isn't them finding out about the marriage the whole purpose of this thing?" Olive asked.

"It is," Megan agreed. "But we want them to learn about it when we are ready for them to learn about it." Megan turned her gaze to me. "I need you to buy Olive a ring. Do it before you leave. We want her to be seen wearing it."

"We'll go and choose something together?" I offered to Olive.

Before she could answer, Megan jumped in. "No. We don't want anyone to talk about this. You know what, forget what I said. They'll probably be trailing you, and we don't want to give them that tidbit yet. Talk to Alvin, he'll handle everything."

Seemingly satisfied with her own plan, she nodded to herself and gave us more details on when we should be seen and how we should act out in public.

"I'll print you out a list before you leave. I want you to be photographed almost everyday at any of those places until you leave for London."

"When is he leaving?" Olive asked Megan.

"I'm right here you know, you can look at me, too," I suggested lazily.

Her cheeks held an appealing blush when she finally looked at me. "Sorry."

I gave her a long look. "I'm heading to London next week. It's only for a few days."

"And you are going with him," Megan added, looking at Olive.

"I am?" she squeaked.

"Yes. And you'll start wearing your ring at the London premiere. If you get questions you can answer them as long as you keep the answers short—but don't talk about getting married —and change the subject back to promoting the movie. You two being there together will be good PR for the movie, too. Other than that, I don't want you to talk to the press about Olive before you leave. When you are being photographed here in the city, just be yourselves, smile for the cameras…I don't know, maybe hold hands, but keep it mild. We want everyone to be talking about you, and so far no one is sure if you are together or not. Seeing you two at the London premiere with a ring on her finger will be an answer enough on its own."

"Don't I have to sign anything?" Olive asked when Megan was done with her instructions.

Megan glanced at me with a quirked eyebrow. I stared back.

"Jason's lawyers will handle that part," she answered eventually. Keeping her stare on Olive, she leaned forward. "It'll be in the contract, but you can't talk about this to anyone. Not your parents, not your friends. Don't even repeat it to yourself after this point. If it gets out that this was arranged, it will undo everything we are trying to do."

"Well," Olive muttered, wincing slightly.

Megan's voice was harsh—harsher than I would allow her to use when speaking to Olive—when she asked, "Who did you tell?"

"Megan," I said in low voice, silencing her.

"I mentioned it to Lucy, but I swear she won't tell a soul, Jason," Olive rushed to say, her eyes focused somewhere over my shoulder.

I ducked a little and caught her eyes. "It's okay. I trust you, and if you trust her…" I shrugged. "It's done, Megan. So move on."

By the time we left Megan's office after going over a few more details of how we should act in public, both Olive and I were pretty much brain dead.

"Wow…" Olive breathed out once we were sitting in the car and just staring out the windshield. I didn't even attempt to start the car. "Who knew I had to be careful about so many things. I mean, come on, was she really serious about me looking a little too long at any other actors? Or the part—which was my favorite part, by the way—where she said I'd have to discourage you if you wanted to have a quickie in London?"

"I'm afraid she was very much serious. Also, *my* favorite part was about you looking at me—oh sorry, not *looking*"—I watched her out of the corner of my eye as I continued—"*gazing at me adoringly* in the photos. You think you can look at me adoringly? I wouldn't mind working on it."

"How thoughtful of you my soon-to-be-hubby."

"Ah," I groaned and closed my eyes. "Call me anything but hubby. For some reason, I hate that word. Hubby, hubster…" I shook my head. "Just no. Call me husband," I said in a husky voice before I noticed what I was saying.

She chuckled. "Fine, I'll find another pet name. How about myyyy… Well, looks like I lost a few brain cells in there, can't think of anything right now. I'll come up with something, don't worry."

I smiled to myself. "Can't wait to hear it, sweetheart." That was definitely something I would look forward too.

"Are you ready to back out yet?" I asked mildly as we silently watched a few guys point and whistle at my Spyder as they walked past.

She twisted in her seat to face me. "I said yes, Jason. I want to help; I won't back out. But if you change your mind…"

"No," I replied after a brief pause, and then I let my head drop back on the headrest. "You're still the only girl I want to get fake married to."

She gave a short, amused laugh and rested her temple against the headrest. "Yay?"

I turned my head to find her studying me. A second later, I was tugging her hair, stealing another sincere smile from her.

"In a few weeks, it'll all die down, don't worry," I reassured her. "And it won't be all bad, I promise."

"I'm not worried. Not exactly. I mean, it's probably every girl's wish to get married to you these days. Fake or not, it'll be... something. So, no, I'm not worried. But I think you should be."

"Why?"

"Well, if we can't tell anyone about this," she shrugged, her lips kicking up at the corners. "I'm not going to be the one who tells my parents I got married so hastily. If I have to lie, so do you."

Now it was my turn to wince. "I think I can charm your mom and dad, but Dylan... Yeah, I'm not looking forward to that talk."

Closing her eyes, she faced forward again. "So, we are getting married right after we get back from London. It's going to be a quick thing at your home. No friends, no nothing. That night, I move in with you, and when the filming starts for *Soul Ache*, I'm to accompany you to the movie set for the first few days so they can get more candid shots of us and essentially start promoting the movie right when the filming starts."

"That pretty much sums it up," I muttered, rubbing my eyes.

"You're not Isaac and I'm...not Evie, they get that though, right?" she asked a little hesitantly when I started the car.

"In their eyes, we will be whoever they want us to be, Olive."

CHAPTER TWENTY

JASON

D o you know what happens after you start acting like you're in love with a girl? Or, hell, forget about being in love, do you know what happens when you act like you're dating each other? Falling for each other? No?

Let me tell you what happens: you start to get lost in your own fucking game. You begin to think you're *actually* dating each other. What the fuck are you supposed to think when you're holding hands, looking into each other's eyes, laughing, and just fucking enjoying your life?

Only, it is a special kind of hell where you can't reap the benefits of dating as you would if you were actually *fucking* dating.

The days after our meeting with Megan passed in a flurry of activity. As much as I hated seeing myself on every media outlet out there, I couldn't deny the fact that I didn't mind it that much when Olive was in the same shot with me. After looking at so many damn photos of the two of us together, laughing, smiling, and holding hands—always holding hands—I could see what Tom and Megan had initially seen.

We looked good together.

Happy.

I was afraid I was starting to believe in the lie we had so meticulously created. I was starting to believe that Olive belonged with me and only me.

Late night movie date?

Check.

Shopping at the farmers' market?

Check.

Coffee date?

Check.

Lunch date?

Check.

Dinner date?

Check.

We were following Megan's instructions to a T, and as we went through her list one by one, we had a whole crew of paparazzi following us everywhere—and when I say everywhere, I mean *everywhere*. They all seemed to have forgotten about my sexcapades and chose to focus on our new love instead. Judging by all the articles and videos everyone kept posting, people were loving it. Everyone who read Olive's book—which was a large number of people—were rooting for Olive to win my heart. They all liked the idea of their troubled movie star falling for an ordinary, girl-next-door type.

What they didn't know was that Olive was nothing short of extraordinary.

———

AFTER A LONG FLIGHT TO LONDON, we finally made it to our hotel room. "Is this our room? Or should I say palace?" Olive asked after turning in a circle and taking everything in.

"High ceilings, big windows, two freaking balconies."

I chuckled. "I take it you approve."

"I definitely approve. I'm very happy that you're picking up the bill, though."

Keeping my eyes up and away from her ass, I trailed after her and listened to her comments about every room in the suite.

"Jason!" she gasped once she reached the main bathroom. She looked over her shoulder to make sure I was following her. Not so fortunately for me, she had it all, especially when she bent forward to check out the…the… I couldn't even see what she was trying to look at. Her shirt rode up and all I could see was that damn ass of hers.

"Jason, did you see this?"

She had righted herself and was looking at me, her green eyes sparkling. I knew she was excited about every little thing because even the plane food had made her happy.

"Everything is all compartmentalized, it's so cute. Isn't it cute? And they keep giving us free champagne, and snacks, and Danish pastries. I'm literally in heaven right now."

I didn't see any of it; all I could feel was her getting under my damn skin.

After she had eaten two of my pastries on top of her own, she had fallen asleep all snuggled up against me.

I hadn't moved an inch the rest of the flight.

"Yes?" I asked, focusing on her face again.

"There is a vintage clawfoot tub in here." Her voice echoed in the tiled bathroom.

"Great," I muttered, quickly turning away from her before I lost my damn mind. *The things I could do to her in that tub…* I didn't need a visual of her standing next to it.

A few minutes later she found me in my room. "There are only two bedrooms here," she commented from the doorway.

I lifted my brow and stared at her. "Two isn't enough? How many did you expect to find?"

"No, it's not that. It's so big, I just assumed it would be more than two. There is a dining room so if we want to invite our non-existent friends over for dinner, that will be useful I guess. Anyway, you're taking this room?" she asked as she entered the room and sat on the bed. "The other bedroom is bigger; why don't you take that one? I'd be more comfortable if you took that one."

When we'd landed at the airport the sky had already been darkening, but I still parted the blinds so the city lights would illuminate the room without me having to switch the bright lights on.

I turned around to move out of the room, but Olive was sprawled on the bed, looking up at the ceiling.

"Okay, give it to me." *Oh, how I wish I could.* "What is our itinerary for tonight? Is it something like this? At 8, exit the hotel, make sure to get photographed hand in hand with Jason Thorn. At 8:30, enter the restaurant, hand in hand with Jason Thorn. At 9:30, exit the restaurant, laughing and clinging to Jason Thorn."

Grinning, I sat down next to her and looked at her upturned face. "I didn't know my hand was causing you such grief."

"Your hand… Holding your hand is no grief at all. It's just weird how detailed she is on her lists, as if she has to mention that I need to smile when I'm looking at you. What does she think I'm going to do? Slug you in public or something? And, hell, maybe I'm having a moment and I just want to look at you for a second."

My fingers stopped playing with the ends of her soft hair. My voice came out husky when I spoke. "Tell me more about this moment and I'll try to answer as best as I can."

She turned to her side and squinted her eyes at me. Before she could answer, my damn phone vibrated with a new text.

"It's Megan. We have a car waiting to take us to dinner. Apparently she is joining us."

Olive groaned and covered her eyes with her arm. "She is going to go over her game plan for tomorrow. We're screwed."

———

THE DINNER WAS EXACTLY what Olive had predicted it would be: Megan giving each of us detailed instructions on what to say, what not to say, etc. Toward the end, she focused completely on Olive and explained what would happen at the premiere the next day. When neither Olive nor I could keep our eyes open any more, she agreed to end the night and we all returned to our rooms.

I eyed the alarm clock on my left side and noticed it had been only eleven minutes since I had left Olive alone on the balcony after giving her a quick kiss on her forehead. It was the closest we had gotten to a real kiss so far, always a forehead kiss, or some-times an even more innocent cheek kiss. I'd already discovered that I preferred forehead kisses over the cheek kisses. The way she looked at me after I gave her one always undid something inside me, so I took what I could get.

Another minute passed. Was she still talking to her friends? It was the first night we'd be sleeping under the same roof, and I was having trouble guiding my thoughts away from that fact.

Finally, I heard a door being clicked shut, then soft footsteps took her farther away from my room to her own bedroom. *Maybe I should've found a suite with only one bedroom.*

I took a deep breath and let it all out.

When I heard Olive's ear-piercing scream, I was out of my bed and running for her in seconds. As soon as I hit the living room, she collided with my bare chest, knocking the air out of me.

"What is it?" I asked urgently, my heart racing in my chest. When she kept shaking in my arms, trying to catch her breath, I gripped her elbows and pushed her away from my body. "What's wrong?"

Her chest rising and falling rapidly, she met my eyes.

"Someone is in my room." Her breath hitched. "The closet."

Just as she finished her words, I heard a soft clatter coming from her room. I gripped her arm tighter. "Go to my room. Now. Call the hotel security." She nodded sharply, but didn't move. "Go, sweetheart. It's gonna be okay," I said, softening my tone. She ran without questioning me further.

When I entered her room, I caught the faint smell of Olive, the scent of her perfume: fresh apples and flowers. As I walked father in, a heavier smell clouded the one I was starting to recognize whenever Olive was near.

"Hotel security is on their way. If you don't want to get in more trouble, you should come out of there."

A slender blonde strolled out of the walk-in closet at my words. She was wearing a black lingerie set that left nothing to the imagination. I made sure to keep my eyes on her face and not an inch below that.

I balled my fists and took a deep breath.

"How did you get in?" I asked, trying so very hard to keep the anger that was burning inside me out of my voice.

What if Olive hadn't noticed this person's presence in her room and this lunatic had managed to hurt her?

She shrugged and offered me a small smile. It wasn't the first time some fan or stalker had paid a hotel employee to get into my room, but having Olive here with me…

It changed things.

Her eyes roamed my naked chest and she found the courage to take a step toward me as she licked her lips. I crossed my arms over my chest.

"I guessed you would bring her here with you, but I wanted to give you options tonight. I'm game for a threesome, too," she said.

I clenched my jaw and had to force myself to not throw her out on her ass on the spot.

"Jason? Is everything okay?" Olive's softly spoken words came from right outside the room.

"It's okay, Olive." I raised my voice. "Open the door so security can get in here as fast as possible."

Turning to the lunatic, I saw the shocked expression on her face. "Perhaps you want to put on your clothes before more people see you like this."

"But…but I love you," she said, taking another step forward. "Please, give me a chance. I really love you, Jason! I've watched every one of your movies a hundred times!"

I gritted my teeth and turned away from her to wait for security.

"I'll do whatever you want, Jason. Just give me one night, please," she begged instead of putting clothes on. "I only want one chance. I'll let you do anything you want to me. I don't even care if you fuck me in front of a bunch of people. Whatever gets you off, I'm down with it."

Hearing raised voices coming from outside the room, I walked out without glancing back at her. I was doing my damnedest to ignore her words. She was still begging me, her pleas becoming desperate. The head of the hotel security, Daniel…something, who I had met as we checked in, reached me before I could get to them.

"What's the problem, sir?"

"Someone managed to get into the room and hide in the closet. I suggest you take her out of here immediately or I'll be pressing charges."

"That's impossible. Our security—"

I held up a hand. "I don't have time to go over this with you. She obviously found her way in. Get her out of here, right now." His eyes hardened and before he could move toward the room with the two other men that were standing right behind him, the girl came running outside, still in the same getup.

"You took him from me," she cried as she ran toward the door. While I was thinking she was finally getting out, one way or another, my eyes caught something in her clenched fists: a taser.

She was running toward Olive.

I growled Olive's name, trying to warn her as my heart leaped to my throat. Before I could reach Olive where she was standing next to the open door or take out the fucking lunatic, one of the security guys tackled the girl down on the hardwood floor and restrained her hands behind her back, forcefully prying the weapon out of her hands.

Once I reached Olive's side, I was shaking just as much as she was, if not more. Holding her face in my hands, I forced her to meet my gaze. "You okay?"

Her mouth opened, but no words came out. She gave a small nod.

I buried her face in my chest and willed my heart to slow down.

She is okay. She is fine.

"Get her the *fuck* out of here," I growled when the security guys seemed to be taking their sweet time with the wailing girl.

I pulled Olive as far away from the door as possible. Her skin was cold under my touch.

"Sir, do you want us to—"

"Get out," I roared, finally fed up. Thankfully, they obeyed.

Before the last one could close the door, Megan peered in through the small opening. "What the hell is going on here? What's with all the yelling?" She looked over her shoulder. "Did someone try to get in?"

Letting go of Olive for a second, I walked toward the door and closed it on Megan's face. I was in no condition to talk to her.

This time I was gentler when I held Olive's face in my hands. She lifted her face and her eyes locked with mine. "I'm so sorry, Olive." She had stiffened when I'd touched her again, but seemed to relax as I slowly caressed her cheeks with my thumbs. I didn't like the fact that her face was still pale, but she didn't seem to shake any more.

She grabbed my forearms. "It wasn't your fault. I think I over-reacted a little. It's just…" Her eyes broke contact. "When the closet door opened and I saw her reflection in the mirror…"

"Don't apologize, sweetheart," I said gruffly. It was my own damn fault for not bringing my own bodyguard. "I'm sorry, Olive," I murmured again and pulled her against my chest.

A few seconds later, her arms tentatively closed around my waist and the tension quickly left my body.

"You took ten years off of my life," I muttered against her hair. I was holding her head in place, right over my heart.

"It's okay, Jason. Calm down. I'm okay."

Did she even know how much she had scared me? "Don't do that again," I said, pulling away so I could look down at her. "Don't ever stand around like that again."

Her brows drew together, her coloring slowly coming back to her face. "I was wait—"

"Don't argue with me either. You should've waited in my room after security got here."

Her frown deepened and I matched it with my own.

"You're sleeping with me," I announced before she could get a word in.

That made her frown disappear completely as her pretty little mouth dropped open.

So many things to do with that mouth.

So many things to say looking into those captivating eyes.

"What do you mean?" she asked, her eyes narrowing when I let her go and gently pushed her toward my room.

"The bed is big enough, Olive. You'll sleep in my room with me."

"Okay," she replied, finally starting to walk.

"That's it? No argument?"

"Well, I did get scared, and it was your fan scaring the shit out of me after all, so the least you can do is sleep with me—to protect me of course, sooo…yeah, I'll gladly sleep in your bed." She looked at me over her shoulder, her eyes all innocent. "It's not like you'll touch me, right?"

Holding back my laugh, I shook my head. "No touching, don't worry."

"Phew." She whistled, pretending to swipe imaginary sweat from her forehead. "For a second there I was out of my mind with worry. Let's go to bed, then." We stopped next to the bed, my hand barely touching her back.

"Oh," she said, fully turning to me as she stood between the bed and me.

There was a chance that I was standing a little too close to her.

Her gaze dropped down to my chest and her eyes slightly widened as if she was just realizing there was a half-naked man right in front of her. When her eyes started to trail lower, my skin prickled and I had to fight with my body to not react to her beautiful wandering eyes. "I…I should take a shower first so I'll just…" Her eyes jumped between my eyes and collarbone. "I'll head to the other room and grab…my things. I'll be right back." She patted my arm and ran away.

Chuckling, I got into bed.

Twenty minutes had passed when she finally put her knee on the right side of the bed and climbed up next to me. There was too much space between our bodies for us to ever come in contact, but instead of lying on the very edge of the bed like I was doing, she quietly got under the covers and settled in the middle.

I tensed.

Maybe she just wanted to lay in the middle so we could share the covers without having to pull on them? Or maybe she was a turner, and to avoid tumbling down, she needed to fall asleep far away from the edge? Either way, I would stay on my side so it was okay.

Everything would be fine.

Another ten minutes passed and thanks to Olive's tossing and turning, I was still wide awake.

Every single time she turned, moved, fluffed her pillow, or quietly sighed, my body got a reminder of her presence and of course acted accordingly. Hell, even her breathing was starting to get to me.

Groaning, I turned to my right to see her back facing me.

"Jas—" she started to whisper, but before she could finish my name, I reached out, splayed my hand on her stomach—thank god she was at least wearing something—and pulled her back against my chest.

She gasped and her body stilled. For a moment, I didn't know what I should do with my hand, but then I decided to rest my palm on the bed, still keeping my arm against her stomach, caging her in. At least this way she would stop tossing and turning and we would finally go to sleep.

"Jason? Are you sleeping?" she whispered, not turning her head.

"What do you think?" I muttered.

"Sorry. I can leave if you want—"

My chest still cushioning her back, I pulled my hips a few inches back—just to make sure she wouldn't feel anything she wasn't supposed to feel—and gave her body a gentle tug with my arm.

"Go to sleep, Olive."

"Oh, okay," she murmured.

A few minutes later, just when I was about to fall asleep, she started to wiggle her bottom. The little minx managed to rest her ass right above my dick. One wrong move and my already raging dick would have been resting right against her round, shapely ass—not that I had spent much time looking at it…

While her breathing had deepened shortly after she'd made sure her ass was perfectly placed to torture me, it took me hours to fall asleep, battling with the urge to move forward, just a few inches, just to let my dick cop a feel.

———

MY EYES STILL CLOSED, I took a deep breath and smiled to myself. I could feel the morning sun filtering through the open blinds, warming my skin. It felt good. The other thing that felt more than good was Olive's scent in my room.

When I tried to lift my arm to stretch, I noticed a heavy weight on it. Opening my eyes, I found my nose inches away from Olive's forehead.

Shit!

At some point in my sleep, I had cradled her in my arms and her leg had somehow gotten thrown over me, pressing my morning wood into my stomach. I tried to see if I could move away, but it only made matters worse. When Olive's hips moved and her thigh pressed firmer against my dick, I couldn't hold back my groan.

Shifting in place, she snuggled closer and buried her face in my throat.

Oh, fuck me for fuck's sake!

With my free hand, I reached to grab her thigh and push it down, but my hand rested over…her bare skin? Before I could stop myself, my hand crept up and my fingertips touched the side of her underwear.

Sweet Jesus…

Had she been naked when she'd gotten in bed with me? Was she crazy?

I tipped my head down and looked at her through my half-closed eyes. She still had her shirt on, but it was all bunched up around her waist.

Dropping my head back on the pillow, I sighed and belatedly noticed that I had started massaging her thigh, right under her ass.

After stilling for a second, I pulled back my hand quickly.

She made a soft, sweet noise in her sleep and tried to climb on top of me.

"Oh god," I groaned quietly. I managed to hold her in place before she could climb up on my lap. When she suddenly pulled her leg away and turned to her other side, I sighed in relief. We weren't touching. Don't get me wrong, her ass was still free of her shirt and if I dropped my eyes a little lower, I could find heaven, but I was able to restrain myself.

I palmed my cock, and yeah, I had one hell of a morning wood I would have to take care of in the shower. Propping myself on my elbow, I looked down at Olive and sighed.

She looked so innocent in her sleep, so beautiful, and she was going to be my wife in just a few days.

Just to see if she would wake up, I touched her arm with my fingertips and gently trailed them down to her wrist.

Nothing.

I made my way back up to her shoulder, but she only burrowed deeper into her pillow.

Feeling like a proper creep, I decided to get up and take care of myself in the shower before I did something stupid. No reason to play with fire.

Leaning down, I placed a small kiss on her temple, and she released a soft moan.

A noise that my dick liked a little too much.

Bad idea, Jason. Worst fucking idea.

Rolling away from her, I jumped into the shower and took care of my wayward dick under the hot water.

CHAPTER TWENTY-ONE

OLIVE

After spending almost the entire day on my own because Jason had things to do, we were now in a limousine with Megan, heading toward the theater where the screening for the premiere would take place.

"You remember everything I told you, Olive?" asked Megan after her talk with Jason was finally done.

It took a lot for me to not roll my eyes. "Yes, Megan. I'll let Jason do most of the talking while I just smile and try to look pretty next to him." I held up a finger as if I'd just remembered something. "Oh, sorry, I almost forgot—I'll also make sure to somehow show off my ring without appearing like I'm shoving it in everyone's faces."

Jason chuckled and extended me his hand, palm up. "We're almost there, come on."

Smiling sheepishly at him, I took his hand. I still couldn't meet his damn eyes. I tried not to think about the talk I'd had with Lucy just that morning.

Me: I SLEPT IN THE SAME FREAKING BED WITH
JASON!

Lucy: Did you see his dangly bits?! Start describing. Now.
Me: No, Lucy! I didn't see his…anything. And, if I do ever get the privilege of seeing it, I'm not calling it "dangly bits".
Lucy: You're no fun. Then what the hell were you doing in his bed? Tell me you didn't watch him sleep like the creeper you are.
Me: Sometimes I question our friendship.
Lucy: It'll pass, don't worry. Come on, spill it.
Me: Long story short, there was a crazy fan waiting in his room, which happened to be my room. After she was removed, he wanted me to sleep with him so he could keep me safe.
Lucy: Swoon. Did you hear the thud? I just fainted on the floor. I'm calling you!

Before I could type in that I couldn't talk, her face was already lighting up my screen.

"I'm supposed to get ready for hair and makeup in a few minutes, I can't talk," I said as soon as I answered her call.

"Hello to you, too, my best friend. Jeez. Hair and makeup you say? Will you even remember my name in a few days?"

"I was the one who texted you just a few seconds ago."

"Well, I couldn't show my excitement through texts, you had to hear my voice. You wanted to hear my voice, didn't you?"

I opened the balcony door and stepped outside to make sure no one could hear me.

"Ok, you did good. I have more to tell, but you can't freak out okay? Because if you freak out, I'll freak out, and I can't freak out."

"Jesus, you're already freaking me out with all the don't freak outs."

"I really have to go before they come in. I don't want to

enrage Megan. Anyway, like I told you, we slept in the same freaking bed," I said, jumping up and down a little. I was getting excited just talking about it.

"Yes, yes. Keep going, keep going!"

"In the middle of the night, I woke up because I felt something on my leg."

"Whaaaaat?" she screeched on the other end of the line, and I had to pull the phone away from my ear. "Was it his dangly bit?"

"No, Lucy. His dick didn't magically grow legs and walk over to me. He was still asleep, but his hand was on my leg, and he was…" I lowered my voice and looked down at the floor. "Massaging my thigh."

Lucy gasped. "He touched your leg. This is scandalous. Go on. I love this."

I bit my lip to keep from grinning. "Then he pulled my leg over his lap and I—"

"Oh my god!" Lucy screamed before I could finish my sentence. "He pulled your leg over his cock! You felt his cock! Jameson does that when he is awake!"

"Thanks for stealing my thunder," I muttered, but I was still smiling.

"Olive?" Jason's voice pulled me out of my thoughts. "We're here. You ready to do this?"

I looked out his window and when I saw what was waiting on the other side of the door, I suddenly didn't feel so good after all. I was getting used to the paparazzi—I even had my own favorites among them—but this? I could understand why Megan was so hell bent on making sure my entire focus was on Jason and only Jason.

"Hey," Jason said softly next to me. I looked at him, my panic barely held at bay.

I was screwed.

"You okay?" he asked.

"We don't have time for this right now, Jason," Megan interjected.

"I have all the time for Olive. If you're so determined to get out there, you're more than welcome." He gestured to the door with his hand.

Megan took a huge breath, gave him a death glare, and said, "Try to be quick." Then she was out of the car, leaving us alone.

"You okay?" he repeated.

"There are so many people out there," I replied, my eyes still focused on all the people screaming beyond the red carpet.

Jason's fingers caught my chin and my attention shifted to him. "I won't let you out of my sight. Would that make you feel better?"

His eyes were so gentle on me. He cared about me more than he cared about everything that was waiting for him out there. Someone knocked on the window and I jolted in my place.

I looked out through the back window of the car and saw that we were holding up the line.

"Don't mind them." Jason turned my head to him again; this time, his thumb gently brushed the underside of my bottom lip.

I took a few deep breaths and nodded to him. "I'd really appreciate it if you didn't forget about me out there."

"Olive," he murmured, his head slightly tilted to the side. "I'm afraid it's too late for me to forget about you at all." My eyes dropped to the dimple.

Did he mean that?

While I was busy being stupid about a damn dimple, someone yanked open his door and leaned into the car.

"Mr. Thorn?"

"Come on," Jason grumbled as he pulled me by my hand. "Let's get this over with so you can see me kill a bunch of guys with no shirt on."

I closed my eyes and, with his help, stepped out.

All the screaming and yelling that erupted all around us as soon as they spotted their favorite actor forced me to open my eyes and face the music.

Jason's hand tightened around mine for a brief second as he searched for something in my eyes; whatever he saw must have satisfied him because he walked forward and gently tugged at my hand to follow him.

With my free hand, I furtively smoothed down my full skirt as I tried to keep up with him. Oh yeah, I was wearing a *freaking* white Burberry dress that I didn't even want to know the price of. Jason had had his own stylist, Jewel, choose something for me as well, and after going over my options, we had decided to go with the Burberry dress. It was the most beautiful thing I'd ever put on. The strapless bustier top fit my skin perfectly and did wonders for my breasts while the full skirt managed to make it look even more feminine. I never wanted to take it off, especially after I'd caught Jason sneaking peeks at my breasts more than a few times.

However, since he had such an anguished expression on his face whenever his eyes dropped lower than my chin, I couldn't be sure if he loved the dress as much as I did or hated it.

Next to Jason Thorn, who was wearing a black suit that made every single woman in his vicinity lose their mind a little, I'd actually felt adequate before we had left the hotel. But now…as my eyes landed on his costars and other actors and actresses that were either giving interviews to the press or posing for pictures, I felt as small as an ant among them.

When our feet hit the red carpet, Jason pulled me to his left, toward the screaming fans. I couldn't even guess the number of them. The barriers and the strategically placed security guards seemed to barely hold them back the way they pushed at each other to get closer to Jason. Some of them were crying.

Jason never let go of my hand as we walked toward them, but at some point a guy wearing a gray suit approached us to talk to him in quiet tones and then Megan was pulling me away from Jason, forcing me to drop his hand. Briefly, he glanced at me over his shoulder with a small frown on his face, but then had to face his fans and sign anything and everything they shoved at him.

A movement on Jason's left caught my eye and I saw a kid, barely older than eight or nine, running toward Jason. He had managed to slip away from one of the security guards, but before he could get to Jason, another one caught him. The commotion must have caught Jason's attention—as it did everyone else's since the kid was yelling and struggling to get out of his captor's hold—because he turned and motioned to the guy to let go of the kid. He kneeled in front of the boy when he ran to him. We couldn't hear what they were saying to each other, but the kid was beaming at Jason with barely contained excitement. He shoved something in his hand and Jason signed it with a smile on his face. The kid looked my way and said something to Jason that was funny enough to make him laugh. The kid dropped his eyes from me, but Jason caught my eye and sent me a wink as he messed up the kid's hair. The same security guard came and escorted the boy back to his dad. After that, he chatted some more and signed a few more arms.

When I thought he was finally done, he looked at me over his shoulder and motioned for me to come to his side.

I looked at Megan, but she had her back to me and was busy on her phone, so I shrugged and tentatively walked toward Jason. It was impossible to hear anything he was saying, but as I got closer, I saw that he was holding something thick in his hand. A book.

My freaking book.

Doing my best not to show my bafflement, I made it to his side and looked at him, at a loss as to why he wanted me there.

His warm hand touched my neck and he leaned down to whisper in my ear, "They want you to sign their book."

"Me?" I mouthed to him when he looked down at me.

He nodded, smiled, and handed me the book. Someone came to my side and handed me a pen. In a daze, I signed more than twenty books.

Twenty freaking books!

When Megan appeared at our side to tell Jason that we needed to keep moving, Jason grabbed my hand in his—which made everyone scream even louder—and we made our way across the carpet so the photographers could take Jason's photos.

There were so many flashes going off, so many people yelling Jason's name—*and* my name.

I felt like I was in a dream, or maybe it was a nightmare; I couldn't decide.

When we were standing right in front of the cameras, Jason's hand landed on my back and he pulled me closer to his front. Per Megan's instructions, I lifted my hand to show off the ring and put it on Jason's stomach—a hard stomach that contracted at my touch, a stomach I had eyed for a good amount of time, and maybe even touched once or twice while he was sleeping the night before.

Just when all the flashes were about to blind me for eternity, one of them yelled, "Jason! A kiss! One with a kiss!

I tried so, so hard to not react, to not grin like the Cheshire cat, but when Jason gazed down at me and I tilted my head up to meet his eyes, I had the biggest smile on my face.

While everyone around us was still yelling, Jason's hand touched my cheek and every single person around us disappeared for me. It was dead quiet in my mind. It was happening. I was seconds away from kissing my dream guy.

I watched his lips descend as my heart tried to force its way out of my chest. My little butterflies were getting ready for the takeoff of their life.

But…

But it didn't happen like it had happened in the dreams I'd had about Jason ever since I could remember. Not even close.

While I was waiting for the very best first kiss in the history of first kisses, Jason only gave me a peck. A freaking *peck!* His lips pressed against mine for only two seconds, three tops.

I felt cheated.

And, well, since I'd dreamed about kissing him for such a long time—*such* a long, long time—I had a hard time not showing the disappointment I felt on my face. For a second there—a very quick second—I might have scrunched up my nose in distaste right after he pulled away from me. Just as quickly, I put a smile on my lips and let him pull me away to another station where he would be giving short interviews to numerous media outlets.

Following Megan's instructions, I stood back a little and did my best to keep a genuine smile on my face.

I couldn't even fool myself into thinking he just didn't like PDA; the guy had been pictured in way worse situations. I couldn't even count how many photos I'd seen throughout the years where his tongue was down the throat of some actress or model.

Evidently, he really did see me as nothing more than a friend. Hell, even I could've done a much better job at kissing my friend.

"You're not smiling. Smile," Megan warned me from her spot next to me.

I showed her my teeth and she sighed, shaking her head.

When Jason was done with all the interviews, the time came for him to join his costars for the group shots.

Close to the finish line, right? After the most disappointing kiss in history, what else could happen that would ruin a beautiful night even more than it already had been?

Jennifer Widner could happen, folks. And she actually did happen. She appeared out of nowhere and took her place next to

Jason and their other costars. She could've stood next to any of the others, but, nope, she chose Jason, and she put her hand on his chest just like I had done minutes before.

Imagine my surprise when she caught my eye and winked at me.

I was standing way off to the side so I couldn't see Jason's face to tell if he had seen her wink. They posed for a ton of pictures and when Jason came back to my side, he still had his dimpled smile on his face.

Me? Not so much.

————

AT THE END of the night, after all the craziness had ended, we made it to our hotel room in one piece. I bid Megan a good night and thanked her for all her help. Without her firm instructions, I would've looked like a fish out of water, at least more than I already had.

After Jason and I entered our suite and he made sure to lock the door, I put a few paces between us and looked at him with a tired smile on my face. "It was a beautiful night, Jason. Thank you for everything." Not exactly sure what I should do, I put my hand on his arm, hesitated for a moment, and then leaned up to give him a soft kiss on his cheek.

When I backed away, his dimple was out to play, but I was done for the night. I didn't even have enough strength to appreciate the way he was looking at me, his eyes traveling my body from head to toe, or how good he looked with his shirtsleeves all rolled up, or how...the list went on. Reaching down, I pulled my heels off my feet and winced in pain.

My feet were gone. Dead.

"You never said what you thought about the movie."

"Oh, I didn't? Sorry. It was amazing. You were great. Thank you for bringing me here."

His smile brightened his face.

Lifting the shoes up in a wave as I backed up, I said, "I'm heading to bed, so goodnight. And again, thank you Jason." He'd had the security check every inch of the suite so I knew we were fan-free that night, which meant I had no reason not to sleep in my very own room.

His brows drew together. "You're going to bed, now?"

"Megan said our flight changed and we're leaving early tomorrow." I shrugged. "Also my feet are killing me, so yes, I'm ending the night." I gave him another small wave and turned around, but his voice stopped me before I could escape.

"You're sleeping in there?" His voice wasn't exactly harsh, but it wasn't as soft as it had been seconds before either.

I looked over my shoulder. "Yeah. Goodnight Jason."

Striding directly to the bathroom, I filled the magnificent clawfoot tub with hot water, took off my equally magnificent dress, and sighed with relief as soon as my toes sunk into the water.

———

IN THE MIDDLE of the night, I woke up when I felt something moving in my bed. For a second, I was confused, but then I realized it wasn't a dream. I screamed and tossed the covers at whoever was in my bed—as if that would be enough to scare away the intruder—and rolled away to jump down and somehow get to Jason.

When a strong hand landed on my stomach and dragged me back against a hard chest, I lost my breath.

"Stop yelling," Jason grumbled behind me.

"Jason?" I whispered. "Jason!"

My heart still beating against my throat, I slapped at his hand where it still laid on my stomach and yelled a bit more just for good measure.

"Are you crazy? I almost had a heart attack."

"How would I know you would wake up?"

"What do you mean *how would I know you would wake up?*" I tried to roll over to face him, but his arm tightened around my waist and drew me closer against him.

This time I lost my breath for an entirely different reason.

"Don't move. I'm trying to sleep."

"Oh, and what did it look like I was doing? Cartwheels?"

When he just grumbled under his breath and otherwise kept silent, I asked, "What are you doing here, Jason? Couldn't you have knocked and woken me up before you crawled into my bed? I thought one of your crazy fans was in bed with me, thinking I was you!"

"Well, it wasn't. It's just me. What the hell is that noise?"

"What? Oh, crackling fire and wind in the trees."

"Crackling fire and…wind…in the trees," he repeated.

"Yes." I turned my head to look at him over my shoulder. He was giving me a 'you're out of your goddamned mind' look. "What? It relaxes me before I fall asleep," I said, taking offense.

"Can you sleep without it?"

"Of course. I just like listening to it."

My body was all stiff, but his hand caressing my arm slowly helped me relax and settle back into him.

He put his chin on my shoulder and eyed my phone where it sat next to my pillow. His hot breath was tickling my neck, but for the most part I managed to stay still.

"The wind is kinda creepy, Olive."

"I can change it to rain."

Pressing his face deeper into my neck, he chuckled.

"Let's hear that one."

Quickly, I stopped the wind and changed it to 'rain on roof'.

He hummed to himself for a few seconds then approved. "I like this combo much better."

"There is waterfall or ocean, too."

"No, keep the rain and your crackling fire. Do you remember how you used to sit by your window and listen to the rain with your eyes closed?"

"Of course I do." But how did he?

"You always had a smile on your face when you did that, your mind miles away. Your mom used to get so frustrated with you when you walked out in the rain without an umbrella. You got sick every single time, but nothing could stop you."

"Yeah," I agreed in a thick voice. "And I remember you trying to stall her whenever you saw me trying to sneak out without her noticing."

"Well, it's hard to trick your mom. It's a two-man job."

We were silent for a while after that.

"I think the AC in my room is broken. I didn't see the need to call someone up just to check out what's wrong when we have another perfectly warm room."

"So…?"

"So, we have to share the bed for another night. You can go back to sleep now."

"I can still hear my heartbeat, Jason. I'm pretty sure I won't be going back to sleep any time soon."

"Let me see," he whispered, and suddenly his hand was moving upward from my stomach toward my heart.

Carefully skipping my boobs—*darn it!*—his hand rested over my heart.

"Hmm, you're right; I can feel your heartbeat."

I couldn't speak. No words whatsoever.

He took a deep breath against my neck, causing my entire body to shiver, and said, "Go to sleep, Olive." Then, finally, his hand moved away from my heart and went back to my stomach. Maybe a minute after that, his breathing evened out and he fell asleep.

Just like that.

I stayed awake for hours.

Engaged to a bad kisser?

Did you see the new photos of Hollywood's most talked about couple? While they were photographed all over the city last week and generally looked happy together, things seem to have taken a bad turn for Olive Taylor.

The new author and Hollywood's heartthrob attended Jason Thorn's latest movie premiere in London last night. While they both looked amazing together and stole their fans' hearts by signing everything that was handed to them, it all changed when it was time to pose for the cameras.

For days now, rumors have been swirling that the new couple is considering tying the knot after losing so many years that could've been spent together. In the second photo, you can clearly see that Miss Taylor is proudly sporting a diamond ring on her finger. We are thinking the rumors are true! How many of you ladies would die to be in her place?

But then, the unthinkable happens. When the couple is asked to share a kiss for a photo, Jason gives her a peck! A peck, people! The handsome star, who is known for his sexual prowess, who we've seen devour numerous women on the big screen, gives Miss Taylor only a peck! And the

funny thing is you can see the disappointment on her face
so clearly.
We were definitely expecting a much more heated kiss
from the couple, and considering the look on Olive's face
after the whole thing was over...dare we say Jason Thorn
is a good actor, but actually a bad kisser in real life?

CHAPTER TWENTY-TWO

OLIVE

It had been exactly a week and a half since we had returned from the movie premiere in London. A week and a half since all the tabloids made the picture of me—the one nobody could seem to stop talking about—their cover. While Jason never even mentioned the existence of it, Megan had been fuming. She had called me more than a few times just to make sure I was aware of how much I was screwing things up for Jason. After that specific conversation, I'd expected to get a call from the man himself where he would gently let me know that our fake wedding thing was off.

That call never came.

While we barely saw each other the week after getting home, I'd kept myself busy with packing and writing the first few pages of my new novel. As much as I was happy that my muse was back, I was just as unhappy about the fact that I couldn't tell my mom and dad or even Dylan about what was going on in my life. At first, they hadn't believed that something was going on between Jason and me and chose not to listen to the press, but after they saw the photos of the premiere, they had called and asked me point blank if everything was true. I hated lying to them, but I had no other option if I wanted a chance to make things real with Jason.

Needless to say, neither one of them were happy with me. While my dad only spoke to me for a few seconds, my mom was…she was sad and worried that I was making a mistake. Because the filming for *Soul Ache* was about to start, I couldn't even go to them until Jason had free time to come with me because there was no way I was facing them alone. No way in hell.

So, that morning, in Jason Thorn's millions of dollars' worth of Bel Air home, I had officially become Olive Thorn. Other than Lucy, Tom, and Megan, there were no witnesses to our holy matrimony. Even Char couldn't make it because she had a full day of exams.

Two hours after our 'wedding', Jason had left me with Lucy because he had to be on set for rehearsals and some other stuff. A while after that, Lucy had had to leave for a class.

Which left my newly married ass all alone in Jason's home. As the hours passed, I gave myself a tour of his house and happily discovered that he had a huge media room with incredibly comfortable leather seats. After walking around aimlessly, in and out of his house, I forced myself to sit down next to the pool with my laptop and get some words in.

When the sky started to darken and I was still alone, I decided that it would be a good idea to start celebrating my very own wedding day with a drink. Then one drink led to another, and then another.

I did awesome. Happy fucking honeymoon to me!

The next thing I knew I was dialing Lucy's number.

"Being Jason Thorn's wife is not"—I hiccupped—"as glamorous as I thought it would be."

"Are you drunk?" Lucy asked.

"So what? So what if I am? Were you having sex with Jameson? Because if you were, good for you. Good for everyone who is having sex. Technically it's my honeymoon, and do you know how much sex I'm having right now? Nada. Zilch. Exactly that much. Think about that. Your mind is blown, right?"

Lucy laughed for a good minute. "Yours sounds blown, all right," she said, still chuckling. "I think you should slow down on the drinks."

"You would think that, right? I mean, if Jason Thorn can't blow your mind, who the heck will? But is he here blowing my mind right now? Nope. My vagina is perfectly untouched by a Jason Thorn penis. Hell, even my lips are untouched."

"I thought he would come back by now." There was a rustling at the end of her line and she murmured something to someone.

"You were having sex with Jameson! I knew it! Everyone is having sex right now!"

"Do you want me to come? And just for the record, you horny newlywed, I wasn't having sex with Jameson. We were…we were just lying in bed. He is sleeping actually."

I sat up straighter and almost knocked down my champagne glass. "You're falling in love with him!"

"Okay, now you're just rambling nonsense. I'll be there as soon as I can."

"No," I whined, taking the last gulp of my champagne. "I wanna come to you. I'm seconds away from going to his room and just rubbing myself all over his sheets. I can't stay here for long."

"It sounds like you already did that."

"Not exactly. Soooo, would you like to tell me about how you are in love with Jameson but pretty much scared out of your mind to hope?"

Silence.

"Ok. Hold tight. I'm coming to get you."

———

"HE SMELLS SO, so good, Lucy. I smelled everything in his room. It was so, so good. Why don't you smell like him?" I leaned forward in her arms and tried to sniff her hair. "You still don't smell like him."

"I'm thinking that's a good thing right now. Try to stay still for a minute! We're gonna fall down the stairs then you'll never get to smell him again."

"I can't fall. I want to smell him and lick him all over."

"Good, then help me a little so we can get you up these last few steps and in a bed."

I hummed a song that was stuck in my head and managed to make it in front of our apartment's door with Lucy's help. "I did it!" I yelled, lifting up my arms. "I did it! Now, what do I win? One night with Jason?"

Lucy's hand clamped down on my mouth. "Be quiet for god's sake," she hissed, and instead of taking out her key, she knocked on the door.

Marcus opened it. "What is going on—"

"Marcus," I cried and threw myself in his arms.

Catching me at the last second, he glanced at Lucy before looking down at me.

"I got married," I announced as I shoved my ring in his face. "See?"

"I do see," he said, pulling me up in his arms as I started to slide down.

"What's wrong with her?" he asked to someone over my shoulder. I looked back and remembered that Lucy had brought me back home. Then I noticed that my hands were touching bare skin.

I frowned at Marcus' naked chest. "Why are you not wearing anything?"

"I think you lost the privilege to ask that, don't you think?"

My frown deepened. "Why should I lost privy-le…privilg—"

"Oh, stop it you two," Lucy exclaimed from behind my back. "Either help me get her in, or get out of our way so I can—"

Before she could finish her words, I was up and in Marcus' arms.

"Whoaaaa," I chuckled. "You never carried me before, Marky. Why didn't you ever carry me? I don't think I'm feeling so good," I added, resting my head on his shoulder.

Charlotte was leaning against her doorframe, her face unreadable. "Char, I missed you today," I said, holding out my hand to her, but she shook her head and closed her door.

"Where are you going?" asked Lucy, following us hurriedly. "Take her to my room."

"What's wrong with Char?" I asked, but both Marcus and Lucy ignored me.

"Marcus, are you hearing me?" she repeated.

Marcus opened his door, carried me to his bed, and gently placed me in the middle.

I curled into myself and murmured, "My stomach is doing something inside."

"What do you think you are doing, Marcus?"

"I'm taking care of her. Someone has to."

"What the hell do you think I was doing?"

"You're being too loud," I said, cringing and grabbing on to the sheets so I could stop spinning.

"Come on, Olive. Let's go to my room."

"Let her be," interjected Marcus. "Jameson is still in your room and Olive's room is practically empty. She needs to sleep it off. Where the hell is her so-called husband?"

"That's none of your concern, Marcus," I heard Lucy say.

Someone sat down beside me and started to brush the hair away from my face. It felt nice. Why couldn't Jason brush my hair away, too? It must've been Marcus. I couldn't remember Lucy having such big hands. "I think it is. Doesn't look like you are doing a very good job of looking after her, Lucy."

I groaned and turned my back to them. I was too tired to listen to them bicker.

CHAPTER TWENTY-THREE

JASON

Fuming, I stood in front of Olive's old roommate and ex-boyfriend, trying my best to not deck the guy.

"Get me Olive," I growled for the second time.

"She is not in a state to see you right now, man. I suggest you come back in the morning." He tried to close the door in my face.

I had come home late, only to find an empty bottle of champagne and Olive's laptop next to the pool, but no Olive.

When I'd tried to call her, I found her phone in her own room right across from mine. Worried out of my mind, I'd gone through her phone, called her friend Lucy, and learned that she was at their place.

I hit the door with my palm and forced him to open it. "Olive," I yelled into the apartment. Instead of Olive coming out, a sleepy-eyed Lucy appeared behind the douchebag.

"What's going on here? Jason? Are you here to get Olive?"

"Yes," I gritted through my teeth, keeping my eyes on Marcus. "Can you tell her that I'm here?"

Grabbing on to Marcus' arm, Lucy tried to pull him back, but he wasn't budging. That son of a bitch had his eyes on me, too.

"Have you lost your mind, Marcus? He is her husband for god's sake."

He gave an unamused laugh. "As if I would believe that was true after the way she came here."

My eyes flew to Lucy's with a different kind of worry. "Is Olive okay? Did something happen?"

"As if you care about her," Marcus spat.

Lucy's face softened. "She is fine, Jason. She just drank a little too much. She is sleeping it off, that's why I said on the phone that you could come and get her in the morning."

Fed up with the idiot, I bulldozed my way into their apartment.

"Hey!" he yelled after me.

Just come at me boy, I thought. *Come at me so I can take it out on you.*

"Where is she?" I asked, looking at Lucy.

Charlotte, the other roommate, was watching everything unfold calmly in front of an open doorway. I took a step toward her and she shook her head. "She is sleeping in Marcus' room."

I whirled on Marcus, my patience completely gone. "You son of a bitch! Did you touch her?!"

"What do you care? You're nothing to her." He raised his voice and puffed up his chest, coming toward me. Before I could reach him and mess up his pretty little face, Lucy grabbed my forearm.

"Stop it, both of you! He didn't, Jason. Jeez." She shot an annoyed look at Marcus. "No one did. I was sleeping next to her. Come on," she explained in a rush and pulled me toward another closed door.

My hands were itching to lay it on the guy, but I let Lucy's small frame pull me away from him.

I entered the room after her and saw Olive sleeping in the

middle of the bed, her legs pulled up into her stomach. All my anger melted off me and my heart settled down. I would have to sit down and think about what that meant.

Putting one knee on the bed, I slid my arms under her back and knees and lifted her up in my arms as gently as possible. I took a deep breath and caught her beautiful scent.

Her eyes blinked open and a sweet smile spread across her face. "Jason," she mumbled quietly. She rested her head against my chest and closed her eyes again.

She reeked of alcohol.

I cleared my throat to soften my tone. "It's me, sweetheart. I'm taking you home."

"I don't wanna go," she murmured. "We were having sex." She looped her arms around my neck more securely and pushed her face farther into my neck.

My body responded to her scent as it always seemed to do lately, but I shook it off. *Not here.*

My frown back in place, my gaze snapped back to Lucy to see her barely holding back her laughter.

"What the hell is she talking about?" I forced out with a growl.

"Nothing, nothing," she said hurriedly. "I'm assuming she was dreaming of you two having sex. She was blubbering about honeymoons on her way over here."

What?

"Oh."

Well, ok then.

Carrying her back to the living room, I saw Marcus waiting in front of the door, his hands crossed against his chest, his face dark with anger.

"Don't you *ever* get in my way again," I said in a low voice when I paused next to him.

"I don't care who the hell you are, but when you end this charade and leave her in a mess, I'll be the one taking care of her."

Lucy reached around him and opened the door for me, but I couldn't move from my spot. I was on the edge, having trouble just letting him go without doing some damage.

"You should take Olive home, Jason," Lucy said, still holding the door open for us. "She is shivering." I looked down at Olive and saw that her arms were covered in goose bumps.

Not meeting Marcus' gaze again, I said a quick thank you to Lucy and drove back home as fast as I could so I could get Olive back in her bed, where she belonged.

PARKING my car in the garage, I rested against my seat and let out a deep breath. Olive was curled up next to me, snoring softly. Rounding the car, I opened the door and called her name.

"Olive, we're home. Wake up sweetheart."

"Go away," she mumbled without even opening her eyes, keeping her back turned to me.

"Olive, baby, can you help me so we can get in the house and go to bed?"

No answer.

Ok then…

I leaned down and carefully cradled her in my arms again. She didn't even hesitate to put her arms around my neck and snuggle closer.

"You're so warm," she mumbled, her lips moving in a soft caress against the skin of my neck, causing me to grind my teeth together to keep myself from moaning or worse… A moment later, she fell asleep in my arms.

Getting a barely conscious Olive back in the house proved to be harder than I'd thought it would be. When I finally did manage to get us inside without any permanent damage, I faltered between the doors of our rooms. I should've put her on her own bed, but I wanted to keep an eye on her throughout the night, just in case she got worse. From what I could smell, she'd had more than just a bottle of champagne on her own.

When I put her on my bed, she didn't even open her eyes to see where she was. I reached out and switched on the small bedside lamp just so I could see if she was all right. The soft yellow light illuminated the room and helped me to see Olive's face more clearly. My eyes fell on her clothes, and I tried to decide if I should take them off. Deciding against it pretty quickly, I rubbed the back of my neck and let her be, heading to the bathroom to take a quick shower.

I returned to the room and found her trying to unbutton her jeans and not doing a very good job of it, though she had been successful with taking of her shirt—thankfully, her bra was still on. It was another lacy number where I could see through and make out her aroused nipples, but at that point anything was better than nothing.

"Olive, stop." I hurried to her side and put my hand on hers. "Stop."

A small line appeared between her brows and she squinted at me. "Hot. I want it off." For good measure, she kicked her legs and fumbled with the fly of her jeans.

I slapped my palm on my forehead and turned off the light before I reached for her jeans.

As my fingers made contact with her soft skin of her stomach, a tingle went through my spine and I had to close my eyes. My dick twitched in my briefs, cursing me.

I wholeheartedly agreed.

Now that she had decided to be helpful, she tilted up her hips into my hands and helped me ease the jeans off down her legs. I kept my eyes away from her body the whole time. To stay busy, I turned my back to her, folded her jeans, and put them on my dresser. Then I reached for the shirt she had thrown right across the room and folded that too.

When I faced the bed, I could easily make out Olive's form lying on her face right in the middle. Her panties were white lace too. They looked wonderful on her full, rounded ass. Nothing flat on my Olive. Nothing whatsoever.

For a moment, when I could finally peel my eyes away from her ass, I wondered if she enjoyed sleeping sprawled across the bed just to torture me, because it sure seemed like she did. I picked up an old shirt of mine from my closet to put on her. As hot as she seemed to think the room was, I didn't think she would be very happy to find herself in just her underwear when she woke up.

It wouldn't hurt me to have her covered up either.

Bringing back a glass of water from the kitchen, I woke her up so she could take a few sips. Instead of taking the glass from my hands, she closed her own over mine and drank it all in a few big gulps, all the while grumbling to herself.

As soon as she was done, she plopped onto the pillows again. After struggling with the covers, I managed to pull the shirt over her and sighed in relief.

That wasn't so hard now was it?

Getting into bed was much easier for me. I made sure to stay on the far side of the bed and kept my eyes on Olive to make sure she was still breathing. I must have fallen asleep because I jolted awake when I felt Olive's hair tickling my arm. When I looked down she was lying half over me and…was she…rubbing herself on my leg?

Christ!

I groaned and reached down to grab her thigh, but in a

maneuver you wouldn't expect from a drunk she had managed to climb onto my stomach.

"Olive," I hissed when I felt the dampness of her underwear on my lower stomach. Her eyes half open, she glanced down at me and drowsily asked, "Are we having sexy yet?"

Despite the dangerous situation I had found myself in, I chuckled and then let it turn into a groan when Olive's hips started to move over me. I tightened my fingers on her thighs and stopped her. If she did another downward move, my dick would be in hot water.

"Sweetheart, what are you doing?"

"I wanna consummate now."

I groaned louder and closed my eyes so I could focus for a second. Olive's small hands landed on my chest and she started to bunch up my shirt. "Off," she ordered.

"Nothing is coming off," I said, finally coming to my senses and gently tipping her off my body and back onto the bed. Instead of fighting me on it like I expected her to, she sighed and muttered, "I need it." Then she started to lift off her own shirt.

I gripped the hem and pulled it down. "Your clothes are staying on too, Olive."

"But I want it so much, Jason." She looked at me in the dark, her eyes glazed and her forehead puckered. Her hands let go of the shirt and found their way to my lips, then my cheeks. "I used to love watching you smile," she whispered, half closing her eyes as if she was imagining our childhood. Her face took on a wistful expression. "I used to look at you when I was sure no one would notice and just wait for it to appear. Your dimple, I mean. It made me so giddy. Will you show it to me, now? Lucy said I should lick it." She lifted her eyebrows. "Can I?"

Shaking my head, I smiled. "Sweetheart, you are drunk. How about we go to sleep?"

She huffed and punched the mattress lightly. "But I want…"

"What do you want?" I asked distractedly as I brushed away the strands of hair she was trying to blow away from her face.

"I want Jason." She uttered the words so softly and in such a way that it reminded me of a girl making a birthday wish, eyes closing tightly just before blowing out all the candles. Such an innocent and simple wish, yet all the more powerful to render someone speechless.

Then just like that, a switch went off and her voice turned husky. "I want to come." Whimpering softly, she lifted her hips off the bed.

"Olive, you have no idea what you're saying. Let's go to sleep so you can sober up, okay?"

"Can you give me my toy, Jason who is not Jason? I really need it." Before I could ask what the hell she was talking about she grabbed my wrist and pushed my hand into her underwear.

Death.

Pure, sweet death.

I was going to burn in flames, both in hell and in life.

I closed my eyes and tried to breathe through it, but it only made matters worse when I inhaled in her scent. Don't judge me —I did try to pull my hand away, but she was faster than me, and before I could react she flattened her hand over mine.

"I'm soaked," she moaned as she started to touch herself with my fingers.

"Olive," I hissed when I felt her wetness all over my fingers. "Olive, please stop." I tried to pull my hand away, but she held on to my wrist with her free hand to make sure it stayed where it was.

Pushing my forehead against her temple, I whispered. "Olive, you're killing me, sweetheart. Please, let my hand go."

God.

Her legs fell open and she pushed one of my fingers firmer against her clit.

Her scent was driving me crazy, her soft panting reaching right down to my dick as if she had her mouth wrapped around me. Pulling my hips back just in case she decided to go for my sweatpants and got ideas because I was hard as a rock, I jerked my hand away from her wetness before she could stop me again and brushed a kiss on her temple.

"You're still drunk, Olive. You don't know what you're doing."

Unexpectedly, she fully turned to me and buried her face against my throat, her weight forcing me to fall on my back. When I felt a wetness on my skin, I held her jaw back and looked at her face.

To my utter shock, she was silently crying.

"Baby, what's wrong?" I asked, clearing her tears with my thumbs.

Her beautiful eyes met mine and she broke my heart into very, very small pieces. "I just want to consummate so they won't take him away from me." She sniffled and hid her face against my neck again.

Jesus. How could she still be drunk off her ass? Exactly what had she had while I was gone, and for how long?

"Baby," I whispered, trying to calm her down.

I knew this wasn't my Olive talking, but if she hadn't been so drunk, we could've...hell...done something about this. Talk? Fuck? Whatever she needed.

"Can I have my toy now?" she asked, still sniffling.

Goddamnit!

Maybe she slept with a stuffed toy or something?

I had my fingers crossed, but...

"Is this toy you're asking for...is it something you use to make yourself come, sweetheart?"

Her tear-filled eyes met mine as she nodded and nibbled on her bottom lip.

There was no way I was going through her stuff to find a plastic dick. There was also no way in hell I was letting myself have her, no matter how much my dick disagreed with me.

"How about we cuddle?" I asked. Girls loved cuddling, didn't they? And the idea was very appealing to me too when the person I was going to cuddle was Olive.

"Okay," she murmured and turned in my arms.

I let out a breath. If she wasn't so drunk I would've loved nothing more than giving her what she needed, but not like this where she would barely remember we had done something.

She settled into my arms a little more heavily, no doubt sleep slow claiming her. I wrapped my arms tighter around her and breathed her in.

Then I brushed another lingering kiss on her temple and let her curl into me. I glanced down at her and her eyes were closed. I closed mine too and relaxed. Soon, her breathing evened out and she fell asleep in my arms.

It had been a long time since I'd felt the way Olive was making me feel—*if* there had ever been a time...

I'd missed something. I'd missed what was happening between us. She wasn't Dylan's sister in my eyes any more. She was my Olive, just like the very first day we'd met. And now she was my wife.

Every time she looked into my eyes with her heart wide open, she was pulling me in deeper. As much as this whole thing had started as a charade, I didn't know if I would be able to let her go when the time came.

I curled myself around her small frame and tucked her closer against my burning body. It wasn't enough. Slipping my arm under her head, I pulled one of her legs over my thigh and made sure she would stay just like that.

With a soft smile on my face, I whispered, "Sweet dreams, wife."

It took a moment for that single word to hit me in the gut.

It took another to feel how right it sounded.

It was a shame she wouldn't remember anything past the point of me carrying her into her new home when she woke up the next morning.

CHAPTER TWENTY-FOUR

OLIVE

"How could you not tell me this before today?"

"Megan sprung it on me at the very last minute, Olive. Don't worry, it'll be fun. You'll like it."

"Are you sure? Are you very sure that I will like it, Jason?" I narrowed my eyes at him and watched his lips twitch as he focused on something on his phone. I heard a chuckle come from beside me so I turned my gaze to Alvin and lifted a brow.

I had met Jason's assistant just a few days before when we'd literally run into each other at the house. I didn't know much about him, but he seemed to be an okay guy. He was definitely on top of everything. From what I had seen for the past few days, he was practically running Jason's life. Kudos to him.

"Did you know?" I asked him.

"Of course he knew, Olive. He arranges my schedule."

"What the boss says," Alvin agreed with him.

"Great. Awesome. Neither one of you thought it would be helpful to mention ahead of time that I'd be in a magazine shoot. As in, maybe, I don't know, a few days *before?*" I kept fidgeting with my hands.

"Stop fidgeting. Other than making you freak out like you are doing right now, how would it have been helpful?" asked Jason.

I gave him a disbelieving look. "If I could've started freaking out a few days before, right now I would be much calmer, Jason. Also, doesn't Megan need to instruct me or rehabilitate me or some crap like that? How am I supposed to know what I can say and what I can't?"

He finally lifted his eyes to meet my gaze. "You don't need instructions for a photo shoot, Olive. Just be yourself, and I'll handle the rest of it."

Photo shoot. Every time I heard the word, I started shaking all over again.

Apparently, Megan's idea of announcing our happy marriage to the world was to announce it through the most fucking popular women's magazine on the planet. I learned that there had been a talk of doing a live interview, but thankfully that idea hadn't taken hold. A photo shoot was the lesser evil in my book, but it didn't mean I was over the moon with that outcome either, especially when I learned about it the morning of.

"We're here," Alvin announced as our car stopped in front of a relatively small industrial building.

I released a big breath and exited the car after them.

"Holy crap!" I whispered when we stepped inside the building. It was a fully furnished loft, and it looked spectacular—apart from all the people running around, that is. As I took in everything around me, I forgot all about my nervousness. Putting his hand on the small of my back, Jason guided me farther in.

Seconds later, before I could take in my fill, Alvin was walking toward us with quick steps and a woman by his side.

When had he even left our side?

I forgot all about the loft and focused on the woman next to him. By the time they were standing in front of us, she had practically eye-fucked Jason and had a salacious grin on her face.

"Hello, Mr. Thorn." Jason reached for the woman's outstretched hand and shook it.

"Please, call me Jason. It's Julie, right?"

Her grin turned brighter when she realized Jason remembered her name.

She nodded. "Yes. We are so excited to work with you today."

Finally, they let go of their hands and she continued. "Our makeup and hair stations are ready for the both of you. As soon as you're ready we can begin the shoot and then the interview will take place on the first floor, after we have the shots."

I cleared my throat and caught her attention.

At last.

Her cheeks flushed, but only slightly. "Nice to meet you, Olive. I'm Julie."

I shook her hand and tried to give her a genuine smile. "Nice to meet you, too, Julie."

She clapped her hands once. "Okay. Let me take you to hair and makeup, then I'll introduce you to our photographer." She was still talking directly to Jason. Apparently, I was just an afterthought.

Jason grabbed my hand and my heart gave a small jump. I was getting used to the annoying thing catching me off guard; I kept telling myself that he was just a guy, but the heart wants what it wants, right? Well, mine was dead set on throwing itself at Jason's feet until he picked it up for himself.

Loser heart of mine.

I resisted the urge to roll my eyes and trailed after them.

Almost two freaking hours later, we were finally ready. Thankfully, they kept my makeup on the lighter side, murmuring that they were after a natural look since I was already a 'nobody'. Okay, maybe they didn't use exactly those words, but, trust me, the meaning was there.

Whatever. I rocked the natural look.

Then started the wardrobe decisions. There were racks of clothing. *Racks*. They spent more than an hour deciding on the right wardrobe for us. At one point, they asked me if I'd be okay with being covered up in a white sheet while Jason was half naked, but Jason vetoed that idea before I could. Considering they ended up choosing only three outfits, the whole process seemed a bit excessive to me. Then again, what did I know?

The first outfit we all agreed on was a dress similar to the one I'd worn at the London premiere. Nothing too risqué, not too much cleavage, not too much legs, but definitely a little playful. The second one was for a casual look they were going for with black jeans and a white t-shirt that would be tied at the back, showcasing a bit of my stomach.

The third outfit...that one was my favorite of them all. It was white, backless, had cutouts in the front, and was very formfitting.

It was perfection.

How it would look on me? I had no idea.

They wanted me in the third one first. A girl from the team came to my side and hurriedly showed me into a makeshift fitting room where I could change into the dress.

I got into the dress, all right, but I decided not to go back out there. While the dress looked amazing on the hanger, on me...it was too much. The back was almost showing my butt crack, and the front...well, the front was showing too much breast without showing too much skin. When I had asked for the bra, the girl had just shaken her head. I could almost make out my nipples.

"Olive?" Jason's voice came from right outside. "You ready?"

"Jason," I whispered, crossing my arms against my chest as if he could see through the thick curtain. If he got a look at them, I knew my nipples would give him a show. "I can't go out there like this."

"What do you mean like this?"

"I mean–"

The beige curtain parted and Jason walked straight into me.

"Whoaa," he said, grabbing on to my shoulders as I wobbled. Once we were okay to stand on our own, he let go of my shoulders and took a step back. "What's wrong?"

"Jason," I started miserably, my face falling. "It's too much. They won't give me a bra and my breasts are..." I opened my arms to give him a look and his eyes bulged.

"Whoaa," he said again, his eyes getting bigger.

"Yes, exactly. And then my back..." I turned and looked at him over my shoulder. "It looks so bad on me."

By then his brows were up to his hairline and his eyes were glued to my ass.

"My ass looks huge, doesn't it? Jason, please. I don't wanna do this. I'm not cut out for this."

When his eyes stayed on my ass and he started rubbing his forehead, I faced him again and pulled on the long sleeves of my dress.

"Christ," he said.

"Christ, what? What?!" I raised my voice. "They'll make fun of me. I'm not fat. It's just this dress..."

His eyes finally met mine and he tilted his head. "What are you talking about Olive?"

I rubbed my eyes. "You look like that," I explained, gesturing to his body, then to mine. "And I look like this..." I could feel the tears gathering in my eyes.

Did he need more explaining?

His voice gentled. "Sweetheart, I'll ask again. What are you talking about? You look...you look fucking stunning. If I could, I would..." His eyes dropped down to my breasts, but then quickly back up. He took a step toward me and held my face in his hands. "Don't get me wrong, I'm not happy about the dress either, but I'm afraid it's not for the same reasons. I don't want anyone to see you in this." Another glance at my chest. "It's a good thing there are mostly women out there. I'll go crazy if they spend another hour choosing another outfit. What do you say we go out there, give them a few good shots, and call it a day, huh? Then we can meet your friends and head to the party. You were looking forward to that, remember? The faster we wrap this up here, the faster we'll get to your friends."

With my freak out, the small party had completely slipped my mind. The production company had closed down a bar for that night so the cast and crew could get together and mingle before the filming started a few days later. I was assuming most of them already knew each other, but when Jason asked if I wanted to go and maybe take the girls with me, I'd jumped at the idea.

"You promise I don't look that bad?"

Something flashed in his eyes and his voice was gruff when he answered. "Promise."

He held out his hand for me and I took it without hesitation.

"We'll start the shoot on the second floor," the photographer, Amelie, said once we were by her side. "Then depending on the shots, we'll take a few down here or maybe on the stairs. We'll see how it goes."

Jason nodded his agreement and guided me toward the stairs with his hand on the bare skin of my back. The way my entire body ached when he was touching me…it was something else.

Amelie and her small team went ahead of us, and I stopped once we reached the bottom of the stairs.

"Jason," I whispered and tugged at his hand to get his attention before he could start climbing up. There was something different in his eyes when he was looking at me, something that was making my heart do funny things, but I brushed it away. "If you don't want me to flash Alvin and everyone who is still downstairs, there is no way I can go up these stairs with this dress. Unless I bunch it up and—"

Without a warning, Jason leaned down and lifted me up in his arms. I was too late to hold back my scream as he started up the stairs. My hands flew to my back to make sure everything was covered, but Jason's forearm was already taking care of that little problem.

Everyone was looking at us—even Alvin, who was trailing behind us, had a small smirk playing on his lips as I clung to Jason's shoulders. Taking advantage of the situation, I closed my eyes and rested my forehead against his warm neck. It was all I could do to not trace his bulging biceps with my fingers. Before I could savor the moment, we were at the top of the stairs and he gently put me back on my feet. I swore I could hear every woman in the loft release a sigh and fall a little bit more in love with my husband.

Jason cleared his throat and distractedly reached for my hand again.

"Okay. I want you guys in front of this wall," Amelie said, placing us in front of the concrete wall.

More blinding lights, great.

Taking our place, I looked at Amelie for more instructions, but what did she do? She lifted her camera and started taking pictures. Baffled, I looked up at Jason and he smiled at me.

"What am I supposed to do?" I hissed at Jason. I tried to force my lips into a smile as I looked at the camera, but I could only guess how awful it looked.

Then Jason's lips were at my ear and he whispered, "You're supposed to love me, my beautiful wife."

Tingles...

My mouth dropped open, but Jason's expression didn't even waver. His eyes on me, he leaned against the concrete wall and pulled me flush against his chest, my front to his front. Now everyone had a clear look at my barely covered ass and naked back, but at Jason's words I'd already forgotten all about that.

"What?" I whispered, keeping my eyes on his face.

"Perfect," the photographer announced from somewhere behind me. "I want to capture your natural chemistry. Please, Olive, try to relax a bit more and forget about us."

Be quiet lady.

Jason buried his face in my neck and spoke softly—only for my ears. "They have no idea that we're married, but they know we're engaged." He lifted his face from my neck and looked into my eyes. "You should look at me like you love me, Olive, the way I'm looking at you."

Say what?

Had he lost his mind in the small amount of time it had taken him to get dressed in a white shirt and black slacks?

He lifted his eyes from mine and looked over my head. "Amelie, is it okay if you give us a few seconds?"

The clicking stopped.

Jason kissed my nose. "You'll have to be a little more convincing if we want them to think we are in love. I'll have to... touch you."

"Touch me?" I squeaked.

His eyes dropped to my lips and he nodded. "And you'll have to touch me like you actually like me." Reaching down, he took my hand and put it on his chest.

"Of course. You're right," I said, barely recognizing my own voice.

"It'll be over soon. You won't suffer for too long, don't worry."

"Sure. No suffering. Over soon. Got it."

"You ready?"

I relaxed my shoulders and nodded. Act and look like I loved him? *Child's play.*

When he gave the okay, the shoot started up again.

Jason straightened from the wall and took me with him. His

hand still on my back, he kept me close to his body, my breasts properly squished between us.

"Olive, can you look at the camera while Jason is focusing on you?"

I took my eyes off Jason and looked at the damn camera.

"Great. Now place your hands on his chest and slightly lean into him."

I was already plastered to the guy, how was I supposed to *lean* into him?

I chanced a glance at Jason and my heart stuttered. Was this how he would look at me if he was in love? His eyes heated, his lips slightly parted, his breathing uneven.

I closed my eyes and sucked in a breath. I could do this. I could just let myself enjoy his closeness without messing this whole thing up.

I wanted to play, too.

Not even hearing what Amelie was saying, I slowly slid my hand up from his chest and ghosted my fingers over his dark stubble, right where his dimple was hiding. His eyes darkened, and I was pulled even more firmly against his chest.

Whoa! My nipples liked that very much.

To his questioning look, I said, "I want to play, too."

I rose on my tiptoes and stopped when I was a breath away from Jason's lips. "Do I look like I'm in love with you?" I asked quietly, my eyes firmly focused on his parted lips.

Take it. My lips are right there. Kiss me. Just once.

He didn't.

Keeping his heated gaze on mine, he kissed the corner of my lips. "We look like we're crazy for each other," he whispered, his hand tightening at my back. His head tilted forward and his lips ghosted on my throat. "We look like we can't bear to take our hands off of each other."

With a quick maneuver, he turned me against the wall and rested his forehead against mine. I hissed and bit my lip when the cold concrete met my bare skin. Arching my back, I rounded my arms around his neck and made sure to push my breasts against his chest.

Amelie was to our right, making sure to capture every intimate moment.

What did *she* see through the lens? Could she see that we were only playing?

His hand curled around my waist and he gave me a smirk right before he pulled my lower half against his own. Now, it was only my head pressed against the wall.

When I felt his…hard on…cock…penis…dangly bits (as Lucy would say)…I groaned and closed my eyes.

So he wasn't exactly oblivious to me. That could count as a good start, right? I could work with that.

"We look like we are about to fuck each other," he whispered into my ear.

My eyes closed on their own and I kissed his cheek, right where his dimple was; I knew I could find it even when my eyes were closed. "You're fucking me right now, Jason."

Because he was. He might as well have pulled my dress up and entered me right there, right in front of everybody. My body was sure as hell ready to take him.

He nipped my chin with his teeth—not too soft, not too hard —and I sucked in a breath. He drew his head back and ordered me to open my eyes in a husky voice. I did as I was told.

Because I was a good girl like that.

What I saw in his eyes… Everything around us melted away. All the lights, Amelie, Alvin, every single person in the building melted away and it was just us. It was just *my* Jason and me. Not the movie star, not Jason Thorn whom every woman was salivating for. Right at that moment, he was just mine.

My dream boy.

My childhood crush.

My first love.

My only love.

And now my pretend husband.

An eternity passed.

I bit my bottom lip.

His eyes flared. "Is it that good, Olive?" His eyes held me captive just as much as his body did.

"The best," I whispered achingly.

Slowly he lowered his head again and captured my bottom lip between his lips. Then I felt his tongue gently licking that said bottom lip.

Please, insert another one of those 'My body is ready gifs'. Holy moly!

"Place your hands on his chest," whispered Amelie next to us.

Holy shit! Where had she come from? Had she heard us?

I didn't even care, just did as I was told. I slid my hands down from his neck, making sure that my fingertips grazed his skin beneath his collar and stopped when I felt his erratic heartbeats.

I heard a few more clicks.

"That was amazing guys. Wardrobe change," Amelie announced beside us, breaking our connection. I was still in his arms, he still hadn't let me go, but he eased himself off of me. I swallowed and Jason's eyes slowly cooled down.

Damn, but he was a good actor.

The same girl came and swept me away for a wardrobe change, which was probably for the best.

The rest of the photo shoot was tamer, and instead of going at it on our own, both Jason and I followed Amelie's instructions. It felt safer to do so. I got a forehead kiss, and another one on my cheek.

When we sat down for the interview and told them that we were actually married, the looks on their faces were priceless.

CHAPTER TWENTY-FIVE

JASON

We had a quick dinner where Lucy and Olive managed to make me laugh multiple times with their stories before we headed to the bar where the cast and crew were meeting up. More than a party, it was a way to reconnect with each other and get to know the new people before filming ate up all our time. If Olive was sad that Charlotte couldn't make it, she didn't show it, but I could see that something about her friend's absence in her life was troubling her. I didn't ask questions.

While Lucy had preferred jeans and some number with a lot of cleavage, Olive was wearing a sparkly, metallic gray skirt with a casual white shirt. Her hair was still damp from the shower she had taken after the shoot and she barely had any makeup on, and she looked perfect in my eyes.

Still reeling from our photo shoot, I was having trouble looking away from her. Every little detail seemed to matter somehow. The way her cheeks were flushed from laughing so much, the way I caught her looking at me under her lashes, the way her eyes sparkled whenever I reached out to hold her hand. It was becoming impossible to not notice every little thing about her.

Impossible to not like everything I was seeing.

I had been forcing myself to sleep in my own room ever since she had cried in my arms before coming on my fingers that night, but my patience was starting to wear thin.

I was seconds away from prying her legs open and taking her for myself. Every innocent look, every innocent touch, every secret smile…everything just pushed us closer to our inevitable.

Chugging down my second beer of the night, I kept track of Olive and Lucy from the corner of my eye. I wanted to give her alone time with her friend because even I could see how much they were missing each other. They hadn't stop talking ever since Lucy had stepped foot in the car. I hadn't meant for my schedule to keep her away from her friends, but in my line of work, you got used to not having your freedom.

They were doing tequila shots and chasing them with beers. She didn't look like she was drunk, and she certainly wasn't acting like it, but I couldn't be sure. If they had another round of shots, I was going to interfere. As much as I would have loved to deal with drunk Olive again, I wanted her to be stone cold sober when we got back home.

An hour into the party, a few of the crew members had decided to set up the karaoke machine and proceeded to sing their hearts out, becoming the night's de facto entertainment. Every now and then, they were hopping back onto the stage to torture everyone's ears. Other than them, no one else had picked up the mic, which was a blessing if you asked me.

I was sitting at the bar with the assistant director, Tyler Cameron, a guy I had worked with before and respected, when I first heard Olive's voice through the speakers.

"Hello everyone, I'm Olive." She coughed and tapped the mic with her finger.

Someone let out a loud whistle.

"I believe that's your wife, Jason," Tyler said, looking over his shoulder. He was the first guy at the party that I'd told that we were married. Tyler wasn't a guy who would repeat it to anyone else, especially after I'd asked him not to.

Wife. Yes. Right. I was married.

I turned in my seat to face the stage. "That she is," I said, my eyes taking in the curves of her body. Leaning back, I rested my elbow on the bar and took a gulp of my beer.

There was a smile in her voice when she said, "I just lost a bet to my friend Lucy there." She pointed to a beaming Lucy and got a whistle from her. "So as the loser, I'm supposed to make your ears hurt for a little while. I hope you can bear with me. It's a slow one, so you should be okay."

"Is her voice any good? I don't think I can handle any more screeching for the night," Tyler said as he gave his full attention to Olive.

"Oh, she's good. Don't worry."

"You look okay, Jason," he said, eyeing me cautiously before Olive started her song.

I took my eyes away from Olive as she tried to get on the barstool. "What do you mean?" I asked.

"I know better than to believe anything I read in the tabloids, but after all those photos and videos…well, you looked like you were a bomb ready to go off at the wrong move. I'm glad you're back with us, and if she is the reason…well, good for you."

Instead of answering him, I grunted and gave all my attention back to Olive.

As always, she hadn't been able to get on the barstool, so when she started Ed Sheeran's song "Kiss Me", she was standing up, one hand wrapped tightly around the mic, the other resting on the barstool.

After a while, when the song pitched higher and her sweet voice charged through the space, everyone seemed to be shocked into silence. Tyler spoke up again. "She seems to be good at a lot of stuff, your wife."

I nodded; that was all I could manage at that moment.

Somewhere in the middle of the song, after her eyes had finally found mine in the crowd, her voice turned soft and husky as she gently ordered me to kiss her. I held her eyes because I needed that connection since it felt like we were busy falling in love with each other. She was seeing me, and maybe for the first time, I was seeing her too. Her voice called to me as much as her eyes did, but then she hid those beautiful eyes from me, and I found myself crossing the room to get to her.

I wanted her to look at me.

I wanted her to see *me* when I was kissing her.

And I needed her to kiss me back.

When the song ended and she opened her eyes, I was standing right in front of her. She smiled at me as if she'd known she would find me there waiting for her.

Taking another step, I closed the space between us. Prying the mic out of her hands, I laid it on the barstool. My hand curled around her neck and I asked, "Do you see *me*, Olive?"

The question was important to me, her answer even more so. It wouldn't be the movie star Jason Thorn kissing her into oblivion in a few seconds. It would be me. Jason. Her friend. The man who wanted to make her his.

A shiver went through her body as she lifted a shaky hand to put on my cheek. Her voice was nothing more than a whisper when she answered me. "I've always seen just you, Jason."

Then my lips were on hers, and her lips were on mine. We kissed long enough to cover years. In front of everyone, her lips became mine and I took her breath for myself, because I needed it more than she did.

I was aware of the whistles and all the applause, but I couldn't hear, couldn't feel anything beyond the woman in my arms. In my mind, it was just the two of us. Standing in the middle of a dark room, we were in each other's arms, where we had locked ourselves in and tossed away the key without a second thought. She tilted her head and my tongue slid deeper into her mouth.

It wasn't enough.

Burning with the need to consume her, I gripped her waist and leaned my body over hers, forcing her to arch her back, and kissed her more desperately.

Harder.

Deeper.

I put everything I'd started to feel for her in those past few weeks into the kiss and offered it back to her.

Our first kiss.

I wanted it to be good for her, change her world in some way. I wanted it to be her best first kiss of all the first kisses she had experienced.

It was my first time touching her heart after all; she needed to remember every second of it.

Her arms went around my neck and her fingers slid into my hair.

I groaned.

She whimpered into me, her body shaking with fine tremors.

She would remember it all.

When I wanted more from her, I slid my hand up and reached for her ponytail to pull her head back, just enough so she could catch her breath while I kissed the edges of her mouth where she hid those secret smiles, the ones she saved for when she was writing on her laptop, lost in a different world she was creating from the start, brick by brick. I wanted to own those secret smiles just as much I wanted to own her beautiful heart. I wanted to be the reason for their existence.

When she ignored everyone and captured my mouth for herself, I went willingly, giving her more of my tongue and taking just as much from her.

Then I kissed her again.

And again.

And again.

And again.

I kept one of my hands on the back of her head and let the other one slowly cup her ass so I could pull her more firmly against my rapidly lengthening and throbbing cock.

If we hadn't been clinging to each other, the hunger I felt for her, the way my world was spinning…it would have brought me down to my knees.

My heart was ready to be hers if she wanted to take it for herself and keep it for an eternity.

I couldn't stop.

Not when my body was aching to feel her hands on me.

Not when her mouth was giving me something I was desperate to have from her and only her, even though I hadn't realized I needed it.

Especially not when she was clinging to me as if I was breathing life into her.

Then she was pulling away and looking at me with lust and a little bit of surprise in her eyes.

"Hello," she whispered hoarsely. I nipped at her lips and she gave me one of her secret smiles.

My first one.

"You sure took your time," she said, hiding her face against my neck as soon as the words left her delectable mouth. Her warm breath was whispering her longing against my skin.

Ignoring the room full of people around us, I asked, "You've been waiting for me to kiss you?"

She came out from hiding and looked into my eyes with the sweetest grin on her face. "Ever since I was a little girl." Kissing me on the cheek, she added, "Thank you for making my dream come true."

My heart ached with love for a little girl who in some ways

had always belonged to me. "Was it worth the wait?" I asked, my voice gruff, my heart thundering in my chest.

She scrunched up her nose, her eyes focused on my lips. "The jury is still out. You think we can try again, maybe?"

"Guys?" Lucy whispered urgently, just below the stage.

Olive stiffened in my arms for a moment as if she'd just remembered the bar full of people we were giving a show, but I caressed her back and she melted against me. Then we both glanced at Lucy.

"I'm fucking loving what is going on here"—she motioned between Olive and me—"but people have been filming the whole thing. Since you look like you're ready to go at each other on stage, I thought maybe you'd want to know before you start losing your clothes."

Shit!

"We should leave," I said to Olive and quickly got her down off the stage. No matter how quickly we left, I knew we would be the talk of the night. With the videos and the news of our marriage, maybe even more so in the coming days.

CHAPTER TWENTY-SIX

OLIVE

I let Jason pull me behind him as we exited the bar and came face to face with a handful of paparazzi swarming us. The biggest grin I'd ever sported in my life fell off my face and I reached for Lucy's hand so she wouldn't fall behind as the flashes started to go off inches away from our faces. Jason's hand tightened on mine and he slowed his pace, falling a step behind us to herd us toward the private parking lot. I glanced at Lucy and saw that she was keeping her eyes down and trying to keep up with our almost running pace in her spiked high heels.

The paps kept asking me questions instead of Jason, and I felt my panic spike when they started to close in on us. When one of them—a blond guy with the complete surfer look—got a little too close for my comfort and caused me to almost knock Lucy down in my haste to get away from him, Jason let go of my hand and shoved the paparazzo with a not-so-gentle push on his shoulder. I let Lucy pull me closer, but Jason had stopped walking to face the man, so we had to stop, too.

"Don't put your hands on me, man," the guy said with a half growl as he lowered his camera. "Just doing my job here and taking a few pics of the pretty ladies."

Was he *goading* Jason?

"I don't care what the fuck your job is. I don't want you getting in her face."

I curled my hand around Jason's arm and tried to force him to keep walking before things escalated between them.

The jerk smirked and said, "Ease up man, maybe she *needs* someone to get in her face. I hear you're not quite doing it for her."

A few of the others let out low chuckles and kept taping the whole thing. They were eating it all up. Jason took a step forward, and then another as his muscles kept tensing underneath my hand where I was trying not so successfully to hold him back.

"Olive, do something or he's going to lose it," Lucy murmured urgently in my ear.

"Jason," I said sharply when I saw his hands had balled into fists. "We need to go."

His eyes still on the smirking idiot and his jaw set, he gave me a sharp nod and started forward again. The paps kept following us and even though they were keeping their distance this time around, the questions kept circling around my reaction to his lackluster kiss at the premiere.

I was half tempted to stop walking and just fling myself in his arms so we could have a repeat of our first kiss—obviously the one we'd just had that night, because there was no way I was accepting the premiere kiss as my first from him—and shut them the hell up, but getting out of there as fast as possible seemed like a better idea.

Maybe I'd have a chance to maul him in public some other time?

Reaching the car and driving away from the small crowd didn't help Jason loosen up at all. As much as Lucy did her best to lighten our moods, Jason didn't utter more than a few words.

As soon as we dropped Lucy off, Jason reached for his phone and called his publicist without speaking a word to me.

"Megan. Yeah. Sorry for interrupting. I'm calling to give you a heads up. A few people from the crew took videos of Olive and me kissing on stage. Yeah, we were at the crew party. Fine."

I quickly realized that I didn't like them doing damage control about something that was so damn near magical to me. Rubbing my hands on my thighs, I turned my head and watched the cars passing by us.

I wondered where they were going, who they were going to reach at the end of their journey. Maybe they weren't going anywhere, just sailing through life.

You're not even making any sense, Olive. Shut up your babbling mind.

"Yeah, I know," Jason clipped. "We didn't promise exclusivity to the magazine with the marriage thing. Sure. Go ahead and make a comment on the videos then. No. That's not all."

He paused before letting out a big sigh. I felt like an intruder listening in on their conversation, but it wasn't like I could get away to give them privacy either.

The best day of my life was slowly being ruined by damage control.

"Someone must have tipped off the paps because a small group of them were waiting for us when we left early. One of them got a little too close to Olive so I gave him a shove."

I closed my eyes and rested my head on the window.

"No. He damn near tripped her," Jason shouted suddenly. Despite being right next to him, I couldn't hear what Megan was saying. I could hear her rising voice all right, but I couldn't make out her words.

"I'm not apologizing," Jason growled at her. "I won't have anyone crowd her just because she is too polite to tell them to back off. I called to give you a heads up. Now you know. Do whatever you want with it."

With those last words, he hung up on her.

For the rest of the ride, he didn't speak to me, so I didn't think it would be a good idea to force a conversation on him. Maybe he was already regretting kissing me? Or maybe he had been playing and I was too dense to notice we were acting? Could he be that cruel? Or maybe he was angry about the paps mentioning the photo from the premiere that made so many headlines...

If he was angry about that, I didn't know how to fix it. I'd waited for him to say something about it the day the picture had gone online, but I was too chicken shit to mention it on my own. When he didn't bring it up and chose to act like nothing was wrong...well, why poke the bear right? However, maybe if I apologized, he would soften at least enough to speak again.

Gaah... He was making both my heart and my head hurt with his loud silence.

We spotted the paparazzi lying in wait in front of his house the moment he turned the corner onto his street.

"Damn it!" Jason growled, speeding up toward the gate before they could get between the car and the gate and block our entrance.

I shielded my face with my hand as they started to light up their flashes to get a glimpse into the car. I had no idea if they could see through the black windows or not, but in any case I wasn't in the mood to force a smile.

Jason managed to get us in without any problems.

"Either there is something new going on that we don't know about, or they know we're married," Jason said as he drove the car up the driveway.

Soundlessly, I nodded in agreement.

After the short ride up, when we were safely tucked away from unwanted eyes, I jumped out as soon as the car was parked.

Jason had given me my own key to the house, but I still waited for him to let us in. No matter what he said, this little palace was his, not mine. I was more like a glorified roommate than a wife.

When Jason came up next to me, I avoided eye contact and waited for him to unlock the door.

Truth be told, I had planned to run to my room and hide there for a few months, but as soon as we walked in and Jason closed the door behind us, he grabbed my hand and pinned me to the wall.

My breath came out in a whoosh as my back hit the wall, hard.

"Jason," I gasped, shocked.

He captured my face in his hands and my heart skyrocketed when I saw the look on his face.

"Do it again," he growled.

My eyes on his, my breathing hard, I quietly asked, "Do what, Jason?"

"Kiss me like that. Again." It almost sounded like a threat.

I swallowed and looked down at his lips. "That wasn't me," I whispered, my voice barely functioning. "You kissed *me*." I fisted my hands and pressed them against the wall. My body was shaking with years of want and need for him.

God, I'd wanted this boy to look at me like he was looking at me at that moment ever since I'd learned about how a boy should kiss a girl. He was my perfect guy.

"Oh, no, sweetheart," he said as he ran his nose against my neck, breathing me in. *He* was breathing *me* in! "That was all you."

His lips ghosted over mine and I took a quick, sharp breath. When he backed off an inch or two, taking his warmth away, I found myself going after him like a puppet being played.

He tilted his head. "Kiss me, Olive," he repeated again, his eyes locked on mine.

Starved for him, I launched myself into his arms. My arms went around his neck and I roughly pulled him down to my lips. That was all the invitation he needed. He pushed me back against the wall and let me take what I wanted.

When I tilted my head to deepen the kiss and tasted his tongue on mine, he groaned. Bending down, his hand reached under my skirt for the curve of my ass and he hoisted me up against the wall.

I squealed into his mouth, but he didn't break our kiss. That was the point where he took over and gave me something I'd never had with any other guy.

I wrapped my legs around his waist and held on tighter, threading my fingers into his hair and pulling on them slightly.

He groaned, a sound that was so rough and delicious that it vibrated through me and caused even more heat to pool between my legs, an area that was now in close contact with his jean-clad cock. I tightened my legs around him, dying to get a little more friction against his hardness. As if he knew what I needed, his hands tightened on my ass and he thrust his hips right where I needed him. *Pronto!*

He broke our kiss and I took a big gulp of air as he grazed my jawline with his teeth and then moved down over my throat. His breathing was just as erratic as mine was. When he gave me another thrust, hitting the—perfect—spot, I gasped and threw my head back, hitting the wall with a thud that probably caused me to lose more than a few brain cells.

Being kissed by him was worth every one.

Then his lips were on mine and suddenly we were moving. I held his face in my hands and took as much as I could from his lips. I didn't even care where he was taking me as long as he kept kissing me like that.

When my ass hit something solid, I opened my eyes and looked around while Jason's hands were working to get off my panties under my skirt. We were in the kitchen area and I was sitting on the kitchen island.

Hot!

I was about to score big time!

The panties got caught up in my shoes and he practically snapped them off, startling another gasp from me. The lights coming from his backyard were enough for me to see his dark eyes burning with heat. Heat for me. His big hands kept caressing my thighs, but otherwise he let me have my look as we panted, out of breath.

His eyes still on me, he licked his lips, slipped his hands in between my thighs, and spread them wide open, making space for his body.

I leaned forward and rested my forehead against his. Our eyes were open and I was falling so deep with him—no turning back, done for life deep.

"Will you be wet for me when I touch you?" he whispered against my mouth. His fingers were toying with me, caressing an imaginary trail from my knee up toward my pussy, never quite touching, but getting too damn close for me to sit absolutely still.

My heart beating out of my chest, I nodded. "*So* wet," I whispered.

"Good," he muttered in a thick voice, and finally, *finally* his fingertips touched me right *there*.

My eyes closed. I moaned and threw my head back.

His hand left me and he cupped my neck, bringing my forehead back to rest against his.

"No, baby. I want you to look into my eyes when I make you come. I want you to remember."

As if I could ever forget him touching me…

He gave me his finger again, but this time, he didn't caress or play. He pushed two of his fingers inside me, literally taking my breath away, and pressed his thumb firmly against my clit.

My legs shaking, I closed my eyes and took a deep breath. He wasn't moving and I needed him to move really bad. It wasn't going to take more than a few seconds for me to come. A few thrusts and I was going to lose it.

"Please," I whispered and cupped his face, staring into his eyes like he wanted me to do.

"You want me?" he asked, his voice unrecognizable.

"Yes," I sighed. I'd wanted him for years. I'd longed for him when he was sleeping in my brother's room, so close but still far away. Then when years had passed, I'd longed for him secretly, watching his movies, holding him close to my heart even when he was impossible for me to have. "Yes," I repeated with more feeling.

"Then kiss me, Olive."

This time, I didn't hesitate. Holding his face to my lips, I kissed him softly. His fingers gave me a small thrust and his thumb rubbed my clit, just as softly as my kiss. I hooked my legs around his waist and pulled him closer to me. Tilting his head with my hands, I kissed him deeper. It was still soft, but I thrust my tongue deeper into his mouth to taste all of him, to play with his tongue.

His fingers started thrusting deeper, my wetness seeping out of me all around his fingers, and I mewled into his mouth as I tried to push my hips forward to take more of him.

When he hit a specific spot, I tore my mouth away from his and held on to his shoulders, my fingers curling in.

"Holy crap," I whispered, spreading my thighs wider. "Jason."

Warmth started to creep all over my body, every inch of my skin erupting in goose bumps. I was almost there, so I told him exactly that.

"I'm so close," I murmured, my eyes close.

He added another finger into me and I arched my back.

So fucking close.

It was going to be one of those long, intense orgasms. Nothing crazy, at least nothing *too* crazy, but still one of those sweet, I'm burning all over in a good way kind of orgasms.

He gave me his fingers with slow, deep thrusts as his thumb ghosted over my clit, making me practically lose my mind.

Letting go of his shoulders, I leaned back and propped myself on my hands, opening my legs even wider, asking for more.

"Jason, please," I mumbled when he didn't quicken his pace and let me fly.

"You need it hard?" he asked with a low growl to his voice.

I bit my lip and nodded.

"Tell me," he ordered. "Tell me what you like."

I opened my eyes and gazed at him, barely holding myself together. To hear the friction his fingers were causing, to know that he was aware of how wet I was for him... Knowing I was blushing, just a little, I spoke when I was still getting lost in his intense gaze. "Harder. Faster."

That was all he needed. His fingers went deeper, his thumb pressing harder. A soft moan escaped from my lips, mixed with his name, and I felt it happen. It started right between my legs and spread through my entire body. My toes twitched and I groaned louder as Jason kept thrusting in deeper, stretching me open and pulling more and more out of me.

It lasted longer than any other orgasm I'd ever had, and it was just with his fingers.

I was more than ready to try out his cock.

When I found it in me to open my eyes and look at Jason, he was a sight to see.

Breath uneven, eyes blazing, he kept working me until the last tremors left my body. Then he took his fingers out of me and his hand went behind my back, pulling me to his waiting lips.

His kiss was savage. We bit each other, licked each other, completely devoured each other. We took as much as we gave. It was amazing. The best of the best. I thought it couldn't get any better.

Twisting my hair around his hand, he pulled my head back. I knew my cheeks were flushed and my lips were swollen, but I needed more. I was hungry for more of him.

I let my hand slowly drop from his shoulders to his chest, then toward the thick bulge in his jeans, the bulge I could barely make out in the dark. When he realized where my hand was going, he caught my wrist and stopped me.

"Not done with you yet."

With those words, he took off my shirt and gazed at my full breasts slightly spilling out of my bra.

His hands reached for my breasts, but he didn't take the bra off of me. Instead, he cupped them, slightly lifting their weight up as if he was sizing them.

"I want to do so many things to you, Olive," he said when he could take his eyes off my breasts.

"I want you to do so many things to me," I whispered back, my heart picking up speed.

He quirked his eyebrow. "Do you, now?"

"Yes."

"Good. I'll do every single thing that is possible to do to you. Is that good for you, my Olive?"

My brain tingled. I was starting to love how he sounded when he was calling me 'Olive'. I nodded. Finding a little courage, I added, "I want everything, Jason."

His eyes went half-closed and his lips kicked up at the edges. "And I want just you, Olive. Lie down, then. You made a mess on my fingers and I need to clean you up."

I flushed and hesitated for a second. *Should I apologize?*

"Come here, sweetheart," he said, noticing my reluctance to lie down.

When I was in his face again, he cupped my cheek and kissed my tingling lips, coaxing me to open up to him.

"Will you let me taste you? Because your scent is making me crazy and I need to lick you up pretty bad." he whispered into my mouth.

While I was distracted, his fingers pulled down the cups of my bra and he twisted my nipple with one hand, causing me to groan and whimper.

When our lips parted, he spoke gruffly. "Lie down for me, baby."

I did. A little timidly maybe, but my back still hit the island.

Jason spread my legs open and stared down at me, his eyes moving over my breasts, and then slowly down.

He nudged my pussy open with two of his knuckles, spreading my wetness all over. Then with a slow slide of his fingers, he spread what was left on them over my nipples.

When his mouth closed around the hard peak and he sucked, my eyes fluttered closed and an electric shock ran through my body, causing me to twitch. While he was still devouring my breasts, licking and biting, he gently lifted my legs and pulled them over his shoulder, letting the backs of my knees rest on his shoulders.

Then his hands held my hips and his head dipped lower, biting and licking on his way. When he had finally reached his goal, I was a quivering mess.

"Such a pretty pussy," he whispered, his hot breath on my sensitive flesh doing all kinds of things to me.

Then he licked me, from bottom to top, pressing his tongue firmly against my clit and then swirling it around. I arched my neck and swallowed.

Looking at me as he dropped small kisses on the inside of my thigh, he asked, "How many men have you let touch you like this?"

"What?"

"How many men have gotten to see you like this? All wet, hot, and pink?"

Dammit... Again with the blushing. I had dated three guys in total and apart from Marcus, you could barely call them men. One was from high school after Jason had left us. The other one I'd only dated for a few months my first year in college. Out of all of them, Marcus was the only one who had gone down on me, so how did I even answer his question?

He quirked his eyebrow. "You're counting?" His mouth lowered and he sucked my clit.

My body quivered again.

I shook my head. "No. I just...I'm not sure how to answer."

He pushed a single finger inside me and waited for my answer.

"Only one went down on me," I said softly.

"Marcus," he guessed menacingly.

I wasn't going to answer *that*.

He added another finger. "Jason," I whispered, a new orgasm already looming ahead.

"From now on, he doesn't get to touch a single hair on your head," he growled from between my legs and started lapping up all my juices. My body shuddered and my hands reached for his hair, my fingers roughly grabbing anything that was long enough to hold on to.

I couldn't decide if I was more turned on by the fact that there was a legitimate possibility of him being jealous of Marcus or by how good he was with his tongue—probably a healthy mix of the two.

His licks become firmer and he started to swirl his tongue around my clit as his stubble did wonders, scraping against my tender flesh. Lifting my hips up to his mouth, I moaned and my fingers tightened in his hair, holding him down.

Realizing what I was doing, I quickly let go and Jason stopped what he was doing.

I'm telling you, he was making magic.

"Don't hesitate with me. Not now, Olive," he said, lifting his head from between my legs. His lips were all red and glistening. I wanted to devour him, and I was planning to. "Grab on to my hair and do whatever the hell you want to do to me."

Ovaries explosion!

I lifted my hands and threaded my fingers through his hair again, slightly gripping. His eyes held mine captive the entire time. I had a feeling he needed to have me as much as I needed to have him, which was mind-boggling.

His tongue stroked through my folds and I started to have trouble keeping my hips down. He yanked me forward, my ass almost resting on the edge.

When he covered my clit with his mouth and started to suck in pulses, I cried out his name, pushing and pulling at his head.

It was too much.

"Jason…I can't…oh, god…you have to stop."

He pushed two of his fingers back inside, curled them up, and found my G-spot. I fell over the edge again, just like that. Legs twitching, body shaking, my cries ringing in my ears…I'd like to think it was a beautiful sight, but I knew it wasn't. Finding purchase on his shoulders, I lifted my hips up and down, trying to prolong it as much as I could.

When it was all done and I stopped contracting around his fingers, all my bones had fallen out of my body and I had become a very happy noodle.

Jason's head lifted from between my legs, but not before he gave me one, last, slow lick, sending a slight tremor throughout my body. When I felt his lips against mine, I smiled lazily and sucked his tongue into my mouth.

He moaned and let me play with his mouth for as long as I wanted.

Then I was in his arms again, my legs barely wrapped around his back, one arm circling his neck, the other gripping his hair in a tight fist, and we were moving.

I was as high as a kite, all dopey and smiley. I doubt I would've minded if he'd taken me to hell in his arms.

When my back hit a soft mattress and I bounced, I opened my eyes to see that he had brought me to his room.

There was just enough light coming from outside for me to watch him take off his shirt and then go for his jeans. While he kept his eyes on me, I propped myself up on my hands and chose to watch him undress for me.

Those abs…

Second Ovaries explosion.

I had a very detailed plan of how I was going to lick and kiss every line.

"Move up, Olive," he said, gesturing with his chin before he took off his briefs.

And it was a good thing, too, because I wasn't sure if I could watch him take off his briefs and not say something that would surely embarrass me, so I pushed myself up toward the pillows. The moment I was settled down, Jason was crawling on top of me, his hands on either side of my face.

When our gazes met…

I was a goner.

His eyes still staring down at me, he reached to his left and opened a drawer, presumably taking out a condom—I'd already gone through his room and knew that's where he had a few of them lying around.

He put the edge of the foil packet in my mouth and pulled it away when I had it between my teeth.

"Put it on me, Olive," he murmured against my neck, dropping the condom on my stomach.

How was I supposed to move my arms or any part of my body when he was kissing and licking my skin like that? When I didn't move, he nudged my neck with his nose.

"Please, Olive. I can barely hold it together."

With shaky hands, I reached for the condom I couldn't see, and then reached down and touched something hard and thick, something that bobbed. Before I could attempt to put it on him, Jason's lips were on mine and he was groaning into my mouth. Forgetting about the condom, I slipped my arms around his shoulders, but before I could get into it, he stopped and pulled his lips away.

"Don't stop. Put it on, baby." His voice was so thick, so seductive.

"But, how am I—"

He pushed my legs open with his knees and then his cock was stroking my pussy.

Oh my god...

I groaned and let my legs open wider for him.

"If you want me inside you, look at me and put it on," he repeated again.

Barely holding his stare, I reached down and grabbed the thick length of his cock, stroking it once, twice.

Growling deep in his throat, Jason bit on my neck, gently sucking the skin.

Because I was dying to have him inside me, I stopped playing and slowly rolled the condom on him.

And rolled.

And rolled.

And rolled.

Holy crap!

The moment my fingers left him, Jason pushed his hips forward and the head of his cock pushed at my opening. I gasped with equal amounts of pleasure and pain.

From somewhere in the house, Jason's phone started ringing.

"Don't think about it," he murmured and pushed in a little bit deeper.

I didn't think about it. I arched my neck and moaned quite loudly.

"More?" he asked in between my heavy breathing.

"Yess," I moaned as he kept pushing in without waiting for my answer. Then he was retreating and easing back in again.

My body getting used to him, I tried to hold his stare to let him see how good it felt to have him go deep in my body.

When the head of his cock hit that magical spot, my eyes fluttered closed and he stopped moving. No retreating. No pushing back in.

I was completely full, in every way that counted. It felt like my whole body was trembling under him. He dropped to his knees but kept his body over mine. I sensed his fingers pushing my hair away from my face and then his lips were against my temple, leaving a tender kiss. I opened my eyes and gazed into his.

"Olive," he whispered.

One word.

How could he affect me like he did? How could one word out of his mouth touch my heart like that?

"In all the ways that matter, I'm your first, Olive. Do you understand?"

He didn't have any idea how right he was. In all the ways that mattered, he was my first, and after this whole deal ended, he would probably be my last. No one…nothing would ever make me feel like he was making me feel right then.

I nodded.

His eyes open, he touched his lips to mine. Gently, softly. I closed my eyes to hide my feelings and kissed him back. He pulled his hips back and pushed in deep. Hard.

"You're perfect sweetheart. You're perfect and now you are all mine."

My brows snapped together and I gasped into his mouth. He didn't break the kiss.

Another deep thrust rocked my body forward and he ate up my moan.

"Jason," I groaned when he gave me enough space to breathe.

"Is it just as good for you?" he asked. There was something hidden in his voice, something that told me he was surprised.

I gave him a lazy grin.

He smiled back. "Look at you taking me all in," he said softly. "Good girl."

Another deep thrust and my breath hitched.

"You're so fucking deep," I gasped.

"You like it, sweetheart? You like it deep?" Knowing what he was doing, he hit that spot and I whimpered. "Sweetheart," he muttered, getting my attention. "Talk to me."

"It fee-els soo go-od," I whimpered. To my horror, I felt a tear slide down from my eye and into my hair.

Jason cupped my face and wiped the coming tears with his thumbs.

"Easy, baby."

"I'm sorry," I whispered as he kept working his cock into me, his movements gentle. "Just…a little overwhelmed, I think."

"I know," he murmured as he kissed my closed eyes. "I know, baby."

He took me, body and soul. Soft, long strokes alternated with hard, shallow ones. I was spent. Our moans echoed in the room and every noise he made spurred me on more.

"You're creaming around my cock. Are you gonna come for me, beautiful?" Jason asked. His mouth was next to my ear, his heavy breaths warming my neck and sending shivers through my entire body. All the while he was sliding his cock as deep as it could go.

"Jason, it hurts so good," I whispered as I held on to his forearms, digging my fingers into his flesh, trying to move my hips with his thrusts.

The pressure inside me was building and building and building… It was driving me crazy.

Completely out of my mind.

"Jason, I'm gonna come," I gasped.

"Yes, baby, I can feel it. I can feel you squeezing my cock already."

"Faster, please."

"No."

One deep thrust.

"This will feel better. We have no reason to rush. Just let it go, sweetheart. Give it to me."

He kept working his cock into me at his own pace, not quickening, not slowing down.

I slid my hands up and onto his shoulders and felt his muscles straining under my hands. He was solid under my fingers, so real, and he was having a hard time holding it all together, just like me. I managed to move my hips under his body and suddenly the head of his cock hit where I needed it to hit and I lost it.

"Kiss me, Jason," I gasped, my hands tightening on his arms. He took my mouth and I let it all go. I let it all seep out of me. Everything I had been holding on to for such a long time.

When I started to contract around him more violently, my orgasm ripping through my body, Jason buried himself deep into me and started grinding. The intensity of my orgasm swept through my body and I started crying again. As my tears slid over our lips, I cupped his face and kissed him deeper, giving him my tongue.

My body was shaking like a leaf.

"Shit, baby." I felt his groan vibrate through my entire body and he started ramming into me. Hard, deep strokes that managed to pull something more from me. Another small shock went through me and then Jason was emptying himself in me.

My chest filling with a warm feeling, I nipped at his lips until his hips slowed down and he let out a long groan. Burying his face against my neck, he stilled inside me. After dropping small kisses on my skin, he lifted his head and gave me my dimple.

"Hey," he whispered.

Propping myself up on my elbows, I arched my neck and kissed his scruffy cheek, right where his dimple lived to torture me and the entire human population.

When my head hit the bed again, he was smiling even bigger.

"How are you feeling?" he asked, a touch of worry in his voice.

"Perfect," I answered, grinning up at him.

"I have to take care of the condom."

"Now?"

He kissed my nose. "Yes, sweetheart." He gently slid out of me, his cock still semi-hard, and then he was off the bed, heading toward the master bathroom.

Without him filling me, I felt so empty. What now? This wasn't how I'd imagined my night would end. What would happen now? Was this a one-time thing for him? After having him and knowing how it felt to have him…if I didn't have him again, would I die from heartache?

Was that how it worked?

Before I could think of something to say, he was back by my side, gathering me up in his arms and settling us under the covers.

It didn't escape my notice that he had put on a pair of briefs before getting into bed.

I lay still, not even moving an inch.

He was silent, but his hands were sliding up and down my arm. What did that mean?

It felt good to be in his arms again. Yeah, I was naked and he was not, but it was still good. He hadn't left me alone in his room. It was something.

I should've opened my damn mouth and said, what now? Or anything really. But I didn't. Neither did Jason.

I had questions, but I feared his answers.

But why didn't *he* say something?

Not too long after he got in bed with me, his arm stilled over my waist and he fell asleep.

Jason and Olive captured on video while engaging in a passionate kiss!

Oh, boy! Ladies, did any of you not take a cold shower after watching the video of Jason Thorn kissing Olive Taylor on the stage? We don't know about you, but we sure did. Several of them.

As if that's not enough, we are hearing rumors from a source close to the couple that they quietly got married in Jason's Bel Air home and are trying to keep it on the down low so they can ease Olive's family into the unexpected marriage. Our source reveals that Jason was too anxious to have an extended engagement and instead decided to surprise Olive with a stress-free wedding. Everyone believes they are truly smitten with each other.

While a lot of Jason Thorn fans are shocked and not sure what to make of the rumors, Olive's own fans seemed to support this union wholeheartedly. After watching that kiss, we don't think the rumors are false at this point.

And can we talk more about the video, please? Oh, what we wouldn't give to be a fly on the wall in Jason Thorn's home to watch what happened when they were alone... After a kiss like that, not only did Jason show everyone what a passionate kiss is supposed to look like, he also showed that Olive Taylor is quite possibly the luckiest girl in the world. As if we didn't know that already...

As they left the bar where the cast and crew were having a party before the filming for Soul Ache started the next day, Jason almost got into a fight with a photographer because they got a little too close to his sweetheart. Who knew he would be a jealous hubby after all his discretions?

For nearly the past two years, Jason Thorn has been known for his sexual appetite. Do you think Olive Taylor—or should we say Olive Thorn—will be his only focus, or will the star have more distractions every now and then?

CHAPTER TWENTY-SEVEN

JASON

I woke up feeling like my blood was humming in my veins. My hands met soft flesh and I groaned. I was burning from the inside out. My hips flexed, and I heard a small moan.

Smiling, I let my hands wander up a pair of thighs.

"Mmmm, what are you doing?" I murmured and squeezed Olive's hips, where she was sitting a little higher than where I would have liked.

Feeling her lips trail kisses on my chest, I opened my eyes and looked into her sparkling green ones. Hesitantly, she pressed her lips over mine and sat up straight stare down at me. Freeing my right hand, I gathered her hair in my fist, held it away from her face, and pulled her back down. When she parted her lips for me, I kissed her the way she was always supposed to be kissed, the way she deserved to be kissed. She moaned and opened her mouth wider, turning the kiss into liquid lust.

"Is this okay?" she asked quietly.

"It'll be better if I can get inside you," I murmured and felt her smile. "You're not sitting where you're supposed to sit."

"I wanted to wait for you."

Hell, she was welcome to wake me up every morning by

climbing onto my dick for a ride, but I'd take waking up with her lips trailing kisses on my skin too.

I nipped her lips and she stopped, her breathing ragged, her hips restless.

Holding on to the back of her waist, I flipped us over and had her under me in a second and then I was finally inside her.

"You should've woken me up if you needed me, baby," I whispered as I thrust into her for the first time. She hid her face in my neck as she let out a long, sexy moan.

Her legs were hugging my hips, but with my second thrust she let them fall open and lifted her hips in sync with my leisurely thrusts.

"I just…"

She bit her bottom lip, her eyebrows drawing together.

"You just, what, sweetheart?"

She gazed into my eyes with such longing that I couldn't look away from her.

"I just wanted to make sure last night wasn't a dream."

I thrust as deep as I could go and reveled in the way her body trembled under mine as she arched her neck and let out another deep groan.

"And you decided to drive me insane to get back at me?"

"Yesss," she hissed, throwing her head back when I grinded into her.

Her pussy was so damn hot, sucking my dick in, squeezing me. Not able to stop, I pulled back and filled her again and again.

Her hands were roaming my chest, her touch waking something inside me. When I started pounding into her, her breaths came out in gasps and she let out sultry, incoherent mews.

Each time my cock disappeared inside her, ripples of pleasure rocked my body.

"Jason," Olive moaned under me, her hands over her head, palms resting against the headboard. I slowed my pounding and roughly pulled down her bra. Why had we not taken it off the night before? Oh, right, I had barely been able to think, let alone care about losing the bra. As long as I had access to what was underneath, I hadn't cared, but now I wanted it off. I wanted every inch of her skin on mine as I buried myself into her.

"When you were writing those sex scenes were you thinking of your boyfriend?" I asked, my voice all fucked up.

She hesitated.

"Answer me, Olive."

I pulled out my dick, loving the way she tried to grab on to it with her muscles, then slammed it back in.

"No," she gasped, grasping the bed sheets with small fists.

"Who were you thinking of?"

"I can't tell."

"Oh, you will, sweetheart."

I dropped my head to her breasts and sucked her nipple in my mouth as I started grinding into her. I loved how she arched her back to feed me more.

"Do you want me to stop?" I barely held back my hips. She looked gorgeous under me, taking my cock so nicely.

The little witch started to move her hips under me.

Gritting my teeth, I said, "You can get yourself off, baby but it won't be the same as how I'm going to get you off on my dick. Who were you thinking of, Olive?"

"You," she whispered, turning her head away from me.

I started throbbing inside her, so I picked up my pace again, driving into her.

"So what they say is true, you really were thinking about me when you wrote Isaac," I said conversationally as if even thinking about it wasn't kicking up my heart rate.

Her eyes were lazy when she opened them to look at me.

"Yes," she whispered, her voice scratchy.

"Do you want me to talk dirty to you, baby? Like Isaac?"

Leaning down to her ear, I stopped when my lips were only millimeters away and breathlessly whispered, "Do you want me to take you hard, too? Fuck you into oblivion?"

As an answer, she tangled her hands behind my head and took my lips, playing with my heart like no one else ever had.

A bold caress of her tongue and everything went hazy. Wrenching my lips away from her mouth, I straightened my arms and looked down to her.

"All you have to do is ask, sweetheart. I'll give you everything you need."

My body surged into hers and I looked down to watch my thick cock disappear into her sweet heat. I catalogued every curve and dip of her body. She was so damn tight and already breathless, her clever hands touching every inch of my body she could reach.

When I realized my control was shot to hell, I got off of her to stand on my knees.

"Hold on to the headboard, baby."

When she reached up and curled her fingers on the headboard, I hooked my arms under her knees and put her legs over my open thighs, making sure to hold her legs open for me.

Wiping off the sweat on my forehead, I grabbed her hips and slowly fed my dick to her pussy, reveling in her loud swearing and moans.

"Oh, god," she mumbled when I was all in.

"Fuck, yes," I said in reply.

Then my fingers dug harder into her flesh and I fucked her like I hadn't fucked her the night before. While the night before had been amazing, it had been more than just sex. This…this was pure pleasure. It was hard, deep, and definitely out of control.

I loved it.

She loved it.

Every time I surged into her body, I bottomed out. I was

drinking in her sharp cries and gasping breaths. When her head hit the headboard from the force I was pounding into her, I tried to slow my pace down but it was too late, for both of us.

"Fuck, Jason…shit, fuck… Yes, yes, please…"

Her eyes rolled back into her head and her body froze under my hands. Her release coated me in a rush and I groaned louder than her cries.

She took a gasping breath.

Then another.

As I kept pounding into her, she slowly came down from her orgasm, her legs relaxed, and she opened her eyes. It was enough to ignite something inside of me, so I let it all go and joined her in oblivion.

I was trying to catch my breath and slowly keep thrusting into her when she splayed her fingers over my contracting abs, looking at me as if she was ready to lick me up and eat me. Out of my mind with need for her, I dropped to my elbows, held her head in between my hands, and gave her the rawest and most passionate kiss I'd ever shared with anyone.

When we were half-dead, I dropped a kiss on her nose and tried to ignore my throbbing cock. I was ready to go all over again.

"We need to repeat this a few times a day. You okay with that, sweetheart?"

As an answer she kissed me and in the middle of our kiss gave me a lazy smile.

"Also, when my brain is functioning, remind me to ask how you managed to roll a condom on me without waking me up. Or maybe we can talk about not using them at all if you're ready for that."

"I vote on not using them at all," she murmured in a soft voice.

I smiled. "Good. We'll handle it as soon as possible."

It was by far the best morning I'd ever had in my entire life.

WHEN WE GOT to the set, everything was ready for the first day of the filming. Olive was beside herself, her beautiful eyes taking in everything with a contagious smile on her face. Before I had to go in for makeup and hair, I introduced her to the director Tanner Pace and a ton of others. When I had to leave her with Alvin to go and run lines with Lindsay Dunlop, I felt a small ache in my heart. I wanted to keep her by my side at all times, have her hand in mine, lips on mine, permanently.

However, I couldn't do that.

After an hour of rehearsal with Lindsay, I checked the trailer but couldn't find any trace of Olive or Alvin in there. Walking around the lot, I found them both munching on fruit and candies, next to the craft service area.

"Jason!" Olive exclaimed when she saw me heading their way. Her smile hadn't diminished a bit, and her excitement was just as contagious as her smile.

"There you are," I said when I reached their side. Hooking my arm around Olive's waist, I leaned down and took a bite of the strawberry in her hand. Then I lowered my head and captured her mouth in a quick kiss.

When it was over, her eyes were half-closed and glazed; maybe it hadn't been such a quick kiss after all. Licking her lips, she murmured, "Strawberry. Yummm."

I laughed and said hi to the electricians, who were getting coffee from the other end of the set up.

Keeping Olive close to my side, I faced Alvin. "Didn't you guys make it to the trailer yet? I looked there first."

"Olive wanted to see the set first."

Olive scrunched her nose and gave Alvin an apologetic look.

"Yeah, sorry about that. It's hard to explain how it makes you feel when you see something in real life that was created in your mind." She turned those green eyes at me. "You should've seen Alvin's face when I teared up. Even the bed covers on Evie's bed have the same feather pattern I wrote in the book, Jason. That's the bed where they shared their first kiss."

I smiled down at her. "The author approves, then? Does she approve the leading actor, too?"

She nodded enthusiastically. "I definitely approve the leading actor. I approve him the most."

"I wanted to show you around myself, but I'll settle with showing you my trailer. Since you brought your laptop with you, I'm assuming you'll want to write?"

"Yes, I figured I'd find a quiet corner. I didn't want to be in your way the entire day."

"You wouldn't be, sweetheart. I spend most of my time in the trailer in between takes, and I enjoy watching you write." I gathered her hair and dropped it back over her shoulder. "You want to go see it now?"

I tried not to look too eager, but I was dying to get her alone for a few minutes. That kiss hadn't been enough to quench my thirst for her, and it had been a few hours too many since the last time I'd had her naked and writhing in my arms.

"Boss," Alvin interrupted before Olive could give her answer. "As much as I love to spend time with your lovely *wife,* I'm afraid I need to leave so I can take care of the house while you're not actually in it. Is there anything else you need from me here?"

"Right. Did they assign a production assistant already?"

"Yes, I talked to him. He should've already dropped the call sheet in your trailer. Anything else you need, you let me know."

"I'll be okay. We'll talk later. Right now, I'll go spend some more time with my lovely wife."

Alvin left and I walked through the studio lot with Olive toward where most of the trailers were kept.

"You're kidding, right?" she asked once we were standing in front of the two-story monster.

"Why would I kid?"

"This is gigantic, Jason."

"It's not mine, actually. I don't care that much about having a big one. The production company offered for me to use this one during filming, and since I knew you would be coming with me, I thought you'd enjoy having a bigger space to yourself. Come on, I'll show you inside. You'll be more than comfortable enough to work in here."

Resting my hand on her back, I urged her to move forward.

"So you're saying I can come to the set with you and work in your trailer? Whenever I want?"

I met her gaze. "I assumed you'd want to come with me. If not to write, then maybe to watch the shooting."

She averted her gaze, but not before I saw her brilliant smile. Walking ahead of her, I ripped off the call sheet the production assistant had secured on the door and unlocked the trailer.

"They don't go in?"

"Not when I'm not in here. You saw what happened in London. Even though this place is pretty well guarded, I wouldn't trust anyone in here." I held out my hand for her to take. "You should keep it locked when you are alone in here, too."

Holding on to my hand, she took the narrow steps up and entered the trailer.

"Holy crap, Jason. I'm in love with your home, but this…this is pretty close to love too."

Wanting to feel her body close to mine, I wrapped my arms around her abdomen and rested my head on top of hers. When she placed her hands over mine, I was grinning like a kid.

Get it together, man.

"This is the lounge area," I explained, standing next to the white leather sectional. I took a few steps forward, shuffling her with me. "Through here, there is the makeup station/office area and a small kitchenette, as you can see." I took a small step forward and let my hips rest against her so she could feel how much I was affected by our closeness. I heard her quick intake of breath when my erection nestled against her fucking fantastic ass.

Better speed this up.

"Through the other door, there is a bathroom and wardrobe area. Upstairs there is a screening room." Done with the tour, I turned her in my arms, pushed a button on the wall to close the door that separated the lounge area from the office space, and backed her up against it.

By then, I was more than ready to have her again.

Touching my lips to hers, I waited to see what she would do. She kissed me back, but it was softer than what I wanted. Not wanting to scare her away on day one, I kept it soft, but still let my tongue out to play with hers. By the time we were done, she was breathless and I could see red flames in her green eyes.

My voice was huskier than I expected when I spoke. "Are you okay with everything that's been happening?"

Seeing her red, swollen lips did something to me, so I reached up and traced her soft lips with my thumb.

She avoided looking at me but nodded her head. I leaned in closer and whispered into her hair. "Can you look at me, baby?"

Then she did, and fuck me, but she was beautiful. I went for her lips again, and this time she was just as eager as I was.

Her hand timidly reached under my shirt and she rested it against my stomach. Involuntarily, I thrust my hips into hers. Before I could lift her up and take her to the couch, someone started pounding on the door.

"Jason, Tanner needs to talk to you about some changes he wants to make in the first scene."

"I'll be right there!" I yelled.

I rested my forehead against Olive's and sighed. Focusing on her parted lips, I discreetly rearranged myself. "I don't think I can make it more than a few hours without having you again," I whispered over my frantic heartbeat.

What was happening to me?

"Go," she said, taking her hand away from my skin and placing it on my chest, over my shirt. "I'll snoop around in your trailer some more. Your tour was pretty lame."

"All you need to focus on is me, woman."

She laughed and halfheartedly pushed at my chest. "Go. Will you come back and take me to watch the first scene?"

Reluctantly, I let her go and rubbed my face. "Let me check the call sheet."

She came to the table with me and looked at the paper over my arm. "Oh, the first scene is the same one you read at the audition. I thought it would be the first time they saw each other on the empty street."

"Movies are almost never shot in sequence. Since I'm in LA and don't have any other shoots, they don't have to schedule the scenes around me, but I think Lindsay has another commitment and she'll have to be away from the set on certain days. They'll want to take care of the scenes we have together first."

"Ok," she said, her eyes still taking in the call sheet. I smiled and handed it to her.

"Do you want to keep it, maybe?"

"Yes!" She ripped it out of my hands and turned her back to me.

I laughed and pulled away her hair so I could brush a small kiss on her neck. "I'll be back to get you for the first scene, sweetheart. Be good."

Why couldn't I keep my hands and lips away from her?

Twenty minutes later, I headed back to the trailer and collected Olive so the PA could drive us to the location.

Leaving Olive to sit on my chair behind the cameras, I took my place in front of them. Half an hour later, Lindsay was in place and we were ready to start.

Before the director could call out *action,* I glanced back at the spot where I had left Olive, but I could barely make out her face with all the lights that were directed at us. Closing my eyes, I relaxed my body and thought about Isaac. Hearing Olive's voice in my mind, I took in every detail she'd given me about him. She had sounded like she was actually in love with him, but I understood that kind of commitment all too well. She wouldn't be a good writer if she couldn't fall for her characters, the good and the bad.

I relaxed my shoulders and let out a deep breath. When I opened my eyes and looked at Evie, I was Isaac, the Isaac Olive had given her heart to.

"*Action!*" Tanner yelled.

It all began.

———

TWO HOURS OF SHOOTING LATER, I found myself next to Olive, gripping her hand tightly, her grip on mine just as strong.

"I have an hour in between takes," I said as I checked the watch on my wrist. "You want to head back to the trailer? I could use some quiet." I needed to get her alone.

She followed me without a peep.

The PA dropped us off at the craft service station and I got myself coffee and Olive some tea. Since the trailer wasn't far away, I sent the PA away so I could have Olive to myself as we walked the short distance.

A big group of people exited one of the warehouses that was

on the way to my trailer and swarmed around us. We had to slow down our steps and let them pass toward the small fake town. I figured they must have been taking a break from shooting.

When Olive suddenly stopped moving, I halted and glanced back at her.

"What's going on?" I asked as she jerked her hand from mine and started waving it in front of her face. "Olive, what are you doing?"

"Is that a bee?" she squeaked, hurriedly backing away.

"I guess so. Why? What's wrong?"

"Oh my god, there are more!" she yelled and jumped on the bench that was closest to her.

By then a few people had stopped and started watching her, trying to understand what the commotion was about.

I jogged to her side. "Olive stop jumping, you're gonna fall and break your neck."

"Jason! Jason, you have to help me!"

Yup, there were only two bees, though these two were persistent suckers.

"Baby," I said, chuckling. "Quit waving your hands around and jumping away if you don't want them to sting you."

"They're coming after me! How can I stop! Get them away from me, please."

"Okay." I sighed and caught her behind her knees. Without hesitation, she jumped into my arms and wrapped herself around me, her face hiding in my neck.

She whimpered and I had to bite back my laugh.

"I didn't know you were afraid of bees, Olive."

"Are they gone?" she whispered into my neck. I could barely make out her words.

"Actually, they are still flying around, but I won't let them get to you, don't worry. No one's taking you away from me, not even these evil bees."

She groaned, but her hold on me was more relaxed. "Don't make fun of me. I've never been stung by a bee, so if they sting me, I might die within minutes."

This time I couldn't hold it back; I laughed, tightening my hold on her waist so I wouldn't drop her. Feeling eyes on us, I glanced behind me and saw a few people taping the whole spectacle with their phones.

Great. More media coverage was exactly what we needed.

"I'm probably allergic. That must be why they are waiting to get to me. Are they gone? If not, wave your hands so they won't get close to us." Olive was oblivious to what was happening around us so I quickened my pace, knowing she wouldn't want to be filmed while wrapped around me. Also, even if it made me a bastard, I liked her wrapped around me. If they filmed it, photographed it…so what? She was my wife after all.

"I'm pretty sure if I wave my hands around that'll only piss them off more, and then they'll steal you away from me."

Lightly, she hit my shoulder and muttered, "I said don't make fun of me. I'm dead serious."

I patted her ass and smiled into her hair. "I know, baby. It's okay, we're almost at the trailer. I'll protect you."

"Are we going to the hospital?"

"Olive, they didn't even touch you, sweetheart."

"But what if one of them is in my hair? If he is anywhere near my head, I'll be dead in seconds."

Her nose was tickling my neck, but then I felt something different.

"Olive?"

"Yes," she mumbled back.

"Did you just sniff me?"

Her body tightened again. "No. No. I *sniffled.* I was checking to see if I was about to cry. You know, readying myself just in case."

"I see."

My body shaking with laughter, I managed to open the door to our trailer and carried my wife inside. Walking toward the couch, I gently lay her down on it.

With a smile glued to my face, I looked down at her. She genuinely looked scared. Pushing her bangs away from her eyes, I said, "Don't move a muscle, beautiful."

Before I could extract myself from her arms, her hand reached up and touched my dimple. Tilting my head, I kissed her finger and left her side so I could go to the bathroom and brush my teeth. I had kissed Lindsay, or I should say Evie, a total of twenty times. I didn't want the lingering taste of her in my mouth. It wasn't that Lindsay wasn't a professional about it, I just wanted Olive's taste back.

As soon as I was done, I was crawling on top of her and reaching for her lips. She hadn't said anything about the filming, and while I was curious to hear what she thought about the scenes we had shot, kissing her was higher on my priority list.

Nudging her lips open, I sneaked my tongue inside her mouth and gently tilted her head back so I could sink into her. I didn't know how long I kissed her liked that, drinking her in, memorizing her scent, but when I slid my erection against the seam of her leggings, her little moan reached through the thick fog that was blinding me.

Ending the kiss, I rested my forehead on hers and listened to her heavy breathing.

"What did you think?" I asked in a heavy voice when I could think more clearly.

"You were amazing," she whispered as she looked into my eyes with her heart shining right at the edges.

Amused, I asked, "Lindsay?"

She made a cute, funny face. "I think I'm okay with the fictional Evie having her happy ending with Isaac, but watching it in real life...actually watching her kiss you soooo many times, and from so many different angles? Not so sure about that."

I laughed and kissed her again.

"That's why I was dying to get you back here. I think I prefer to kiss the author."

"How does it work exactly? I mean, how can you not feel something for her and then go ahead and kiss her like that?"

"Like...what?"

"Like you wanted to eat her up?"

"I want to eat you up, Olive. Can I?"

"I'm serious, though."

"Baby, nothing about those kisses was intimate. Didn't you see how many times we had to stop to make sure the director was happy with the angle and the lighting? It's Isaac and Evie kissing at that moment, not Lindsay and Jason. Now, I really want it to be Jason and Olive kissing," I murmured into her ear and left a trail of small kisses on her neck.

Arching her neck to get more, she lifted her hips.

I groaned and pushed her hips back down to the couch with my hand. "I'm afraid if we start with that, I won't be able to get back to the set."

Ignoring my warning, she pulled me down by my neck and kissed the fuck out of me.

By the time there was someone banging on the door, I was fucking her through our clothes.

I wrenched my lips away from hers and snarled at whoever the hell was at the door.

"Starting the scene in ten, Jason!" someone yelled from the other side. It sounded like the AD.

I rested my head on Olive's shoulder. "Be there in a minute."

Watching how fast her chest was rising and falling gave me immense pleasure. *I* did that to her. *I* took her breath away.

Pushing up with my hands, I looked down at her flushed face. Her eyes were dilated.

"I love this look on you, Olive," I said, feeling so many things all at once.

"What look?" she asked breathlessly.

"This look that says, *I've been fucked so very well.*"

She laughed. "I don't remember being fucked."

I lifted an eyebrow. "You don't? Maybe we should amend that."

Her expression serious, she nodded. "We definitely should. I want you so bad, Jason. In me. On me."

I groaned and hid my face against her throat. They pounded on the door again.

"We need to leave."

"I'll stay here. The kissing and all that was starting to get to me. Plus, I want some of it to be a surprise when I'm watching the movie. I feel motivated enough to write more so I should take advantage of that."

"Ok, sweetheart." I kissed her nose and slowly backed away from her body. "If I can't come back in between takes, I'll make sure to have somebody bring you lunch."

"When does shooting end today?"

"I think closer to eight. Tanner wants to shoot some of the street shots today. Why do you ask?"

Sitting cross-legged on the couch, she straightened her shirt and looked away. "No reason. I thought maybe when we get home, we could..." Her words trailed off.

"We could what, baby?"

She stayed silent but bit her lip, drawing my attention.

Placing my hands on either side of her hips, I got in her face and asked again, "We could what, Olive? What do you want from me?"

She lifted her eyes and met my gaze. "I want you."

"You got me."

"Did I?" she asked, tilting her head.

I nipped her lips and she squealed. "Does my wife want her husband to fuck her? Is that what you are trying to ask?"

Her gaze softened and she placed a hand over my cheek. "Can he?"

"Oh, baby," I murmured, breathing in her unique scent. "You want to be properly fucked, don't you?"

"Mr. Thorn? Everyone is waiting for you on set. What should I tell them?" This time it was the PA they had assigned to me—you could tell from the uncertainty in his voice.

"For god's sake! I'm coming," I shouted again.

I sighed and said to Olive, "Hold that thought until I get back."

By the time we were shooting the martini shot, it had already gotten dark outside and I hadn't seen or heard from Olive for hours. After a quick talk with Tanner and Lindsay about the next day's schedule, I was heading straight to her, hoping that she was still in the trailer.

I unlocked the door and got in, but couldn't find her on the first floor. Heading up to the screening room, I found her curled up on the corner of the couch, her laptop on her lap, her fingers tapping furiously. When I got close enough to see her face, I noticed the tears falling from her eyes.

"Olive, what's wrong?"

She flinched and her fingers stopped moving for a moment as she looked up at me.

"Sorry," she sniffled. "I didn't hear you. Can you just give me a second? I need to finish this scene."

"Of course," I said, a little dumbstruck. I sat down. She gave me a small smile and then turned her eyes back to the screen.

Sitting beside her, my hands were adamant that she needed them on her skin, so I reached out and gathered her hair on the other side of her neck. Small goose bumps appeared on her skin, but I doubted she even noticed me touching her.

After several minutes passed and she was done with whatever was making her cry, she twisted in her seat and faced me. My hands were on her face in a second. "Sweetheart, why are you crying?" I asked, wiping away her tears. She must've been crying for a long time for her eyes to be so red and puffy.

She gave a miserable laugh and wiped at her face with the back of her hand. "Her father...her father died."

"Aww, baby, whose father died?" I brushed a small kiss on her mouth, tasted her salty lips, and leaned back. I was still stroking her jawline, quite possibly to assure myself that she was okay.

"Maya's," she replied as fresh tears started spilling down her cheeks. Noticing my questioning look, she clarified. "The new book I'm working on. Maya is the heroine. Her father had cancer, and she was with him...his last night, holding his hand, and then he never made it to morning. He knew...he wasn't going to, and he loved her so much."

Her breath hitched and the tears started coming faster.

"Oh, baby," I whispered with a small chuckle, and then she was in my arms, her face buried in my neck. She was so warm, so beautiful, both inside and out.

"And then," she continued. "And then she met this jerk in a hotel and he heard her crying from next door and barged into her room when..." Another sniffle. "When she was reading her father's letters."

I stroked her hair and then her back. My heart was breaking into a million pieces as she cried her heart out for her characters.

"That's good though, isn't it?" I asked softly. Pulling the rest of her body into my lap, I let her straddle me and plaster herself to my chest as I started to stroke her thighs to calm her down. "She won't be alone. I'm sure you'll make the guy help her."

She put her small hands on my shoulders and lifted her head

up. "He'd been a jerk to her before that so they don't like each other that much, but he'll be worried when he sees her crying."

I brushed her hair back so I could see her splotchy but still beautiful face. "Will they fall in love?"

She gave me a small smile. "Very much so."

"Good for them," I whispered, loving how she was looking at me. Her eyes had a vulnerability in them, yet it made her look all the more powerful somehow.

"But first she'll ask him to have sex with her," she said, her smile turning wicked. That's when I realized exactly where she was sitting. Returning her smile, I gathered all of her hair in my hands and dropped it back over her shoulders.

"I thought they didn't like each other, little Olive. Does she really want him to have sex with her?"

She nodded eagerly and wiggled her sexy ass a little back so she could settle down more firmly on my newly awakening erection.

"I bet her lips look so beautiful all red and swollen, just like yours do now. I bet he jumps on that idea." I gripped her chin and pressed my thumb on her bottom lip, pulling on it gently.

She rolled her hips and I had to drop my head back and close my eyes to hold it together. Resting her cheek on my shoulder, she whispered, "Not really. He didn't want to take advantage of her when she was upset, but she'll change his mind."

"I bet she will. I bet he can never say no to her," I said, not moving my head an inch. If I looked down at her and those lips, I was going to lose it.

Her warm lips pressed against my neck and my hands tightened on her thighs. When I felt her body lean away from mine, I opened my eyes to see her reaching for her bag. I steadied her hips to keep her where she was.

After struggling to find something in her bag, she whipped out a condom, looking pretty proud of herself.

I chuckled and pulled her chest back against mine. "You want me to make it all better baby?"

Another hip roll and a firm nod.

"Up," I said, spanking her ass lightly. "Take off your pants and climb on."

Her eyes glanced at the narrow staircase, and I spoke before she could start worrying about people coming up.

"Everyone knows not to come up here, sweetheart, and I locked the door when I came in. Don't worry."

I unbuttoned my jeans and lowered the zipper. She only hesitated for a second or two, but when she saw my dick proudly standing up, waiting for her, she was rolling down her leggings and stepping out of them in a heartbeat.

My blood roaring in my veins, I quickly rolled the condom on and held out my hand to her. She climbed on and I grabbed her waist as I lowered her down on me.

That feeling.

That first slide where she took me into her body and her eyes fluttered closed... It was the most erotic and beautiful thing I'd ever seen on a woman's face. Her eyes still closed, she bit on her lip and gave me a half-smile as if she was drunk. Hell, she hadn't started moving yet and I was already feeling dizzy. Instead of going all the way down, she held on to my shoulders and lifted herself up, keeping the head in her body. Then on the next downward move, she sank all the way down to my base and we waited until her legs started shaking.

I never stopped touching her, stroking her thighs, pushing my hands under her shirt, caressing her bare skin.

Oddly, it was even sexy to be half-clothed with her. It felt forbidden to slide my hands under her shirt and in between her thighs. Every moan, every tremble belonged to me. When she rested her palms on my pecs and started rising and falling faster and faster, it was all I could do to not spill myself inside her before she could find her own release.

She looked amazing. The lip biting, the half-lidded eyes, her pussy hugging my dick so tightly, the eye contact, the moans...I was simply mesmerized.

I was falling deeper and deeper for her and we needed to have a serious conversation if this kept picking up speed.

Suddenly, she slowed her movements and leaned down for my lips. Instead of kissing me as I was expecting her to do, she stopped when our lips were touching. "Why are you looking at me like that?" she murmured.

"Is my baby shy?" I asked in a heavy voice.

She hid her face in my throat again, but kept working my cock into her pussy.

Putting my hands under her ass, I urged her to take me deeper and faster.

When she let out a long moan, I asked, "That good, baby, huh?"

"Yesss," she whispered, her fingers threading into my hair. Her lips grazed my ear. "I love it when you talk to me when we are doing this."

I pushed her hips down and forced all of me into her. "When we do what, sweetheart?"

She tried to move up, but I held her down. "Tell me, baby. When we do what? I want to hear you say it."

She licked my earlobe and then whispered, "When you *fuck* me, Jason. Is that what you want to hear?"

I slid myself a little down and Olive squealed in my lap, rounding her arms on my neck.

"That's exactly what I want to hear, baby," I said with a growl and started fucking her from beneath.

She groaned and moaned. She curled her little fingers around my biceps and held on for the ride as I stretched her open and took everything she was willing to give me. While I made her see stars, I kept talking to her, revving her up more, enjoying the way she got all wet around my dick.

Closer to the end, she whimpered my name, her breath hitching.

"I love how you take all of me without a single complaint, Olive. I love it. I love it," I murmured into her ear.

When we came, we came together.

My teeth grazing her neck.

Her fingers clutching my biceps.

My hands gripping her hips, holding her in place.

Her whole body trembling.

CHAPTER TWENTY-EIGHT

OLIVE

"Lucy, what are you doing?"

Her head peeked out from behind the fridge door. "I'm alley-catting. What does it look like?"

I stared at her unblinkingly from my spot on the couch.

Her smile widened. "You see what I did there? Alley? Jason? Alley-catting?"

Silence.

I heaved a sigh. "It wasn't as funny as you would think, Lucy."

It was a Thursday and Jason had left at 5:00 AM for an early shoot. Their schedule was intense and I wanted nothing to do with it—not that I didn't enjoy spending time in his trailer and focusing on my writing, but I could barely focus when he was around me.

"Oh, come on, it was. Don't break my heart by saying I'm not funny. I don't want to spend my entire night telling jokes to everyone around me to assert my funniness."

Ignoring her, I asked, "So, how is it going with the new room-mate? Char's friend, Lily, right?"

"Yes, Lily." She scrunched up her nose as if she had smelled something bad. "Not that sure about her. I'm giving her more time."

Finally closing the fridge door, she plopped down next to me and handed me an apple while she clutched a bowl of blueberries in her hand.

I looked at the apple in my hand and then to Lucy. "What is this for?"

"Now that you are getting it on the reg, you need to eat healthier to keep up with Jason Thorn." She cocked her head, but stared intently into her bowl. "Because you do need to keep up with him don't you? He is a machine in bed, isn't he?"

I raised my brows and took a bite from my apple, but otherwise stayed silent.

Picking up a blueberry, she gave me a side glance. "Well?"

I shook my head. "Sorry, I'm not falling for that. No sex details. Already told you that, I don't know, a thousand times today?"

She put her bowl down on the couch and pulled her legs up to face me. "You're no fun at all, Olive. How am I supposed to live vicariously through you if you don't give me the details? What did I ever do to you to deserve such cruelty?"

I took another bite of my apple and picked up my laptop from the gargantuan ottoman. Before I opened it, I twisted to face Lucy.

Her eyes were expectant, her excitement written all over her face.

"Let's make a deal," I said.

"Great. Let's. I love deals." She held out her hand to me.

I took her hand and stared straight into her eyes. "You tell me about Jameson and I'll give you a few *small* details about Jason."

She shook my hand enthusiastically. "Done. You already saw Jameson's penis, so you know that he is hung."

Squeezing my eyes shut as if that would erase the memory of

that image, I held up my hand, palm out. "Not that. God, no. Not bed details. I think I heard more than enough from the next room to have an idea of how he is in bed. Tell me what you're *doing* with Jameson." I winced when I saw the look on her face. "Not in the literal sense. Tell me if you are in love with him." Then it was her turn to wince. "Tell me what's going on, Lucy. Ever since this book stuff and Jason stuff happened, all we ever talk about is me. Even though I'm quite aware of how much you love talking about those particular subjects, I'm more interested in your life."

"Nothing exciting is going on in my life. I like yours much better." She popped a few blueberries into her mouth and averted her gaze.

"Lucy, please, just tell me why you won't date the guy. He is crazy for you."

"How do you even know he is crazy for me?"

"Please," I said, fighting the urge to roll my eyes. "Have you even seen how the guy looks at you? I'll admit he is hot as fuck." She gave me a quick grin. "And still he is like a puppy following you around. You keep kicking him out of your bed, but whenever you turn around he jumps right back in."

"He really is hot as fuck. We did good, didn't we?"

I waved my hand dismissively. "I have no idea what I'm doing right now, but you definitely did good. You should hold on to him, Lucy."

She put down her bowl of blueberries and sighed. "If I talk about the annoying bastard, you'll give me a few details about how Jason is in bed?"

"Yes."

"Fine. This is called blackmail by the way, if you didn't know."

I quirked my eyebrow and waited for her to go on.

"*Fine*. I never intended to sleep with him more than once, okay? Then it just got out of control. And you don't see him at school; it's not like he is running around after me. He is flirting with everything that moves and has a vagina. I have no idea why he keeps coming back for more."

"Are you sure about the flirting? I mean, do you know if he is sleeping with anyone else? If he is, I have no idea how the heck he is keeping up."

"Of course I'm sure. I don't think he is sleeping with anyone else though."

"I think he is trying get your attention with all the flirting. I'm telling you, that guy is head over heels in love with you. He is just waiting for you to do something about it."

She rose up from the floor and went back to the kitchen. "I'm going to use this state of the art espresso machine and not talk about freaking Jameson any more." She pointed her finger at me and wiggled her eyebrows. "And I believe you owe me some details about your beloved husband. Gimme."

"Pfff," I snorted. "Husband my ass."

Playing with the buttons on the espresso machine, she looked at me over her shoulder. "Get your ass over here so I can actually hear you."

Reluctantly, I lifted myself up from the comfy couch and made my way toward her. No way in hell was I going to try to sit on those bar stools though. I pretty much hated all six of them with a burning passion.

"Okay, you have a limit of two questions. Choose wisely." I leaned over the counter and rested my chin on my hands.

"Stop grinning, you dork." She laughed at my expression. "Okay. Just let me think about it for a second. Closing her eyes, she donned her thinking face and started humming. "Okay, I won't ask if he was any good, because, duh…your lips are about to split from all that grinning you're doing. I won't ask if you came, because again…duh… I feel like I wanna ask how long he lasts…nah, I won't ask that either."

My grin turned into laughter. "Come on. I said small details. Ask something that's been eating at you for all these years."

"Fine. Is he big? I just gotta ask that." I opened my mouth to answer but she covered my mouth with her hand. "No! Don't say it; *show* me how big."

"Okay." Grinning, I lifted my hands and slowly started parting them. Her smile got wider and wider.

"Yowza! Damn woman. What is that eight, nine inches? You lucked out. Damn."

Blushing a little, I laughed. "Okay, do you have a second question?"

"Crap. If I'd known you were actually going to answer them, I'd have made a list. I can't decide on the best question when you put me on the spot. Okay, does he talk when you're, you know… doing it? I mean, is he a dirty talker? Because if he is, I might just pass out right here in his kitchen, and then you'll have to nurse me back to health and I'll get to stay here."

"You don't have to pass out to stay here, Lucy."

Already fanning herself, she said, "Go ahead, answer. He is a dirty talker, isn't he? He has to be."

"Yes."

Her eyes almost popped out of their sockets. "That wasn't a yes or no question, woman! You have to give me more than that."

"Sorry."

She dropped to her knees and put her arms on the edge of the island I was leaning on. "Pity me, Olive. For the love of our friendship. Please."

"Yeah. No way."

She took a deep breath and slowly let it out. "I hate you. Okay. Okay, I can live with this. Holy shit, but you are lucky."

Was I?

He was definitely beyond amazing in bed, best I'd ever had, but was I really lucky?

"I'm not so sure about that. I mean, is he just sleeping with me because he can't sleep with anyone else right now? Are we dating now? Are we husband and wife? What the hell are we?"

"Easy there." She got up from the floor and made it to the espresso machine again. "You'll figure it out." She glanced at me over her shoulder. "Eventually. I'd say, just keep living in the moment for now. My money is on you staying married, though, just so you know. I saw you guys together. There is no way he'll let you go." Turning her back to me, she played with a few buttons on the machine. "Do you have any idea how to work this thing?"

"Not at all, but I would assume you have to plug it in first."

She huffed and went for the kettle. "Tea it is then." Her phone pinged with a new text and she abandoned the kettle to get to it.

"Who is it?" I asked when she made an annoyed sound.

"No one." She dropped the phone back in her bag and came to my side. "The tea will have to wait though. I have to head out."

"Is everything okay?" I straightened from the island and faced her.

She rubbed her eyes and bounced on her toes. "Look," she started.

"Uh-oh." That was not a good start to any conversation.

"No uh-oh. It's just that I'm not sure if I should tell you this or not. I mean it shouldn't affect you in any way...but maybe it will... Ah hell."

"Cough it up, Lucy."

"I saw Marcus and Char kissing," she blurted out all at once.

"Marcus and our Charlotte?" I frowned. "No way. Are you sure it was them? I mean...how...when?"

"Since they were doing it in our living room...yeah, I'm pretty sure it was them."

"Whoaa..." I took a step back and leaned against the edge of the bar stool, making the damn thing scratch the floor. "I did *not* see that coming. Do you know how it happened? I mean, *our* Char with *my* Marcus? Really?"

"Your Marcus?" Lucy asked gently.

"You're right. Not mine, I guess. Could that be why she's been shutting me out lately? Did she think I would get mad or something? She barely responds to my calls and texts. I assumed it was because of her workload, but now…"

"To be honest, I had no idea either. I think Marcus still has a thing for you. He always did, even after the break up. You should've seen him when Jason came to collect your drunk ass. I thought for sure he was going to clock Marcus with the way he was acting. Then again, from what I saw, it didn't look like he was kissing Char for the first time either."

"I don't feel anything for Marcus. Not any more," I said carefully. *So why does this leave a bad taste in my mouth?* "But, it wasn't like Char didn't see how sad I was after he dumped me. She was right there with us almost from the beginning. Was she lusting after him all this time?"

"I have no idea, babe. I want to hear more about that myself, so don't worry, I'll let you know what I learn. Char is not so chummy with me either ever since Lily moved in, but I'm good with Marcus. I'll ask him and see what's going on."

"What do I do? Do I say anything to her if by some chance we talk? Not that she is dying to get in touch with me." I met Lucy's gaze and asked, "Am I overreacting? If they are in love, I'd be happy for them, but isn't it weird that this happens just a few weeks after I move out? It just feels weird."

"Don't think about it, okay? You have other things to focus on right now. If Char chooses not to talk to you because of Marcus, screw it. I'll talk to Marcus and we'll know more about what's going on."

I nodded. "Sure, but you don't have to. I mean, it's not our business, is it?"

"I have to leave, but we'll talk later, okay?"

I hugged her tightly. If there was one thing I didn't like about Jason's house, it was that Lucy wasn't living it with me. "I miss you," I murmured into her hair.

"Oh, babe, I miss you, too. Especially your comfy breasts." She stood next to me and peered outside. "You guys could always adopt me, you know. I wouldn't mind calling Jason *Daddy* at all."

"Ah, please, get out."

Holding her hands up, she backed away. "Just a suggestion. You guys are in a marriage now; you shouldn't make a big decision like that without talking to your hunky husband."

"Sure, I'll do that."

She gave me a miserable sigh. "As if you leaving is not bad enough, now I'm forced to sleep on the couch when Jameson stays over. No comfy breasts, no spooning…"

I stalked her toward the door with a big grin on my face. "Poor Lucy. I'm getting all the spoons. And I'm begging you, please, sleep in the same bed with the poor guy. At least give him that much."

She narrowed her eyes at me. "You're the worst friend on planet earth."

"Thanks, I try."

———

IT WAS hours after Lucy had left and I'd stopped wandering around the house trying to decide if I should call Char to see what was going on or not. It wasn't that I was jealous; I knew Marcus had dated other girls after me—he had even brought a few of them home. It had stung, but I hadn't been jealous. Hell, I was fake married to my childhood crush, who was I to have an opinion on their lives?

But, being with my friend? Kissing her? Sleeping with her??

I wasn't feeling very motivated to get back to the story I was working on, but I forced myself to sit down and get some words in since I had planned to write until Jason got home. When the scene turned from emotional to another hot sex scene, I thought it would be a good idea to get on tumblr and do some research, look at some erotic pictures and...you know, get motivated.

Since I knew Jason wouldn't be home for at least another three hours, I connected my laptop to his ginormous TV via Bluetooth and started scrolling through some tasteful black and whites. After jumping from one tumblr site to another, I found a new site that had all kinds of audio recordings—masturbation, edging, threesomes, fisting (*holy shit!*), dirty talk, moans, and good ol' mf having sex.

Curious and admittedly excited, I pressed play on one of the 'dirty talk' sound clips and immediately flinched when a deep voice echoed in Jason's house: *You like getting your pussy fucked up by this big cock, don't you?*

I was scared out of my wits. I had no idea that Jason had in-wall speakers in the house. I lowered the volume, but it was still an...experience, to say the least.

Not liking the girl calling the guy 'daddy' and mewling unnecessarily, I stopped that one and pressed play on another clip. And then another.

And another.

And another.

I didn't mind watching porn, but I didn't like going through a million videos just to find something that would actually excite me. I wasn't after a storyline or anything like that, but when the girl is screaming all over the place, faking it, or you don't find a guy attractive, no matter how many inches he has, it is hard to get into what they are doing.

So, having the freedom to imagine whomever I wanted to

imagine while I listened to sexy skin slapping, some dirty words, and pretty good moaning, I was a happy girl.

Once I found a ten-minute, homemade sound clip of a guy that was groaning and moaning just as much as the girl was, I closed my eyes and pictured Jason and me having sex.

That right there? Instant arousal.

Opening my document, I started to put down the words and soon enough I was lost in them.

"Boo!"

The moment I felt someone's breath on my neck and heard the voice, I screamed at the top of my lungs and tossed my laptop right over my head.

By the time I realized it was Jason who had scared me out of my mind, I was already standing in the middle of the ottoman, holding my chest and begging my heart to stay put where it belonged.

"What did you do that for? Are you crazy?!" I screamed, still breathless.

Jason was rubbing his head and looking at me as if I was the one who had lost her mind. "You throw your laptop at my head and you are calling *me* crazy?"

My laptop.

"Oh no!"

I jumped down from the safety of the ottoman and ran for my laptop. "No, no, no, no." I couldn't lose all the stuff I had written.

Before I could get to it, Jason leaned down and lifted it up from the floor. I jerked it out of his hands as soon as I was next to him. While the screen was shattered in the top left corner, the document I was working on was still open. *Thank god.* I hadn't lost everything I'd spent hours working on.

"Are we watching porn, my Olive?" Jason asked with a suggestive voice from behind me, and just like that, the little scare I had experienced seconds before turned into something else.

Something like *terror*.

I groaned and dove for the TV, which was displaying a gif of a very sexy dude hammering into a pretty brunette on the screen. However, it was a failed attempt because Jason was quicker than me.

"Not so fast my little Olive," he murmured as he curled his hands on the edge of the couch and successfully caged me in. As if all of that wasn't enough to cause major mortification, the second Jason pinned me between the couch and his gorgeous body, the couple in the speakers picked up speed in their love-making, making all kinds of skin-slapping noises, groaning, and cursing. It sounded like someone was going at it inches away from our faces.

Jason took my laptop from my hands and gently tossed it on the couch.

"Well, my beautiful wife, isn't this something to come home to."

"Oh my god," I groaned and clutched at his shirt with both hands, then proceeded to push my forehead against his shoulder. I could've happily hidden there for years.

When Jason's chest started to shake with quiet laughter under my head, I burrowed closer.

"Please, just kill me," I grumbled into his shirt.

"Oh, I couldn't, sweetheart," he said, nudging my chin up with his fingers.

He had *that* look on his face, that specific look that perfectly matched the erection I was feeling against my hip.

The woman's moans reached their crescendo and she finally came.

Hallelujah!

Seconds later, her partner joined her with his own release.

Then blissful silence.

Why couldn't have they finished just a few minutes earlier so Jason wouldn't think I was a pervert? Was that too much to ask?

"So…" Jason broke the silence as he looked down at me expectantly.

"Welcome home," I said, forcing a smile on my red face. "How was shooting today? Did anything interesting happen on set? Which scenes did you—"

He interrupted me, which I thought was quite rude.

"I don't think those are the right questions to ask today, my dear wife."

That last word… It melted my heart *and* my brain.

"Are you horny? I'm not taking care of you?" he asked while I was trying to recover from completely melting into a puddle.

"Huh?"

"You heard me." He tucked a hair behind my ear, his fingers lingering on my skin.

"I was just doing research," I mumbled, unable to look into his eyes.

"Research, huh?"

"Yep. There was a sex scene and I needed a little inspiration… and I…well, I thought it would be more authentic if I was in the mood."

"Hmmm." He finally broke our eye contact and bent down to nuzzle his nose against my neck as he breathed me in.

Hot guy sniffing me alert!

Every single hair on my body stood up and my body—acting completely on its own—arched toward him.

"Let's see if you are properly in the mood then."

In my next breath, his big hands were at the back of my thighs and a loud squeal left my lips. I quickly wrapped my arms around his neck as he lifted me up.

"I'm getting used to this whole carrying me away thing," I murmured, still avoiding his eyes.

"I just want you to get the whole experience right, you know, feel it in your bones kinda thing, so you can write a good sex scene."

"All for the greater good, you say?"

"Exactly."

When he dipped me down and my back met the couch pillows, I thought he would dump me there, but instead he kept one of his hands firmly around my waist, reached for my laptop, and opened the site that had the sound clips.

"What are you doing?" I asked, my voice tinged with a bit of panic.

"Just want to see if I can make you scream louder than her. How long is this thing?" he asked after pressing play on the same one that had been playing when he'd busted me.

Still hugging him with my arms and legs, I answered his question. "Around fifteen, twenty minutes, I think."

"We will definitely beat them," he murmured as soft licking sounds filled the house.

"Are we in a race that I'm not aware of?" He straightened us up and started to head toward his bedroom.

I'm telling you, hearing sounds—especially licking and slurping—coming from the walls was the weirdest thing ever.

"Don't you want to play with me? Scream my name while I'm pounding away at you?"

I groaned. Even if the audio-porn hadn't done the trick, Jason was definitely getting me there with his words. "That does sound good, but…"

"No buts, sweetheart. Let me help you with your research."

Then my back hit his bed with a thump and his lips took my mouth in a scorching kiss.

With frantic hands, I reached for his shirt at the same time he reached for mine. I took his off in a hurry as soon as he gave me an opening and he took care of mine even quicker. Seeing the outline of his cock straining against the thick material of his jeans did nothing to help me calm down and take it easy as I struggled to open the damn button.

In seconds, he had me completely naked under him. When I was breathless from his kiss, he stepped off the bed and took off his jeans and briefs all on his own. His dark eyes never once strayed away from mine.

His erection—or whatever you called that monster—was standing up proudly as my attention focused on the thick vein I was dying to trace with my tongue.

Putting his hands under my knees, he slowly pulled me to himself, toward the edge of the bed. In seconds, my legs were being spread open and his head was right between my legs, licking me clean.

When he was done—or more accurately, when *I* was done for —he crawled on top of me, his erection incredibly hard and warm against my leg.

"Point one for us," I murmured, my voice a little hoarse from all the begging and moaning. The girl was still begging for her release.

"You were soaking wet, Olive. Was that all for me, or was it the audio that got you this hot?"

"Both, I think," I said, looking away from his persistent gaze.

"You are full of surprises," he murmured and licked my lips, parting them open so he could slide his tongue inside.

In the background, when the girl came in a rush, Jason was still lazily kissing the fuck out of me.

"Now that they caught up, what now?" he asked as he pressed small kisses on my jawline. His fingers were doing something wicked to my nipples as he made his way down toward them.

The sounds of skin slapping and other wet sounds filled the room and before I could order my brain to answer his question, Jason said, "I think I know what that sound is."

The next second, I was flipped onto my stomach and Jason was kneeling over me, my legs closed up between his thighs.

"Push your ass up for me, beautiful."

I did what I was told. Then his chest was plastered to my back. He was burning up, or maybe it was me?

"Thank you," he murmured against my neck and pulled all of my hair to one side.

The guy in the audio let out a long groan as he kept fucking the girl.

Jason licked my earlobe into his mouth and gently bit into it. "Is this making you hot, baby?"

"Yes…" I moaned, lifting my ass up to invite him in.

"You are burning for it, aren't you, sweetheart? You want to be fucked like her?"

Out of words that would make any sense, I nodded.

"Can you hear how hard and fast he is fucking her?" A gentle bite on my neck and my eyes fluttered closed. The guy really was going at it at full force, making the girl cry out with pleasure. "Shit, baby. I bet she is on fucking cloud nine right now. Can I fuck you harder than he is fucking her?" he whispered, his soft voice causing all sorts of shivers to run through my body. His fingertips were tracing my spine when he asked, "Do you want me to?"

"Yes, Jason. Please," I mumbled.

Then he was off my back, and I heard him tear open a condom and roll it on. Next his hands were massaging my ass cheeks. "One day, your ass is going to be the cause of my death," he mumbled almost to himself, guiding his erection into me, stretching me wide open. I groaned as loud as humanly possible. I tried to push up on my knees to force him to slide it in faster or maybe to get away from him; I had no idea what I was doing, only that my body had come alive and I could feel every soft touch, every little pressure against my skin.

And boy was there pressure.

He pulled slightly back, but then pressed his entire length into me.

My legs were shaking when he pressed his knees against my hips, caging me under him. I lifted my arms up and hugged my pillow, burying my face into it.

When his abs were pressing against my back and his elbows were propped on either side of my shoulders, I took my face out of my pillow.

"It must feel good having all of me inside you like that. Being inside you…" He took a deep breath. "Fuck, but it feels amazing, Olive."

"Too good," I managed to say in a whisper.

"I think I owe you an orgasm. They are ahead of us, sweetheart."

"What?" I had completely forgotten about the audio couple. Every inch of my skin was prickling with awareness under Jason. I was too far gone to hear anything other than his breath and my own heavy breathing.

He pulled back, almost to his tip, and pushed back in—hard.

My breath hitched. "Yes!"

"You liked that, huh?"

Another hard thrust and I was clawing at my pillow. He picked up speed.

As he kept fucking me into pure bliss, he lowered his head next to my ear and said, "I think I would love to come home to this every single fucking day for the rest of my life."

My heart stopped.

Then it started back up again as my orgasm caught me off guard when Jason pushed all the way in and started grinding into me.

My screams were definitely louder than the girl's, I can tell you that much.

There will never be enough words to describe sharing the perfect moment with the person you love, with the person you've been in love with for most of your life…but…as sweat dripped down from Jason's forehead onto my shoulder and his hips kept slamming into me through my spectacular orgasm, I decided that I didn't need any words.

Hearing his deep moan, knowing that he was enjoying it just as much as me was enough on its own.

He slowed his movements and I managed to stop trembling underneath him. His teeth grazed my shoulder and another shiver went through my body. I was a mess.

"Ah, sweetheart… The sounds you make when you come for me? So fucking dirty."

A deep thrust from him and a shameless mewling from me.

"I love it. I can feel it my bones. And the way you clench on my cock, the way you pull me in? It kills me every single fucking time." He kissed my neck and gently slapped my ass, pulling a gasp out of me. "I think we are caught up on the orgasms. Do you want me to lick you all clean again, as I'm guessing from the sounds they are making they are doing too, or do you want to ride me?"

He pulled out of me, but his heat didn't leave my body.

"Have to say, my vote is on you riding me, baby. I want to watch your face when you come all over my cock. I can always lick you clean at the end."

I didn't make him ask twice. While we could still hear the guy licking his girl, I pushed Jason onto his back and sunk down on his cock.

"Yes, sweetheart. Oh, fuck! Yes. Just like that, Olive. Take it all in, baby." My hands found the headboard and without playing around, I started riding him. I was all shaky and definitely was muttering some obscenities at some point, but it was all perfect. Being with him felt perfect. Our kind of perfect.

Beautiful.

Just like I'd always dreamed.

When I came all over him, I let him watch what he did to me, what he gave to me.

Everything.

"IF I'M NOT HELPING you with your research in one way or another the next time you're writing a sex scene, I think we're gonna have problems sweetheart."

At the end, we had held on longer than the audio couple, I had come more times than I could count or remember, and each time I'd been louder than her.

We had definitely won, on all counts.

"I think I'm having a stroke or something. I can't feel certain body parts."

Jason chuckled and his finger trailed down from my shoulder toward my hip. I was already half passed out and lying on my face. When his finger hit the curve of my ass, he pushed the covers off my back and his hand started massaging. I tried to wiggle away from his hand, but before I could...

"Hey," he admonished me with a serious voice. "You're staying right there."

I groaned. "If you start doing that, I will start feeling things, and I'm not sure I'm functioning enough for that."

Continuing to massage my ass firmly, he kissed my neck and shushed me. "Thank god the audio doesn't replay itself; it's dangerous to listen something like that with you around."

"Mmmm," I mumbled, acting like I was half-asleep.

"Come on," he said in an amused tone. "Don't get shy with me. I love that you like playing. You were burning for me the entire time. I bet hearing them be so vocal didn't hurt either."

He gathered me up in his arms and I nestled against his chest. It wasn't even seven o'clock, but I snuggled in closer.

When I didn't make any comments, he chuckled again and brushed a kiss on my temple. "Okay, have it your way. For now. What did you do today? I missed you on set."

"Lucy came over for an hour or so." Then I remembered that I hadn't asked his permission for that. "Is that okay? Her coming over?"

"Of course it's okay for your friends to come over, Olive. You don't need my permission for that."

"But I know you said you don't like having people in your personal space."

"I meant industry people. Unfortunately, I don't have that many friends. It's hard to trust people when you are out in the open as much as I am, and since I prefer a relatively quieter life , I don't have that many people close to me. Speaking of friends, there is someone I met very early in my career, Devlin. He lives in New York so I don't get to see him that often, but he is opening up a club/lounge here and he invited us. Would you like to go? We can invite your friends, too. I feel bad that you're having trouble meeting with them without a sea of cameras following you around."

I extricated myself from his arms, pulled the cover over myself to make sure nothing was showing, and stared at the ceiling.

"If you're okay with it, that could be fun. Lucy would love to come, and maybe I can convince her to invite Jameson, her on-again, off-again one-night stand. But Charlotte...I'm not sure about that right now."

Jason propped himself up on his elbow and looked down at me.

God... What was it about this guy that affected me so much? Even when he wasn't showing off that damn dimple of his, you kept staring at him just for the sheer pleasure of it, and of course the promise of that dimple wasn't something to turn your nose up at.

"Is everything all right with you two?"

Forcing myself to look away so I wouldn't tackle him and climb on for one last ride, I said, "Apparently, Lucy saw Char and Marcus kissing in the apartment."

"And…"

"And she is my friend. Isn't there supposed to be a girl code of some sort that says you shouldn't date your friend's ex?"

His tone was different, both softer and tighter at the same time when he asked, "Do you still have feelings for Marcus? Are you jealous of her, Olive?"

I glanced at him. "The answer to the first question is a definite no. Being jealous? Not sure, but I don't think so. Marcus and I… We've been over for a long time, and…heck. No, I'm not jealous of him. It's just sort of a weird thing for Charlotte to do behind my back. If she had at any time told me that she had feelings for Marcus, I would've gotten over it, and if they love each other…I would be happy for them. I mean, she hasn't even talked to me about it so I have no idea what's actually going on. Just a few short months ago, the day I was meeting with the production people, Marcus came to my room to tell me he thought we would get back together once I'd finished my book. And now he is with Char? I don't know. It's not anger or jealousy I'm feeling. It's something else, but I'm not sure I can name it."

"I understand. The way Marcus acted when I came to get your little drunk ass from their apartment, I wouldn't have guessed he had his eyes on anyone but you."

"Yeah, I heard about that from Lucy, too."

"Well," he started as he got up from the bed, completely naked.

Don't look, Olive. Don't do it.

But of course, I looked.

At least don't look down.

Oh, but I did.

"The invitation is open; you can invite whomever you want to invite. Devlin will have a VIP room reserved for us so we'll have privacy."

CHAPTER TWENTY-NINE

OLIVE

Two days later, we were getting out of the car in front of Devlin's club, Mad Play. The logo for the club was two Ms intertwined with each other in a geometric shape. I had no idea what it meant since it wasn't the initials of the club, but it was cool as hell.

Jason and I had met with his friend over dinner before he headed to his club ahead of us. Even though we had barely spent an hour together, he was very charming throughout the entire dinner—maybe a little too charming, the kind that would sweet talk you out of your panties if given the chance.

Imagining him wreaking havoc in New York with a single Jason had led to a multitude of scenarios going through my mind. Those two would break hearts left and right, and they probably already had. On a side note, I had loved how Jason had introduced me as his wife. I wasn't sure if he would let him know this was all a play for the public eye. Since my best friend knew, I'd assumed he would share that with Devlin, just like Alvin was in on the whole thing.

Speaking of Alvin, he was supposed to meet us at the club with his girlfriend, but as far as we knew he hadn't made it yet.

The biggest surprise of the night, however, was getting a text message from Lucy that said Char and her friend Lily were coming with her. Not having any idea how that would go down, I decided not to dwell on it for the time being.

Since there would be drinking involved, Jason had a driver drop us off. When I saw all the paparazzi huddled in front of the club, I held on to Jason's hand tighter and exited the car right after him.

Wrapping his hand more securely around mine, he put his other hand at the small of my back and guided me toward the entrance. The bulky guard at the front didn't even check our names as we were ushered in before the paparazzi could swarm us.

"Does it ever get easier?" I asked, slightly breathless from jogging the short distance. The music was loud enough that Jason had to lean down to hear what I was saying. I repeated my question when he was close enough.

"The paparazzi, the constant following…does it ever get easier?"

He shook his head in a distracted manner and curled his arm around my waist, pulling me close to his body as a beautiful blonde approached us with a smiling face. Of course, she only had eyes for Jason and ignored me completely. I was getting used to it.

Really.

I definitely didn't wanna gouge her eyes out or anything.

That would be gruesome.

"Hello Mr. Thorn. My name is Drew. We were waiting for you. If you can follow me, I'll take you to Devlin."

Jason didn't reply, gave her a stiff nod, and pretty much shattered the girls dreams, judging by the look on her face.

Smug, I stood a bit straighter and gave the girl a brilliant smile when she finally gave me a dismissing glance.

Fuck her.

After walking through a hallway filled with mirrors and lights, we found ourselves at the mouth of the club where you could see the sea of bodies dancing under the flashing lights. A remix of the latest song by The Weeknd was blasting through the speakers and from what I could see, it looked like everyone was having the time of their lives.

As we started following the girl, skirting around the gyrating bodies, Jason positioned me in front of him and kept his hands on me at all times.

Trusting him to guide me in the right direction, I took out my phone from the small clutch in my hands and sent a quick text to Lucy asking if they had arrived.

By the time we made it to Devlin's side and the blonde gave Jason one last longing look, Lucy had texted back, saying they were already inside. After sending one last text that asked her to meet us at the bar area where we were, I gave all of my attention to Jason.

"Your friends are here?" he asked as soon as I tucked my phone back into my purse.

"Yes. I told her where we are." I looked around me and noticed that no one was bothering Jason. No one was coming at us, begging to take a picture with him or have him sign any of their body parts.

"Marcus?" he asked, his voice tighter than I would've liked.

"No," I said shortly and turned my eyes to Devlin. "Are you sure it's safe for Jason to be down here?"

Devlin let out a sexy laugh. If Jason hadn't been my Jason, the guy I wanted to have babies with, I would have been content with just watching his friend. "Aww, how sweet of your little wife to be worried about you, Jason," he yelled to be heard.

Jason's thumb brushed the underside of my breast.

"So, what do you think of my new place?" Devlin asked, opening his arms.

Sure, let's ignore little Olive.

Despite feeling annoyed at being dismissed again, I had to admit, his *place* did look amazing. The general color scheme of the venue was black, white, and gold. There were white balloons dipped in gold paint floating around the place and my hands were itching to steal a few of them.

"It looks amazing," I said, looking at the female bartenders that were wearing pretty gold dresses. The guys were wearing black slacks with white button downs, complementing the girls perfectly. The whole concept was simple, but sexy.

"What she said," Jason said with a sexy chin lift.

Looking satisfied with the answer, Devlin nodded. "What can I get you guys?" he asked, leaning toward us.

"I have to be on set tomorrow so I'll only have one and I'll take that later," Jason answered his friend before glancing down at me.

"I'll have a Long Island," I murmured, looking up at him.

God, was it a good time to lick that dimple? Or those lips, I would have been content with licking those lips...

Smiling at me as if he could hear my thoughts, he fitted his hand around my neck and brushed a small kiss at the edge of my mouth.

"Happy?" he asked, showing me a bit of his dimple.

Holding on to his forearm, I leaned up and kissed his dimple as my answer. When I leaned back, his dimple was out full force. Taking my drink from Devlin, I rested my back against Jason's chest and listened to them talk as I waited for the girls to find us.

Despite the thumping music, I heard Lucy yelling my name before I actually saw them. Jason took my drink from my hand before I splashed it all over my pretty dress.

"You look amazing," I said to Lucy, twirling her around to

check out her dress. She was wearing a black lace dress with a plunging neckline. Surprisingly, it wasn't that short. "I'm guessing Jameson is coming?" I asked, lifting an eyebrow.

She rolled her eyes, but her lips tipped up with a smile. "Maybe."

"Maybe is good. I'll take those odds." She gave me a brief hug and then I saw Char and Lily coming through the crowd behind us.

When Char spotted me, she gave me a small smile. For the life of me I couldn't see anything wrong with it. Letting go of Lucy, I hugged Char and said hi to Lily. I'd only seen her a few times around campus, but she looked kind.

After the girls said hi to Jason and Devlin, they ordered their drinks. When Jason's arm sneaked around me while I was talking to Lily, I turned my head to look at him, but his attention was on Devlin telling him a story about their mutual friend.

"Can we talk for a few minutes when we find a quiet spot?" Char asked, leaning toward me.

I smiled. "Of course."

So what if they were together? I wasn't Marcus' keeper, and if Char actually had feelings for him, even if they'd started when we were dating... Well, I hoped they were happy, or at least would be. So, I would listen to her and be okay with whatever she wanted to tell me.

"Come on. Let's dance," Lucy said, pulling Lily to the dance floor with her. Motioning for me to follow, she turned her back and started dancing with a more than ready to let loose Lily.

"Do you want me to show you the private rooms, Jason?" Devlin asked, saving me from humiliation. As much as I loved the atmosphere of a club, I wasn't the best dancer out there. Sure, I could shake my ass, do a dip, jump around, and that sort of stuff, but I wasn't drunk enough to jump on the dance floor quite yet.

"You can stay with your friends if you want," Jason said, pushing my wavy hair away from my face.

I fitted my hand into his. "No, I want to come with you."

After letting Char know that we were going up to check out the private rooms, we left the girls downstairs and followed Devlin up to the third floor where the VIP rooms were located.

"There is a security guard waiting right outside every occupied room, and you'll have your own bartender to prepare you whatever you want from the bar," Devlin said, letting us into a dimly lit room.

To my surprise it wasn't cut off from the rest of the club at all. At the right side of the room, there was a small balcony with a railing where you had a bird's eye view of the entire club. Since the private rooms were located only on the left side of the building, there was no way anyone could see who was in the private rooms or what they were doing in there. I doubted anyone looking up from the dance floor could make out anything in the dark either.

A huge leather sectional covered an entire wall and in front of it, there was an equally big leather ottoman. The chandelier that hung from the ceiling was the only light source in the room. In the far left corner of the room there was a small bar, fully loaded, presumably for those A-listers who didn't want to waste time waiting for their drinks to arrive.

A security guard came inside and pulled Devlin to the corner of the room, speaking in hushed tones.

"You want to bring your friends up here?" Jason asked, coming to my side as I took in the room. "It's nice, but you will be pretty isolated from the crowd, though."

"Guys," Devlin said, grabbing our attention. "Is it okay if I join you later? The guys are having a problem at the door. I better go handle that. Please, invite your friends up and use the room in any way you want, Olive. If you call out to Anthony, who is guarding the door, he'll make sure to send a bartender up here."

"Everything okay?" Jason asked.

He gave him a nod and patted him on his shoulder. "Nothing to worry about. A few uninvited people making a ruckus outside. I'll come back when things are more settled down, okay?"

Devlin left and I braced myself on my elbows on the railing as I gazed down at the dance floor. The DJ changed the music and the dark notes of Katy Perry's "Dark Horse" filled the space. It was a more erotic remix of it, the bass lower and more powerful.

When I couldn't hear Jason, I looked over my shoulder to see him closing the door and turning the lights off. Then he came toward me and positioned himself behind me. His arms went around my waist and he straightened me up from the railing.

"Don't hang over the railing like that," he murmured next to my ear. I turned my head and showed him my neck. When he ghosted small kisses on my skin, I could feel his lips tip up to a smile.

"Thank you for inviting my friends," I said, feeling the music working its way into my bloodstream.

Jason must've felt the change in my mood because his hands started traveling lower and when he got a hold of my hips, he pulled me back and let me feel his lengthening erection.

"You look beautiful. I like your dress." He bit into my earlobe and I couldn't hold back the moan that escaped my lips.

"It's one of the dresses your stylist left with me for the London premiere." I was wearing a black and brown Alexander Wang V-neck dress. More than sexy, I felt beautiful in it. The hem of the dress was also shaped in V, and there was an open slit in the back, too. Feeling Jason's shirt brush my bare skin through that small opening heightened my pleasure.

"Hmmm," Jason murmured. I guess he didn't care about the dress that much. "We should get your friends up here. I don't think I'm a fan of sharing you, but we did invite them after all." My toes curled in my shoes from the pleasure his words were causing.

I linked our hands together and pulled them back up to my waist, or more like just under my breasts.

"I'll go get them," I said, closing my eyes and moving my hips along with the rhythm of the music.

I didn't want to go anywhere.

"Does my baby want to play again?" Jason asked as he bent his head down to my neck and gently sucked on my skin.

I groaned and let him push my lower body against the railing. "Don't say that when we can't do anything about it." Letting go of his hands, I lifted mine up and wound them around his neck. Pulling his head down to my lips, I kissed him slowly. Then with a growl he slipped his tongue inside my mouth and took things further.

The music pounding in my head, I already felt drunk. The funny thing was, I had only taken a few sips from my drink.

"Who says we can't do anything about it?"

He gripped my chin, a little more aggressively than I was expecting, which only caused more wetness to seep into my panties. He kissed me until I was seeing stars behind my closed eyelids. When one of his hands skimmed my dress and cupped one of my breasts, I moaned into his mouth and threaded my fingers into his hair.

When we separated to take several gasps of breath, I was smiling.

"What are you smiling at?" he asked, his voice raspy from all the kissing.

"Nothing." He gave me a disbelieving look. "Nothing," I repeated. "It's just, I think I like kissing you a little too much, and somehow you seem to like it almost as much as I do."

"And that surprises you?"

"Yeah." He wouldn't understand, but yes…finally kissing someone you'd longed to kiss for so many years and actually having him kiss you back with just as much passion…it was indescribable. The only thing I could say was that it did something to your heart, something that knocked you on your ass with the unexpected force of it.

"My heart is beating just for you, Jason," I whispered against his lips as I made sure to look into his eyes. Did he understand how much I loved him? How long I had loved him? Because I could almost feel it pouring out of me.

The door opened and the connection between us broke.

Lucy's head appeared in the doorway. "Is it okay if we come in?"

I took a step away from the hot body that was plastered to my back and went to open the door wider so the girls could get in. Lucy had the biggest grin on her face, but managed to keep her mouth closed.

Two tequila shots and one and a half Long Island Iced Teas later, Char pulled me away from our little group to the small bar at the corner.

"I know Lucy told you that she saw us, but it's not what you think, Olive," she said, putting down her pink cocktail on the glass surface.

"Honestly, I'm not thinking anything. I'm trying not to. If you guys have started something, I'll be happy for you."

Her eyes hardened for a moment, but before I could even guess what it was that I saw in her eyes, it disappeared. "You don't understand, Liv."

Again with the name…

When Lily let out a big laugh that reached across the room to us, I looked over my shoulder to see her laughing with Jason and Lucy. I smiled when Jason caught my eye, took a sip of his drink, and gave me a wink.

Char touched my arm so I turned back to her again.

"Marcus and I..." Stopping mid-sentence, she picked up her drink and took a big swallow. "We might have slept together... while you were still with him."

My stomach dropped and my eyebrows reached almost up to my hairline. I swallowed and gently put my drink down.

"Please say you didn't do that."

She gave me a small, sad smile. "I don't know how it happened, Olive. I swear to you, it wasn't more than a few times, but I know that doesn't make it any better. I'm sorry I haven't told you before today."

A few times?

"You slept with Marcus while I was still with him? When you knew I loved him? No way Charlotte. You wouldn't do that."

"You guys were growing apart." She took a deep breath. "Remember the time you went back home to San Francisco for a week, after one of your fights?" I didn't say anything, didn't even nod. She sighed. "It happened then. We were both half-drunk the first time it happened—not so drunk that we didn't know what we were doing, but you know...it made it easier to overlook the fact that you were together, I guess."

How nice of them.

"I'm assuming not so drunk the other times it happened," I said in a stony tone.

She shook her head and looked down. "I'm sorry, Olive. I never thought this would happen to me."

"To you? What happened to *you*, Charlotte?"

"You're my best friend, Olive. Do you think I was thrilled to realize I had feelings for my best friend's boyfriend? Can you understand how much it hurt to see him with you after what happened between us?"

"Wow. Should I say sorry for the inconvenience?"

I took a step back.

She grabbed my arm and stopped me before I could get away from her.

"Please don't be angry with me, Olive. You didn't love Marcus. We both knew it. You never loved him like you love Jason."

"How can you decide that for me, Charlotte? Of course I loved Marcus. Maybe I should remind you that he was the one who dumped me, not the other way around." I pulled my arm back and she dropped her hand. "Why did you think it was a good idea to tell me this now? Why bother? So much time has passed and you can actually have Marcus all to yourself. Why not just keep it to yourself?"

"I think Marcus is holding himself back because he thinks you'll go back to him. Whatever you decide I wanted you to have all the facts. We got together—"

I lifted my hand up and cut her off. "I don't think I want to hear anything more Charlotte." I shook my head in disbelief. "Are you about to tell me that I should talk to Marcus and tell him that we are never getting back together? Is that why you told me this? To make sure I would never go back to him if Jason dumped me?"

"Girls? What's going on?" Lucy came up behind us. I hadn't realized that our voices were carrying over to them.

"Olive," Charlotte said, ignoring Lucy. "It's not like that. I didn't think you—"

"That's the problem, I don't think you are thinking at all," I said and turned my back to her. "Can we go down to the bathroom or something?" I asked Lucy. I was just realizing that my hands were shaking. She looked into my eyes and nodded without asking anything.

My eyes were starting to water.

I glanced at Jason, but he was in a conversation with Lily, his brows furrowed, so I slipped out before he could see the state I was in. I didn't want him to think that this was about Marcus.

Lucy grabbed my hand as soon as we were out of the room and steered me downstairs.

We found a bathroom one floor down that was just for the private rooms, so as soon as we got in, Lucy guided me to sit down on the bench in front of the mirrors. If my mind hadn't been reeling with what Char had just told me, I would've enjoyed the décor in the bathroom, but unfortunately, I could barely see Lucy kneeling in front of me.

"What's wrong, Olive? What did Char say?"

A few tears escaped my eyes and slid down my cheeks before I could wipe them away. "She slept with Marcus while we were still together."

Lucy straightened up then sat down next to me. "Say that again?"

I nodded and wiped away more tears. Why was I even crying? Was I really sad because Marcus had lied to me, had cheated on me with my friend? I thought about it, but it didn't take hold. It wasn't what Marcus had done that was breaking my heart. It was Charlotte.

I got up and started to pace in front of Lucy. "Why am I even crying? This is so stupid."

"Can you start from the top and tell me exactly what she said to you?"

I nodded and told her everything Char had said.

"I'm sorry, Olive. I don't know what to say. All I can think is where the hell was I when they were sneaking into each other's rooms?"

"Looks like I was wherever you were. I would never have thought Char would do something like this."

"Are you going to talk to Marcus?"

A girl stumbled into the bathroom, heading straight toward the stalls.

"Why would I?" I asked, getting out of the way before she could take me down.

Lucy's phone started to vibrate in her hand, so she held up a finger to me and answered her phone.

"Jameson, where are you?" Her brows drew together and she shot up from her seat. "What? Which hospital?"

At her words my body froze.

"Yes. I understand. Thank you."

Ending the call, she sat back down, then shakily tried to stand back up.

"Hey, easy there," I said, helping her up. "Tell me what he said."

Instead of answering me, she said, "He was supposed to be here by now."

"Lucy," I snapped my finger in front of her face a few times. "Focus. What did Jameson say?"

"It wasn't Jameson. It was a nurse. Jameson was in an accident, he…he is going into surgery in half an hour."

I waited to hear more, but she just stood there, staring at me helplessly.

"Come on, we are leaving," I said, pulling her along with me.

We exited the club in a hurry and jumped into the first cab we saw sitting at the curb. Thankfully, there were no paparazzi around to capture our departure.

"Jason," Lucy said in a tearful voice. "You didn't tell Jason you were leaving."

"I know. I don't have my phone with me so I'll have to text him from your phone. Let's just focus on getting to Jameson before he goes into surgery, okay? The hospital is close enough, we should make it there in time." I gave her hand a squeeze. She hadn't let go of it ever since we'd run out of the bathroom.

Her grip tightened on mine and I heard her breath hitch.

"Can we please go a little faster?" I begged the cab driver.

Lucy dropped her head on my shoulder. "You were right, the other day. I love him," she confessed, then more heatedly, added, "And I hate him for making me fall in love with him."

"Baby," I said gently, trying not to laugh. "I'm sure he is already aware of that fact. Even your professors know."

"I always push him away." Her voice broke. "I didn't even tell him that I hate him. He should know how much I hate him for making me fall in love with him."

Maneuvering my arm from under her head, I hugged her to me and held on. "If he doesn't know—even though I'm pretty sure he does—you'll tell him before he goes into surgery okay? He'll be happy to finally hear the words from your mouth. We're almost there, sweetheart."

As soon as the cab dropped us at the emergency entrance, we rushed inside and found a nurse that could help us. We made it to his side just before they took him into the operating room, but seeing him unconscious and all banged up didn't help Lucy calm down at all. Before they could wheel him away from us, I heard Lucy's heated whisper, *since you made me fall in love with you, you better get well soon so I can torture you for what you did to me!*

His doctor assured us that even though his injuries were serious, they weren't life threatening. Apparently, his motorcycle had collided with a speeding car. He had a broken leg and multiple fractures to his shoulder blade and forearm along with various cuts and bruises.

"Tell me he is going to be okay, Olive," Lucy said once we sat down in the waiting room.

"He *is* going to be okay, Lucy. You heard his doctor, he is in good hands." She nodded and kept silent.

"You should call his friends," I said after some time. "I'm sure he'd like to see them once it is okay for him to have visitors."

"Here, I forgot." She handed me her phone. "You should call

Jason first. I'm sure he is wondering where the hell you are. I'll call Jameson's friends after that."

I took the phone. "I'll be right back. Don't move from this seat."

Meeting my eyes for the first time since we'd gotten the phone call, she gave me a small smile. "Thank you, Olive."

I huffed. "For what?"

"For holding me up. For running out of there without a second thought." Her eyes started to water, but she had a small grin on her face when she said, "I'm not sure I could've left Jason Thorn behind for you."

"I'm sure enough for both of us. You wouldn't leave his side for a moment. You made that pretty clear." I said. "And save those crocodile tears for Jameson; I'm sure he'll be happy to see how much you care."

She gave me a laugh; it was shaky, but I would take it. "That bastard would like that, wouldn't he? He would probably puff out his chest and let everyone know that I cried for him." Sighing, she shook her head. "Go ahead and call your husband. I'll wait right here."

Not wanting to go too far away from Lucy, I found a quiet corner where I could still keep Lucy in sight and quickly dialed Jason's number. It rang several times and then his voicemail picked up. I left him a short message that explained where I was and what had happened and asked him to call me back before he came charging in there. It was his friend's night and he didn't have that many friends around him; I didn't want him to leave abruptly when there was nothing he could do at the hospital.

Taking my seat next to Lucy again, I shook my head at her. "He isn't picking up. I left him a voicemail and I'm sure he'll get back to me when he sees it."

We settled down in our seats and the waiting game started.

After four hours, Jameson was out of surgery.

After those same four hours, there was still no call from Jason.

———

AT 5:30 AM, I was using Lucy's key to get into the apartment, and I was doing some major praying and begging to anyone that was listening up there that I wouldn't come face to face with Charlotte or Marcus. When I managed to sneak into Lucy's room without waking anyone up, I sighed a breath of relief. I didn't actually know if anyone was home, but to be on the safe side, I tried my best not to make any noise and packed up a change of clothes for both Lucy and me. I left the building just as quietly as I had come in.

At that moment, I was more worried about not hearing back from Jason. At first, I'd thought maybe he was angry at me for not letting him know I was leaving with Lucy, but then I thought maybe he wasn't angry at all but just couldn't come to the hospital because everyone would recognize him. I also thought that was a lame excuse.

But then, why wouldn't he call me back? Why wouldn't he respond to any of my voicemails? Had something happened back at the club that I wasn't aware of?

Maybe an earthquake had hit?

When I made it back to the hospital, Lucy was sitting exactly where I had left her.

"Any word from the doctors?" I asked as I put down the small bag on the seat in between us."

"Still in ICU. They'll let me know when I can see him. I left voicemails for a few of his friends, I'm sure they'll get down here as soon they get it."

"His family?"

She shook her head and finally looked at me. She looked

better than before, but I could see that she was struggling to sit up straight. What a cluster fuck of a night for both of us.

"He has an aunt and a grandma, but they live in Florida. I'm not sure if they'll be up for the travel. I'll let him call them himself. Why didn't you change your clothes back at the apartment?"

"Wasn't sure if anyone was home." I gave her a half-shrug and tightened my hand on the bag's handle. "Didn't want to risk waking them up with the noise."

She nodded and turned her head to the nurses station. I rubbed my eyes and rose up from my seat. "Come on, we stick out like a sore thumb in these dresses. We'll be back in a minute."

I guided a reluctant Lucy toward the restrooms and quickly changed into more comfortable clothes. While the leggings and flats were actually my own stuff I had left at the apartment when I was moving, the baseball tee was hers and it sat a little too snug on my chest.

"How are my leggings not cutting off at your knees?" Lucy asked once she was done changing.

"They're not yours," I explained with a smile. "Some of mine. I must have left them behind."

"Oh. Okay."

"Lucy, you don't look so good. How about you rest your eyes for a few minutes while I wait to hear back from the doctor?" She linked her arm with mine and we walked back to our seats.

"You don't look so fine either," she pointed out.

"Thanks. How kind of you," I said in a flat tone and she gave me a small chuckle. I'd take that one, too. "Come on, if the doctor comes out, I'll wake you."

Once we reached our seats, Lucy noticed a doctor wearing scrubs talking to a middle-aged woman and her hand tightened on my arm.

"It's not the same doctor, don't worry," I said, patting her hand. It didn't escape my notice that the woman was crying a bucket of tears.

"Thank you for coming with me, Olive," she said again as we sat back down.

"Where else would I be?"

She took a good look at me, then rested her head on my shoulder and closed her eyes. "I bet by the time I wake up Jason will call. Here, take this." Reaching for her pocket, she handed me her phone. "It's on vibrate so keep it on you."

"Thanks," I said, turning the phone over and over in my hands.

In a few minutes, she was out like a light. While Lucy slept on my shoulder, the waiting room filled and emptied several times. None of the voices disturbed her sleep.

Early in the morning, when the doc came to take her back to Jameson's room, she almost looked like her normal self.

I chose to wait in the waiting room for a while longer. A few minutes after she left, her phone started going crazy with notifications in my hand. Thinking it was either Jason or one of Jameson's friends, I swiped at the screen.

Busted!!! Is It Already 'The End' for Our Favorite Newlyweds?

*Last night, Jason Thorn and his blushing bride attended
the opening of Jason's friend Devlin Parker's nightclub,
Mad Play. Until now all we've heard from several sources
close to the couple is that they are intensely happy and in
love. Do you remember those set photos we shared only a
few days ago where Jason was carrying Olive to their
trailer? Well, folks, seems like there is trouble in paradise.
We got these photos from an anonymous source who was
in the nightclub while the incident occurred and managed
to capture Jason Thorn getting cozy with a blonde who is
most definitely not his wife. As you can see in the first
photo, the girl is sitting on his lap and whispering into his
ear while his head is resting on the wall.*

*While the couple was pictured together entering the club,
at this moment we don't know when Olive Taylor left the
hunky actor alone. It appears that not all is well with
Hollywood's latest favorite couple.*

*Let's face it, none of us would mind sharing a bed with
Jason Thorn, but we were over the moon about his
marriage to the bestselling author, Olive Taylor. Their love
story, the book, Jason being her first crush...our point is,
we were definitely rooting for Olive to steal Jason's heart*

for good. However, these recently leaked photos showed us again that a Hollywood marriage does not equal long-lasting wedded bliss.

We all know how the saying goes: 'A leopard can't change its spots.' Maybe the fate of this short marriage was sealed from the very beginning. What do you think?

So far, Jason Thorn's PR team is refusing to make any comments on the photos and we are still trying to locate Olive Taylor to get her side of the story.

CHAPTER THIRTY

JASON

"You need to wake up, man."

Was that Devlin? What the hell was he doing at my house? "What?" I croaked, trying to push through the fog and open my eyes. "What are you doing here?"

Fingers snapped in front of my face, and then I heard Alvin's voice. "Do you think we should call a doctor?"

"Alvin? What the fuck?"

I forced my eyes open and had to close them right back when the bright lights pierced into my brain. I groaned and covered my face with my hands. "Somebody shut off the fucking lights!"

"It's daylight boss, I don't think we can shut that off."

Shielding my eyes with my hand, I squinted up at Alvin's worried face, then looked around. I was lying on a couch... I jolted up and that brought all kinds of pain to my head.

Jesus! How many drinks did I have last night?

"Where are we?" I croaked.

"In my suite," said Devlin with a suffering sigh as he handed me a bottle of cold water.

"Thanks," I mumbled. I drank the whole thing to the last drop and dropped the bottle on floor. When I was done, I cleared my throat and looked around at my surroundings again. "Why are we in your suite?"

Devlin glanced at Alvin.

"Fuck," I cursed, dropping my head into my hands. "My head is pounding. What time is it, Alvin? Am I late to set?"

"Jason," Devlin said in a serious tone.

"Yeah? Haven't you ever heard of blinds, you little bastard?"

"How do you feel, Jason?" he asked instead of giving me an answer. *Shit.* I was seconds away from vomiting all over their shoes.

"Brutal. I suggest you point me in the direction of the bathroom. Right now."

When I was done puking my guts out, I felt worse than I had when I'd woken up, if that was even possible.

I stumbled out of the bathroom. "Alvin, what time is it?"

"Sit the fuck down for a minute," Devlin barked.

"Keep your damn voice down for fuck's sake. What the hell did you give me to drink last night anyway?"

"I didn't give you a damn thing, Jason."

I plopped down on the couch again and started massaging my temples. Alvin was still hovering around, but Devlin sat right across from me. He didn't look any better than I did.

Frowning, I turned to Alvin. "Where's Olive?"

"Look," Devlin cut in before Alvin could say anything. "Look, Jason. You're in trouble. Hell, I'm in trouble."

"Explain," I ordered, steeling myself. If he had done anything to Olive, if he had said anything to upset her—

"I've been questioning my staff, the ones that came in contact with you in the club. And— "

"Why?"

"Shut up and listen. We think someone spiked your drink."

"What?" I thundered and scrambled up to my feet. "Where is

Olive, Alvin?" I yelled, ignoring my brain cursing me for the quick movement.

"We don't know, boss," Alvin answered quietly.

"What the fuck do you mean you don't know? Her friends? Where are they? Ask them."

"Look," Devlin started again, and I took a step forward. If he said look one more time, I was punching his goddamned face.

"I was late last night. When I finally made it to the club and Devlin escorted me up to your private room, I found you being a little too friendly with one of Olive's friends," Alvin explained, stealing the words from Devlin's mouth. "I don't know what happened, but I know you wouldn't cheat on Olive. Not like that."

My eyes widened in shock. I raked my hands through my hair and turned to Alvin. Devlin was sitting with his head bowed, quiet.

"Are you fucking with me? Fuck! I wouldn't. Never. I didn't. Damn it!" I growled as I picked up a vase that was on the table close to me and threw it at the wall, bleakly watching it shatter into pieces.

"What did you see? What was I doing?" I asked through gritted teeth. I was trying to speak calmly.

"She was in your lap, man."

Goddammit!

I started pacing and when the wall was right in front of me…I just punched it.

It seemed like a good idea in that moment. With the fury building inside me, I could've brought down the whole building down just with my hands.

Ignoring my bloody knuckles, I slowly walked back to the couch and sat down. My heart was racing out of my damn chest.

"Please explain," I finally said when my breathing was under control and I didn't feel like killing anyone and everyone.

Alvin sat down on the other end of the couch, keeping his

eyes on me the entire time. "I don't know much, Jason. That's how we found you. Don't you remember anything? She was in your lap and you were making out, I assume. I don't know, man. Maybe not? Her hands were all over you and you were just sitting there dazed."

"Which one?"

"Which one, what?"

"Which one of her friends?" I gritted between my teeth.

He glanced at Devlin so I lifted my head to look at him, too. "Lily," Devlin said after thinking about it for a minute. "I remember Olive introducing her as Lily. One of the blondes."

"No one was in the room?"

"Just you two. Could she be the one who spiked your drink? Because none of my staff would do something like that. I hand-pick them, you know that. And even if they could, why would they?"

"She is Olive's friend for fuck's sake, why would she do something like that?"

"Exactly how much do you remember?" Alvin asked again.

I thought about it. What the hell *did* I remember? I remembered going up to the private room with Olive. I remembered kissing her, wanting to do much more to her than just kissing. I could still feel her lips on mine, her hands in my hair. She always trembled when I kissed her, as if my touch sent small shock waves into her body, and I loved drinking it all down. I simply loved being near her, touching her...

I shook my head.

"Not much. I don't remember Olive leaving. I remember talking to Lucy and Lily, but that's it. Did you call her?"

Alvin grimaced, and I hated it. "We couldn't find your phone, but her handbag was next to you, and her phone was in it. But," he added hastily before I could explode all over again. "I called

Lucy. She isn't answering right now, but I'll keep calling. Don't worry, Jason."

"Tell him the rest," Devlin said darkly.

"What rest?" I glanced between them.

Another grimace. This one was worse. If I never saw Alvin grimace like that ever again, it would be too soon.

"Someone leaked photos of you and the girl. Every media outlet is running with the story of you cheating on Olive."

CHAPTER THIRTY-ONE

OLIVE

I contemplated getting on a bus, but I had enough money to hop on a plane. I was a damn bestselling author now; the least I could do was buy a plane ticket back home without counting every cent in my bank account.

So I did just that.

First, I raced to Jason's house. Being married to a fucking actor had its perks, like how you didn't have to carry your wallet with you when you were going out with said actor. The smallest clutch could hold your phone and maybe a lipstick, but that's it, which is why I had to stop by the house to grab a few personal items, a change of clothes, and of course, my ID.

I didn't want to think about it, but it was hard not to notice that he hadn't come back home. Where he'd spent the night...I didn't want to think about that either.

By 12:30 PM, I was in San Francisco.

At 2:00 PM, I was standing in front of the door of my child-hood home, where this whole mess had started.

I took a deep breath and lifted my arm to knock on the door.

My dad opened the door, and we spent a few silent seconds

looking at each other, which only caused my lips to tip down and tears to start flowing freely down my cheeks.

"Baby," he sighed.

I wiped at my tears angrily. Why was I even crying?

"I know you are angry at me, but—"

I burst into more tears.

Pathetic, I know.

But then, I was in my dad's arms and he was whispering the most beautiful words into my ear.

It was worth being a pathetic little wimp. There, I was safe.

It felt so good when he was hugging me so tightly. I could let go of everything and know that he would take care of his girl like he always did. Who could hurt you when your dad had his big arms around you? Who would dare break a little girl's heart? Didn't every woman feel like a little girl when their dad gave them a good hug? Didn't everyone just want to stay there until the monsters went away?

No?

Well, good for you and your independence then. Pop some champagne and celebrate. Congrats, you made it into adulthood. Me, not so much. I would take my dad's hugs over anything.

"Logan, who is at—Olive? Oh, sweetheart."

When I heard my mom's voice and felt her hand softly brushing my hair, I buried my face harder into my dad's chest and let them love their little girl.

CHAPTER THIRTY-TWO

JASON

After living through the worst morning of my fucking life, we had finally found Lucy at the hospital with her boyfriend. She looked like a mess herself, and I couldn't imagine what she'd gone through while waiting for her boyfriend to come out of surgery. I'd learned that Olive had been with her the entire time, which was progress since we couldn't find her anywhere. She had left with Lucy and spent the entire night at the hospital while I was out of it.

It was a miracle we even managed to get *that* out of her mouth. She had seen the news coverage and was just as furious as I was, if not more. The only difference was she was ready to attack *me* and have *my* balls for her friend, not the bastard who had spiked my drink or taken the photos.

It took some time, but we explained what was going on and she looked like she wanted to believe us. After some begging on my part, she told me that Olive had flown to San Francisco hours ago.

At 10:00 PM, I was on a plane—fuck waiting for a private jet—flying to San Francisco.

———

IT WAS weird being in the neighborhood where you spent a big and very important chunk of your childhood. All the houses looked the same as I remembered; even the damn air smelled like it had back then. The house my mother had decided to take her own life in was still the same, too. Sure, it looked more lived in, and there were flowers that hadn't been there when I was a teenager, but it was right where it had been, tucked among the memories I wanted to forget.

I hoped the family who was living in it now was a happier and more functional one than ours had been. I hoped the kids who were growing up in the house weren't witnessing their mother slowly losing the light in her eyes for no good reason. I hoped that they had another house they could spend their time in if things weren't going that great for them, someone to care about them like Logan and Emily had cared about me.

Right then, standing in front of their house in the middle of the night didn't feel as scary as I had thought it would feel when I was on the plane. It was more like coming back home, and that was a good feeling for someone who hadn't had a good home for most of their life, someone who had lost both his parents along the way and for a very long time hadn't had a real thing to hold on to when things got rough.

Maybe it wasn't as scary as I had initially thought it would be, but I was still a mess. Apart from feeling like a mess, I also *looked* like a fucking mess.

After spending ten minutes in front of their house, not knowing how Olive's parents would react to seeing me, not knowing if Olive would even agree to see me, I sucked it up and knocked on their door.

When Dylan opened the door and his eyes hardened when he saw who was standing on their porch, I was still trying to get over the shock of seeing my best friend after so many fucking years.

Dylan didn't have that problem.

My lips spread out in a smile, but that was a mistake because his whole body tightened. Instead of being happy to see me again like I'd hoped he would be, he stepped out of the house and quietly closed the door behind him.

"What are you doing here, Jason?"

"Dylan. Shit, man." I tried to stop my smile from spreading out more, but...hell, he was my best friend, and it had been years since I'd seen him. "Man, it's really fucking good to see you."

His expression didn't change.

"I'll ask again. What are you doing here? Don't you think you did enough damage to her already?"

I dropped my smile, but it was too late to brace for the impact his words caused. If he wanted to act like a piece of shit, so be it. So could I.

"I can see that you don't care to see me. I guess it's a good thing I didn't come to see you either. I'm here for my wife."

"Wife?" He gave a humorless laugh. "Cut the crap, Jason. We both know that it's just a game for the public even though she refuses to admit that. You are using her to look good and she is too stupid to care about it even though she knows it herself."

"You don't know anything about us, Dylan."

"About *us?* There is no *you and her*, Jason. Do you know that she is in love with you? Hell, she's been in love with you for most of her life. Are you going to keep playing this game, knowing it will kill something in her when you finally get bored with it?"

I lowered my head and squeezed my hands into fists.

"I don't want you to see her, and I want you to turn around—"

"I don't care what the hell you want, Dylan," I said in a low voice. He stopped speaking. "I will get through that door even if I have to deck you to do it."

He lifted an eyebrow and crossed his arms against his chest. "Try it," he said. "Give me a good reason to fuck up your—"

"I'm in love with your sister, you idiot." I took a step forward, getting into his face.

His eyes narrowed on me and he took a step forward with clenched fists. "You lying son of a bitch."

Before he could do anything, the door behind him opened and his father walked out.

"That's enough, Dylan," he said in a gravelly voice, shutting the door gently.

I froze. My hands flexed and I swallowed.

In front of me stood the man I had idolized, a man who knew how to take care of his family, a man who didn't shy away from showing his love to his children, to his wife…even to the neighbor's kid.

Just like the houses around us, he looked just the same. He had more white hair and the smile lines around his eyes were deeper, but those big shoulders, the stance, and everything else that made him who he was just the same.

Hell, why did he have to come out? I couldn't deck Logan. I would happily get into a fight with Dylan, but not with his father.

I took a step back and tried to loosen up my muscles.

"I don't like the reason you are here, but it's still good to see you, Jason," Logan said after forcefully moving his son out of the way. There was a small smile playing on his lips. Maybe I still had a shot at getting to Olive. Maybe Logan would believe me.

Feeling like a seventeen-year-old again, I rubbed the back of my neck and looked down at the ground. Surely I wasn't tearing up…right?

"You have no idea how good it is to see you, too, sir."

He nodded. "I'm assuming you're here because you want to see Olive?"

I gave Dylan a hard look and kept my eyes on him as I answered his father's question.

"Yes, I'm here for Olive."

"You're not seeing her," Dylan said as he took another step toward me.

The bastard was just itching to get his ass kicked.

"Dylan, that's enough," Logan cut him off again. "Simmer down." Turning to me, he said, "Let's have a talk before you see her, is that okay?"

"Of course," I agreed as we both sat down on the porch steps. Wisely, Dylan chose to stand next to the door instead of getting in my face. If he thought he even had a chance of stopping me from going in to get Olive, he was in for a surprise.

I would fuck him up without a second thought.

"Olive is not saying much, so you'll have to be the one to tell me exactly what's going on here, Jason. I want to hear it in your own words, not some speech your people prepared for you."

I frowned. "I'll tell you anything you want to know. I won't hide anything from you."

"That's not the vibe I got from Olive. I think she was trying to share as little as possible with us."

I shook my head and rubbed my forehead. "That was before."

"And now? Did something change?"

"Yes." I rubbed my forehead some more. "Yes, everything changed."

"You married Olive so it would look good for you, is that true?"

I flinched. *Jesus!* An interrogation was not what I needed.

"Yes." I sighed. "Yes, my publicist thought it would save my career after everything I'd done. When I saw Olive and acted like…and then everyone else saw us together…"

I didn't finish my sentence.

"I see. And now? What is different now?"

I lifted my head and looked into his eyes. I couldn't decide if he was angry with me or not, but I answered honestly. "I fell in love with your daughter, sir." Looking over my shoulder, I gave Dylan a hard look. "That's what changed."

"And you think my daughter loves you too?"

Breaking eye contact with Dylan, I faced forward again. "I don't know," I admitted. "But I'm hoping that the answer is yes."

"So why is she here? We saw the news. If you are in love with her like you say you are, what happened?"

I told him everything that had happened the night before, except the part where my dick was roaring to get into his daughter's tight little body in public, of course. That I kept to myself.

The more I talked and explained everything—not just that my drink had been spiked, but everything that had happened between Olive and me—the more Dylan's stance relaxed and he got closer to us.

After I talked for I don't even know how long, Logan smiled, patted my shoulder, and rose up from the steps.

"I'll leave you two friends to catch up. Olive is sleeping, but you can stay here tonight and talk to her in the morning, Jason. I'm sure Emily would love to see you, too."

Stopping next to Dylan, he added, "She isn't a kid any more Dylan. She is old enough to make up her own mind about Jason. Don't interfere."

When he got inside and closed the door, Dylan took his dad's spot.

"So you really love her, huh? Have you told her that?" he asked, sounding tired.

I already felt dead on my feet.

"How nice of you to believe me now," I said a little pointedly as I glared at him. Fuck, I was too damn tired to fight with him if he decided to be a jerk about this. "Give me a break. I just realized it today. I spent my entire day trying to find out where she was hiding."

"You sound surprised every time you say it, and you keep saying it over and over."

"If you have a problem with me being in love with her, keep her out of it. I don't want you to say anything that will upset her," I grinded out, looking at the house across the street. I wondered if Mr. and Mrs. Kealey still lived there.

"You're protecting *my* sister from me?"

"Yes," I said simply, giving him a hard glare. "You never knew how to keep your mouth shut around her. I won't let you say something stupid and break her heart. I don't care if you are her brother or not."

He cocked an eyebrow and gave me a look I couldn't even begin to name.

"Huh," he grunted.

We were silent for several moments.

"What are you doing in San Francisco, anyway?" I asked when the silence became too heavy. I wanted to go in and talk to Olive, but Logan had said she was sleeping. Was she okay? Was she angry? Sad? Disappointed in me?

"*My* wife's best friend had a baby. We're visiting for the weekend."

That made sense.

More silence.

"Did you feel anything for her when we were kids?" Dylan asked.

I had asked myself the same question over and over again, but I still didn't have an answer.

"I don't know," I said with a sigh. "I don't think so. I mean she was my Olive, too, you know. I was your friend, but I enjoyed being around her as much as I enjoyed being around your sorry ass." That made him chuckle, so I relaxed more. "But, no. I wouldn't call it love. She was too young. Yeah, maybe she had a crush on me, but it was probably because I was the only boy that was around. I don't think it was anything big."

"You would think so," he said as he kicked a small stone with his foot.

"What does that mean?"

He shook his head and rubbed his face. "It was more than just a crush, man. I was constantly warning her away from you without being too obvious about it. Do you remember a girl texting you, just before your...before you had to move?"

I thought about it, but I couldn't remember anything specific.

"Someone from our class?"

"No. A random girl."

"How the hell am I supposed to remember that?"

"It was Olive."

"What?" I turned my head to look at him so fast that I heard something snap. Then I chuckled. "I think I would know if Olive texted me. I had her number."

Another annoying sigh. "I think she borrowed the phone from her friend or something. My point is, she was trying to talk to you. Even back then, she was taking risks just to be close to you. I have no idea what her plan was with texting you, but—"

"And you know this how, again?"

"I'm trying to tell you, you idiot. You told me you were texting with a girl, then when you were downstairs I went into Olive's room to check on her and found a phone in her bed. Since it wasn't her own phone, I poked around, and imagine my surprise when I found your texts."

"What did you do, Dylan?"

"What do you think I did? I took your phone and texted her."

CHAPTER THIRTY-THREE

OLIVE

When I first realized that I'd fallen asleep, there was still daylight outside and I could hear Dylan's raised voice coming from downstairs. Ignoring him, I pulled the covers over my head and resumed my sleeping. I didn't want to do anything else anyway.

The second time, I woke up because I was suffocating under the covers and it was still daylight. Switching to a lighter cover, I lost some of my clothes, too.

The third and fourth times were because I was uncomfortable in my own skin.

Then I started tossing and turning too much. I simply hated everything. At least it was finally dark outside.

The fifth time… The fifth time I woke up because someone was getting in bed with me.

I didn't open my eyes, but I knew it was Jason; I'd know his scent anywhere. My body tensed, but I tried not to make it too obvious and tried even harder to keep my breathing under control.

Dylan was pissed off enough for the entire family; he wouldn't have let him in the house, let alone climb up in bed with me, so what was he doing here? I didn't have to wait too long for an answer.

"Your mom fixed me the couch, but I sneaked up to your room," Jason whispered. "We have to be quiet so your idiot brother doesn't bust in here trying to protect my wife from me." He paused. "You have no idea how weird it is to be back here, Olive, but to be sneaking into your room like this...for some reason that doesn't feel weird."

I didn't move, but he continued.

"Olive..." There was a long sigh. "When did I start missing you this much, sweetheart? When did I..." Another sigh. "I was so worried when Alvin said they didn't know where you were."

More silence.

Slowly, he pulled the covers down, and his fingertips touched my bare shoulder.

Damn it! Why had I thought it was smart to sleep in a tank top and my underwear? I should've let myself suffocate in peace. When his fingertips reached my hip and he realized that I wasn't wearing much underneath the covers, he sucked in a breath and let the cover rest on my thighs.

My heart beating in my throat, I waited to see what his next move would be. Maybe he had come to say we had to get a divorce? If these were our last moments, I wanted to savor every second of it.

I know what you're thinking, but did you hear the part where I already acknowledged the fact that I was pathetic?

"Is your heart still beating just for me, Olive?" he asked softly, his voice low and sweet.

I closed my eyes tighter.

"I wonder if you can feel my touch in your dreams...if that's why your heart is beating so fast."

His soft words a whisper on my skin, I let his fingertips trail every inch of my body, seducing my heart before my mind could put a stop to it.

"I missed you, baby. If I kiss you, Olive…" I felt the touch of his warm lips on my shoulder just before he moved closer. A shiver went down my spine and I was too late to hold in my small gasp. Jason continued as if he hadn't heard me. "If I kiss you will you wake up and play with me? I want to feel your lips on mine so badly, Olive. Will you please stop pretending to be asleep, baby?"

He knew I was awake. Too tired for games, I opened my eyes to a dark room. "What are you doing here, Jason?" I whispered after some time.

"Will you look at me, sweetheart? Please."

I turned to face him, but we were a little too close for my comfort, my childhood bed being too small to keep a respectable distance between us. Still, I backed away until I was lying on the very edge of the bed. I kept my eyes down on the sheets.

"Can I tell you what I remember from last night? Will you listen to me?"

"Do I have any other choice? You are in my bed and I have no other place to run to."

I could barely see with the only light coming from outside, but he still lifted my chin so I could look at his eyes. I focused on the stubble on his cheeks.

Because I'm a rebel like that.

"I never want you to run away from me again. If you do, I will always come after you. I want you to remember that. That being said, I will never give you a reason to run away from me either."

Again, I stayed silent.

"The last thing I remember from last night is going up to the private rooms with you and trying to figure out what I could say to convince you to let me have you up there."

His fingertips touched my lips and I flinched. He ignored it and gently stroked my lips.

"Then I kissed you, Olive, didn't I? I always remember kissing you."

I would never forget how it felt to have his lips on mine either. It would always stay with me.

Damn those tears rushing to my eyes!

"I also remember talking to Lucy and Lily, but after that I remember nothing, Olive." He paused for a minute. "Do you know where I woke up this morning?"

I flinched again and braced myself, but instead of continuing with his story, he brushed my hair back.

"You're shivering sweetheart. I wish you would come closer so I could warm you."

I didn't move. When he was satisfied with my hair placement, he sighed and picked up from where he had left off. "I woke up in Devlin's hotel suite. Alvin was there, too. They think someone spiked my drink because I was acting weird, and when I woke up I couldn't even remember where you were."

I tensed.

"Will you come closer so I can hold you in my arms? You're about to fall off, and I'm afraid Dylan will barge in to protect you from me."

"He knows you're in my room?"

"Not yet, and I'd like to keep it that way."

He linked his hand with mine and gave it a gentle tug. Reluctantly, I scooted forward. When I was close enough, his hand sneaked around my waist and he pulled me flush against his chest, resting his head on top of mine as I discreetly breathed in his scent.

His long sigh sounded like he was relieved.

"I don't know how I'm going to make you believe me, Olive, but I hope you will. While I was sleeping it off, Devlin questioned his entire staff, but other than that one drink, I didn't have anything. No one could've slipped anything into my drink because the bartender prepared it in the room, you saw it yourself."

Somewhere in the house, someone opened a door and we fell silent, our bodies tense with the interruption. A few seconds later, the bathroom door opened and closed.

When the coast was clear again, he continued, talking in hushed tones. "I took Alvin with me and went to your apartment to look for Lucy, but she wasn't there. When I found Lily instead, I kinda lost it. I might have scared her a little, but it was worth it because she admitted to messing with my drink with Charlotte. According to Lily, it was Charlotte's idea to take pictures of me to leak to the press. I don't know how much of it is a lie, but that was what she was going with."

I hadn't even realized I was crying until Jason lifted his hand to softly wipe away my tears.

"As if they hadn't done enough damage, one of them also called the tabloids as an anonymous source to say that our marriage was fake."

Bewildered, I shook my head. "It couldn't be Lily. I don't even know her all that well. But I swear to you, I didn't tell Charlotte either. Only Lucy knows."

"It's okay sweetheart, it doesn't matter. Megan pulled some strings and they won't take the tip seriously." His lips touched my forehead and instead of pulling back, he stayed just like that.

"I brought your phone with me. Why don't we call Lucy and you can hear it from her, too," he whispered.

Reaching behind, he took something out of his back pocket and handed it to me. My phone. I barely had any battery left.

I dialed Lucy's number.

"Lucy? Hi."

"Hey, babe. How are you holding up?"

"Shouldn't I be the one asking you that? How is Jameson?" I tried to talk as quietly as possible.

"He is awake now. He is already making my life miserable. Frankly, I'm more worried about you right now. You promised you would call me when you made it home."

"Yeah, I'm sorry. When I saw my dad, I just…"

"It's okay, Olive, I understand. I'm assuming lover boy made it there and that's why you are calling."

My lips twitched, but that was all I could manage.

"I don't know exactly what he told you, but he is telling the truth, my little green Olive. I talked to Charlotte a few hours ago, or more like fought with her. The night I brought you to the apartment and Marcus carried you away to his room, well, that's apparently when she realized Marcus would drop her like a hot potato the moment you wanted to get back with him. I think that's why she told you that she'd been with Marcus while you guys were still together. If you ask me, I have my doubts about that after everything that's happened since yesterday."

The more Lucy talked, the more confused I was getting. Messing with someone's drink was a whole different ball game then just cheating, or made up cheating, or whatever. Heck, where had she even found a pill that would mess Jason up like that?

"My take is that she told you about the cheating so you wouldn't go back to Marcus, and she messed with Jason so you couldn't have him either. The worst of it is she made it sound like she did you a favor because it was 'bound to happen anyway'. The bitch has no idea Jason is in love with you."

"You are the only one who thinks that."

"Oh please, it's only you who doesn't think that."

"My battery is dying, I have to go, Lucy. Can I call you tomorrow?"

She made a sound that clearly meant she was annoyed with me. "Fine. I'll call you later. Don't be stupid about this, Olive.

You better have good news for me tomorrow. And try to ask him what he thinks about adopting me. He is even hotter when he is fuming. Be a good friend for once and ask him."

She hung up while I was still shaking my head.

I pushed my phone under the pillow.

"So?" Jason asked into the silence. "Do you believe me?"

"I didn't have to call Lucy to confirm what you said, Jason. I believe you. This type of stupid drama is supposed to happen with the costar you are working with. I'm supposed to hate Lindsay, not my best friend. She is supposed to fall in love with you and then mess with our marriage."

"Is that what is supposed to happen?" he murmured, a small smile curling around his lips.

"Yes," I said miserably. "That's what happens in books. There is always an evil costar or ex. It wasn't supposed to happen like this. I'm really sorry for what my—"

His lips crashed into mine and the angels started singing above us.

With his unexpected movement, I gasped into his mouth; he made sure to take advantage of that opening and slipped his tongue inside. I clutched his shirt and pulled him closer to me, his fingers biting into my flesh, but right when I was getting more into the kiss, he pulled away.

"That's all I wanted to hear," he said roughly, his hot breath mixing with mine.

I slowly pried my fingers open, let go of his shirt, and took a deep breath to clear my mind.

"This is not a game any more, is it?" I asked.

"I thought about that on my way over here. I'm not sure if it ever was, baby."

"So what happens now?"

"Tomorrow, I'm taking you home with me."

"And then what? We act like nothing happened?" I twisted away from him and plopped onto my back. "I'm not sure if—"

"Don't finish that sentence. Yes, we act like nothing happened because nothing happened. You are my wife, Olive. You already made the mistake of saying yes, and I'm not letting that go. You can't take it back."

See if I'm letting you go, buddy.

In my next breath, Jason was on top of me and was making himself a place in between my legs.

When I felt his erection, I gasped. "What are you doing?" I asked in panic, glancing at the door over his shoulder.

"Falling in love with you."

"Right now? You're falling in love with me right this minute? Sure."

Dipping his head down, he gently nipped at my lips.

"No, you little smartass. I already fell—a little too hard if you ask me. Now it's your turn."

"My turn for what?"

"To say you love me so I can close my eyes and fall all the way."

"I didn't exactly hear you say you love me so why am I saying it? I think you should say it first."

He tilted his head and this time lowered it slowly, giving me the option of stopping him. When our lips were barely touching, he murmured, "Kiss me, Olive."

Without meaning to, I lifted my head up and gently kissed his lips. The bastard was playing with me. "What's with the ordering around all of a sudden?"

"Shut up and kiss me, woman."

"I thi—"

He shut me up and kissed me, for several minutes—several *glorious* minutes. When it ended, we were both breathless. "Say it. Please," he murmured again, ghosting small kisses around my lips.

"I love you, Jason Thorn," I admitted.

I've loved you for a disturbingly long time.

My heart was going crazy. The butterflies he had awakened in me the very first day I'd seen him were multiplying by the second, and I felt sick.

And vulnerable.

And hopeful.

So very hopeful.

His eyes closed and then he rested his forehead on mine. "The night I came to the bar and saw you singing with your friend… that's when I started falling for you."

"Can you say the actual words?" I asked.

He smiled down at me. "I love you, my beautiful little Olive. My wife."

Breathe in.

Breathe out.

Keep repeating that. You can do it!

"Okay. That was okay," I said, patting him on the shoulder and barely holding back a heart attack.

He chuckled quietly. "So my love is acceptable?"

I made a noncommittal sound. "Eh, sure. Why not?"

He started kissing my neck while he was still chuckling, so I closed my eyes to keep my sanity. "You are more than ten years late, but damn if it isn't good to hear those words in this room," I whispered quietly.

His hand sneaked under my top and he started stroking my waist, slowly moving upward. "What else did you want to hear *or* do in this room? I'm all about making your dreams come true."

Suddenly the door to my room opened and I saw Dylan's shoulder. He was trying not to peek in.

"You've been in here for an hour now, you son of a bitch. Did you think I wouldn't notice? How about you get your ass out of my sister's room and we have a nice little chat, you piece of shit!" Dylan whispered furiously and closed the door without waiting for an answer. Not a second had passed when he opened it again. "I'm waiting for you!"

Burying my forehead against Jason's neck, I quietly laughed.

When the door had opened the first time, his hand had frozen on my skin, his whole body going taut, but as soon as Dylan closed the door, he started stroking again and sighed.

"I guess I wasn't as sneaky as I thought I was."

"I guess not," I said and started laughing again.

"He's not gonna make this easy on me, is he?"

I dropped my head on the pillow and looked at his handsome face. "Doesn't look like it."

"I thought I would be happier to see him, and for a second there I thought I was, but it looks like I was wrong," he said with another heavy sigh. "At least it wasn't your father who busted us. Thank god."

I smiled without saying anything.

He fell silent, too, and smiled back at me.

"I love you so very much, Jason," I said, having a hard time keeping it in.

His smile grew bigger.

"There's that dimple," I mumbled, reaching with my finger to touch it.

"You like it?" he asked roughly.

I nodded.

"There are a lot of things I like about you, too, wife."

"Like what?" I asked breathlessly as I lost myself a little bit more in his eyes.

"Like that little birth mark you have on your waist," he murmured, his fingertips finding it in the dark as if he had painted it on there. "Like that little smile you always have on your lips when you are writing and you think no one is looking at you."

There was a rude knock on the door and Jason sighed.

"Do you know what else I learned today?" Jason asked conversationally as he pushed himself up with a sigh. "I learned that you texted me when I was eighteen, pretending to be someone else."

I lost my breath and my smile melted off my face. "Wh-hat?"

"Interesting isn't it? Because I certainly thought so. And you know what? Apparently I texted you back saying my friend's sister was being sticky, clingy or something like that."

By then he had already gotten out of my bed and was standing over me as I held the covers in a death grip in my hands.

"You know why I can't remember what my exact words were? Because—wait for it—it wasn't me who wrote them. Hilarious, isn't it?"

"What?" I repeated again. "What do you mean, it wasn't you who wrote them?"

"Oh, you didn't know? It was your loving brother trying to protect you from me. Or maybe the other way around, who knows with him."

"You can't be serious."

"Oh, but I am sweetheart. I am."

I threw the covers off and scrambled out of my bed. "I'm gonna kill him!"

I only managed to take two steps and then Jason pulled me back against his chest.

"Easy there tiger. We can kill him together, but first wear some pants so he won't have a legitimate reason to kill me first."

I turned in his arms, rose up on my tiptoes, and kissed him passionately until his hands were framing my face and tilting my head to the side. I could've easily fainted with the intensity of it.

"I'm not sticky or clingy?" I asked once I could find the willpower to stop.

"I loved you. You were my little Olive. I would never call you clingy. And…" He let go of my face and suddenly lifted me up in his arms. "Now that you are all grown up, I don't mind you being sticky at all. In fact, I can't wait to get you home so you can get sticky all over me, sweetheart."

EPILOGUE

"Jason!" I lifted my head up and saw my wife running toward me.

My heart rate spiking up, I met her halfway. "What's wrong, Olive? What happened?"

She held her chest and tried to catch her breath. "How could...how could you not tell me about...just a second, I think I'm having a heart attack." She bent down and rested her hands on her knees.

I grabbed her shoulders and straightened her back up. "Olive, talk to me, what's wrong?" She waved her hand dismissively. "Give me a minute, I'm angry at you."

"What the hell for?"

"How could you not tell me that Adam Connor, *the* Adam Connor had moved in next door? Why did I hear it from Lucy instead of you? I trusted you, damn it!"

I blinked. "Sweetheart, I don't keep tabs on the neighbors. I didn't know Adam was moving in next door any more than you did."

Her eyes widened slowly, making her look comical as she

stared up at me. "You know him? You said Adam, like you actually know him," she whined. "You know Adam Connor?"

She was trying the pathetic act with me. Again.

I tilted my head and gave her a pointed look. "Try not to faint over another guy in front your husband. It's not a good look on you."

Her little fingers curled around my shoulders and she dropped her forehead against my chest. Taking advantage, I immediately wrapped my arms around her and pulled her closer.

Wearing a goofy smile, she looked up at me. "You'll introduce us? I mean me? And yeah, maybe, Lucy, too? Both of us? To Adam Connor? To *the* Adam Connor who is going to live right next door to us with his lovely kid? You will won't you? Ah, I knew I loved you for good reason!"

"Olive," I sighed. "Your husband is a movie star, too, woman. How fast are you kicking me to the curb for another one? You don't see me running around to find other authors."

She patted my cheek and sighed. "Can you introduce us soon? I don't want to find Lucy hiding in the bushes trying to get a look at him over the short wall."

I shook my head and forced her to turn around. "Come on, it's time."

She huffed, but started walking in front of me.

"Tell me again why I have to be part of this prank you all are playing on Lindsay?"

"Because you are helpful like that?" I was steering her toward our trailer where the makeup girls would put a wig on her so she could bear a passing resemblance to Lindsay. What she didn't know, however, was that the prank was actually for her.

"When are you guys shooting the last scene?" she asked as she slipped her hand in mine. "I want to be there to watch that one. I want to hear Tanner yell, *That's a wrap, folks!*"

"We'll start that one right after the prank."

"And when are you going to share what the prank really is? I'm gonna wear a wig and do what exactly? Jump on her or something?"

My impatient little firecracker. "You don't have to do anything sweetheart, just standing there will be enough for the prank to work." Lifting her hand, I kissed the back of it.

It wasn't like I was lying to her anyway; all she had to do was stand on top of an X and do one simple thing. She gave me a side-ways glance, but entered the trailer cooperatively when I gave her backside a little push. I couldn't wait to get her home that night.

Half an hour later, the sun had gone down, and it was completely dark outside when we emerged from the trailer. I walked her back to the set where the last scene of her movie would be shot.

"People are giving me funny looks, Jason," she hissed, leaning closer to me. "I thought you said there would be other people looking like Lindsay."

"It'll be okay sweetheart," I assured her.

When Tanner saw us, he motioned for me to keep walking with his hand. From what I could see, everyone was exactly where they were supposed to be and they were waiting for us.

"I have a surprise for you, baby," I said, once we were standing on top of the X taped on the ground.

"Jason what's going on?" she asked urgently when the crew turned the low lights on and we were in the spotlight.

"We are shooting the last scene."

Her eyebrows rising, she pulled at my hand, but I wasn't letting her go anywhere, not again. "What do you mean we are shooting the last scene?" she squeaked.

"I love you, Olive," I said, taking pleasure in watching her heart shine in her eyes. She did that every time I told her I loved her, and I told her how much I loved her as often as possible.

I was just as pathetic as her.

"And I love you," she said back.

"This was our story from the very beginning, Olive. If you hadn't written this book, I would've never found you. Hell, maybe we were written for each other from the very first day we met, but it would've taken me a long time to find you on my own." I kissed her nose. "So thank you for finding me. Thank you for writing yourself into our happy and inevitable ending." I kissed her again. "I talked Tanner into letting me shoot this scene with you. Everyone will think it's Lindsay, but when we watch it together for the first time, we'll know that I'm kissing the woman I love and no one else."

"Jason! Get ready. We'll start with camera two for the first take!" Tanner yelled at us.

Olive's face softened and her eyes filled with tears. "You're going to kiss me? In front of the cameras?"

I pushed the hair behind her ear. It wasn't anywhere near as soft as her own beautiful hair, but it would have to do. "You say that as if I never kiss you, wife."

"You don't kiss me nearly enough," she murmured against my lips. She wasn't fighting my pull or trying to escape any more, so I pulled her more firmly against my chest.

I was smiling when I murmured, "I'm trying to do my best, but I keep falling short apparently. Maybe you should take matters into your own hands."

"Everyone lock it down!" Tanner gave his last warning and the set fell silent.

"What now?" Olive whispered. She was having a hard time standing still.

"Now," I said, framing her face with my hands so the camera couldn't pick up the small differences between my Olive and Lindsay.

"The curtain!" Tanner yelled; seconds later cold fake rain started to soak into our skin, making Olive squeal loudly.

"Jason! I'm going to kill you!"

Not letting go of her face, I smiled into her eyes.

"You're turning out to be quite the murderer, baby. I thought a pluviophile like you would appreciate this. It's a small change to your book, but I thought…"

"It's perfect," she said, tilting her head back and laughing. "They are pretty much hosing us down with water, but I'll take it. Are you really mine?" she asked when she had hair plastered all over her face.

"Action!"

"I am, sweetheart," I whispered against her lips as my chest tightened. "I love you so much, Evie," I said, knowing Tanner would pick up our words and use them when he was piecing everything together.

Fake rain pouring down on us, I kissed her softly and slowly, countless times. At one point, Tanner switched cameras, but there was no one that could pull Olive away from me. She was mine. I wouldn't let anyone take her away, not evil little bees and certainly not Adam Connor.

Every time we came up for a breath, I whispered her how much I loved her and how much I wanted to get into her pants when we got home. As soon as she was smiling, I would kiss her tenderly, drinking in her happiness.

When her body started shaking against mine, I hugged her tighter to myself.

"I kept my promise to you," I said, kissing the edges of her mouth as she took deep breaths. The world faded away and it was just the two of standing in the middle of a fake road. "I told you that I would never forget you Olive *Thorn*, and it looks like my heart never did, sweetheart," I tugged a piece of her hair, the familiar gesture making her lips wobble. "My world is a less scary place with you in it, baby. I will kiss you a thousand times every day if that's what it takes to keep you in love with me for the rest of our days."

Her tears mixed in with the rain, but she was still smiling up at me when she said, "You stole my little heart with just one dimple, you sneaky little thief. I never managed to fall out of love with you after that. I don't think I know how to."

"I never want you to learn. I'll give you as many orgasms as you want along with the kisses."

I kissed her.

"Why do I feel like you are trying to sell yourself to me? I might consider taking you if you promise you'll do me in the screening room at your house. Maybe we can do it while we are watching something? Or listening? And I want to do it in the pool at least twice. Then I want do it in Devlin's club, in one of those private rooms. And maybe we can—"

I kissed her again. "I see you're gonna work me like a slave. You know that they are recording us, don't you?"

Her eyes widened in shock and I heard a few chuckles coming from the crew members.

"Kill me. Someone strike me with fake lightning, anything, please. It will look perfect for the movie. The author died while filming the last scene. Think about the box office numbers or whatever the hell…"

I chuckled and went for her lips again as Tanner changed angles and told us to keep going.

Leaning into her ear, I whispered, "I will fuck you anywhere and any time you want, Olive. Crook your little finger at me, and I'll take you in a heartbeat, baby."

"Jason, give me another kiss and we'll wrap this up. Hold her face in your hands and go for it," Tanner's voice echoed to us.

"These lips?" I touched her lower lip with my thumb. "I never want you to feel someone else's lips against what's mine. I am it for you, Olive, the one, the right one—whatever you want to call it, I'm that."

"Action!"

I kissed her some more, taking my time and tilting her head in my hands, sinking deeper into her until I didn't know if it was her breathing life into me or if it was me being greedy and taking everything she was giving me so freely.

When I was done kissing her, I knew my hands weren't shaking because of the cold.

"I love you, Olive," I whispered, out of breath at last.

"Surprisingly, you've been the best kind of heartache, Jason Thorn." She smiled against my greedy lips and everything was perfect in a way it had never been before.

"That's a wrap, folks!"

The End.

If you loved Lucy and would be interested in her story, keep reading to glimpse into the first chapter of her standalone book. Fair warning: If you enjoyed *To Love Jason Thorn*, chances are you'll love Lucy's story too.

CHAPTER ONE
LUCY

I believe in love. Wholeheartedly.

Seriously, don't shake your head like that. I do.

I can picture those of you who already know me snickering. Well, don't.

There is no need for that, and frankly, it's kinda rude, don't you think?

Here, I'll say it again: I genuinely believe in love. I know all about its magic. Good and bad. I know the world seems bigger when you're drunk on love. I know it mends broken hearts, makes you deliriously happy, excited, hopeful…terrified, sick…a whole list of things that make this complicated world we are living in a better place.

For example, my best friend Olive. She has loved her husband ever since she was a wee bitty kid. She even asked Jason to marry her when she was six years old. She was six, people—six! Isn't that just the cutest thing you've ever heard? Then when they found each other years later, his movie star self swept her off her feet. Love works for her, big time, and it looks good on her too. She deserves all the love in the world.

Me? Love hangs a bit loose on me. Essentially, it's not quite the best fit.

So…what I'm saying is, love can do anything and everything…as long as you don't have a curse hanging over your head like I do. Oh, and you have to be willing to let love into your life, open that heavy door that leads the poor guy into the maze that is your heart, so to speak.

That's the tricky part, isn't it? You have to let love in. You have to open yourself up, share your least lovable parts, the deepest, darkest corners of your soul. That's the only way to experience real love. They feed us that shit as early as possible, or so I've heard. Our surroundings are an ongoing commercial for love. Share yourself with someone, be true, be honest, and if they love you for who you are then you are golden.

Enjoy the confetti shower that just blasted in your face.

You found real love. Good for you.

Sucks for the rest of us.

Now…do *I* let love in? Nope. I try my hardest not to, thank you very much. Been there, done that. If you are asking me what my problem is if I do indeed believe in love…well, if you are so curious about it, my problem is that my dear old friend '*love*' doesn't love me back. Never did. Probably never will.

I'd say it's quite rude of her, but…I've made my peace with it —at least I thought I had until I went and fell for Jameson.

Enter the hot bad boy covered in ink. College love.

If you haven't guessed it yet, I have all kinds of daddy and mommy issues. As if all of those weren't enough to fuck up my life, I have grandma issues to top it all off.

Blah blah blah…

Now you're starting to think I'm boring, and we can't have that.

Let's talk about one-night stands instead. Those are fun, right? You're skirting around love, smiling at each other, feeling all dizzy and ditzy with the excitement that you might score a good one, enjoy the feeling of having someone else's skin on yours, his hot breath, the heat, that blasted bliss you get to experience for a few seconds when he manages to hit that sweet spot—*if* he hits that sweet spot. Those are all awesome things, I agree. Hell, I encourage you to experience all those feelings, especially if he has some good inches on him.

Don't be a bitch; be a calm, happy waterfall.

Roar at life. In life.

Don't be closed off; be as free as a raindrop.

Most important of all: *live*.

My greatest advice to you all is, whatever you do, don't go back to the spectacular one-night stand you had just to satisfy your traitorous body's needs if you're trying to stay away from love, have your fun, live a little, love someone for a single night and then move on. Because if you keep going back to the same guy, oh, I don't know…about a hundred times…eventually what *will* happen is that you'll start to have feelings for said guy.

Look at that—I have a heart after all. Didn't expect that, did you? So you start to fall in love just like I did. Slowly. At first, you might feel a trickle of something you can't name because of how well he wields that huge cock of his (by the way, that's called an orgasm, not love). He'll zap you with all kinds of feelings when he is using it on you. And yes, he'll be that good; heart-breakers tend to be good in the sack.

More for you to cry over when they're done with you. Goody, right?

But then you'll foolishly start to put more meaning behind the Big O you experience every time he is near you with that monster cock. And then his smile will start muddling the waters, or the way he touches your face, or the way he looks at you when you take off your shirt in front of him—all smoldering and shit. Then those wicked words of his will make their way into your heart *and* brain. And maybe, just *maybe,* you'll start to feel safe because he seems to genuinely care for you. Then somehow, before you have the chance to back up…before you even realize what your heart is doing behind your back…

Boom!

You're in love.

Congrats. And, well, fuck you, dear heart!

Now you can thoroughly enjoy the misery that will surely follow suit.

Of course, I can't speak for everyone, but at least that's what happened between me and Jameson, my one and only college love, so go and blame him for the love vomit.

It had been exactly six days and twenty-one hours since he'd left Los Angeles and moved to Pittsburgh to start his stupid new job at his stupid new firm, leaving me behind, a little heartbroken, and essentially homeless.

If you're wondering how I managed to fall in love with this Jameson who broke my heart…let me rewind a bit. I met Jameson in a study group for our economics class. Contrary to popular belief, I wouldn't jump into bed with someone I'd just met—and I didn't. At first, I just enjoyed the view and chose to somewhat salivate over him…because that's always fun, isn't it? Oh, the anticipation, the coy looks, all those knowing smirks. Then a few weeks later we just tumbled into a bed that was nearby. Just like that, I swear.

Completely accidental, I tell you.

I recall seeing some ink on his chest and forearms, and then he turned around and I saw those tight buns. Suddenly we were in a bed and he was giving me and my lovely vagina the time of our life. I've already mentioned how good those monster cocks feel, haven't I? I wouldn't have minded if he were a tad bit thicker, but, oh well…I guess you can't have it all in life.

So, I went back for more. I remember telling myself, *Just one more time, Lucy, and that's it*. I sincerely thought it would be a crime not to experience that level of hotness again, and I'm no criminal. What could *possibly* go wrong, y'know…

Then somehow we ended up having those one-night stands a few times a week. So, technically he wasn't a one-night stand, but I'd still like to call him just that. He also proved to be a tough cookie when he started to fall asleep in my bed before my brain would start working enough to remember why I needed to kick him out of it.

Funnily enough, that's how I used to end up going for sleepy time on my best friend Olive's boobies. Sleeping and cuddling with your one-night stand is a big no no. The best part; Olive's boobs were The.Best.Freaking.Pillows.In.The.World! Trust me on that. So soft, yet so firm. It was basically magic, but that's a story for another time.

Long story short, I'd started to fall for Jameson. I thought maybe it was time for me to give good ol' love a spin and see if I was still cursed or not. True, I wasn't necessarily expecting a happily ever after at my first try because real life is rarely all unicorns flying around and farting rainbows in the clouds, but hell, I hadn't been expecting a sudden cut and run either. I was just dipping my toes into the water, not trying to electrocute myself.

So, yup, still cursed.

No love for this gal. Hurray…I guess.

"Hello? Lucy? Ah, there you are. Is there a reason you're talking to yourself?" Olive asked as she appeared at the end of the hall where I was dumping a trash bag filled with Jameson's clothes. I straightened up and let out a deep breath as I took in her appearance. The yoga pants and baggy white shirt she was wearing were practically her uniform when she didn't want to think about what to wear. And baggy or not her boobs still managed to look good. Her strawberry blonde hair was in a messy bun on top of her head and looked like it had seen much cleaner days. My guess was she had come straight from her writing cave.

"No reason at all. Just entertaining myself," I answered, clearing the invisible sweat off my forehead with the back of my hand. "What are you doing here this early? I thought you were coming around later. And is there a reason why you look like you haven't showered in a week?"

She was in the process of looking through the trash bags I had lined up against the wall that contained the clothes Jameson had chosen to leave behind. At my question, Olive's head snapped up and her lips spread into a wide grin.

"Not a week, but maybe two days? I only have a few chapters to write then it's officially The End for the story." She shrugged and went back to her rummaging, looking for God knew what. "Who has time to shower anyway?"

It wasn't a question, but I answered her anyway—under my breath of course. "People who like to be clean instead of smelly like you maybe?"

"And to answer your ungrateful question," she continued. "I came early because I'm *the* best friend anyone could have. Why do we have to go through his clothes? Why didn't the bastard take them with him?"

"*We* aren't going through his clothes, *you* are. I've already gone through them. I'm just gonna leave them outside. Jameson texted to say his friend was coming over to take care of them. I don't care either way."

"Or we could burn them to make a statement." She kicked one of the bags toward the door and reached out to lift up my small, bright yellow weekend bag.

"And what statement would that be exactly?"

"I don't know…to show him that we are a united front against him? And it would be therapeutic for you, too."

"Right. How about we stick to moving me out of here as quickly as possible instead."

She shrugged and grabbed the bag I was holding out to her. "By the way, I'm pretty sure Jason would've said something if I smelled. And look who's talking—you look like death warmed up. Your beautiful blue eyes are practically dead. Even your dark hair somehow looks…darker."

I clasped my hands over my heart and batted my lashes. "Aww, thanks, my little green Olive. You look lovely too, with your greasy hair and sleepy eyes. Combined, it all does wonders for your complexion."

A small smile playing on her lips, she shook her head and carried the bags downstairs to her car. I opened the bathroom door and checked the medicine cabinet to make sure I hadn't left anything behind. Then just to be safe, I checked the bedroom again. When I was sure everything was packed and ready to go, I carried my last suitcase into the living room where Olive was waiting for me with a full bottle of tequila.

"I brought this," she said, using her hands to present the bottle to me, as if that baby needed any extra presenting.

Taking a few steps to make it to her side, I snatched the bottle from her hands, ignored her gasp, and plopped my ass down on the shit-colored sofa, as I liked to describe it.

While I was busy trying to screw the top off, Olive sighed and dropped down next to me. I took a quick gulp and screwed up my face when the precious liquid burned my throat then handed the bottle back to her waiting hands.

She'd been my friend for three and a half years, and I doubted anyone else knew me better than her. She was a writer—a crazy successful author who'd made the bestseller lists with her very first novel. My favorite part was that she was the lucky, lucky wife of the hottest actor in Hollywood, who had also been her childhood crush. You'd think that shit would only happen in books, but nope, she did it. She scored the hottest guy. I liked to think I'd given her a small nudge in the right direction, encouraging her to go after what she wanted, but her chemistry with the guy was off the charts, so I knew with or without me, they still would've ended up together. And, well, despite being a hotshot celebrity, Jason Thorn was one of the good ones. He was completely in love with Olive—otherwise I would have totally organized a sneak attack on him to get his paws off my best friend.

"So…" Olive started after she took her own gulp of tequila and coughed a few times. "What was the subject of the conversation you were having with yourself when I walked in?"

I took another sip, a big one. That one definitely went down easier. "Actually, I was reminiscing about your pretty boobs and thinking how come you're so selfish about sharing those puppies."

She quirked her eyebrow at me and pulled her legs up to get comfortable. "Who said I'm selfish? I share very nicely with my husband."

I gave her a genuine smile. "Are you ready to share exactly *how*? As in with details? Like what's his favorite position? Doggie? Does he take care of your boobs? Is he nice to them?" I knew she wouldn't share—I had tried before; I didn't understand why, and it never stopped me from trying to get answers. Plus, it was fun watching her squirm. That's what friends got for hoarding important details like that.

"Sorry, no bueno."

Doing my best to give her my version of the evil eye, I offered her some alcohol. She passed, which was good for two reasons. One, more for me—yay—and two, well, she got out of hand when she got drunk.

"Not to sound like an ungrateful friend, but I thought you said you'd come around two PM, not ten AM. And you came bearing gifts too. Are you being nice to me 'cause I'm a victim?"

She looked clueless as she glanced at me. "A victim? A victim of what?"

"A victim of love, of course," I returned, acting outraged. "I got chewed up and spit out—and not in a sexy way."

She rolled her eyes and gave her attention to the phone buzzing in her handbag. After checking the screen, she sighed. "Sorry, my poor victim of love, I need to take this. I'm scheduling meetings with potential agents."

"You go ahead and do that, and I'll keep doing this tequila."

As soon as she left the room, I closed my eyes and let my head rest on the back of the sofa.

So Jameson was gone. So I wasn't in a relationship anymore. Whatever, right? I'd never planned to get into one in the first place. I should've been happy. I should've felt better knowing I'd been right about the existence of a curse on our family.

Did I feel anything like happiness at that moment?

Not even close. But I knew I would live, so there was no point in acting like my life was over. Thanks to my family, I'd seen worse. Jameson was a saint compared to them.

When Olive came back, I tried to avert my gaze so she wouldn't focus on my watering eyes.

Oh, shush! I hadn't been silently crying or anything, I was just allergic to the damn apartment.

"How about we get out of here?" Olive asked softly.

Apparently I hadn't been quick enough to look away. I wiped away a lone tear and took my last sip from the bottle. As much as I wanted to get sloppy drunk with my best friend and possibly start a big fire and make voodoo dolls with big junks, we couldn't. Adulting sucks big balls.

"Yeah. We should do that," I agreed.

Olive reached for the bottle in my hand, and I reluctantly gave it up, after a short struggle, of course.

"I'll hold onto this, and we'll continue later."

"Promise?"

"Promise." She narrowed her eyes on me. "Hell, you know what? I'll even let you cuddle me."

Perking up, I wiggled my brows at her. "And while I'm cuddling you, will you be cuddling your pretty husband?" I sat up straighter. "Olive Thorn, are you granting me a cuddling three-some because I'm a victim of love? If so, I'll totally take that."

ABOUT THE AUTHOR

Writing has become my world and I can't imagine myself doing anything other than giving life to new characters and new stories. You know how some things simply makes your heart burst with happiness? A really good book, a puppy, hugging someone you've been missing like crazy? That's what writing does to me. And I'm hoping that reading my books will leave you with that same happy feeling.

Everything you'd ever want to know about me and my books is on my website. I'd love to see you there!

www.ellamaise.com

To get the inside scoop of my books, extra materials, and to be the first one to know when I have a new release, you can sign up for my newsletter!
(Only sent a few times a year.)

Newsletter Sign Up